The Chain Mistress

By

Rebecca Bryn

'The light of kindness and goodness in our heart is ultimately what we must tap into. We do not so much "fight the darkness (of hate and bigotry)" as we illuminate it when we unite our own inner light with the inner light shining in our fellow brothers and sisters.' – **Aimee Ginsburg Bikel**

Apart from the political figures of the day, the characters in this novel are fictitious, and no likeness is intended to anyone living or dead.

Dedicated to the memory of Sarah Knight, much-loved mother, wife, daughter, aunt, sister, and daughter-in-law.

A victim of Covid-19 – Always in our hearts.

***

Prologue

Hawley Heath, England 1920

Bright hearths illuminated the inside of Mrs Kimble's chain workshop. Sparks flew from hot iron beaten between hammer and anvil. It was sweltering and noisy, and smelled of sweat, hot iron, and breeze – the small coal used in the hearths: the sounds and smells of Emma Taylor's childhood ever since she could remember. She was thirteen and would leave school soon to work full-time, but her early years had already been spent here while Mom worked making chain at this very hearth.

She brushed a spark from her cheek and raised an arm to pull the lever on the bellows that fed air to her hearth. The breeze glowed brighter, and the length of rod in her tongs changed from red to yellow. The rod withdrawn from the heat and laid on her anvil, she cut it to length with a single blow of her chisel, hammered the length into shape and turned a link. She threaded the link through the end of the last one, reheated it, and fire-welded it closed, and then gave the still-hot link a twist and checked that it lay perfectly flat with the others.

Another link done; another chain finished. She quenched it to cool it and mopped sweat from her eyes with the back of her hand before reheating the rod for the first link of her next chain. If she didn't make enough, she'd be letting down Mrs Kimble. She worked on, her hands and body moving with a rhythm that had become second nature, while her mind wandered beyond the soot-blackened walls to dream of places she'd seen in picture books but would never see in reality, chained as she was by the hammer, tongs, iron rod, and anvil of her trade.

2

'Let's have a look, Emma.'

She stepped aside for Mrs Kimble to examine her work. If it wasn't good enough, she wouldn't be paid.

Mrs Kimble fingered the chain she'd just thrown into her box of finished items. 'Good work, Emma. You'll make a fine chain master, one day, or should I say chain mistress.'

She frowned. 'Chain mistress?'

Mrs Kimble looked flustered. 'I shouldn't have said nothing. It ain't my place, Emma. You ask your mom and dad – Matthew Joshua put the factory in their hands, not mine.'

Matthew and Marion Joshua were her grandparents, but it was Mom and Dad who now owned the factory and Heath Hall. If anyone was to be a chain master after Dad, it would be her younger brother George as he was older than Theo. The Black Country didn't have chain mistresses, and anyway, she had other dreams.

She'd ask Mom. She pushed the thought to the back of her mind and bent back to her work. She had a quota to fill and dreaming of cool, fresh air, wide open spaces, and foreign lands wouldn't get it filled.

**

Rosie Taylor smiled as her daughter stood before her, hands on hips, with determination written all over her face. 'What is it, sweetheart?' Whatever she wanted, Emma wouldn't be put off.

'Mrs Kimble said I'm to be a chain mistress. What does she mean.?'

Her smile faded. 'She shouldn't have said that.'

'So, I'm not to be a chain mistress?'

3

'Yes. You are, but –'

'What about George?'

'George isn't a Joshua.'

'And I am?'

'By birth, yes. You know this, Emma. You're also a Taylor.'

'But –'

She patted the sofa beside her, unable to put off the explanation any longer. 'As Willis's only child, you will inherit Matthew Joshua's estate when you are old enough. It's a long way off, and I wanted you to have a childhood, not be concerned about the future. Mrs Kimble had no right to tell you.'

'But what does it mean?'

She took a deep breath. 'Heath Hall, the factory, the chain workshops. the farm and land, and much of Hawley Heath will belong to you when you are twenty-one. It was a condition of your dad and me having the estate after Matthew and Marion died.' She swept an all-encompassing hand around the room. 'All this will be yours. There are conditions to be met, but essentially, it will all belong to you.'

'Mrs Kimble's chain workshop?' Emma looked around the room as if taking in for the first time the luxury neither Rosie Wallace nor Jack Taylor had been born into.

She pushed away memories of giving birth on a blanket on the floor the night the dredger had brought up Willis's body from the canal. 'Yes, and Scraggs' workshop and some of the workers' houses and chain workshops.'

'So, if I'm to own Mrs Kimble's workshop, why am I working there under her?'

'With property, power, and wealth come responsibility. Your workers will depend on you for their livelihoods as much as you depend on them for their labour. How will you know what you can expect from a worker if you haven't learned every aspect of your trade and laboured with them? Mrs Kimble is a good teacher, and I should know.'

She smiled at her daughter's serious expression. 'You have so much to learn, Emma, if you're to provide work and welfare for the men and women who will depend on Joshua and Son. This is something your grandfather never really understood. He was a chainmaker once, but he let profit blind him to the hardship his workers suffered. You had rickets, because Jack and I couldn't put food on the table despite the hours we worked. We didn't even have a bed to sleep on. You have to understand why you can't let that poverty and exploitation – slavery – ever happen again.'

She paused, aware she'd been on a soapbox reliving the heady days of striking and picketing for a living wage. Tuppence ha'penny an hour was all they'd asked for and Matthew had stubbornly refused to pay it. Emma had every ounce of Matthew's stubbornness and Marion's wayward courage.

'But, if I'm to own all this, what about Bonnie and Grace, and George and Theo? What will they get?'

'They get the freedom to do what they want and make their own way in the world. This inheritance is a double-edged sword, Emma. The factory and the welfare of our workers is a huge responsibility.'

Her daughter looked sombre. 'I shall do my best, Mom.'

She hugged Emma. 'I know you will, sweetheart, but it's a long way off, and no one expects you to do it alone. Dad and I will be beside you every step of the way.'

5

They would need to be. Once it was common knowledge that Emma would inherit the factory, every gold-digger in the county would be after her money.

Chapter One

Hawley Heath, England 1928

Rosie looked around the office that had been her responsibility for so many years. The family solicitor had drawn up the papers in readiness, and they'd an appointment with him this afternoon. All Emma needed to do was sign, and all this, the factory, Heath Hall, and the houses and chain workshops in Willis Street and beyond, would belong to her.

She and Jack had worked so hard for so many years to build the factory into an inheritance worth having and instil into Emma how important it was to provide jobs and welfare for local families, but what was it they were giving her? A secure future or a noose around her neck?

Emma looked up and smiled as if she knew her mother was thinking about her. She'd grown into a beautiful young woman with a caring heart, though she sometimes reminded her of Marion with her restless nature and reckless disregard for her own safety – and she had Willis's dark hair and eyes.

She waved back and turned away to fight once more with the order book and paperwork Jack so hated. No matter how she looked at it, the pages were no fuller of orders, and wages must still be paid.

Since the end of the war, the lack of need for new ships had plummeted the shipbuilding industry into steep decline, and with it had gone the orders for cable chain for anchors. The slump also affected the rolling mills and blast furnaces, and the amount of coal needing to be mined. The Black Country, so dependent on its heavy industry, had plunged into mass unemployment and desperate poverty.

Orders for heavy chain and rattle chain were at an all-time low. With the coming of tractors, trace chains for harness were a thing of the past, and they relied more and more on small chain, much of which still went to America.

Electrically welded chain had taken the place of handmade chain, being cheaper to produce, and the little backyard workshops, where she'd learned to make cow, trace, and dog chains at her mother's side, were closing one by one as the older women died or retired, their hearths never to be relit.

While she wouldn't wish another war on her worst enemy, peace wasn't putting food in workers' bellies, and the whole of Europe was still in a state of political and economic flux. Only five years ago, the French had invaded Germany, occupied the Ruhr district, and seized industry and towns in the Rhineland.

Disarmed under the Treaty of Versailles, and unable to defend itself, Germany was being taken apart piece by piece as pressure grew to separate the Rhineland from the German Republic and establish an independent Rhenania. A vigorous movement in Bavaria campaigned for an independent Catholic monarchy there.

She sighed at matters outside her control that might yet come back to haunt them all. War or peace, change had come uncalled, and they must change too or be left behind.

She rubbed her hands over tired eyes.

'Mom? Are you all right?' Emma stood at her side and put an arm around her shoulders. 'What is it, Mom?'

She looked up into a concerned face. 'It's…' She wanted to say it was nothing to worry about, and not Emma's problem, but today it was. 'I've been racking my brains for something we can make other than chain, Emma. I didn't want to worry you, but…'

'But?' Emma squeezed her shoulder. 'I'm not blind, Mom. I've seen men wandering the streets looking for work, I've read the newspaper reports about the general strike and the hunger marches, and I know we're not getting the big orders we used to get. All the factories are in the same situation.'

'The only manufacturing that seems to be booming is the motor car industry in Birmingham.'

Emma's eyes widened. 'You're not suggesting we make cars? We wouldn't know where to start.'

'No, but there might be some part of the process we could provide, the way we helped the country by filling Mills' bombs during the war?'

Emma frowned. 'And Grandma Joshua paid the price for that.'

Haunting guilt drove her to make life as good as she could for Marion and Matthew's granddaughter, Willis's daughter. She was failing at that as well.

Emma broke into her self-recrimination. 'It wasn't your fault, Mom. Grandma Joshua was a brave woman. She put her life in danger for the sake of others – for the vote for women and for the war effort.'

Marion's sacrifice, throwing herself in front of Sarah when a spark ignited spilled aluminium dust, had made up for her misdemeanours. She'd been easier to forgive in death than she had in life. If Emma had forgotten the childhood trauma of Marion pushing Jack down the stairs, it was all to the good, and she wasn't about to remind her. Marion had possessed both courage and determination, and she'd admired her for that. 'You are so like her, sometimes, Emma. She'd have been very proud of you.'

'So, what are we going to make, Mom, if we don't get orders for chain? Not cars, they're just for the well shod. Something to help ordinary working folk. Something they can afford.'

'Like what?'

'Bicycles!'

'What?'

'Bicycles. Theo and George are always messing with bicycles. Cheap transport for men travelling to work. They're having to go farther and farther afield to find a job now, and bus and tram fares are expensive day after day. Bicycles would solve their problem if we can produce them cheaply enough.'

'Joshua and Son, Cycle Manufacturers? What do we know about bicycles?'

'No, not Joshua and Son.' Emma nodded towards her brothers, their muscular arms raising the hammers that shaped the links. 'Taylor Brothers, Cycle Manufacturers. Theo and George need something of their own. They may only be fifteen and eighteen, but they're both mad about cycles and motorcycles. Give them room in the factory and let them take a cycle apart to see how it's made. Bending, welding, or braising tube can't be so different to bending rod and welding chain.'

Oh, the optimism of the young. She couldn't bring herself to quash Emma's enthusiasm. At her age, she'd been the same, looking to improve her family's lot without a thought to the cost or difficulty, and for a cause to fight. Emma's restless energy needed an outlet, a cause. Perhaps this would satisfy it. 'We could take out some of the unused hearths to make room. I'll talk to your father.' She paused. 'No, if you feel you need advice, ask him. This is your future, the future you'll build for your children.'

Emma sighed. 'I know it's what you expect, Mom. I'd love children, but to be honest, I've not met a man I could spend the rest of my life with.'

'Not even the young man you saw yesterday evening?'

Her daughter pulled a face. 'Especially not him. You were lucky with Dad.'

Luckier than Emma would ever know. Who but Jack would have forgiven her stupid affair with Willis and loved Emma as his own?

Emma hugged her. 'We'll be all right, Mom. We have a good work force, skilled men and women who aren't afraid of hard graft. I just need to find something different for them to do.'

She kissed Emma's cheek relieved she'd taken up the challenge. It was time for the younger generation to breathe new life into the factory and Hawley Heath. The business would be in safe hands, for whatever direction Joshua and Son took in the future, Emma would make an excellent chain mistress.

***

Emma lifted down the tin box from the top shelf of the wardrobe in the room that had been her grandmother's. Inside, along with an envelope and newspaper cuttings, was a brooch, and judging by the colours of the stones, white, purple, and green, it was a suffragette brooch. She rubbed it on her sleeve and the stones sparkled. Were they genuine diamonds and emeralds? She pinned the brooch on her blouse. If Marion Joshua had left everything to her, then this was hers to wear.

She'd never owned jewellery; Mom never wore it, hating shows of wealth when others had less, especially now when so many were out of work. Having been raised in poverty, without even a bed to lie in, Mom was acutely aware of class inequalities and had instilled a sense of social justice into her children. The rest and maternity home at Heath Hall, free for the women of Hawley Heath, had been part of her life for as long as she could remember and a condition of her inheritance.

The faded envelope was addressed to Frau M. Joshua, and the

11

newspaper cuttings told of suffragette 'outrages'. Grandma helped bomb St Paul's Cathedral? Against a report of the burning of a church, her grandmother had scribbled a note.

I set the fire against the wooden screen, and I could see the smoke for miles. Now the church misogynists will take notice of women.

Next to a report of Sir Henry Curtis-Bennett receiving a letter bomb, Marion had drawn an explosion. Had Grandma been so careless of others' lives?

A shudder ran down her spine as a vague memory surfaced from long ago. Dad at the top of the stairs, raised voices, and Dad falling. She'd run and hidden, and Mom had come and found her. What had happened? Had Grandma Joshua pushed Dad down the stairs? She shook the feeling away. Why would she give everything to him and Mom if she'd hated him that much?

Beneath the newspaper cuttings were a number of thin black books. Diaries? Day-to-day accounts of household trivia could wait, but the foreign envelope was intriguing. She was curious about her forebears, and photographs of Matthew and Marion showed strong features – Joshua was a Jewish name, wasn't it? Perhaps the letter would be a link to a relative.

Frau M Joshua… The stamp was foreign. She could make out Deutsches Reich under the smudged postmark.

30th April 1907,

Börneplatz

Ostend,

Frankfurt am Main,

She'd have been just over three weeks old.

My dearest Marion,

I am devastated by your news, although after these months of waiting, hope of finding your darling son alive was fading. I am at a loss for words to convey my sorrow, although I have said the blessings. I know you and Matthew aren't practising Jews, but not to have the burial according to our family's customs must still be difficult.

The letter confirmed her Jewish heritage. She'd been raised in the Church of England, like Mom and Dad, but she had no great religious belief.

How are you bearing up? How is poor Matthew? Oh, my dear cousin, what a terrible burden for you to bear. You say there will be an inquest according to English law, and I hope it gives you some answers and some peace. I shall pray for you. May God comfort you among the other mourners of Zion and Jerusalem.

Your loving cousin,

Dvorka.

Frankfurt was in Germany. Other than that, she knew nothing of the town. Dvorka, whom she was assuming by the tone of the letter was a woman, was obviously fond of her cousin. Had anyone told her of Grandma's death? With Matthew and Willis both dead, who would even know Grandma Joshua had a cousin in Germany? After twenty-one years, would Dvorka still be alive?

There was only one way to find out.

April 5th 1928

Heath Hall,

Hawley Heath,

England

Dear Dvorka,

My name is Emma, and I'm Marion Joshua's granddaughter, Willis's daughter.

How did you tell a complete stranger their cousin was dead? She was being a coward. Twelve years on from Grandma's death, with no letters from her cousin, the woman would have guessed. Still, it would comfort her to know that Grandma died a heroine.

I found your letter today in a box in Grandma's wardrobe, or someone would have written to you before.

The truth is we know nothing of the Joshua family and didn't know you existed. I wish I had better news of Marion, your cousin, but I must tell you she died in 1916, sacrificing her life to save one of our workers from an explosion. We all miss her, and I hope one day to have her courage and make her proud. I expect you know she was a suffragette and was faithful to that cause until they abandoned protests at the outbreak of war.

Would war be a touchy subject, given the deep shame Germany felt at being defeated? How would she feel had Germany defeated England? She shuddered. It didn't bear thinking about.

She'd keep the letter short and to the point - conciliatory.

I hope this letter finds you well and you will feel able to reply. I would love to learn more about my German relations.

Kindest regards,

Emma Taylor.

She hesitated and then added (*Joshua*). She'd explain why her name was Taylor if Dvorka asked. Having addressed the envelope, she ran down the stairs and left it in the box of mail to go to the post office.

Chapter Two

The diary slipped from Emma's fingers and landed with a thud on the floor. She shook her head, unable to take in what she'd read. Mom had killed Willis? Her mother had killed her father? She tasted bile, hot with anger and betrayal. Her parents had hid this horror from her, and Grandma had kept their secret for the sake of her granddaughter, but this was a truth that could send Rosie Taylor to the gallows.

She slammed the front door behind her and ran out into a chill April morning. She was the child of a rapist and a murderess. What did that make her? Why had she looked in those damned diaries?

She ran on down the hill towards the town, past chestnut trees that pushed their candle flowers upwards from the tips of their branches, past pale primroses, bright violets and celandines, and burgeoning bluebells, scarcely heeding the beauty she cherished. At the bottom of the hill, she stopped to catch her breath and then hurried on along Willis Street towards the factory.

Joshua and Son, Chainmakers

The name picked out in dark bricks took on a new and darker meaning. Mom's dalliance with Willis had resulted in his death, her picketing of the factory had doubtless contributed to Grandfather Joshua's heart attacks, and then she'd seen off Grandma Joshua in the Mills-bomb factory.

She'd never known Matthew, but Dad spoke of him with a certain fondness.

She should go in and take her rightful place as chain mistress, but she couldn't face it. How could she look Mom in the eye and pretend she hadn't read Marion's diary? Instead, she strode on towards the canal and past the smoke-blackened buildings that confined her small world. The air was cleaner, and the sun got through the smoke more often, since the mines and blast furnaces were less busy, and even the weeds struggling to grow along the gutters were greener, but life had become as grey and muddied as the canal.

She smelled the canal before she saw it. The hard-packed mud of the towpath slammed the soles of her feet, and the bridge ahead of her framed barges in a tight semi-circle, their broken reflections barely visible in the stinking water. Victoria Street had been renamed Willis Street, so this must be the bridge where her father had died, or, at least, where they'd found his body.

Stopping beneath the bridge, she leaned back against the cold bricks of the arch and contemplated the water that had hidden the tragedy for so long. How could her parents have been so cruel as to push her father into the canal and leave Grandma worrying so?

She huffed a hot breath. 'Under the bridge...' She'd heard the term used about girls who were *"no better than they should be"* and went under the bridge with boys who felt entitled to *"sow their wild oats"*. Was this where her father brought Mom? Was this the awful place where Emma Taylor's miserable life had begun.

Joshua and Son. It was a name with a dark past that Taylor's should have had no part in running, but could she run it by herself and give it a brighter future without their help? Emma Joshua. She straightened. She wasn't a Taylor, not anymore – Grandma Joshua had finally got her way. And if, one day, she found a man she could love and had a son, Joshua and Son would be reborn.

"Love, cherish, and obey". No, she wouldn't marry. She wasn't willing to grant any man the obedience – the marital right – her wedding vows would give him. She might have the right to vote, but what had women gained when they still had no rights over their own bodies in marriage? She hadn't been deaf to the talk of wives forced to have children they didn't want by husbands who *"had to have their way"*. Contraception was expensive, and marriage for many was little more than legalised rape. If she had a child, it would be out of wedlock. Huh, wedlock! Even the word told of its imprisoning intent.

And what about Mom and Dad – Jack? She couldn't just ignore them. This was something she had to face head on. She let her anger carry her back along Willis Street towards the factory, not sure if she was most furious with Mom or with Willis, whether she was more angry with her family than she was ashamed of them. Either way, she needed justice for her father and to atone for the dreadful things Willis, Marion, Mom, and Jack had done.

***

Rosie had taken her place at her forge, stepping back from the office, which was now Emma's territory. She turned a link, fire-welded it, and glanced at the door. Emma hadn't yet come to work, and she'd been forced to spend half the morning in the office and had answered the telephone several times.

She took a drink of cold tea from her bottle, bent back to her work, and lost herself in the repetitive motion of heating the rod in her hearth, cutting the iron to length, and hammering, shaping, and welding the links, one through another to make the snake of chain. Other women worked at electrically welded small chain, and Jack and the remaining men toiled with sleeves rolled up and shirts sticking to their backs, finishing a rare order for replacement pit chain. The heat and the noise she'd grown up with was a comforting, companionable din that made sign language more useful than words. She'd missed this sense of companionship, working alone in the office.

A tap on her shoulder jerked her out of her rhythm. Dark, angry eyes stared into hers. Emma gestured her towards the office, and she nodded and laid down her tools. Something had upset her daughter.

She hurried after her and into the office, mopping beads of sweat from her brow. Emma stood behind the desk, shaking.

'Emma, what is it? What's happened?'

Emma shook her head as if clearing her thoughts; her hands made tight fists, her knuckles bled white.

'What's happened? Emma, tell me.'

'The truth about my father.'

'What's all this about, Emma? What is it you want to know?'

'I read Grandma's diaries. They were in the tin box in the wardrobe.'

Marion had written diaries? Oh, hell. Sweat trickled down her back and between her breasts. 'The box was locked.'

'I found the key.'

'And what did Marion write?' Her fingernails dug into her palms. Please, God, she hadn't written the truth.

'You killed my father.'

There it was. The bald truth she'd never wanted Emma to know.

Emma slapped her palms on the desk and leaned forward, breathing heavily. 'You killed my father!' She swept papers off

18

the desk. 'You killed him and left him to rot in the canal. You're evil. I hate you!'

Oh, Emma. 'It wasn't like that, sweetheart.'

'Don't you *sweetheart* me. I want the truth, all of it, now!'

'You won't like it, Emma. I've been trying to protect you from this all your life.'

'Protect me? Protect yourself and Jack, more like.'

She winced. "*Jack*". He'd always been Dad. 'Sit down, Emma I suppose you're old enough now to cope with the truth. I'm sorry you have to hear it though.'

Eyes hard as the iron they forged, Emma waved her to a chair as if she were an employee, which she supposed she was now. 'Go on.'

'If Marion wrote it, you already know.'

'I want to hear it from you.'

She shook away the cold brick of the canal bridge and the fog, the stink of the water, and the feel of hard iron in her fist. 'I'll start at the beginning. Willis was our fogger when I was still working with Mom in the cinder yard, before the houses collapsed into the mine tunnel. He was older than me by about five years and very handsome and charming. I loved Jack even then. We were always going to be married. He looked out for me, always had. I was fifteen, old enough to marry, but Jack didn't ask me. I was young and foolish, and I thought to make Jack jealous.'

Emma stayed silent. She wasn't making this easy.

'Willis had an eye for the girls and didn't need any encouragement. He said if I went under the bridge with him for a kiss and a cuddle, he'd make sure our jobs were safe and Mrs

Kimble had the best orders. We were desperately poor. You have no idea.' Her voice caught at the memory of hunger pains in her belly and watching her mother drive herself beyond exhaustion. 'We lived on bread and bacon fat, you had rickets when you were little, and we had no beds to sleep on and only the clothes we stood up in. Matthew Joshua owned us lock, stock, and barrel. They didn't call us *the white slaves of England* for nothing.'

'That doesn't justify murder.'

'It wasn't murder, Emma. Listen to me, for pity's sake.' She took a deep breath. 'I was naïve enough to believe a kiss and a cuddle was all Willis wanted. Of course, when we got under the bridge, he wanted more – much more.' A hot pulsing reminded her of losing her virginity, of becoming a woman. 'I didn't know that Jack was waiting until he could afford to ask me. I thought he didn't want to marry me. Of course, I got pregnant. Mom and Dad were furious, but Mom wouldn't let me get rid of the baby.'

'You wanted to abort me?'

'Yes... No... I don't know. We couldn't afford another mouth to feed, and Willis – I was going to tell him, but I caught him having sex with another woman – a married woman – and he just laughed at me. He made it clear he wouldn't marry me even if I was pregnant, not that he ever knew about you.'

'But he might have done the right thing if he'd known.' Emma's expression tore at her heart. 'You should have told him.'

'Yes, I should have, but I was hurting and scared. I wanted nothing to do with the Joshuas. It was complicated.'

'So complicated you had to hit my father over the head with a mooring pin?'

Marion really had put down all the gruesome detail. Obviously,

20

she'd left out Willis's misdemeanours. 'I told Jack I was pregnant.' She brushed away tears. 'He was broken-hearted, I couldn't have hurt him more if I'd tried, but he agreed to marry me and say you were his, born early, to hide your identity. I didn't want a feckless man like Willis in your life.'

'Well, you made sure of that.'

'Emma, please. This is hard enough.' She swallowed. 'Jack had a fight with Willis and threw him in the canal – he pulled him out again before he drowned, but Willis was furious. He was determined to pay him back any way he could. He found a way after I married your dad.' She held up a hand to prevent Emma refuting Jack was her father; he was the only father she'd ever have. 'After your Grandad Wallace had his accident at work, money got tighter, and Willis's demands grew. He put up the rent and demanded we paid it immediately. Of course, we didn't have the money, and he knew that. I didn't have a choice but to do as he wanted, Emma.'

Emma's face betrayed no emotion. Did she believe her?

'Sweetheart, my only option was to meet Willis under the bridge and let him have his way, or we'd all face a winter on the streets, and not just us but Kimbles, and Spraggs where Jack worked, as well. Do you wonder I didn't want Willis in your life?'

'Yet you took me to see Matthew and told him I was his granddaughter?'

'You remember that?'

'Only vaguely. It was in Grandma's diary.'

'It was when Matthew refused to pay the legal wage. I hoped to persuade him. I thought that if he saw how thin you children were, he'd relent. He threw me out.' She grabbed at a breath and hurried

21

on before she lost her courage. 'Jack followed me out the night I went to meet Willis. He knew something was wrong. He saw us under the bridge and knew I didn't want what Willis was doing. Jack knocked Willis to the ground, and they rolled across the towpath. Willis was on top as they reached the edge of the canal. He pushed Jack's head under the water and held him there. I pleaded with him to let him go. I scratched his face and tried to gouge his eyes, but he wouldn't let Jack up.'

Her breaths came in quick gasps. 'There were fewer bubbles of air breaking the surface of the water. Jack was drowning. I tugged a mooring pin from the ground and hit Willis hard. He slumped to the ground, and I jumped into the canal. Jack's head was still under the water, and I didn't know if either of them were alive or dead, but I rolled Jack back onto the bank. I thumped his chest, and he spewed canal water. Willis wasn't breathing.'

She wiped more tears from her eyes with her sleeve. 'Jack said I wasn't going to the gallows for Willis. He rolled his body into the canal and there it stayed until spring, when the dredger found it.'

Emma's brow made tight, angry creases. 'According to Marion, Jack and you found the body. Why would you draw attention to it?' At least, she'd listened, not that she could have got a word in edgeways.

'It seemed like a good diversion. It was me who spotted it – him. My idea we should report it. It was the shock and fear that brought on labour. Jack used that to hide your parentage by saying the birth was two months early. He took me home and then went back to the canal. When he was sure it was Willis, he went to tell Matthew. It was probably the bravest thing he'd ever done, and he did it all for me, because I was a stupid young girl who allowed herself to fall for Willis's arrogant charm.'

A tense silence settled over the office, broken only by the muted sounds of hammers on iron and the pulse of the steam bellows and steam hammers.

'Emma?'

Emma shook her head, her fingers fiddling with a brooch on her lapel. It looked like a suffragette brooch. 'I don't know, Mom. I don't know.'

'We have always loved you, Emma. You are not your father, even though you look a lot like him.'

Emma dry-washed her hands. 'I don't know who I am anymore. I don't know who you and Dad are.'

'You're Emma Taylor, and we love you, sweetheart.'

Emma wiped her eyes with the back of her hand. 'But I'm not, am I? I'm Emma Joshua, and you killed my father.'

'He raped me, Emma, and tried to kill Jack. He wasn't fit to be your father. Jack has been the best dad you could ever have. I never meant to kill Willis. I only wanted to save Jack's life. You do believe me, don't you?'

Emma's face was a study in conflicting emotions. 'I don't know.'

'You think I could kill someone in cold blood?'

'What about justice for my father, for Grandma Joshua? What about truth?'

The truth. 'The diaries. What are you going to do, Emma?'

'I don't know if I can forgive what any of you did. I'm a Joshua, with Joshua blood in my veins, not a Taylor like Bonnie and Grace and the boys, and I shall never know my real father.'

23

Chapter Three

Rosie waited for Jack to finish his link and then motioned him outside. Jack turned to face her. 'What's up?'

'Emma knows I killed Willis.'

'What? How?'

'She found some diaries in a box in Marion's room. She knows everything, Jack.'

'Is she all right?'

'She's furious. I tried to explain, but –'

'I'll go and talk to her.'

'No, leave her, Jack. She's angry with you, too. Let her calm down a bit. We just have to hope she sees sense.'

'What do you mean?'

'She wants justice, Jack. The diaries –'

'She won't do anything to hurt you, Rosie.'

'Are you sure about that? She has Joshua blood running through her veins. You've often said yourself she's like Marion, and Marion tried to kill you.'

'Emma isn't Marion.'

'And Willis was a blackmailing rapist with no conscience at all.'

'She isn't Willis.'

'And Matthew was an unscrupulous slave master who cared

nothing for his slaves.'

'She isn't Matthew either. And anyway, Matthew wasn't all bad. He loved his horses.'

'Horses? Face the truth, Jack. If Emma takes the diaries to the police, we'll be gaoled at best, and hung at worst.' She dissolved into tears. 'I didn't mean Willis to die. This is all my fault. I wish I'd never set eyes on the bastard.'

Jack held her close. 'If Emma does go to the police, I shall do as I promised the day Willis died. I shall plead guilty and tell the police it was me who killed him.'

'And I told you, I wouldn't let you do that.'

'What choice do we have? Emma may be angry with you now, but she needs her mother. I'm not her father.'

'Don't say that, Jack. You and Emma are the only innocents in this, and she needs you too. All you've ever done is try to protect us.'

'Emma will do the right thing, Rosie. We have to trust her, and accept whatever choice she makes, but one thing is certain – I shall not let you hang for Willis bloody Joshua.'

***

Emma had tossed and turned all night, her own words racing through her mind. *I'm a Joshua, with Joshua blood running in my veins.* Bad blood, according to Mom, and her assertion was backed up by the diaries. Marion, Matthew, Willis – they'd all been capable of despicable, selfish acts, so what did that say about her character? She wanted justice, but at what cost?

She grabbed the post and hurried to the factory, where she could open it at her leisure. The envelope in her hand smelled of lavender and was addressed to Fräulein Emma Taylor. She closed the office door, sat at her desk, and opened the envelope with not a small amount of curiosity. Would the German branch of the Joshua family be any better than the English one?

Dear Emma,

Your letter came as something of a surprise. Mother passed it to me as she says it will practise my English. I am sad that Dvorka, my oma – grandmother – has been dead three years, but it is lovely to know I have a 'cousin', however far removed, in England.

I remember your grandparents a little from a visit they made to my grandparents when I was very small. Your grandmother sent photographs of Willis when he was about fourteen, which Oma Dvorka showed me when I was curious about family. He was a good-looking boy. Do you have photographs of yourself? I would love to be pen friends and improve my English if you would like to write again and tell me about England.

I am eighteen-years-old and live with my mother in the house in which she was born in Ostend, which is the Jewish part of Frankfurt.

Ostend. Wasn't that the same name as the Belgian port? She read on.

I work in the jewellers' shop of my uncle Saul. My father died in the war fighting for the Kaiser when I was only seven years of age. Things have been very bad in Germany, although they are a little better now, especially here in occupied Germany. Still, no one has any money to spare to buy jewellery, and there is little employment. How is it in England?

I hope you write,

Your 'cousin',

Hanne Samuels.

She folded the letter and slid it back into the envelope, catching the faint scent of lavender again. She would reply to Hanne. The letter was a slender thread that linked her to the family she'd never known. They couldn't all be blackmailing rapists like her father, exploitative slavedrivers like Matthew, or bombers like Grandma Joshua.

Or murderers like her mother. Normally, she'd have rushed to show Hanne's letter to Mom, but she wasn't ready for that yet. Maybe she never would be.

She reached for the next envelope. Her world might have fallen apart, but bills still needed paying, orders needed to be confirmed, and quotes had to be prepared. Men needed jobs, and it was up to her now to see that they had them. It was an intimidating responsibility, but she would fulfil her duty to her workers as best she could – she would be better than Matthew.

She looked out along the factory floor. Mom was hard at work. Dad was dancing the intricate steps that a team of chainmakers moved to, each with their own task in perfect harmony. The noise and the heat were a constant in her life, but for how much longer? Chain factories were closing – Scraggs's chain workshop had shut its doors for the last time now Bernie had retired.

She couldn't change the past, what was done was done, but she could affect the future for her brothers and Hawley Heath. Scraggs's workshop stood empty, and it belonged to her. It would be the perfect place for Theo and George to set up a bicycle factory. Free of the curse of Joshua blood, they'd done nothing to deserve her anger, and it would create much-needed jobs.

The decision made, she picked her way across the factory floor. George was working with Dad. She beckoned to him, and he laid down his hammer. Dad stepped into his place to do twice the work.

'What's up, Em?' George's frown mirrored Dad's.

She beckoned for him to follow and closed the office door behind them. 'Bicycles, George. What do you need to make them?'

'You want me to make a bicycle? Mom mentioned something about this hare-brained scheme. You can afford to buy one, surely?'

'Of course, I can. I want us to manufacture bicycles. What do you need?'

George scratched his head; blond hair like Dad's. 'Steel tubing and rod. A tube-bending machine. Steel-milling machines if we're to make cranks and axles. Steel cutters, tube cutters, thread and die cutters, welding and braising equipment. Rubber for brake blocks. I'd have to strip a bike down and see if we can make the parts. It's a skilled task – more engineering than hitting rod with a hammer. Not that chainmaking isn't skilled, but it's very different in technique.'

There would be a lot for the boys to learn. 'Then do it – find a bike and strip it. You can have Scraggs's place. You can rip out the hearths and set up the machinery there once we know what you need. I'll advertise for men with engineering experience to help get you going. Anything you can't make you must be able to buy in as parts.'

'I suppose. You are sure about this? What do Mom and Dad say?'

'Absolutely sure, and it's nothing to do with Mom and Dad.'

George tilted his head to one side. 'You had a falling out?

Come on, Emma. This isn't like you. We're family. We pull together.'

Her eyes smarted with tears.

George put an arm around her. 'Whatever it is, it'll come out in the wash.'

She smiled to hear one of Grandma Wallace's sayings. 'I'm not sure. Oh, I expect you're right. Now go and fetch Theo and get round to Scraggs's place.' She lifted a key from a row of hooks on the wall. 'This is yours now. Taylor Brothers, Cycle Manufacturers.'

George beamed. 'We won't let you down, Em.'

She ruffled his hair for all that he was taller than she was. 'I know you won't.' Family was family, after all, wasn't it? The price of justice would be the destruction of everyone she loved.

***

Frankfurt, Germany 1928

Hanne Samuels opened the letter from England. It had to be from Emma. A photograph was of a girl of about fifteen with dark, wavy hair, and she was standing in front of a beautiful old house so different from her own apartment home in Frankfurt. This house stood in its own grounds, which were clearly extensive. The family resemblance to herself at that age was striking.

May 10th 1928

Heath Hall.

Dear Hanne,

Thank you so much for your kind letter. Your English is very good. I enclose a photograph of myself. It was taken some years ago in the gardens of Heath Hall. It's a lovely old house, and part of it is run as a nursing home for the women of Hawley Heath. It was Grandma Joshua's gift to her workers.

We have exciting times in England this week. The government has finally reduced the voting age for all women to twenty-one, so I shall be able to vote at the next election.

She frowned. Britain was behind the times. Women in Germany had been able to vote from that age since the end of the war, though she was still too young.

Mom helped campaign for this for many years. Grandma Joshua, according to her diary, took a more direct approach. Did you know she helped set a bomb in St Paul's Cathedral in London? She was a woman passionate about women's rights. Can women vote in Germany?

Marion Joshua bombed a cathedral? She looked across Börneplatz to the synagogue. Who on earth would want to destroy a place of worship that was so important to so many people? She couldn't imagine such a thing happening in Ostend.

My younger brothers, Theo and George, are setting up a factory to make bicycles. There are a lot of men out of work here in England and much poverty. It will give men skilled jobs and provide cheap transport. I have placed an advertisement in the local newspaper for a man with experience in engineering. The boys will need someone to guide them and keep them in order, so I'm hoping for an older man – a steadying influence. Mom says prices have gone up more than wages, and many families are in a worse state than they were before women won a legal minimum wage, years ago – before the war even.

Britain had won the war, but it seemed it had yet to win the peace.

You say things have been bad in Germany, too. Is there

anything I can send you to help? You only have to ask, and if I can do it, I shall. Already, I feel a bond between us. I hope we shall become great friends.

She blinked away tears and blew her nose. Emma was so kind to offer, but she and Mutter were managing, and Mutter would see it as charity. She felt the bond, too. She would write back more confidently now she knew her English was passably good.

Perhaps, one day, we shall meet in person. Wouldn't that be exciting? What is Frankfurt like? I've never been far from Hawley Heath. Have you travelled? How I should love to see foreign lands.

She would invite her cousin to stay. It would be wonderful to meet her and learn to speak English properly. Like Emma, she was already sure they would be great friends.

***

Hawley Heath, England 1928

The photograph enclosed in the lavender-scented envelope was of a slim, pretty young girl with black wavy hair and dark eyes. She was dressed stylishly in a long coat and wore a dark, broad-brimmed hat that hid part of her face.

Emma didn't have friends in England, and she needed a friend, not that she could confide her worries to anyone. To deny her father justice was to live the lie her parents had lived all her life, and yet, Mom had been so young, not so much older than Grace was, and Willis had taken advantage of her. How would she have felt had her sister Grace been raped?

Her blood pumped at the thought of it, and her fists clenched. No man should be allowed to get away with rape. Was death too harsh a penalty?

31

She pushed aside the turmoil in her heart and looked again at the photograph. Hanne had a kind face, and, yes, she badly needed a friend. Her position as Matthew Joshua's granddaughter had set her apart from most of the working girls in the area, even though she'd worked alongside them at Mrs Kimble's, and she'd never made friends among the wealthier families; her roots were working class, firmly planted by Mom and Dad, despite her Joshua wealth.

She'd made promises of help to Hanne when she hadn't really a good idea of her own finances beyond what she'd set aside to get the bicycle factory up and running. She would put that right as soon as she could. Mom would know to the penny. She'd need to talk to her eventually.

May 25th
Börneplatz
Ostend,
Frankfurt,
Dear Emma,

I was so excited to get your letter and your kind offer of help. We are not in such need at the moment, although I see much poverty in other families. The reparations Germany was forced to pay after the war have crippled our economy, even I can see that. People are still angry at the terms of the Treaty of Versailles and believe our country will never recover. But Germany will recover in time, I am sure.

Frankfurt is a beautiful city. We have an apartment near the synagogue on Börneplatz. I would love you to come and see Frankfurt if you are able? Our generation is lucky, as the government lifted the restrictions on Jewish life in Germany before I was born. We have much more freedom than our grandparents had, forced as they were to live in Judengasse, the

32

Ghetto.

You speak of being able to vote. I long for that, although some of my friends' parents see needing to vote means we have a weak government. I think they are too used to doing as they are told and not having an opinion. Anyway, I was too young to vote in the federal election just past. Mutter, mother, voted for the Sozialdemokratische Partei Deutschlands, but there are so many factions in Germany, and apart from the Communists on the far left, and the Fascists on the far right, it seems there's little to choose between many of them. Most parties have seats in the Reichstag, the German government.

Mutter says this makes the Weimar Republic weak, because they can never agree on anything, whereas the Kaiser's control over the army made him strong, and many blame the new government for Germany losing the war and hate them. I don't know if this is true, but there is much shame among the German people for losing, and they look for someone to blame. There were attempts to overthrow the government, Mutter says, by both Communists and Fascists when I was a child, but I don't remember it.

Reichspräsident von Hindenburg has a hard task, although he has the power to rule by decree in an emergency. According to Mutter, this a dangerous thing, and it is fortunate that he is an honourable man. Hermann Müller is our Chancellor.

But enough of politics – I am becoming as bad as Mutter. I have met a nice Jewish boy. He is twenty and his name is Berik, which means bear. Mutter wants us to be married, but I am not sure. I am young still, and there is life to be lived, is there not?

Do you have a young man? Do tell me about him if you have.

Emma pursed her lips. She didn't have a young man when most

33

women her age were married with families. She wanted children – it was the man she wanted to be their father she was missing. Was she being too fussy and risking being left on the shelf?

She reread Hanne's letter with a longing to escape and see Frankfurt for herself. Dad's stories of life aboard HMS *Valiant* during the war with Germany, and his time at Scapa Flow, had always stirred her imagination and her need to see new and distant places.

Sometimes, she wished she were a man and could leave Hawley Heath behind, but barring another war to take men abroad again, even they were stuck in a factory six days a week until they retired – those fortunate enough to have a job, that was. The dole paid precious little. The state of the men standing on street corners begging for work or handouts was pitiable. England may have won the war, but it was in as parlous a state as Germany.

Which brought her back to her role as a chain mistress. She couldn't cure all the ills of the area, and handouts, much as they were needed, were only a temporary answer, whereas a bicycle factory would help long term. She was doing her best, and she was grateful for what she had – for what Marion had bequeathed her, and to Mom and Dad for working all these years to ensure it was an inheritance worth having.

She had her family's lives in her hands, and part of her screamed for the truth to be told, to hurt as she'd been hurt, but what good would that do now? Could she bring herself to be as vindictive as her father had been, as cruelly calculating as Marion, as cold as Matthew – as brave and loving as Mom and Jack – Dad? But whether or not her Joshua blood won out, whatever she decided, it wouldn't mean she'd forgiven any of them.

***

34

Emma faced her parents across the office desk. She couldn't live with this burden of guilt and indecision any longer. She took a deep breath: she was not her father. 'We need to sort this, once and for all. We have to live and work together, after all.'

'Emma, if you want us to leave Heath Hall and the factory, it's your decision.' Her father's face held no smile, no frown of condemnation, just the placid acceptance and trust that was so typical of him.

Had it really come to this? 'No, Dad, Of course I don't. But this lie is tearing us apart. I've heard Mom's side of the story. I've read the diaries. Dad, how could you leave Marion and Matthew to suffer all those months, not knowing if Willis was alive or dead?'

Dad shook his head. 'It was a terrible thing to do. I panicked. It would have been our word against the wealth of Matthew Joshua. All I could think of was protecting your mother. And I was furious with Willis. If you'd seen...' His voice trailed off. 'It was a dark night, foggy – no one would have seen us. I didn't expect his body to stay hidden so long, but once it sank, I couldn't disclose its whereabouts without incriminating myself, and your mom refused to let me take the blame.'

'You'd have gone to gaol for her?'

'I'd have died to keep her safe, Emma, and I still would. For all of you. Willis's death wasn't her fault. He brought it on himself.'

'Mom?'

'If you take the diaries to the police... I won't let Jack hang for something he didn't do. Are you prepared for that?'

Dad took Mom's hand. 'Come on, love. Emma will do the right thing, and like I said before, we must abide by her decision. She's

35

the only relative of Willis's left, and she must do as she sees fit. Let's give her time to think about it.'

Tears rolled down her cheeks as her parents closed the office door behind them and walked hand-in-hand across the factory floor. She'd been mean to Mom, and no one could have a better father than Dad.

She wiped her eyes with a handkerchief and unlocked the small safe in the office. Taking out Marion's diary, she threaded her way between snakes of chain to the far end of the factory. 'Mom?' She tapped her mother's shoulder.

Mom looked round and smiled. 'Are you all right, love?'

She opened the diary and turned to the offending pages. She tore them out and held them out to Mom. 'I'm sorry, Mom. I know you didn't have a choice. I do love you – and Dad.'

Mom laid down her hammer and put the red-hot length of rod back in her hearth. She wiped her hands on her apron before taking the pages. 'What are these?'

'Grandma Joshua's diary entries concerning Willis. I can't lose you, either of you, and while these exist there's a risk someone could find them and use them. Throw them in your hearth. Burn them.'

Mom held them over the hearth. 'Are you sure about this?'

'Aren't you going to read them.'

'I trust you, sweetheart.'

The pages fluttered into the hot coals and blackened, and the past and the Joshua curse curled up in a wisp of smoke and disappeared.

'I love you, too, Emma.' The words were felt more than heard above the din of iron on iron. Mom gave her a hug, and all was right with her world once more.

Now, she must be the best person she could be, like Mom and Dad were.

She'd show Mom the letter from Hanne and see what she thought about them writing to one another. She'd missed Mom's sure hand on the reins of her life. Being twenty-one, an adult, came with decisions and responsibilities she hadn't anticipated.

It was long past time she grew up and faced them. Back in the office, a knock on the door interrupted her thoughts. A man in his late twenties with a thatch of fair hair poking from beneath a flat cap stood outside. She beckoned him in.

'What can I do for you, Mr…?'

'Dudley. Charles Dudley.' His blue eyes twinkled as he removed his cap. 'Most folk call me Charlie.'

She wasn't most folk. 'Take a seat, Mr Dudley. How can I help?'

'I read your advert in the newspaper. Engineering skills?'

She nodded. 'My brothers are setting up a factory to make bicycles. They're young but very enthusiastic. I need someone with experience who could turn his hand to bicycle manufacture.'

The man nodded. 'I'm working in Birmingham at BSA. They make cars and motorbikes, but twelve miles is a long way to travel on a push-bike. I'm looking for work closer to home and there isn't much about.'

'So you'd know what machinery and skills we'd need. We're chainmakers, so this is new ground for us.'

'Would it just be cycles or would it be motorcycles as well?'

'I hadn't thought beyond bicycles, cheap transport for working men and women, but if there's a market for bikes with engines, why not once we get set up?'

'It would cost a pretty penny to tool a factory from scratch. You'd need metal-working lathes and men who know how to use them, as well as welders and–'

'I realise that. I'm prepared to invest in my brothers' venture, Mr Dudley.'

He shifted in his seat as if uncomfortable. 'I wish you'd call me Charlie. I'm not used to such formality.'

The pleading expression on his face made her laugh. 'I'm not usually so formal, Charlie.' She held out her hand in welcome. 'I'm Emma. Do you have references?'

'No.' He got up from his chair. 'I'm sorry to have wasted your time, Miss Emma.'

'Sit, Charlie.' She smiled apologetically; she'd sounded as if she was commanding a dog. 'I'm just Emma. We're all family here. I shall write to your previous employer for a reference. What will they tell me?'

'Hopefully, that I'm a good worker. I've been with them since 1918, when they were making small arms, rifles and such, for the army. After the war I went over to making motor cars and motorbikes.'

'Then leave me your address, or a telephone number where I can contact you, and I'll be in touch.' She pushed a notepad and pen towards him and watched him as he bent over the task. She was almost willing to take a chance on him, judging his character more valuable than his expertise, but this was her brothers' future she was gambling, and common sense decreed a more cautious approach. Was he the right man for the job? Was he married? She flushed hot at the thought.

He looked up, pushed the notepad and pen back across the desk, and grinned as if reading her mind. 'I hope to see you again, Emma.'

She hoped so, too.

Chapter Four

Rosie read the letter Hanne had written to Emma. 'Life must have been difficult for her in Germany. It's hard enough here with so much unemployment, but we haven't had to pay reparations to Britain and France. I read a figure once. I think it was over six billion pounds. How the world expects them to do that when France has possession of their coal mines, I don't know.'

'But Hanne will be all right, won't she?'

'I'm sure she will. These factions she speaks of – they have a democracy now, as we do. The extremists won't get voted into power.' She gave the letter back to Emma. 'It's going to take all countries time to get back on their feet. Ten years is not such a long time.'

'Not long? It's half my life. I still worry about her. Is there something we can do to help her?'

'You offered to help her in your last letter. She says they're managing, Emma, and we have our own problems to solve. Concentrate on this scheme you're hatching with the boys. If you need me to give you a hand in the office, let me know. I'm sure Hanne will ask if she needs help.'

'I suppose. I shall write to her again.'

She sighed as Emma went back to the office, happily unaware of the difficulty of being Jewish in a country like Germany. She'd suspected Matthew Joshua was of Jewish extraction, and Hanne's letter confirmed it. Emma showed Jewish characteristics, more so as she'd grown into womanhood.

She selected a length of rod and placed it into her hearth, reaching for the handle to pump the bellows as she did so.

With her daughter's future in mind, she'd kept a quiet watch on events around the world these last few years. The Jewish people had a centuries-long history of being displaced from countries: Russia, Austria, America, and even England. They'd been discriminated against and banished from Germany in the past, and it could happen again, despite the more relaxed rules Hanne described. The girl's letter had unsettled her more than she wanted to admit.

The rod glowing bright yellow, she removed it from the heat, cut it to length with a single blow, and laid it on her bickon. She was making rings today to be joined to links to make cow chains. It was one commodity still in regular demand across the world, and Joshua and Son had a reputation for quality chains. What would they do without orders from America? Hammering and reheating the rod, she formed the first ring. More blow from the bellows made the hearth spark white, and she fire-welded the iron with her hammer.

She quenched the ring, threw it into a box with the others, and laid a new piece of rod in the breeze. The actions were so well practised, they came almost without conscious thought, and her mind strayed back to Hanne and the letter from Germany.

It was no good. She couldn't concentrate. Tapping Jack on the shoulder, she motioned for him to follow her.

She stopped when she reached the stables, now garaging for vehicles and storage for iron rods. She missed the great Shire horses that had served them so well.

Jack caught her up. 'What is it, now?'

'It's Emma.'

Jack frowned. 'Is she all right?'

'Yes, she's fine. She's been writing to the granddaughter of a cousin of Marion's or Matthew's. I'm not sure which. Her name is Hanne, and she lives in Frankfurt.'

'Germany?'

'Yes. The thing is, she's worried about Hanne.'

'Why?'

'Things are hard in Germany right now.'

'No more than they deserve.'

'Hanne doesn't deserve anything bad. She's done nothing wrong.'

'So, what's the problem?'

'Hanne is Jewish, and Jews aren't loved. Emma is part Jewish, too. I've been watching affairs that might affect her ever since I suspected Matthew and Marion were Jewish. There was an attempt to overthrow the Weimar Republic five years ago. It failed and the leader of the NSDAP was gaoled. It didn't stop his party winning seats in the last election with him as their leader.'

'And this man is a threat to Emma?' Jack looked understandably incredulous. 'How, when she lives in England?'

'Suppose she takes it into her head to visit this cousin? This man compared Jews to a *race tuberculosis of the peoples*. He's even reported as having given a speech where he said *death to the Jews*. God forbid he should ever reach a position of power or influence.'

Jack frowned. 'She's just as headstrong as you were at that age, and we've no chance of stopping her. The Treaty of Versailles was intended to punish Germany, not visiting Britons.'

'But it's the ordinary German people who are suffering. You know what they've been through. The French invaded the Ruhr because of non-payment of reparations –'

'Well, you can't blame them for that.'

'Maybe not, but them taking control of Germany's steel industry has had a disastrous effect on the German economy. The government printing more money made the mark worthless – what value has money when a loaf of bread costs two hundred billion marks? People lost their life savings, and only those astute enough to put their wealth in foreign banks, as many Jews did, escaped the worst of the disaster.'

She'd thought her own life hard when she was a child, when a quartern loaf cost thruppence and she'd earned three shillings and sixpence a week if she worked all the hours God gave. The ordinary folk of Germany had been in a desperate plight.

Jack waved a hand towards the factory. 'Germany isn't alone in having suffered inflation, debt, and unemployment.'

'No, but when a nation needs a scapegoat, it will pick on those least able to defend themselves, those least popular, and Jews come high on the list of potential victims. Even part-Jews, if they look Jewish, might feel the backlash.'

'Rosie, Emma is perfectly safe. Germany was thoroughly beaten and shackled. No harm will come to her or Hanne.'

Was Jack right? It was lovely to see Emma excited at discovering a newfound relation, but she still feared for her daughter and Hanne. Even in Britain, there were people who didn't like Jews, and anti-Semitism, if it took hold, could spread far beyond Germany's borders. Was it because Jews were successful, because they looked, dressed, and worshipped differently, or because they believed they were God's chosen

43

people?

She didn't know, and she didn't care. Her concern was Emma's wellbeing and dissuading her from dashing off to help Hanne.

She went back to her hearth, and another ring clattered into the box. She was worrying unnecessarily. Germany had recovered a lot these past few years thanks to their able chancellor, who'd taken out massive loans to boost their flagging economy. Other countries were trading with Germany again, and, at last, things were looking up for the German people. Hanne would be fine.

***

Emma read the glowing reference from British Small Arms. They would be sad to lose Charlie Dudley. Their loss was her gain if he could set up a new venture. Should she take the risk or wait for someone older? Life was all a risk and sitting on Grandfather Joshua's chair behind his desk wouldn't get the bicycle factory up and running. Before she changed her mind, she telephoned the number Charlie had left.

She spoke to a woman, Charlie's landlady, who promised to get him to call her when he got in from work. She hung the receiver on its bracket and twiddled her thumbs. It wasn't that she had nothing to do, it was that she couldn't concentrate. Should she have asked Mom or Dad to speak to Charlie as well? Now she was being cowardly. What would Grandma Marion have done? She smiled; she'd have told her to fight for her right to decide her own future – or planted a bomb under her chair.

Half an hour of shuffling the orders around on her desk didn't make them any bigger any more than it made the bills smaller. *Diligent and reliable.* That described Dad to perfection. It was what she needed in a foreman to guide the boys, but was it what she wanted in a man – a lover? The thought made her skin tingle.

What would it be like? Mom had warned her so many times about trusting men who might be after her for her position and money that she hardly dared trust any of them. A lover, she reminded herself, a father to her children, not a husband to obey – not that Mom always obeyed Dad.

The ringing of the telephone made her jump. 'Joshua and Son. How can I help you?'

'Is that Emma?'

'Yes, speaking.'

'It's Charlie Dudley. You asked me to telephone you.'

'I did. Thank you, Charlie.' She shuffled the papers on her desk, only to discover the one she wanted was in front of her. 'I've had a glowing reference from your employers. I'd like to offer you the job if you still want it.'

'That's fantastic. Thank you, Emma. When do I start?'

'Your employers require you to work a week's notice, so shall we say a week on Monday? I'll introduce you to Theo and George and show you the space they have. It's going to be quite a lot of work, but I pay by results. I can guarantee you won't earn less than your present wage, and if I'm happy with you, that will increase. Is that a deal?'

'It's a deal. Thank you, Emma. I look forward to working with you.'

She smothered a laugh. 'I hope you're looking forward to working with the boys. They can be a bit of a handful, but they're good at heart and hard workers. I'm sure you'll get along fine. I shall make you factory foreman, and tell them to do as you ask, at least until they've learned the ropes.'

'You can depend on me.'

'I hope so, Charlie.' She truly hoped so. She had a lot riding on Charlie Dudley.

Determined to see what her brothers had achieved at Spraggs's workshop, she put her paperwork in order. Now to face the daily heartbreak. For every two men in work, there was one waiting outside a factory gate looking for employment. She straightened, trying to harden her heart.

'Do you have any work, miss?' She looked into eager eyes. Behind the lad crowded a group of hopeful men.

'I can make chain. Been making it for twenty years.' The old man's face was familiar. Had he worked for them once?

'I'm a good worker, miss.' A youngster with brawny arms, too young to be out of work.

'Please, I've six little'uns to feed.' The wiry little man was almost in tears. 'I'll do anything.'

'I'm sorry. There's no work in the factory at the moment. We're not taking anyone on. I'm so sorry.'

'It's all right, miss. It ain't your fault. I know as Joshua and Son do their best.'

She nodded, grateful to the man for lessening her burden of guilt, and then turned back. 'Do any of you know anything about bicycles, motorcycles, or lathe work?'

One or two of them assured her they did.

'Come back tomorrow. I can't promise anything, but I may have something for you.'

She walked on, hoping Charlie, Theo, and George wouldn't have to disappoint them. It was time she recruited strong arms to hump machinery and for Charlie to train on the metalworking lathes. They needed men to make bicycles and a factory fit for them to work in.

***

It seemed every street corner had a group of men kicking their heels against the blackened bricks of the terraced houses, caps pulled down, and collars pulled up against a chill wind. There was an air of despondency that crept right into her bones. The previous year, the miners of Wales had marched on London, and the year before that there'd been a general strike, but now, these men seemed to have all but given up.

Head down, Emma avoided their stares and hurried on; she couldn't employ them all, and she felt guilty for making sure all her family had jobs at the expense of other workers.

Some would find it hard to find employment, even in good times. Most jobs required two arms, two legs, and reasonable eyesight, and the war had left many men with terrible disabilities and chest problems. It was a disgrace that proud men had no option but to sit on the pavement with a begging bowl just to feed their families. That Dad had come home physically unscathed was a miracle.

She hadn't been old enough to realise how poor Mom and Dad had been before they'd taken over the running of the factory on Matthew's death, but she hadn't been so little that she couldn't remember going to bed hungry, not that she'd possessed a bed when she was a small child, and the hunger pangs in the night had kept her awake.

She was all too aware, now, that Mom had almost certainly gone without sometimes so she and her brothers and sisters could eat, and still she'd suffered from rickets; her legs weren't quite as straight as they should be.

47

With returning soldiers forcing women out of well-paid jobs, many now earned little money in domestic service and sweated labour. Mom and Mary Macarthur had fought for better wages for the white slaves of England, but where were these women now? No better off than they'd been twenty years ago.

She opened her purse and dropped loose change into a begging bowl, barely able to stomach the man's gratitude. Some of these men might not get paid dole even though they were seeking work. If they hadn't paid into the insurance scheme, or they'd been out of work for twelve months, or the hated Public Assistance Committee deemed they had savings – these men had wives and children who went to bed hungry: children who risked having rickets or worse. There must be something more she could do to help.

The door to Scraggs's workshop stood open, and a cloud of dust puthered through it to be blown away on a chill breeze. A crash accompanied a shout, and more dust joined the cloud.

She covered her nose and mouth with her hand. 'What the hell are you doing in there?'

A dust-covered face poked around the door frame. 'Knocking out the hearths like you wanted.'

She followed Theo inside the workshop. Bricks and cement dust lay everywhere. Fortunately, the boys had left enough brickwork to support the chimneys, something she hadn't thought to tell them. 'It might be an idea to leave a couple of hearths in case they're needed.' She coughed and covered her mouth again. 'I've found a man with knowledge of making bicycles and motorbikes. He's been working for BSA in Birmingham, and he's starting work on Monday next. He'll be your factory foreman, and he knows what's needed, so you do what he tells you. We're lucky to have him, and I don't want you two frightening him off.

Understand? His name's Charlie Dudley. Listen and learn.'

Theo fidgeted. 'All right, we'll behave.'

'And I'll send along a few men to help in setting up the factory. Men we can train.'

George nodded. 'We'll need them. Which two hearths should we leave?'

'How about one at each end? They'll provide heat in the winter. And clean and stack these bricks. We can reuse them.'

'Will do, miss.'

'Don't cheek me, Theo. And sweep this dust out. I want this clean by the time Charlie arrives.'

'Yes, miss.'

She cuffed George around the ear and shook her head. 'You two are impossible.'

Hurrying back to the factory, she passed groups of men still hanging around outside. One of them was drinking cold tea from a bottle. She shivered inside her warm coat. What these men needed was food inside them. Hot food.

The land belonging to Heath Hall produced food that went to local shops, not that many people could afford to buy it. She couldn't feed the entire town, but she could help those in dire need with a soup kitchen – it would be a way of making a little food go a long way. She could set something up in the church rooms and get volunteers. There were enough out of work people to man it. It wasn't an answer, but it would provide short-term relief and make her feel she was doing something useful. She was a chain mistress, not a slave maistress.

She crossed the factory to the office with more determination than she'd felt in a while. On the wall behind the desk hung the slave chain her great-great-grandmother had forged, rescued from the chain workshop in the cinder yard all those years ago.

What was it Mom had told her? *Some make chains, and some wear them.* She took the chain down from the wall, the links cold in her fingers. Men and women had been enslaved for life in chains like this, and the women of the Black Country had forged them.

Women might have won the vote and a minimum wage, but there was still precious little equality between men and women, either in pay or freedoms. She was one of the privileged few to have independent means and the option of deciding her own future, and yet, as a mere woman, she still felt like a second-class citizen – still felt the urge to defer to a man's "superior" intellect, expected to obey her husband, expected to accept lower wages and less unemployment benefit, and yet women were allowed to go to university now and train as teachers, nurses, and even doctors.

Allowed to go. She clenched her fist around the slave chain, carried it to Mom's forge, and threw it into the hot breeze.

'What are you doing?' Mom's voice grated, shocked. 'Emma –
'

'This…' She pumped the bellows, grasped the yellow-hot chain with tongs, and laid it on Mom's anvil. Taking a hammer and chisel, she sheared the centre link. 'Breaking the chain. Mom, I won't be a slave. I won't be inferior, not to anyone.'

Chapter Five

When Emma walked through the door to Scraggs – Taylor Bros Cycle Manufacturers as the sign above the door proclaimed – she knew she'd made the right choice in Charlie. He had a way of inspiring George and Theo by explaining why a thing needed doing the way he suggested. Because they understood, they took his instruction and worked with a will.

It had only been a week since Charlie had started work, and already rows of electrical sockets were installed and a bank of enigmatic machinery stood along one wall of the old chain workshop. Outside in the yard, George and two of the men she'd sent along to help were unloading steel tubing and other lengths of metal from a borrowed Joshua and Son lorry. Things were moving apace, expensively, judging by the invoices Charlie had been handing her.

Charlie and Theo were bent over a lathe, the noise of the machine deadening her footsteps. She waited until they switched off the machine and looked up.

'This is great, Em. Look.' Theo held up a piece of metal bar he'd turned into a perfect, graduated cylinder. 'Charlie's teaching me to use the lathe.'

She smiled, delighted to see her brother so enthused. 'So I see.'

Charlie patted Theo on the shoulder. 'That's good for a first try. We can't do much more until we have plans and specifications drawn up, and we need instruments like callipers and vernier gauges before we can do precision work. It's a good start, but you'll have to practise.' He turned to her. 'Emma, we'll need a drawing board and a plan bench before we can start making anything viable. We must come up with a design that's instantly recognisable as a Taylor Brothers' cycle.'

Charlie had an eye for marketing as well as production. She was impressed. 'Order what you need.' If this venture succeeded, and they could expand into motorcycles, it could be a good investment and a long-term answer to unemployment in the area.

She left the workshop in capable hands and walked back to the factory with a spring in her step. Long-term plans didn't feed families *now*, and if she could help the good folk of Hawley Heath through the short term, they would repay her with the same loyalty Mom had earned. Wealth was a privilege, not a right, and she would use it to the best effect she could.

'Mom?'

'Emma.' Mom's eyebrow was almost permanently raised nowadays.

'You're so much better in the office than I am.'

Mom wasn't fooled for a moment. 'What hare-brained scheme are you dreaming up now?'

'I've found volunteers to help run a soup kitchen. I'm not cut out to be a chain mistress. I'd be much happier making and serving soup. And I need to keep an eye on Charlie and the boys.'

Mom pursed her lips. 'You're a very good chain mistress, but if you want me to take over the office for a while… You have to do what you think is right, Emma.' She smiled. 'I'm sure Charlie Dudley needs you to keep an eye on him. He seems like a nice young man.'

She hugged Mom to hide the pink flush she was sure was creeping into her cheeks. 'Thanks, Mom.'

'Only for a while, though.'

She ran back through the factory before Mom changed her mind. Margaret and Elsie were already at the church rooms preparing the mountain of vegetables she'd sent down with Mr Timms. The old man must be eighty if he was a day, but he refused to retire and still tended the now extensive kitchen gardens with the help of a young lad called Jacob.

She'd ask him if he needed more help; it was a lot of work for an old man and a young lad. Mr Timms had provided carrots, parsnips, and potatoes from the winter store in the clamps, onions from the strings hanging in the barn, and fresh spring greens. Made into soup, it should be enough to supplement the meagre provisions of the hungriest of Hawley Heath for a week.

She set up the huge saucepans on the paraffin-fuelled range in the hall kitchen. The oven looked large enough to braise a joint of meat. If today's soup kitchen was a success, they could ring the changes with mutton from the farm; there were always barren ewes or ram lambs not worth keeping for breeding. And bread would fill empty stomachs if the baker would supply quantity at a discounted price.

She set to chopping the vegetables, happy to be doing something worthwhile. Mom and Charlie would see the factories ran to their best ability; they didn't need her.

***

A trickle of hungry mouths on the first day had led to a flood by the end of the first week, and Emma had wondered if they could keep up with demand. They added more water to the soup, served it with a noggin of bread, and asked people to bring their own bowls or mugs. A ticket for the next day's meal, to be handed in and exchanged for another, prevented the greedy from coming back for second helpings later in the day and helped slow the tide. Even charity could be abused, it seemed. On the whole, however, the men, women, and children who turned up with hopeful, hungry faces were grateful for the little sustenance they received and many a 'God bless you, dear' was whispered when she ladled hot soup into proffered bowls.

Charlie and the boys had the bicycle factory up and running, and after intensive training, a small team of men and women had produced their first batch of bicycles. She and Charlie had put their heads together over pricing, keeping in mind that production would get faster as the workforce gained experience, and they needed a competitively priced machine even if, at first, they generated little profit; they weren't the only cycle manufacturers in the vicinity. They'd decided on five pounds five shillings, which undercut some of the other factories, and Charlie had come up with the brilliant idea of allowing monthly or weekly payments.

She'd drafted advertisements for the local newspapers and the better-known cycling magazines, and they held their breaths, awaiting interest. It was nerve-wracking waiting for the first orders, but the boys were riding two of the cycles around the town, allowing people to try them out, and so spread news of them by word of mouth.

They needed sales and satisfied customers to generate capital for more materials, pay wages, and expand to employ more men. She'd done all she could. It was in Charlie's and the boys' hands now.

The soup kitchen ran like clockwork with many helping hands, and she didn't feel needed there, either.

Her thoughts turned to Hanne, as they often did. They'd exchanged letters over the past months, and she longed to meet her cousin in person. She'd devoured any news about Germany with an appetite keener than the hungry at the soup kitchen, and the desire to travel beyond the confines of Hawley Heath grew ever stronger as the weeks passed.

Keen as she was to further the cause of equality for women, there seemed little she could do while there was so much male unemployment. '*Fight the battles you can win.*' Who'd said that? Dad, Mom?

She turned from the window of Heath Hall and the view of spreading chestnuts in full leaf to the small, blue cardboard-covered booklet in her hand. Inside was her photograph embossed with **Foreign Office** and the date. It was her passport to the world, and she was a free woman, so why did she feel the need to ask permission to leave?

She was a chain mistress. It was a job, not a life. Mom and Grandma Joshua had no right to tie her down to a life of servitude – she'd broken the slave chain in two, hadn't she? No, she would go and see Hanne. It was settled, and she'd brook no argument.

Shoulders squared, she strode down the hill and into the factory. 'Mom, Dad, I'm going to Frankfurt.'

Dad frowned. 'What?'

She raised her voice over the sound of hammers and the whoosh of the steam bellows. 'Germany. I'm going to visit Hanne.'

Mom nodded but didn't smile. 'I wondered how long it would take you to fly the nest.'

'You don't mind?'

Mom sighed. 'You're a grown woman, and I can't forbid you to go. As I told you once before, Emma, you have to do what you think is right. It'll be a valuable experience.' Mom motioned her away from the noise. 'Emma, just one thing. Remember you have Jewish blood and be careful.'

'Why does that make a difference?'

'The German people are a proud people, and defeat didn't come easily to them. Many still believe they won the war and were let down by their weak government. After the war, there were a lot of Jews in government positions, positions of power – some people, people with influence, blame the Jews.'

'That's ridiculous. Hanne and her family have lived in Germany all their lives. They're German.'

'I know, but Germans have targeted Jewish people in the past. I know things are better now in Germany, but old prejudices run deep.' Mom smiled ruefully 'They don't like the French, either, or the Communists.'

'I don't suppose any country is pleased to have an occupying army. The French are only protecting their own border, surely?'

'Yes, but there's a lot of bad feeling about them seizing the Ruhr. It's caused a lot of problems for Germany. All I'm saying is, Germany might now be on firmer ground, but the political factions are far from in agreement. There have been attempted coups, violent ones, in the not-too-distant past. Germany is still volatile.'

'I shall be fine, Mom. Hanne will doubtless escort me everywhere.'

Mom brushed a stray wisp of greying hair from her forehead. 'Yes, Hanne will look after you, I'm sure. She knows you're going?'

'Yes.'

'When do you leave?'

'Tomorrow morning. I need to be in London by three o'clock to catch the train for the ferry.'

'So soon?'

'You and Dad have everything in hand here, and Charlie and the boys don't need me.'

'And the soup kitchen?'

'Margaret and Elsie have plenty of willing helpers. Mom, if I don't do this now, before I get tied down...'

Mom nodded, appearing to concede an inward battle. 'Freedom is hard to find once you have a husband and children. You're right, sweetheart. You should go while you can. Time enough to settle down when you come back.' Mom's brow creased in familiar worry lines. 'You are coming back?'

'Oh, Mom. Of course, I am. I may even bring Hanne back for a visit to England if she's able. Mom, will Dad be all right with me going to Germany?'

'The war's in the past, sweetheart, and your dad's used to putting up with wilful and wayward women in his life. He'll miss you, though.' Mom hugged her. 'You have packing to do, and it seems I have a factory to run. Take care, sweetheart. Promise me.'

She kissed Mom's damp cheek. 'I promise.'

***

Emma nodded, trying to keep her eyes open so she wouldn't miss the trees, fields, churches, and houses moving past her carriage window like the pictures on the cinema screen in town. Her heart had ceased the frantic beating on first boarding the train, and now, the regular clackity-clack of the wheels on the track made it hard to stay awake.

'London, Euston. London, Euston.' The conductor's voice grew louder as he worked his way along the carriage's corridor. 'London, Euston, miss.'

She collected her luggage and waited for the train to rattle to a halt, almost throwing her against the carriage wall. London. Heart in mouth, she stepped down onto the platform amid a belch of steam. She looked around, searching for the exit. Signs pointed to street names that meant nothing to her. She hailed a porter. 'Where do I find the train for the ferry to Ostend, Belgium?'

The man pointed. 'You want the train to Victoria and the boat train to Dover.'

She hurried along the platform, wishing she'd travelled lighter. It was almost three o'clock, and if she missed her connections, she'd miss the ferry and have to wait until Saturday for another. The train seemed to be gathering steam.

On the platform at Victoria was a blackboard with the words **State of the sea – choppy**. What did that mean? She was about to find out. 'Is this the boat train to Dover?'

The plump, middle-aged lady looking hot in a fur coat nodded. 'It is. It'll be leaving soon. We'd better get aboard.'

'Thank you.' She swung her bags onto the train, climbed up after them, found a seat by the window, and sank down with a sigh of relief. Travelling was tiring.

She'd been too nervous to eat, but now it was mid-afternoon, and her stomach rumbled. She'd packed sandwiches and a bottle of cold tea. She picked at her food and gave up – *choppy*.

The train rumbled through the suburbs of London and out into open country and neat fields and villages. Her first sight of the sea at Folkestone took her breath away. She'd seen pictures in Mom's old books, but the reality went on forever… How had Dad dared to sail to war?

The train slowed and the sign across the platform announced Dover Marine. The train juddered to a halt and doors crashed open. This was it.

'You look lost.' The porter smiled. 'The ferry's that way, about a mile.'

'A mile?' She looked at her luggage.

'There're cabs out in the street if you don't want to walk.'

The woman she'd met at Victoria was climbing into one. 'Thank you.' She didn't mind walking, but the travelling bags were already making her arms ache. Working in the office or making electrically welded chain instead of wielding a hammer had made her soft.

She hurried, sure the crowd of people leaving the station ahead of her would take all the cabs. A mix of cars and horse-drawn carriages stood outside the station. An open-top bus pulled in behind them. She made for the bus, surely the cheaper way to travel, enquired of the destination, and took a seat near the door. She might have money, but the train from Ostend to Frankfurt was first class only, and frugality was a lesson learned early in life and reinforced by Mom and Dad's example.

The steamer was already docked, and she followed a throng of men and women to buy her ticket and board the ferry. On deck, a stiff breeze tugged at her hair. Was this the reason for fur coats on a warm day in late summer? She would have to look out Grandma Joshua's long coat with the fur collar and matching fur hat next time.

Next time? She had yet to survive this time. The port of Dover slipped away to stern, and for the first time in her life, she was leaving England, following Dad to sea, except she was going to Germany to meet the Hun in peace, not fighting them from the engine room of a super dreadnought.

Chapter Six

It seemed the affluent of England were used to travelling in style, which was more than Emma was. Piles of smart matching luggage, carried by porters or servants, followed imperious-looking couples in tweeds and fur coats. She was too ill-dressed to approach any of them, and the sideways glances from young men and older women suggested they considered a woman travelling alone and unchaperoned was neither wise nor virtuous. Her jaw clamped. Why shouldn't she be able to travel alone? Equality, it seemed, had a long way to go, and parents needed to educate their sons as well as their daughters, if women were to be respected and treated as equals.

Her stomach still rumbled with hunger, but the thought of finishing her sandwiches made her nauseous, and she gripped the rail on deck and kept her eyes on the rolling horizon. The foreign coast's pale blue outline gained strength and grew buildings and a port. Ostend, Belgium.

Eager to be back on firm ground, she grasped her mismatched travelling bags and headed for the landward side of the steamer, before waiting for the ship to dock and the gangway to be lowered. Signs pointed her to the station a short walk away.

'Paspoort, juffrouw.' The officer held out his hand while blocking her path. 'Paspoort?'

She fumbled in her bag for her passport and proffered it, holding her breath. The officer perused it for a long moment, looked her up and down, stamped it, and handed it back. She managed a smile. 'Thank you.'

He waved her on and accosted the next passenger. Breathing again, she hurried to board her train. Her carriage had ten compartments, each small and wood-panelled and equipped with a sofa, table, and washbasin. She chose an empty compartment and claimed the seat by the window. It had already been a long day, and her journey across Europe had barely begun. The train juddered into movement, and the town of Ostend trundled past as the train gathered speed.

'Is this compartment taken?' It was the lady she'd met on Victoria station.

'No, it's just me.'

The woman smiled. 'Edith Chamberlain-Watts. Where are you headed all alone?'

She held out a hand in greeting. 'Emma Taylor. I'm visiting a cousin in Frankfurt. You?'

Edith removed her coat and sank into the seat beside her. 'Vienna. A beautiful city. I visit every year. Is this your first time abroad?'

It was that obvious? 'Yes. It's exhilarating but stressful.'

Edith waved a confident hand. 'You'll get used to it, and I'm here now to guide you. Have you eaten?'

'I brought sandwiches, but haven't had more than a bite. The ferry—'

Edith smiled. 'The dining car will be serving dinner. It will be a long hungry night if you don't eat, Emma. Shall we?'

She followed Edith along the corridor to a carriage with rows of tables, each with their own lamp and set for two. Buildings gave way to fields and woods, and despite her intention to devour every foreign sight, food and Edith's conversation took all her attention.

By the time they'd finished their meal, Brussels was behind them and it was dark outside. An attendant had been into their compartment and made the sofa into two bunks, complete with sheets and blankets. It was more luxury than she was used to at Heath Hall and brought home to her the inequalities between the haves and the have-nots even more strongly. What did Edith know of soup kitchens and unemployment? Her rich husband had left her a wealthy widow.

Edith drew the plush curtains. 'Do you mind if I have the bottom bunk, Emma, dear? Your legs are younger than mine.'

'Of course not.' She hadn't thought to need nightclothes on a train. She washed and climbed the short ladder to her bunk.

'I'll leave the light on, dear. There's a toilet compartment at the end of the carriage, should you need it.'

'Liège. Liège.' The voice woke her with a start. Edith was snoring, peacefully unaware. The train slowed to a halt but soon moved off again, and she fell back into uneasy dreams. She'd barely closed her eyes when she woke to a voice coming closer. 'Herbesthal. Herbesthal. Herbesthal.'

Sleep, it seemed, wasn't to be had, and she was still awake when the train rattled to a halt again and the guard shouted. It was past midnight. 'Duitse grens! Houd uw paspoorten gereed. Volgende halte Aken.'

'Edith. Edith!'

The snoring stopped. 'Where are we?'

'I don't know. I don't speak the language. All I understood was paspoorten.'

Edith swung her legs over the side of her bunk. 'Must be the

63

German border. They change engines here, and there's a border crossing. They'll want to see your passport, so make yourself decent.'

Doors banged open against the carriage walls, and heavy boots thumped along the corridor. 'Reisepass. Reisepass.'

She had nothing to fear, so why did border guards make her feel so nervous? Her compartment door opened. 'Reisepass, Fräulein.' Her heart thumped in her ears as she handed over her little blue booklet. The border inspector stared at her. 'Wohin gehst du?'

'Pardon?'

Edith answered for her. 'She's going to Frankfurt.'

The guard returned her passport. 'Danke.'

She let tense shoulders relax. What had ever made her think she could travel across Europe alone. Thank God, she'd met Edith.

In the early hours of the morning, they stopped at Aachen, then at Cologne where more carriages joined the train, and then at Wiesbaden; they gave up all attempts at sleep. At half-past four as it was getting light, the express pulled into Frankfurt Sud station. She gave Edith a grateful hug, collected her luggage, and stepped down onto the platform. Finding a bench, she huddled into her coat. The other passengers on the night train hurried from the station, but she had a long, lonely wait on a chilly station platform before she could expect Hanne to come to meet her.

***

Frankfurt, Germany late-summer 1928

Franzosen und Belgier nicht erwünscht

The faded words were scrawled on the wall. There was also a

torn poster with the legend, **Juden und Bolschewiki sind heir unerwünscht**. Emma didn't know what the words meant, but the image of an ugly, red-skinned man with an enormous nose and grasping hands suggested it wasn't intended to be friendly. And judging by the depiction of a Star of David, Juden meant Jew. Coloured red to depict a Bolshevik? Mom had said the Germans didn't like the French, Jews, or Communists. How did they feel about the English?

She walked up and down the station platform nearest to the exit to the street to keep warm but still shivered, and not only from the chill of dawn.

'Tu as froid, mademoiselle?'

She looked up into black eyes in a black face. She stepped back, startled. The man was in a soldiers' uniform, so he must be one of the French occupying force, but she hadn't expected a black man. 'Pardon?'

'Vous êtes Juive?'

'I don't understand.'

'Anglais, oui? English.'

'Yes, English.'

He grinned. 'Vien avec moi.' He gestured, rubbing his arms as if to warm them. 'Froid. Cold. Vien avec moi.' He stepped away from her and looked back as if to see if she was following.

'You know of somewhere warm to wait?'

'Warm, oui.'

She smiled, grateful for the soldier's care, and followed him around a corner. It was ill-lit, and she shivered.

'Je te garde au chaud, oui?' He smiled and put a hand on her

65

arm, winked and tightened his grip. 'Les hommes noirs sont de bons amants.'

'Let go of my arm, please.' She tried to shake off his hand, but he gripped harder.

He grinned, showing white teeth, and pushed her to the ground, straddling her so she couldn't get up. She kicked and struck out at him, landing a blow on the side of his head, but he was strong, too strong, and the more she struggled, the more ineffectual her blows became. He grabbed both her wrists and sneered in her face. 'Je vais vous donner un salaud de Rhénanie, Juive.'

The intent behind the strange words was clear. Fear froze her. She was at this man's mercy, and there was nothing she could do to stop him. How dare he do this? In a last desperate bid for freedom, she twisted sideways and brought her knees up, throwing him off-balance.

One hand freed, she hit him hard in the face, and wrenched her other hand from his grip. Taking her chance, she leapt to her feet and ran. Feet pounded after her, drawing ever closer, and she used what felt like her last breath to scream.

A man in a uniform was hauling a baggage wagon across the platform. She hurled herself towards him, almost knocking him off his feet, and his arm came around her waist. 'Let go.' Her breath came in ragged sobs. 'Let me go.'

'Hör auf zu treten. Ich tue dir nichts.' The German held her tight as she kicked and beat her fists on his chest.

The French soldier slid to a halt. 'Elle est à moi.'

A slight figure with dark wavy hair pushed herself between the soldier and his prize. 'Lass sie sein!'

'Franzosenschwein.' The luggage porter pushed the girl aside, and his fist lashed out. The French soldier fell to the platform and lay still, bleeding from his nose. The German released his grip on her waist. 'Du bist jetzt in Sicherheit. Safe now, ja?'

She took a breath, and the German's eyes followed the heave of her chest. 'Thank you.'

'Emma? It is Emma?' The girl's dark eyes betrayed her anxiety.

'Hanne?'

'Emma, I'm so sorry I was late. Are you hurt?'

'Just bruised.' She smiled. 'It's good to meet you at last, cousin.'

Hanne hugged her, and she winced. 'Let's get you home, Emma.'

'You go where, meine Damen?'

Hanne answered for her. 'Börneplatz.'

The man took hold of the handle of his trolley. 'I go, later.' He indicated the parcels and mail bags on his trolley. 'Post Strassenbahn. You ride tram with me, ja?'

'Danke.' Hanne released her. 'It will be safer than walking empty streets with these French soldiers patrolling. Where is your luggage, Emma?'

'Back there.' The black man was still out cold. Was he alive? She wasn't going to hang around to find out or wait for other soldiers to arrive on the scene. She grabbed her scattered bags, followed the man onboard the post tram, and sank into a seat, her legs wobbly and shaking. But for this kind postal worker, she'd have suffered the same fate Mom had endured at Willis's hands.

Her hip and back hurt, and she rubbed sore knuckles. She better

67

understood Dad attacking Willis – and Rosie defending him at the cost of Willis's life. How could any man do that to a woman? Was a woman's right to her own body so abhorrent to a man? She hated her father, hated everything about him. Her clasped hands trembled in her lap; she was not her father's daughter. She was Emma Taylor, daughter of Rosie and Jack Taylor, and she wished she'd never heard of Willis Joshua. She wished she'd never opened that tin box in Grandma Joshua's wardrobe – except then she'd never have met Hanne.

The tram took them past tall, many-windowed buildings with odd, stepped gables and black and white timbered walls. The river sparkled in the early morning sun and lit the facades of the tall houses that lined the road, boats steamed upriver, and the pungent smells of water, fish, horse manure, and coal smoke from steamers and trains mingled on the breeze.

Hanne was chattering, but she had trouble concentrating on what she said. 'There are too many brown babies. We call them "*Rhineland Bastards*", fathered by the French Senegalese troops. They say they rape and mutilate German women. I don't know if this is true or propaganda. Germans hate the French.' Hanne shrugged. 'People believe what they are told.'

Hanne pointed out the synagogue on Börneplatz, and they thanked the kind German and left the tram. Although it was early, the sun was now quite hot and there were people about, some dressed only in shorts.

A group of young boys marched in file behind a red flag. 'Who are they, Hanne?'

'We have a lot of youth movements, some religious, some political. Those are Communists. Mutter says our young men are being indoctrinated.' Hanne shrugged again. 'That group in the brown shirts? They are a branch of the National Socialist German

Workers Party, Nazis for short. Mutter says their leader is a Fascist, not a Socialist, but she sees conflict everywhere. Germany hates communism as much as it hates the French occupation.'

There were girls showing more flesh than the women of the Black Country would ever show in daylight. It was deliciously shocking to see tanned legs, arms, and midriffs.

Hanne's mouth curved in a smile, her eyes alight. 'There's Berek. You must meet him.' Hanne took her by the hand and waved to a tall, black-haired young man with a short beard. 'Berek. This is my cousin Emma from England.'

'Welcome, Emma.' His dark eyes sparkled with humour and kindness. She could see why Hanne loved him so much. 'Are you staying with us long?'

'Not as long as I would like, Berek.' Warmth crept through her cheeks. What meaning would he take from that remark? 'I have seen very little of Frankfurt, but it seems a beautiful city.'

'The Rhineland is a lovely part of our country. The forests, the rivers, the mountains, and castles – and the vineyards. You will love it, I'm sure.'

She smiled, enthused at his passion and hoping she wasn't blushing scarlet with embarrassment. 'I'm sure I shall.'

Hanne appeared not to notice her discomfort. 'Come, Emma, you must be tired after your journey, and you must meet Mutter.' Hanne kissed Berek and waved him goodbye with a gaiety she envied.

Hanne was lucky to have found someone she could love. Love was an ache in her heart made keener by seeing Hanne and Berek so happy. They walked on, their arms linked as if they'd been best friends forever, Hanne chatting in excitement.

There seemed to be an air of careless optimism that was lacking back in England, and there was certainly not the same dreary poverty in Frankfurt that she'd seen in the back streets of the towns around Hawley Heath, but she didn't feel safe – she hadn't forgotten the faded scrawled words or the ripped poster – **Juden. Bolschewiki**. Beneath the sparkling surface, there was a dark undercurrent, a bubbling cauldron of fear, hatred, and mistrust.

Chapter Seven

Hawley Heath, England January 1929

Rosie reread the article in that morning's newspaper with a sense of anger and frustration.

SCOTTISH NUWM MEMBERS' HUNGER MARCH ON LONDON

Unemployed of Glasgow mobilise to rousing send-off on Blythswood Square.

Two hundred representatives from the Scottish coalfields, shipyards, textile towns, and fishing industries joined others affected by the blight of unemployment. Led by a pipers' band, they set out this morning to march five hundred miles to London.

Five hundred miles from Scotland to London in January? They were either mad or desperate, and she knew which. She remembered too well how it felt to be hungry.

Wal Hannington, founder of the Communist Party of Great Britain and National Organiser of the National Unemployed Workers Movement said "We are calling on the workers of the land to stir their slumbering souls and rise against the callous governing class responsible for the terrible plight of the unemployed".

Their cause stirred her soul. The Communist Party would oppose Baldwin's Conservative government, but that aside, hunger and poverty were real, and she doubted Baldwin had ever gone hungry. How she wished Mary Macarthur was still alive to rally support and whisk her off to join the march.

Twenty years ago, she'd have gone anyway, despite Jack's objections. Now, she had to admit she'd become complacent and wasn't as young as she was, but if she couldn't march, she could at least try to rally support.

The men are marching against the clause in unemployment benefit that the Baldwin government is using to throw tens of thousands of young men and women off the benefit scheme, putting families into real hardship. "Not genuinely seeking work" when there are no jobs to be found is not, in this newspaper's opinion, a justifiable reason to withhold Labour Exchange benefit, especially when the Poor Law's Boards of Guardians turn men away because they are able-bodied.

Jack would say '*You can't feed the whole country, Rosie*'. She huffed a bitter laugh. She was doing her best to keep jobs going for their workers, and Emma was working hard providing food for the hungry and new jobs, making cycles. Mr Timms had put even more land down to growing food, and Emma had recruited two desperate young fathers to help with the work, but Jack was right. She couldn't feed the entire country. Hawley Heath was a challenge enough.

The right-wing TUC and Labour leadership have condemned the march, saying it will cause the men hardship, and have asked trades councils and local Labour parties on the route not to offer assistance.

If they were trying to dishearten the marchers, the government had learned little when it came to the determination of ordinary men and women to support just causes. All her life, there'd been strikes for better wages and conditions for the working-class, and not even gunships in the Mersey and troops in the Welsh coalfields had stopped them.

She and Mary had helped fight for universal suffrage and a minimum wage for women. Even though it had taken years to get the laws through parliament, they'd never once thought of abandoning the fight.

She put her head in her hands and raked her fingers through her hair. Maybe she was getting old, but there seemed to be unsurmountable problems everywhere. She worried about her family, especially her firstborn. Since Emma had come home from Germany, she'd been even more restless, evasive almost, and she wouldn't talk to her about her visit. She'd caught her more than once with a faraway expression, as if she longed to be somewhere or someone else. Were they right to land her with the factory and all its responsibilities so young?

'What's up, Mom?'

She pushed the newspaper towards Emma. 'Another hunger march. People must be so desperate, marching in this weather. I wish there was something we could do to help them.'

Emma read the article. 'Can we find out their route? If we can join them...'

'Join the march? A contingent from Birmingham?'

'Unemployment is as bad here as it is in Scotland. If the NUWM calls to rally the workers in support, people will join the cause, Mom.'

They'd rallied to support the women chainmakers in 1910. 'You're right, Emma. Feeling is high against the government's unemployment policy. People are hungry and have lost hope. What else do they have to lose? Their dignity? I keep wishing Mary was here. She'd know who to contact.'

'Telephone the federation, Mom. Someone will know.'

She made the telephone call.

Emma shifted from foot to foot. 'Well?'

'A contingent from the Midlands is assembling in Birmingham on February 7th to march on London. People are joining the cause from all over England and Wales. They intend to arrive in London around the twenty-fourth. We have just over a fortnight to gather support and then a fortnight more of marching.'

Emma's eyes lit. 'Where do we start?'

She smiled, reminded of her own enthusiasm at Emma's age. 'With organising the factory and our orders to accommodate a couple of weeks' possible shutdown. Then with our own workers, of course. This won't be easy, Emma. It'll be cold and hard, and there'll be police and troops to keep order, and they aren't always compassionate or gentle. We can take a little food with us, but between here and London, there'll be little or no union assistance. We'll be relying on the generosity and support of ordinary people, who'll have little enough food and shelter to spare for us. It will be a hunger march in every sense of the word.'

Emma held out her hand. 'Pass me the order book. I'll see who isn't urgent and telephone them to see if they can wait a bit longer.'

'Good. I'll see how many of the workers will want to march and see if we can get the urgent orders out faster.' She chewed her top lip. 'And inform your dad of our decision.'

She crossed the factory floor with more sense of purpose than she'd felt for a while. It was good to have a cause again, something to fight for; she'd missed it more than she'd realised. That Emma would march alongside her was something she'd never dared hope, and it gladdened her to see the spark back in Emma's eyes. She smiled; Matthew Joshua would turn in his

74

grave. Jack wouldn't be too happy, either.

***

Emma turned up her coat collar and pulled her hat down over her ears. A bitter wind blew through her coat as if the fabric wasn't there. She should have worn Grandma Joshua's fur coat, but knowing that most marchers were unemployed, some having been out of work for over two years with no support, and wouldn't have such luxuries, she'd left it in the wardrobe. She was here to offer support and shame Baldwin's Conservative government into paying these poor people dole, not show off her family's wealth, even if that was dwindling. Losing orders for chain, the cost of setting up the bicycle factory, and providing food for the starving had dented their fortunes.

In front of her marched men, women, and children so skinny and ill-clothed they must be freezing – a far cry from the summer before in Germany, the feeling of hope and freedom, and the bronzed, bare arms and legs of the young people there. Some marchers she recognised from the soup kitchen. Behind her, marched Mom, and beside Mom, Dad, who'd decided, much to their surprise, to join them to keep an eye on them. As he rightly said, London was a long way, and he'd only worry about them.

At her side, strode Charlie, Theo, and George. If the twelve miles to Birmingham were anything to go by, the march to London was going to be tougher than she'd imagined. She rolled shoulders hunched against the cold and tried to ignore the pain in her feet. They had it easy compared to the marchers from Glasgow.

According to the newspaper, which reported on the progress of the march from Scotland, various contingents had sent telegrams to arrive at points along the route to encourage the Scots and assure them they were not alone. Perhaps, their contingent would do the same.

As they neared Birmingham, crowds lined the road, cheering them on, and the number of marchers swelled. They reached Victoria Square and stopped in front of the Council House amid a crush of people waving placards and flags.

She caught snatches of song. '*Get up, the damned of the earth. Get up, convicts of hunger... Slave crowd, get up, get up!*'

Police with batons assembled at one side of the square, and the rousing song from the throats of the unemployed grew more strident. A sea of dark uniforms blocked the way out, and the crush of marchers pushed towards them, singing. '*The people only want their due.*'

Batons raised, the police charged.

Men and women fell before them and were trampled underfoot as the crush of people behind surged forward, shouting.

'Emma!' Charlie grabbed her arm and pulled her back.

'Mom? Where's Mom?' She couldn't see her or Dad. 'Charlie, can you see Mom?'

'Jack will look after her. This way, Emma.' Barging against a broad man, Charlie dragged her sideways against the thrust of the crowd, but they were losing ground and being forced forward.

Neither Mom nor Dad were tall, and they lost them in the mass of heads and hats and helmets. Raised batons rained down on the marchers, and fights had broken out between the police and protesters. People were falling like ninepins. They made it to the steps of the Council House and climbed above the crowd.

'I can't see them, Charlie.'

He scanned the crowd. 'Stay here, Emma. I'll see if I can get to them.'

'Charlie, be careful.' But she was talking to empty air. She tried to track him in the crowd, but he was soon lost to sight. 'Dear God, please keep them all safe.'

People were still singing. Didn't they realise people were being beaten and crushed?

'Mom! *Mom*!' She was wasting her breath, but someone was forcing their way towards the steps. 'Charlie?'

A young man climbed the steps, half-dragging an older man. Both had blood streaming from cuts on their heads. The older man was barely conscious. Across the square, she could see ambulances. Men in uniforms pushed through the crowd, which made space for them. There were bodies lying on the ground. The police still blocked the road towards Coventry as ambulancemen carried injured marchers away.

If Mom or Dad or her brothers were injured, the ambulances would take them to safety. She turned her attention to the man slumped at her feet. 'He needs to go to hospital.'

'I had to get him out of the crush. This seemed like the safest place.'

'He needs treatment. You need treatment. We have to get you both to an ambulance.'

The man shook his head. 'I can't carry him.'

She helped the older man sit up and put a hand under his arm. 'We can do it together.'

Supporting the semi-conscious man between them, they plunged back into the crowd and forged a way through. Her arms ached and the young man stumbled and fell. Sure hands took the injured man's weight and relieved them of their burden. More

77

hands helped the young man to his feet and supported her towards the ambulances.

'Emma?'

Theo gripped her arm. 'Mom's been hurt. They're taking her to hospital.'

'Where is she? Where's Dad?'

Theo pointed to two men carrying a stretcher. Dad was hurrying alongside it, holding his head.

She didn't want to ask if Mom was badly hurt – the stretcher said it all. 'Have you seen Charlie and George?'

Theo shook his head.

'If you see Charlie, tell him I've gone with Mom and Dad to the hospital.' Theo released her arm, and she hurried towards the ambulances. 'Dad! Dad, wait!'

Her father paused and looked around. Blood was streaming from his nose, and one eye was barely open. 'Emma, thank God. Your Mom's hurt.'

'Is it bad?'

'She was hit with a baton, and then crushed and trampled. Emma...' His face crumpled. 'Emma...'

'I'll come with you. You need attention, too.'

'It's nothing. She might die, Emma.'

Dad's injury didn't look like nothing, but she pushed towards the stretcher. She didn't recognise the body on it. 'Mom?'

The bloody face turned towards her, an arm raised limply, and swollen lips parted. 'Emma.'

'I'm here. Dad's here. You'll be all right. They'll look after you at the hospital. I shan't leave you.'

'Emma.'

She leaned closer to hear the words.

'March, Emma. They can't – can't do this to us. March, Emma. Promise me.'

'But Mom.'

'Promise me. Take this to–' Mom's lips moved. '–London – the government.'

She nodded and then realised Mom probably couldn't see her. She took hold of the limp hand. 'I promise.'

'We need to get her to hospital, sharpish.' The ambulanceman tucked Mom's hand under the blanket and put her into the ambulance.

'Dad?'

'She's right, Emma. The police and Baldwin's government can't treat the hungry like this. I'll stay with your mom. You finish what we started. Where's Charlie?'

'I'm here, Jack. I'll look after Emma.' A muscular arm came around her shoulders. 'I'll keep her safe.'

Injured men and women lay tumbled around her, more ambulances were arriving, and blood stained the road dark with broken lives. She leant into Charlie's chest, grateful for a protector she could trust as the ambulance drove away, whisking Mom and Dad out of her life. Please God, let her see them both again.

Chapter Eight

As if ashamed of the carnage they'd wrought, the police stood aside as Emma and the rest of the uninjured marchers strode out of the square towards Coventry, voices raised in defiant song.

'The state oppresses and the law cheats. Taxes bleed the unfortunate, no duty is imposed on the rich. The right of the poor is a hollow word.'

That wasn't quite true. Joshua and Son paid taxes, but it was true that they paid as little as they had to, claiming for every little thing as expenses. She'd never thought that wrong, but now, seeing poverty through the eyes of Communists? Hanne and Berek were much better off in Germany than the workers were here. Berek's sister was an accountant, and his cousin was training to be a barrister. Women had so much more freedom and choice in Germany: so much more hope and ambition.

One day, her cousin and Berek would marry, and she would be happy for them, but… her mind returned to Frankfurt as it did so often. She longed to visit again, but there were so many demands on her time and conscience that it seemed like an idle and selfish wish to return to explore the city's ancient streets and the forested valleys of the Rhineland. The truth was, she'd lost her heart in Germany to a love that could never be hers.

'Let's blow the forge ourselves, strike the iron when it's hot.'

Her arm muscles tensed with the memory of hammering chain at Mom's side. 'Please, God, let Mom be all right.' She should have stayed with her.

No, she was doing what Mom wanted, and she'd promised. She tried to match Charlie's longer stride. It was getting dark and large splats of rain made black spots on the road in front of her. She didn't know where they would spend the night or if they'd find food. Her stomach rumbled at the thought, and she shivered as icy rain hit her cheeks. At least Mom would be warm and dry while the rain washed away her blood from the streets of Birmingham.

'Get up, the damned of the earth. Get up, the convicts of hunger.'

Hunger was what this march was about. She'd eaten well before she'd left home. Some of these people had eaten little for days, by the look of them. Keep marching, Emma. She put one painful foot in front of the other and bent her head against the driving rain.

Ahead of her, people slowed and stopped. Where were they? Not Coventry, that was for sure. They hadn't left the outskirts of Birmingham, and Coventry was a long day's march away.

Voices came out of the night, lanterns swung in the wind, and she could recognise the smell of soup from a mile away. They followed the lanterns to a building with light shining from the windows.

'There's hot food for all. No need to push. Plenty for everyone and a floor to sleep on out of the weather.'

She wiped wet from her eyes that wasn't rain. 'Thank you. That is so kind. God bless you.'

'Least we could do, miss. The union might not agree with your march, but we look after our own here. Come in. You must be frozen.'

She took a bowl and waited for the soup to be ladled into it, feeling the warmth of the bowl send prickles through her numb fingers. She slumped onto the floor against the wall and sipped the soup.

Charlie slumped down beside her. 'You all right, Emma.'

She nodded. 'You?'

'All in a day's work.'

'Thank you for coming with me. It means a lot, Charlie.'

He smiled. 'I wouldn't have missed it for the world.' He took a swallow of his soup. 'She's in excellent hands, Emma.'

'I know. She has to be all right, Charlie. She has to. I can't imagine life without Mom.'

Charlie was silent.

'Charlie?'

'I lost my mom when I was twelve. Wouldn't wish that on anyone.'

'I didn't know. I'm so sorry.' Her soup finished, she hunched into her coat.

'You cold?'

She nodded, and he put an arm around her. Resting her head against his chest, she closed her eyes. She was tired, so damned tired. She might have dreamt it, or imagined it, and she couldn't be sure whose voice it was except that it was reassuringly familiar, but somewhere in the dark recesses of her exhausted mind breathed the words. *I love you, Emma.*

She woke cold, stiff, and sore to the sounds of crockery being rattled together.

'Breakfast, Emma.'

She stretched and yawned. The hall was full of people, some still asleep on the floor, some queuing for breakfast, and some doling out mugs of steaming tea, slabs of bread, and bowls of soup. She followed Charlie and joined the queue. That it was the same soup as the night before worried her not a bit – it might well be all the food they got that day. These kind men and women had provided food and shelter, at their own expense, to more than a hundred people on a bitter January night, and for that she would be forever grateful.

***

Emma plodded on, one foot in front of the other, mile after wet and weary mile. On the outskirts of Coventry, gathering crowds waited to greet them despite the weather. Police made their presence felt, standing at intervals along the route wherever people gathered. Worry about Mom kept her mind from the hollow in her stomach and the blisters on her feet, and she kept reminding herself that the marchers coming from Glasgow had already been on their feet for weeks in blizzards, and she'd only managed three days. Mom had warned her it would be a hard and hungry march, but she hadn't realised the toll it would take on her both mentally and physically. She hadn't felt such hunger since she was a small child.

A woman held out a small loaf of bread, and she took it, squeezing the woman's hand. 'Thank you. Thank you so much.' She broke it in half and half again and handed pieces to Charlie, Theo, and George understanding better the value of the soup kitchen back in Hawley Heath. This was life, the only hope of food, for many of the unemployed who had no reason to believe things would get better. This was why she was marching – for a reform in the benefits doled out to the starving.

They arrived in Coventry as a chill wind whistled through the ill-lit streets. There was no hall ready for them to sleep in, no hot soup to warm them. Fat raindrops glistened in the lamplight and boded a storm.

Should they march on or try to find shelter in the workhouse? She shuddered, remembering, when she was little, picking up on Grandma Taylor's fear of ending up in the workhouse. The fear had never quite left her despite the factory's prosperity, and now that times weren't so prosperous? Most of the marchers were too tired and footsore to go on, so they approached the Whitefriars Monastery Workhouse.

The door opened to the tired and hungry crowd. A tall, thin man with an air of authority addressed them. 'Has your union no accommodation for you?'

Why did he think they were here, begging?

'Are any of you sick or destitute?'

A man spoke up. 'We'll all be destitute if the government doesn't pay us dole.'

'Are any of you sick?'

Another man helped a woman forward. 'My wife is unwell. Have you room for us?'

'Your wife may come in. I'm afraid the Board of Guardians have been advised to enforce the ordinary regulations that apply to vagrants, so I am bound to refuse shelter to all but the sick and truly destitute.'

They were being refused entry? She clenched her fists. 'And who advised them?'

'The General Inspectors of the Ministry of Health.'

Fingernails dug into her palms. 'The government hopes to

break our spirits and stop the march!'

Angry voices rose in dissent. '*They can't do this.*' '*We need food and shelter.*' '*Call yourself a Christian!*'

The man held out his hands as if helpless to change his decision. 'The police have been telephoned, so I suggest you disperse before they arrive.'

Charlie grabbed her wrist. 'Think of your mom. We don't need another bloodbath, Emma. We should carry on – try somewhere else.' He raised his voice and waved a hand to the protesters. 'Don't give Baldwin's bastards the satisfaction. We march on!' He began the chorus of the Internationale. '*It's the final struggle. Let's group together, and tomorrow…*'

Defiant voices swelled the song, and the weary band marched on into a bitter, stormy night.

***

They reached Dunchurch before dawn and collapsed onto pews in the church, wet, exhausted and starving. Coughs betrayed those that had caught colds, and some were limping with trench foot from constantly wet feet, but the numbers of marchers had barely dwindled, testament to the desperation of their plight before the march.

Woken by the tramp of feet, and the few hardy souls among the band who were still singing, villagers had come out of their houses and now went along the pews, bearing blankets, bread, and hot drinks. For the second time in as many days, Emma was truly grateful for the kindness of strangers.

They'd walked all night, and no one could go farther without rest. Huddling into blankets, and cuddling up to one another for body heat, she and Charlie settled down to sleep.

Did she imagine those words again and the feel of lips brushing her hair? Was it a dream or real? But her heart belonged in Germany...

She woke with a start and a crick in her neck. And was that the smell of bacon fat? She must still be dreaming. She opened her eyes to pale, winter sunlight slanting through the tall stained-glass windows and painting the pews red, green, and yellow.

Someone had set up a trestle table and women were already slathering thick chunks of quartern loaves with bacon fat. A large tea urn had been pressed into use and was singing promisingly. She forced herself to her feet and folded her blanket. 'God bless the people of Dunchurch.'

'There you are, dear.' The woman was like a little bird – tiny and nothing of her, but she pushed bread and a cup of tea into her icy hands.

'Thank you. You are so kind.'

'It's you who are kind, dear. You're the ones marching to London in the middle of winter for the likes of us. It's us as has it easy. Least we could do to give you a bite of lunch to see you on your way, dear. Least we could do.'

She smiled her gratitude. Breakfast, lunch... Whatever it was, it was welcome.

Refreshed, they set out again, the sun bringing with it a little warmth and higher spirits, even if the sky did promise snow. Daventry, Towcester, Bletchley, Dunstable, St Albans – day after day they trudged on. With the help of strangers and the occasional full stomach, reaching London in time to welcome the Scottish marchers didn't seem so impossible.

They'd checked at the post offices in all the towns they'd

passed through in the hope of a telegram with news of Mom, and finally, at St Albans, one awaited them. She tore it open. **Mom fractured skull, broken arm, recovering well. Carry on to Hyde Park. Give them hell. Dad**

'She's alive, Charlie. Mom's going to be all right.'

'Thank God.' Charlie picked her up and swung her around. He thumbed tears from her eyes and kissed her. 'Emma, I–'

She stopped his words with a finger to his lips. 'Don't, Charlie, please. I – *can't.*'

He drew back. 'Can't? I thought – Emma, you must know I love you. I fell in love with you the first time we met, and I thought you felt the same.'

She hadn't meant to lead him on. 'Charlie, I do love you, but not in that way. You're the kindest man I could ever wish to meet, but I have nothing to offer you. I've fallen in love with someone else. I'm so sorry.'

He brushed her concern aside. 'It's all right. I understand.'

He looked so crestfallen, and she longed to make him happy. 'It's someone I met in Germany. Nothing will come of it. They're promised to another, but it doesn't change how I feel about them. I can't pretend I could love someone else, ever.'

'You'd give up a chance of love here for a man you know you can't have?'

To her surprise, she'd fallen in love almost at first sight, and those dark eyes haunted her dreams. 'I wouldn't come between Hanne and Berek, even if I could. They're happy, and I won't be the one who might spoil that, but I can't imagine ever loving someone else.'

'Yet you might, one day.' He looked so hopeful, like Grandma

Joshua's puppy, Happy, asking for a treat, that she laughed.

'And one day, when you're married with a family, and I'm a lonely old maid, I might kick myself for refusing to try. Friends, Charlie?'

He smiled and hugged her. 'Is there no hope for us?'

She wished there was, it would be so much simpler, but she couldn't change the way she felt. 'I think not, Charlie, but whoever finally holds your heart will be a very lucky woman.'

***

London, England 1929

The last week of the march had been bitterly cold, seldom above freezing, with an easterly wind that went straight through Emma's coat, but today was overcast and warmer in the shelter of tall, closely packed buildings.

Trafalgar Square was a sea of faces come to welcome the Scottish marchers and help take the plight of the unemployed to parliament. Hundreds of marchers and working-class Londoners had assembled already, with more marchers on their way from Newcastle, Sheffield, South Wales, Lancashire, Derbyshire, and Nottingham, as well as Birmingham.

The Glasgow contingent had been on the road for five weeks, and she couldn't imagine the hardships they'd suffered.

A man mounted the plinth. She'd seen his photograph in the newspaper. He was Tom Mann, a self-confessed Communist, of the National Unemployed Workers Movement. Mom had told her about him organising the Liverpool Transport Strike in 1911.

Tom Mann commanded attention. 'We are here to greet the unemployed marchers who have come into London from nine different directions. They have had many hardships, but they have come through well shod, strong, and hearty.'

She wasn't sure how well shod she was. She'd worn a hole in her shoe and had limped the last mile.

'Many of these men have been out of work for a year, some over two years. The government have been increasingly legislating and administering in a harsher manner – these men have paid into the insurance fund, their employers and the government have been paying into the insurance fund, but these souls have been cut off from all relief from the Labour Exchanges, and when they turned to the Poor Law, the Boards of Guardians have told them there is no relief because they are able-bodied. They have nothing! The government don't give a damn, and the politicians don't give a damn, so they have come here to see the ministers. Whatever is necessary we will do. See there, on that banner?' Tom Mann pointed.

She followed the direction of his finger to an enormous banner held aloft by two men.

'That is what they are demanding. Thirty shillings a week to all over eighteen years of age and ten shillings for a wife.'

There would be miners, textile workers, men from the shipyards. Proud men who wanted only to put food on their families' tables.

Tom Mann raised a hand. 'We refuse to take it lying down, absolutely refuse, and if there is fighting to be done – by God, before we talk of fighting the Germans or fighting America, we will damn well fight the capitalists here.'

The crowd erupted, but he hadn't finished. 'When the men arrive, they will need accommodation, and we shall call upon you all to help them. And when their work here is done, they cannot be allowed to march back. Their fares must be paid home.'

That it would be done, she didn't doubt. There was a solidarity of purpose here that she'd never felt before. Was this what it had been like for Mom when the women chainmakers fought the chain masters for a minimum wage and when Mom and Grandma had marched for women's suffrage?

The crowd headed for Hyde Park where the marchers were to assemble when they arrived. Banners held high and bands playing, they lined the streets to Hyde Park.

'Here they come!'

Weary but proud, thousands of men from all over Britain marched towards the park amid thunderous cheers and singing. Baldwin's government would ignore them at their peril.

Chapter Nine

Hawley Heath, England May 1929

Rosie sat with her feet on a footstool and stared out of the window across the fresh, spring grass that fell away to the town below. Her headaches were getting fewer, and her arm had mended, but her spirit had taken a harder knock than her head.

Baldwin had refused to meet with the unemployed marchers, and Emma and Charlie had left feeling they'd achieved nothing. But the support the protest had garnered from ordinary working people had brought pressure upon the government, who'd been forced to stop the thirty-week stamps' qualification, saving a quarter of a million workers from being struck off the dole. It was a triumph for the working class that had dented the Conservative government's impregnable armour.

'Newspapers, Rosie.' Maisie, who'd been Marion's housemaid, still lived in and helped with the cooking and cleaning. Her fiancé had been killed right at the end of the war, and the girl had never married. She was family, now, like all the people who worked for Joshua and Son.

'You're an angel, Maisie. What would we do without you?'

Maisie blushed. 'What would Hawley Heath do without you, Rosie. You must start taking better care of yourself. You're not as young as you were.'

'Thirty-eight isn't that old.'

'It isn't that young, either. There's plenty around here in their graves before that age.'

Rosie shook her head. 'You are a little ray of sunshine, Maisie.'

'Sorry, but it needs to be said.' Maisie patted her arm as if she was a dog. 'What I'm saying is, there's folk around here don't want to go to your funeral yet, and if you keep going on these damn silly marches…'

'All right, I'll act my age. Hand me that newspaper, if reading it isn't too strenuous for me.'

'Rosie Taylor, I do declare you are the most infuriating woman.'

She smiled. 'Thank you, Maisie. That's good to know.'

Maisie turned her eyes heavenwards, flounced out of the room, and closed the door behind her with a sharp snap.

Feeling a little guilty, she scanned the news. It was still covering the terrible disaster at the Coombs Wood colliery near Halesowen a fortnight ago. A fire in the pit had killed eight men. Eight women left to bring up families alone and Lord knew how many children left fatherless.

She turned the page to the national news – there was still rumour and speculation about the stock market wobble on Wall Street, but that was the other side of the Atlantic Ocean and didn't concern Hawley Heath. Her heart thudded.

GENERAL ELECTION DECLARED

The country will go to the polls on May 30th. For the first time, women over the age of twenty-one will be able to vote.

'Emma!'

No answer. She rang the little bell Maisie insisted she use and the girl poked her head around the door.

'Maisie. We can vote! They're calling a general election, and

92

women will be able to vote.'

'Huh, it's taken them long enough.' Maisie put her hands on her hips, a study in determined feminism. 'Now we'll see who wears the trousers in the country.'

She laughed and wiped away tears of joy. 'Tell Emma.'

Finally, after sixty years or more of suffragette and suffragist campaigning, and a full ten years after the passing of the Representation of the Peoples Act, she and Emma could have a say in who governed them, and it wouldn't be a vote for bloody Baldwin and his Conservative sharks or Lloyd-George, whose party had steadfastly refused women the right to vote for as long as she could remember.

That left Ramsay MacDonald and his Labour Party. With the high number of unemployed workers who could all vote, and the treatment of workers during the general strike of a couple of years ago, it seemed likely there would be a change of government.

Over the next few weeks, she followed the election campaigns of each party, and voting day brought with it yet another dry day, sunny, with blue skies and an expectant air of carnival in Hawley Heath. Bright posters daubed on doors and walls were persuasive.

Men and women workers,
your chance at last.
The works are closed,
but the ballot box is open.
VOTE LABOUR IN YOUR OWN INTERESTS!

The whole family lined up in a queue of people waiting in excitement to cast their vote. She gave her name and address and was handed an official ballot paper. She didn't need to read the names. Labour was the only party she could, in all conscience, vote for. She marked the paper and posted it in the ballot box with a satisfaction born of years of struggle against male political dominance and arrogance.

She turned and winked at Emma, who was waiting behind her. 'Stick that in your pipe and smoke it, Stanley Baldwin.'

***

Emma switched on the radio and tuned into the long wave to see if the votes had been counted. It crackled and burst into life, and a voice travelled across the miles. '*The British people have spoken. The British worker has cast his – and her – vote. Stanley Baldwin's government resigned to await the result of the ballot, which we can now declare.*'

'Mom, the government has resigned!'

Mom hurried into the room. 'Shush, Emma.'

'*Ramsay MacDonald's Labour Party has won two hundred and eighty-seven seats against the Conservative Party's two hundred and sixty, and Liberal's fifty-nine, while the other parties netted the remaining nine seats. Three hundred and eight seats are needed for an overall majority. It is not yet known if there will be a coalition with either the Conservative Party or the Liberal Party, or if there will be a hung parliament.*'

'We've won!'

Mom was quick to add caution to her exuberance. 'It's not the convincing victory I hoped for. The Liberal Party will hold the balance of power, and if they decide to support the Conservative Party –'

She wouldn't be deterred. 'But the British worker have had their say. They've given Baldwin a flea in his ear.' It was a beacon of hope and light in a dark time. 'Labour will put the people first.'

94

'I hope so. I wish Mary Macarthur had lived to witness this. She'd have stood for parliament and would have been an excellent representative for workers' rights.'

She squeezed Mom's hand. 'Mary would have been very proud of you, Mom.'

Mom smiled. 'And of you, Emma.'

It was an anxious wait to hear which party would be forming a government, and for days, the radio was seldom switched off. It was June 7th when the news was broadcast. '*Mr Stanley Baldwin has conceded power rather than risk a fragile majority by forming a coalition with the Liberal Party. It is expected that the king will ask the Labour leader, Mr Ramsay MacDonald, to form a minority government. Margaret Bondfield is tipped to become Minister of Labour and the first female cabinet minister.*'

'We did it, Mom. A woman in the cabinet and Minister of Labour, at that. Who'd have thought it?'

'It's a tremendous achievement, but she'll have an uphill struggle to get men to listen to her if past experience is anything to go by.'

'It's a start. At last, we have someone who'll represent women, the way Mary would have.'

For the first time in a while, she felt genuine hope for the future. The new Labour government would get the country back to work. The bicycle factory was going well, and the land was producing food. Now all they needed was an increase in orders for chain.

***

Hawley Heath, England October 1929

Emma's spirits rose with the scent of lavender. She'd been tardy in writing to Hanne, despite her desire to hear from her, and Hanne had taken her time replying. She opened the envelope, eager yet afraid to read Hanne's news.

My dearest Emma,

I'm so pleased that your mother has recovered so well from her awful ordeal. Police in Frankfurt are not always gentle, but I have not witnessed such brutal treatment as you described. I think you are very brave to have marched in such awful weather and for such a long way.

The situation in Germany has continued to improve since you were here. Frankfurt is not quite Berlin, yet, but it is still a bustling and thriving city. Young people here have much to look forward to.

Nothing about Berek.

Sad news is that our chancellor, Herr Stresemann, has died. He has done so much good for Germany in pulling us out of the deep depression we were in after the war. I hope that whoever takes his place will be as good for Germany's future.

Your news of a Stock Market crash in London is bad for England, or so Mutter says – she knows more of these things than I do. Will it affect you, do you think?

The newspapers were full of the scandal. Clarence Hatry, a profiteering businessman whose bankruptcies had somehow made him richer, had been charged with issuing fraudulent stocks, and his business empire had collapsed, sending the London Stock Exchange crashing in a panic that was felt even as far as America. The man now faced criminal charges and was likely to be gaoled, and the fact that the financier was the son of a Jewish immigrant hadn't been lost on the press. People who'd invested faced financial ruin, but so far, the repercussions hadn't affected Joshua and Son.

Mutter and Berek both wish to be remembered to you and hope you will visit with us again. Berek has been promoted and has a big rise in wages. He has asked me to marry him. I always expected that we'd marry, but now it seems very real, and I feel quite nervous. I have said yes, of course. We are to be married next summer. I know you will be happy for us, and we hope you will come.

She put the letter down and sank onto a chair. There it was. She'd nursed a hope of nurturing the spark between them she was certain she'd felt, but Berek and Hanne were to be married, and her love would forever remain unrequited. She was glad that they had one another and were happy, but a tear trickled down her cheek, nonetheless.

Could she sit in the synagogue on Börneplatz and watch the love of her life marry? No, she couldn't without betraying her feelings. She would think of an excuse, wish them well, and nurse her broken heart alone.

***

WALL STREET STOCK MARKET CRASHES

Rosie couldn't miss the headline, plastered as it was across the front of the newspaper. She read on, heart pounding. This could be bad news for the factory.

After Black Thursday comes Black Tuesday. Stock market disaster causes panic worldwide. Bankers' efforts fail to halt decline. Speculators lose life savings.

After days of uncertainty, share prices on the New York Stock Exchange collapsed today when investors traded some 16 million shares. Billions of dollars were lost in the worst

day's trading on record, and anxious crowds gathered outside the Stock Exchange and banks. It is feared that a run on banks will cause many to fail, and it is reported that there have already been several suicides.

Rosie put her head in her hands. As if things weren't bad enough, this had to happen.

She took the newspaper to Jack. 'If the banks fail, what hope is there for business and the ordinary people?'

He read the report. 'Has Emma seen this?'

'Not yet. What are we going to do? We've fought so hard to keep our workers employed. America was our last hope.' Most of their orders for small chain went across the Atlantic to the farmers of America.

'It doesn't sound good, Rosie. If orders drop, are we going to have to lay off workers?'

'I was about to order more rod. Do you think I should hold fire until we know more?' She and Emma had changed roles while her arm mended. Emma was bent over a machine that made electrically welded small chains.

Jack's team worked on without him, making heavier chain, while he checked the stocks of rod; sparks flew, forges burned bright, and the steam bellows breathed life into the flames, but the huge steam hammers they'd installed with such hope for the future stood silent.

'I think we have enough of everything for a couple of weeks, Rosie.'

'The markets may recover as quickly as they crashed. You know what these things are like.'

'Not really, but I hope you're right. You can delay ordering for a week, I'd think.'

Should she worry Emma with this news? It was Emma's factory, her decision… She would wait until she was more certain of the effects of the crash.

She walked back to the office. Many factories had closed over the past few years, but Joshua and Son had kept going, their workers loyal to the last man. If they were forced to close too, what then? Could the cycle factory earn enough to feed the family? Memories of hunger loomed large. If the factory failed and they couldn't afford to pay gardeners, they'd have to rely on volunteers to keep their soup kitchen going.

Putting more men and women out of work didn't bear thinking about. She pushed her worry away. The markets would recover; they had to. She flicked over the rest of the newspaper hoping for a more hopeful article.

The good news was that the Privy Council had declared women were *"persons in their own right"*. As if women didn't know that, but apparently the men who made the laws of the country needed telling that women weren't a spare part attached to, or a lesser part of, a husband.

The next day's news, however, was worse.

AMERICA CALLS IN FOREIGN LOANS

Is this the beginning of a worldwide depression?

Following the disastrous crash on the New York Stock Exchange yesterday, American banks are calling in their foreign loans. Shock waves are being felt worldwide. The UK cabinet is holding an emergency meeting to discuss the implications.

The worst hit among the European countries will be

Germany, who under the Dawes Plan has borrowed heavily from America to finance its industrial recovery.

She couldn't keep this from Emma; she'd be distraught – not just the worry about the factory – Hanne was in Germany. What would this mean for Emma's cousin and her family?

Chapter Ten

Hawley Heath, England 1930

Emma reread the newspaper reports. They were predicting a prolonged slump, and with confidence in investment destroyed, the Black Country was feeling the effects of a self-fulfilling prophecy. One in three workers could have no jobs to go to.

The pile of letters on her desk stared at her. If they were anything like yesterday's, they'd be more order cancellations. People were tightening already restrictive belts and no one, including Joshua and Son, was spending money.

She looked up at a knock on the office door, and Charlie pushed it open.

'Problem, Charlie?'

He perched on the edge of her desk. 'You look as if you have. Can I help?'

She smiled despite her worry and passed him the newspaper. 'If they keep telling us there's going to be a recession, there'll be one. Who the hell is going to risk investing in business, now? No one with any sense.'

He tilted his head to one side like an inquisitive sparrow. 'Are we in trouble, Emma?'

She glanced at the intimidating letters. 'If these are more cancelled orders, I'm going to have to lay men off.'

'And if they're not?'

'You're right. Nothing to be gained by ignoring them.' She slit open the envelopes and read the letters.

'Well?'

'Two cancellations, two accounts paid in full, and one new order. It won't save us, but it'll keep the wolf from the door for a while longer.'

'What about George and Theo?'

'You tell me. Do you have any orders – sales?'

'A few, and we're working on a new grocers' bike for deliveries, but it's like you say – business is wary of investing in new stock. Having said that, we can't sell bikes if we don't make them.'

'How much do you need to produce them?'

He smiled ruefully. 'I have a contact with a chain of butchers' shops in Birmingham. I think I've sold him on the idea of a fleet of delivery bikes. They're cheaper and more versatile than vans, and delivery boys are paid much less than drivers. I need to make ten. If they're seen to be a good investment, he might order more, and there are other grocery shops that might be interested. People have to eat even in a depression.'

'If they can afford to eat.'

'It won't get that bad, Emma. We have to hold our nerve.'

'Have you never gone to bed hungry, Charlie?'

'More than once, Emma.'

'You're right about holding my nerve. I'll transfer some funds into the Taylor Cycles' account. Make every penny count, Charlie.'

'Things are that tight?'

She nodded. 'Things are that tight. We're even adding more water to the soup.'

'I won't let you down, Emma.'

'I know you won't, Charlie.'

He scratched his head. 'It's just an idea, but if you lay men off, they'll have time on their hands. What about making a scrap of land available for allotments?'

'Allotments? Charlie, you're a genius. We can afford seed, and producing food will give the men a bit of their self-esteem back. Tools. They'd need tools – spades, hoes, and forks.'

'And you have iron, hammers, and forges. They can make their own.'

She could have kissed him. In fact, she nearly did.

One letter remained unopened, and she waited until Charlie had left before she read it.

My dearest Emma,

It was lovely to get your letter. We are all well, but the financial crash in America had an almost immediate effect here. Berek has lost his job and few people can afford to buy the beautiful jewellery Uncle Saul sells. Bread is worth more than gold, it seems. We have some savings still, but I don't know how long they will last. Mutter is very worried. I think we may have to postpone the wedding, although Berek insists he will find employment again soon and has set a date for Sunday July 6th. We would love you to be here, Emma, to share our happy day. I pray Berek is right, but every day, more and more people are losing their jobs.

Part of her hoped Hanne and Berek would never marry, but that was selfish and unworthy of her. Hanne's happiness was more important than her own.

People are angry, and they blame the government. Germany has suffered so much since the war, and Mutter remembers the hardship she endured during it – once again, people are in danger of starving. I wonder if we shall have hunger marches as you did in England.

People are turning to the Communist Party and even the Nazi Party, the smallest party in the Reichstag, for a solution. Mutter doesn't say as much, but I think she fears the leader of the Nazis. In the past, he has said awful things about Jews, and they say he's a convincing speaker. They are gaining support while the government argues over how to tackle unemployment. Something has to be done, or I fear there will be rioting in the streets!

Oh, Emma. I've just heard a radio broadcast. Chancellor Hermann Müller has resigned. They've named Heinrich Brüning as chancellor. I think he is a member of the Centre Party. Let's hope he can do a better job for the German people. Rioting, we can do without. Rioting leads to looting, and Uncle Saul's shop would be a target. He is already afraid of raising his shutters for fear of attack. People think we have money when they have none, but we can't eat gemstones or gold. Pray for us, my dearest Emma, as I shall pray for you. These are desperate times.

***

Summer had replaced the spring candles on the chestnut trees with spires of tiny green conkers. It was Sunday July 6th – the day Hanne and Berek were to be married.

She picked moodily at her breakfast, imagining Hanne's excitement. Would she be nervous? What would it be like to be in the arms and the bed of the man you'd married? Part of her had wanted to go to Germany, but she'd made the excuse that the cost of the fare was too much of a luxury in such difficult times. It wasn't entirely a lie. And anyway, she was too busy. They'd opened another soup kitchen to cope with the increasing numbers of hungry men, women, and children.

She gave up on breakfast and took her plate and cup to the kitchen to wash. She scrubbed at it as if she could scrub away her heartache and worry. How long could the family keep going? There was a limit to how much they could dilute the soup and still provide nourishment to the starving, and even if the allotment idea was a success, it would be months before they could harvest the crops. If this went on, they'd be adding grass to the soup!

The home they ran for the sick women of Hawley Heath and the employment of the Heath Hall staff were conditions of her inheritance and couldn't be discontinued to save money – Grandma Joshua hadn't reckoned on a worldwide financial collapse when she'd written the clauses into her will.

And then there was Charlie. Was she being stupid to condemn herself to a solitary life and push him away when he obviously loved her? Could she put the love of her life into a box in her heart and make room for Charlie? He would be easy to love, just like –

'You'll scrub the pattern off that plate, Emma.'

She put the offending article in the drying rack and turned into Mom's arms.

'Oh, sweetheart, what is it?'

It was so many things. 'Hanne and Berek are getting married today.'

'It's a shame you said you wouldn't go to the wedding.' Mom squeezed her tighter. 'Emma, Hanne won't forget she has a cousin just because she's married. She'll still write, and she'll still want you to visit. She may need you even more. Every woman needs a female friend.'

'You think so?' She couldn't tell Mom the real reason she didn't go.

'You should look to your own happiness, Emma. I was married with four children at your age.'

She changed the subject and mopped her tears. 'Mom, we need to talk to the workers on Monday. Unless the older ones retire early, we're going to have to lay people off.'

Mom sighed. 'I've been dreading this, but you're right. If we're going to keep the factory open, we have to cut costs.' It was Mom's turn to mop at her eyes. 'They have been so loyal for so many years. They've given us their working lives, fought for their country, trusted us to look after them, and this is how we have to repay them. It isn't fair, Emma.'

'But what more can we do, Mom?'

'Pray things pick up. Ask if they're prepared to work shorter hours for less pay. Make sure we keep on men with children to feed and don't throw an entire family out of work. We'll get together with your dad after church and see what we can do.'

'Thanks, Mom.'

'It'll be all right, Emma. Things are bound to pick up sooner or later. People will always need chain, and George and Theo's enterprise seems to be working. Charlie's got some orders, I hear.'

'Yes, it's one small beacon of hope.'

'About Charlie…'

'What about him?'

'He's very fond of you, you know.'

106

'I know. He told me.'

'So?'

'It's complicated, Mom.'

'Because you're his employer?'

'No, not that.' How could she tell Mom the real reason – that she'd given her heart to someone she could never have? 'I'm not sure I want to get married.'

Mom frowned. 'But you love children, Emma, and Charlie would be a brilliant father.'

'But I don't love him, not in that way.'

Mom smiled. 'Give it time, Emma. Love can surprise you, sometimes. Now, get ready for church. We're going to have to walk to save petrol, and we can say a prayer for better times.'

'Amen to that, and may they be quick in coming – like before tomorrow when we have to start laying people off.'

'Miracles take a little longer, Emma.'

And a miracle was what they needed.

***

The hoped-for miracle wasn't forthcoming, except maybe it was. When Emma spoke to her workforce on Monday morning, laying bare the factory's problems and Charlie's idea about the allotments, they all voted for the option of working shorter hours for less pay rather than any of them being laid off. It wasn't an ideal solution, but for the moment, it was the best they could do.

Belts were tightened another notch, and spade and fork production took the place of making chain at several of the forges. She smiled, grateful for the loyalty of her workers – maybe she should change the name of the factory to Hawley Heath Garden

Tools Co-operative! Actually, the production of tools wasn't a bad side-line – people always needed tools and more people would be growing food if the depression continued much longer.

She'd sent Hanne and Berek a gift of a hand-embroidered tablecloth, but it was a couple of weeks before she had a letter back from her cousin.

My dearest Emma,

Thank you so much for the lovely gift you sent. It is beautiful and most generous of you, and I shall treasure it always. It is odd to have a new name, but I am now officially Frau Hanne Bergman.

Hanne Bergman. She hadn't even known Berek's surname.

I so wish you could have been here for our big day. It was a lovely wedding with much cake being eaten, in the German style, and Berek and I are so very happy. We are living with Mutter, so my address will remain the same. It is the cheapest option for us all, and Mutter needs the company. I could not bear to leave her on her own.

Berek is still looking for work but is hopeful of a job with a friend of his father, who is an apotheker – a pharmacist, which is Berek's training. Even in a depression, people need medicines. Sometimes, it is not what you know, but who you know. I pray something will come of it as things are very bad here with men queuing for jobs while their families wait at soup kitchens.

I heard on the news yesterday that the Reichstag has been dissolved, which means we shall have yet another election this September. It seems the minority government could not push through the measures they wanted. Already, the parties have begun their campaigning, and there are so many parties to choose from!

108

Mutter says she will attend all the speeches – she is determined to cast her vote for someone who talks sense. I hope someone does. Germany desperately needs a strong leader who has the welfare of the people at his heart.

But enough of me and Germany. Are things any better in England? Is the factory managing to make a profit? I do hope you don't have to let your workers go – it would be heart-breaking when they have worked for Joshua and Son for so many years. It is a difficult time for us all. Stay strong, Emma, dearest, and write to me soon. I miss you.

Your loving cousin,

Hanne Bergman.

She folded the letter and put it back in its envelope. *Hanne Bergman.* She couldn't change how she felt, but life went on, and there were people in England who depended on her.

Chapter Eleven

Frankfurt, Germany August 1930

August had brought with it humid heat, and Hanne was glad to take a tram rather than walk through the sweltering streets to the Festhalle in Hessen. It was a necessary luxury as Mutter was determined to hear every candidate for the election speak and judge them on their merit, and today, walking so far was beyond her. How men could work, even bare-chested, in this heat, she didn't know.

Berek favoured the SPD, the Social Democratic Party and the largest party in the Reichstag, but many people spoke of voting for the KDP, the Communists. Others, to combat the communist threat, vowed they would vote for the far right, the Nazi Party. There were so many parties, thirty-seven in all, she was almost glad she was too young to vote by a few months.

Today, they were to hear the leader of the Nazi Party, one Adolph Hitler. The man was touring the country in a whirlwind campaign of dramatic speeches and was causing quite a stir with torchlight parades, banners, posters, and even special edition Nazi newspapers. Some were hailing him as the saviour of the nation. Germany certainly needed one.

The Festhalle was full almost to bursting when they arrived, and they squeezed in at the back among the people who were standing.

'There must be twenty thousand people, Hanne.' Mutter stared up at those lucky enough to get one of the tiered seats. It was hot in the hall, and airless, and she fanned herself with her hand. 'I hope he's not long in coming.'

The stage remained empty with the central lectern picked out with a spotlight and flanked by huge banners bearing swastikas. Military music blared suddenly, and a procession of Brownshirts with golden banners marched down the centre aisle and onto the stage. The hall echoed with shouts of 'Heil!'

A small, dark-haired man with a clipped moustache walked onto the stage.

'Is that Hitler?'

'Yes – shush.'

The hall was silent, expectant, and the man spoke in a low, hesitating voice that gained in strength. He spoke to hungry minds of national pride and unity, the need to battle for the soul of the people, and to keep down Marxism and form a kernel of hope and strength that would flourish.

His voice rose with indignation. 'We must discard the Treaty of Versailles and stop paying these crippling reparations. We must send the French soldiers back to France and reclaim the industrial heartland of the Ruhr. How else can we expand our territory, so we can feed our sixty-two million people?'

To the unemployed, he promised jobs, to the hungry he promised food, to the industrialists he promised investment, to the workers he promised an end to class distinction, to those who felt shamed and beaten, he promised order where there was chaos, a strong army, and victory.

Hitler thumped the lectern in front of him and raised his voice further. 'As long as there are peoples on this earth, there will be nations against nations, and they will be forced to protect their vital rights in the same way as the individual is forced to protect his rights. One is either the hammer or the anvil.'

He paused to let his words sink in. 'We confess it is our purpose to prepare the German people again for the role of the hammer. We admit freely and openly that if our movement is victorious, we will be concerned day and night with the question of how to produce the armed forces that are forbidden us by the peace treaty.' He raised a clenched fist. 'We will do our utmost to build a great nation for all German people. Our rights will be protected only when the German Reich is again supported by the point of the German dagger.'

The Brownshirts, as one, saluted with their right arm raised. 'Sieg Heil! Sieg Heil.'

Hail to victory. The hall erupted, the noise was deafening, and sweating bodies crushed closer in a frenzied mass. Mutter grabbed her arm and pulled her towards the exit amid 'Sieg Heil' from twenty thousand voices.

Fighting against the tide of emotion, they reached the fresh air outside and could breathe.

'He didn't mention the Jews, Mutter. He said all German people.'

'The man speaks well. He's very convincing, but do you think he meant it?'

'You think he didn't?'

'I don't know, Hanne. I don't know what to think.'

***

Hawley Heath, England August 1930

Emma scratched her head, wishing she'd paid more attention at school to her arithmetic lessons. Both White Star and Cunard were laying down hulls for massive ocean liners – Cunard's Mauritania was over twenty years old. A last-ditch attempt to save the flagging shipbuilding industry? Men's jobs were at stake, and she knew how that felt.

Ships needed anchor cable, cranes and hoists needed chain, and she intended Joshua and Son to put in a favourable tender for any present or future requirements. White Star's proposed Hull 534, to be called Oceanic III, had her keel already laid down and could be the saving of the factory.

'Dad, what sizes of cable chain are they likely to want? I'd like to estimate costs for a range of diameters in the hope they'll find our prices competitive and invite us to tender as their needs arise.'

'We've tendered to them before with some success, but it won't hurt to remind them we exist. Cunard, too – they haven't built a major liner since 1914. White Star's Oceanic III is going to be huge, by all accounts.'

'So how much chain do I quote for and what diameter rod?'

'Titanic's cable chain was three-and-three-quarter inches, if I remember rightly. The links would have been a couple of feet long. Stud chain, of course. Estimate a price by the shackle, but bear in mind a cable chain is likely to be at least ten shackles, and there'll be two bow anchors that could weigh eight tons apiece.' Dad paused. 'You'd have been four when they hauled Titanic's anchor through Netherton. What a sight. It took about thirty horses to pull the dray.' He smiled at the memory. 'Make sure you add that this estimate is at today's steel prices.'

'I'll get Mom to look it over when I've done.'

'Good idea. I've heard rumours Cunard's thinking of building an ocean liner, as well. We can only hope some of the work comes our way.'

113

She went back to her calculations. She didn't need to be precise as she didn't have detailed requirements, but what she did need was a realistic estimate that would look good on paper.

At least, if everything failed, they wouldn't end up in the workhouse. The Poor Law Unions had been abolished and the workhouses turned into hospitals. What the destitute did now, she had no idea. Jump off a bridge and injure themselves?

She pushed her calculations to one side to await Mom's keen eye and opened the weekly newspaper. Headlines stood out across the pages.

Two million unemployed.

Airship R100 makes a successful flight to Canada. 78-hour passage.

Did airships need anchor cable chain to stop them floating away?

Investigation into May explosion at Bibby's oil-cake mill announced.

That brought back sad memories of Grandma Joshua's death. Aluminium powder had ignited when the factory was making Mills' bombs, but no one had thought it necessitated an investigation. The canary girls had been dispensable – casualties of war.

More plays planned after transmission of BBC's first television play hailed a success.

They didn't have a television set. It was a luxury they couldn't justify.

Mental Treatment Act passed. Free voluntary treatment.

If things carried on the way they were, they'd all need free mental treatment. The fact they'd changed the name from lunatic asylums to mental hospitals didn't alter the suffering of the insane.

She sighed. Hanne hadn't replied to her last letter yet, and she longed to hear from her. Was marriage all Hanne expected? Were she and Berek happy? Waiting was driving her... mad.

***

Frankfurt, Germany Autumn 1930

Hanne sucked the end of her pen. She should have replied to Emma's letter ages ago.

My dearest Emma,

I'm sorry I have been so long in writing. Mutter hasn't been well, and I have been looking after her as well as working and caring for Berek and the apartment. I think she took a touch of heatstroke last month, and it made her quite sick for a while.

However, she is much improved now. She dragged me to several political speeches during the hottest weather, and I'm relieved that it's cooler now as she has more speeches in her diary. With thirty-seven parties, these speeches could take all month!

The leader of the Nazi Party is an insignificant little man, but he speaks compellingly and with such hope and passion, I think he may gain many supporters before the election. His party is small, only twelve seats in the Reichstag, but he tells people what they want to hear with great conviction.

Mutter isn't sure we can trust him, but he didn't single out Jews among the people he wants Germany to be rid of – not like the French and the Bolsheviks. He speaks a lot of sense, and it's hard to resist his words. He's quite the showman and almost caused a riot in the Festhalle in Hessen when he was here.

115

His name is Adolph Hitler. Mark the name. I think we shall see much more of him in the future. I doubt he can gain enough support to win the majority of seats from the ruling NPD in this election. We shall see.

There'd been an attack on a Nazi event by the KPD, the Communists, and three people had died fighting the police. She wouldn't tell Emma that. She'd only worry.

How is the bicycle factory going? I hope you are selling lots of cycles. Charlie sounds nice. Is he the love interest you are so shy of revealing to me? Do tell.

I want you to be as happy as I am with Berek. I love you like the sister I never had.

She signed her name. She did love Emma. There had been a strong bond between them from the first moment they'd met, and she worried about her. She smiled. It seemed they worried about each other. But she and Berek were fine and happy, and hopefully, her letter would reassure her cousin.

Postscript. Berek has found a position with his father's pharmacist friend, so that is one less worry.

She folded the letter into a lavender-scented envelope. She felt more hopeful about the future than she had for a while.

***

Sunday, September 14th and the leaves had turned to the yellows and oranges of autumn. Election day dawned overcast and humid and Hanne was up early to do her chores.

Mutter called from the lounge. 'I'm going to vote, Hanne.'

Mutter still wasn't completely over her illness, though she asserted she was well. She might find she needed an arm to lean on. 'Wait for me. I'm coming with you.'

She'd be able to vote herself at the next election. She joined her mother and together they walked across Börneplatz. It seemed the whole of Ostend was out and about, the air busy with hopeful chatter. People were desperate for change. So many were out of work, and those in work had seen their wages cut when taxes had risen. Everyone, it seemed, was anxious to cast their vote.

They waited in a queue at the polling station while representatives of the various parties walked up and down the line trying to persuade voters to their party.

Brownshirts carried banners, red with black swastikas in white circles, and shouted, drowning the single voices of the other parties. 'Sieg Heil. Sieg Heil'.

Hail to victory. The chant was taken up by some in the waiting crowd. If Hitler had this support in every city, the election was surely won by the Nazis.

Next day, she ran to the local newsagent for a paper. The election result was splashed across the front page.

SPD wins another term in the Reichstag.

Nazi Party makes huge gains in seats.

The SPD still had a majority, even if reduced, but the Nazis were snapping at their heels.

The sound of breaking glass made her pause halfway across the Platz. A man with a sledgehammer was smashing the window of a restaurant.

'What are you doing?'

He turned to her with a snarl. 'Jüdischer Abschaum.'

'*Scum?*' She watched in shock as he put the hammer through the shop window next door. From farther along the street came the sound of more breaking glass. The butcher's shop, the newsagent... All Jewish-owned shops.

She ran as fast as she could to her uncle's shop and almost fell in through the door. 'Uncle Saul, men are attacking Jewish shops!'

Her uncle pulled her inside. 'Stay there.' He went outside and lowered his shutters, locking them into place. 'I told you to stay inside, Hanne.'

'What's happening, Uncle Saul? Why are they attacking us?'

He pushed her back inside, glancing behind him as he closed the door. 'Nazi storm troopers celebrating their success in the election – their civilian clothes don't fool me.' He bolted the door and put his hands on her shoulders. 'You must be very careful now, Hanne. Promise me.'

'But why?'

'Persecution of the Jews. It's beginning again, Hanne. It's beginning again.'

Chapter Twelve

Hawley Heath, England October 1930

Sometimes, no news was good news. It certainly felt that way as Emma read the weekly paper. Fourteen miners had been killed in an explosion near Cannock, and the British airship R101 had crashed in France on its way to India on its maiden voyage. Forty-eight of the fifty-four people on board had been killed. Now there were reports of hurricanes, volcanoes erupting, and an earthquake.

Tragedy seemed to follow tragedy. Would the loss of the R101 sound the death knell for the airship industry? The loss of Titanic on its maiden voyage had almost ruined the White Star line.

'Post, Miss Taylor.' The postboy threw a bundle of mail onto the desk and ducked out of the door.

Would there be something from Hanne? She breathed in the relaxing scent of lavender and smiled. Invoices and, hopefully, orders could wait.

My dearest Emma,

Thank you for your lovely letter. It cheered me to know you are thinking of me. I fear we are entering difficult times. As if life wasn't hard enough with unemployment being so high, Mutter's reservations about the Nazi leader, Hitler, may be justified. He has gained a lot of support, and his party is now second in size in the Reichstag.

Hitler – that was the man Hanne had said spoke so convincingly at the Festhalle for the Nazi Party.

His storm troopers celebrated their success by breaking

windows in Jewish shops, restaurants, and department stores. Apparently, the elected Nazi deputies, dressed in their brown shirts, marched in unison into the Reichstag and took their seats. When the roll-call was taken, each one shouted, 'Present! Heil Hitler!'.

Although there hasn't been trouble since, Uncle Saul thinks it is a sign of things to come – more persecution of Jewish people. We are someone to blame for the state of the country, apparently, for being hard-working and successful when many others are struggling, and he and Mutter believe we shall suffer restrictions in what we can do, what we can own, and where we can go.

She couldn't imagine living like that, and yet Hanne's family had experience of this in the past. What sort of restrictions?

It has happened before here. Once, we were only allowed to live in the Judengasse, but that has been demolished now. Most Jews live here in Ostend, and we have our own shops and, of course, our synagogues. We shall keep ourselves to ourselves and hope not to attract hostile attention. Anyway – sticks and stones, as Mutter is often heard to say.

'Sticks and stones may break your bones, Hanne.' The posters and the scrawled writing at the station took on a darker meaning. Was it a small minority who were anti-Semitic, or was it a growing tide of resentment? This Hitler could be a very dangerous man if he allowed, or worse, encouraged, his storm troopers to break the windows of Jewish shops.

On a brighter note, splendid news. Berek and I are expecting a baby next July.

This was the news she'd been anticipating. Berek and Hanne were truly committed to one another now – a baby needed both its parents.

I am very excited, Berek is proud as can be, and Mutter is delighted. I confess to being a little nervous. It's a little late to wonder if this is the right time to bring a child into the world.

I suppose every mother worries like this, but it feels like an enormous responsibility. Still, babies are born all the while and most families cope very well.

Mom and Dad had raised five children, and Mom was one of eight. Hanne would be fine, but she couldn't help the empty feeling in her heart or the surge of longing for a child of her own. It was time she put her impossible love behind her and found someone she could spend the rest of her life with. Someone who could give her the family she wanted.

She put the letter down and tried to concentrate on her accounts. Invoices for iron rod for chain and steel tubing for the bicycle factory, an order that needed quoting for, a reply from Cunard thanking her for her interest and promising to keep Joshua and Son in mind when they were ready to invite tenders for anchor cable, a cancelled order from a company in America who claimed trade tariffs to protect American businesses made British chain too expensive, and an income-tax reminder.

Why did Hanne have to fall in love with Berek?

She let her tears fall. It was madness, longing for someone she could never have. She had to move on for her own sanity. Charlie loved her, and he was a good man who would never hurt her. Could she love him in return?

***

Hawley Heath, England July 1931

'Netherton Pictureland is showing *Madame Guillotine* at the Workers Institute. Do you fancy going, Emma?'

Emma put down the invoices Charlie had given her and looked up. 'I'd like that. I can't remember the last time I saw a film.'

'Saturday night?'

'Why not?'

'It's a date. Meet you at the Blue Bus stop at the end of Willis Street?'

'A date?'

He grinned. 'If you like. My treat.'

She couldn't help smiling back. 'Then I accept graciously.' Not paying her own way felt alien, but Charlie could afford it on the wages she paid him – he only had himself to keep.

His grim widened. 'I knew you'd succumb to my charm, eventually.'

'Charm? Is that what you call it?'

He laughed and went back to his work. She stared after him. He was a good-looking man – strong, honest, hard-working, and clever, and if there was any man she could fall in love with, it would be Charlie. A tiny flutter in her heart was either indigestion or... Other than the all-consuming longing she'd felt in Germany, which she'd tried hard to put behind her, she didn't know what love felt like.

She had to admit, she'd resisted Charlie's charms very well, but a closer relationship with him would distract her from the emotional pain of Hanne having Berek's baby, which was due any day now.

Saturday was baking hot, and she wore a skimpy dress with no sleeves like the ones the girls had worn in Frankfurt. She pulled her mind back from Frankfurt. There was Charlie, wearing a dark suit and tie, his fair hair neatly Brylcreemed.

She waved and hurried to join him in the queue just as the bus arrived.

'You look lovely, Emma. I was afraid you'd changed your mind.' He put a hand beneath her arm and helped her onto the bus.

She hid a smile. If it made him feel chivalrous... She almost had changed her mind, but she wouldn't have stood him up. She had to be honest with him if she was to maintain a friendship with him, never mind have a relationship. Love, marriage, children were topics that needed confronting. But not now. They were going to see a film on their first date, not walking up the aisle.

The hall was filling up. *Madame Guillotine* must be a popular film. Charlie ushered her to the back of the hall and sat beside her. Her heart raced. She'd heard Bonnie and Grace talk about the back row of the cinema.

The lights went down and the screen lit as music played. Charlie put his arm around her, and she nestled into his shoulder. It felt good to be held, a haven for a while away from the worries and responsibilities of life. Louis Dubois, a French revolutionary, fell in love with and married Lucille de Choisigne, a noblewoman. Charlie's lips brushed the top of her head and she raised her face towards him. She heard the swish of the guillotine and the gasp of the crowd, but her lips were on Charlie's, and her heart pounded with desire, not horror.

***

Frankfurt, Germany July 1931

Hanne supported her belly with a hand as she got onto the tram. The seats were all taken, and no one stood to let a heavily pregnant woman sit down. She put her shopping bag on the floor by her feet and leaned against a seat, holding onto the hanging strap. The woman in the seat flinched away as if she was infectious.

The tram stopped, and the woman got off. She sank into the seat thankfully, feeling a slight twinge in her belly. It was so hot and airless, she wouldn't have been surprised to hear thunder.

'Anyone would think pregnancy was catching.' The voice was male, elderly.

She turned to the old man sitting beside her. He had a long grey beard and wore a kippah on the crown of his head. She huffed a derisive laugh. 'I think she was afraid Jewishness was catching.'

He smiled with eyes that had seen all this before. The long walking cane in his left hand explained why he hadn't offered her his seat. 'It is ever the case that we are despised, feared, even. I'm not sure what threat we represent. We are Germans, after all, and fought for our country, and we keep ourselves to ourselves.'

'Mutter says they blame us for losing the war and for unemployment.'

He raised patient eyes to the tram roof. 'And we few Jews in such a large population did it all by ourselves. It is an excuse to hide their own inadequacies.'

She smiled back. 'Still, people believe it.'

He nodded. 'Sometimes, I am glad to be not much longer on this earth, but perhaps I shouldn't say that with you expecting a new life. Still, this old goat is tired, and your little one will be a new generation with hope and aspirations.'

'Old goat?'

'The sheep bleat the words of the shepherd's propaganda. We goats listen to our goatherd and then think for ourselves.'

124

'I would rather be a goat, then.'

'Good. And make sure your little one is a kid, not a lamb.'

'I shall.'

The tram slowed, and a man pushed past her. 'Jewish whore. Fattened on the misery of others.'

'I beg your pardon?' She was pregnant, not overweight, and she wasn't a whore.

The man leaned towards her and spat in her face. 'There are too many Jews. Germany is under the ugly thumb of the impure Jew who has all the money and the power.'

She wiped spittle from her face. 'If that is true, perhaps it is because we have all the brains.'

'The Nazis will answer the Judenfrage. Then see where your evil noses get you. Not on this tram, I'll bet.'

The tram stopped, and the man disembarked, leaving her trembling. She rubbed her aching back. 'What did he mean?'

The old Jew put a hand on her arm. 'Take no notice. Hatred of the Jews comes and goes like high and low tides of self-righteous resentment. We have faced restrictions before and have survived. If we are banned from using trams, we shall walk. If they ban us from shops, we have enough of our own. They can make life difficult for us, but they can't destroy us or our faith.'

The next stop was her own, and she'd be glad to be home safe. She bade the old man a good day and stepped down into a sultry heat. Who thought having a baby due in July was good planning? She carried her shopping the remaining distance to the door of her apartment block. Someone had daubed words in yellow paint across the black door.

TOD ALLEN JUDEN!

Pain swirled through her back and stomach in a huge contracting wave. She bent double, gasping for breath while the pain ebbed. She'd only just made it home in time.

'Berek!'

No answer.

'Mutter!'

Could she manage the stairs? Grabbing the handrail, she climbed one step at a time, resting while pain clenched her belly and receded again.

'Mutter! Berek!'

She left her shopping bag on the tenth step and continued without it, one hand cradling her belly. Five more steps to go.

'Mutter!'

The door to her apartment opened, and Mutter took in the situation at a glance. 'Hanne, child. Let me help you.'

'I left the shopping on the stairs.'

'I'll fetch it. Go and rest on your bed. I'll telephone the midwife and tell her to come at once.'

Grateful to be in loving hands, she sank onto her bed. She needed Berek. She wished Emma was here. Her mind went back to the daubed words on the door downstairs.

TOD ALLEN JUDEN!

Death to all Jews! What kind of world was she bringing her baby into?

Chapter Thirteen

Hawley Heath, England 1931

My dearest Emma,

I'm thrilled to tell you that Berek and I have a baby boy, born on July 16th. We have called him Asher, which means happy and blessed. He weighed a little over three kilograms and has a thick mop of fine black hair, Berek's dark eyes, and Mutter's nose. He is so beautiful, and Berek and Mutter are besotted with him.

Emma turned over the small square of card to reveal a photograph of Asher. Hanne was right that he had Berek's eyes, but she could see Hanne in his little face. And how tiny were those curled fists ready to take on the world?

I am exhausted. A week of sleepless nights have caught up with me today, but Mutter has taken him out for a walk in his pram, so I am resting while I can. I have a mountain of dirty nappies to wash and hang on the balcony to dry. I seem to have become a feeding and changing machine and wonder if I shall ever have my own life back. But I shouldn't complain. They are babies for so short a time, Mutter warns me, so I shall treasure every moment.

What other news? I have been so immersed in pregnancy and babies these past month that I have lost track of what is going on around me.

Did I tell you Hitler was prosecuted for being involved in manslaughter carried out by the Sturmabteilung – his storm troopers – in Berlin last year? The case was dismissed in May, but it shows that there are lawyers prepared to work for those who stand against the Nazi Party. Nazi supporters say Hitler is a man of peace, not a sabre rattler, but he is a passionate man who easily carries people with him.

There was something dark in the spaces between the lines of the letter. Hanne felt the need for the law to protect her against this Hitler? What wasn't she telling her?

I hear Chancellor Brüning visited London last month. He has suspended payment of reparations and was warning about the collapse of the banks in Germany. It was not an exaggeration. All the banks in Germany are now closed. We are fortunate that some of our family's money was not in a German Bank.

Mutter is back with Asher, and he will need feeding, so I shall close and tend to my son. I hope his Auntie Emma will come and visit us very soon. You will love him, Emma.

What of you and Charlie? Will we be hearing of your wedding soon?

How little Hanne understood. She would never know how she felt; it would destroy their relationship, and she couldn't bear that.

What of her and Charlie? They'd been on a few dates and had kissed, but she couldn't take it further unless Charlie agreed to her terms, which wasn't likely. She needed to have a serious conversation with him before he asked for more than she could give.

It was a fortnight before she found the courage.

He caught her staring out of the window in the office. 'A penny for them, Emma?'

She smiled. 'I've been thinking, Charlie. About us.'

He raised an eyebrow. 'Oh?'

'I really like you. You know that, don't you?'

'But?'

'There is a but, a big but. I don't want to marry. I never have, and I never will.'

'Well, that stopped me making a fool of myself.'

'I'm sorry, Charlie. It's nothing to do with you. I —' She couldn't bring herself to admit the truth to him. It had been hard enough coming to terms with it herself. She ploughed on, hoping a half-truth would explain some of her reluctance. 'I've seen so many women who are less than they could be because of marriage. However good a marriage it is, there are sacrifices that have to be made that I'm not prepared to make — can't make. I can't take all a man offers and give nothing in return. That wouldn't be fair, and I couldn't live a lie. I love you too much to do that to you.'

'So, you do love me?'

'Of course, I do. It's just —'

'You don't want to marry me. This chap you met in Germany. Would you marry him if he was available?'

She didn't answer, but her silence was answer enough.

'I get it, Emma. Friends?'

'Always, Charlie.'

'Lovers?'

She had felt something when she'd kissed him. 'I don't know.' How would she know what she was turning her back on if she didn't try it? If Mom had been old enough to make her own mistakes at fifteen, she, at twenty-four, was old enough to live with the consequences of hers. 'Maybe.'

'I can wait, Emma, until you're ready.'

129

'Thank you, Charlie.' She watched him go. Would she ever be ready?

She buried her confusion in the newspaper.

Labour Government Resigns

MacDonald to lead National Government drawn from all parties as suggested by King George earlier this year.

May Report's recommendation to cut government spending forces 'split' Labour out of office.

What did that mean for business, workers, and the unemployed of England?

***

September brought Emma no nearer to a sexual liaison with Charlie. The man had the patience of a saint, but she was afraid of not being in control, or worse, of losing his friendship because she changed her mind at the last moment. Charlie wasn't Willis or the French soldier who'd assaulted her in Frankfurt.

She turned on the radio to distract herself. '*Mad dogs and Englishmen go out in the midday sun…*' Noël Coward wasn't wrong there, but Germans were just as bad, and they wore skimpy clothes most English men and women would never wear. She let the words wash over her and settled to filling wage packets with notes and coins withdrawn from the bank that morning. She wished she could add a bonus – it seemed too little an amount to reward the hard work and loyalty of her workers, her friends.

'*The Chancellor of the Exchequer, Philip Snowden, has announced wage cuts for all government employees.*'

She turned up the volume.

'*The chancellor further announced that there will be cuts in unemployment benefits. Sources suggest the cuts will be in the region of ten percent, half the proposed cut that split the Labour Party earlier this year. The chancellor has not ruled out means testing as a way of deciding who is entitled to unemployment benefit. Three million people will be affected by the proposals.*

'If means testing is confirmed, it will be carried out by the Public Assistance Committees formed by borough councils when the Boards of Guardians and workhouses were abolished last year.'

The dole was only payable for the first six months of unemployment, which was why the soup kitchens were so vital. She was thankful for Charlie's idea of giving over some land to allotments. Contributions of excess vegetables had helped soup content enormously.

A ten-percent cut in what little dole they got was the difference between hunger and starvation for many families. She'd thought Ramsay MacDonald, as a Labour prime minister, would fight for the workers. MacDonald might as well be a fat Tory for all the good he was. He was a traitor who had betrayed the British working men and women who'd voted him into power and trusted him to work for the common good.

The news having ended, she switched the radio off. What did they mean by means testing? An excuse to pay out to fewer people? Didn't the government realise people were starving while politicians ate and drank at their London clubs? They couldn't expect local ratepayers to support the unemployed when most of them were unemployed themselves.

It was government that had called the tune and government who should pay the piper. The National Unemployed Workers Movement wouldn't lie down and let their members be trampled underfoot yet again, and if they called for another hunger march to

London, she'd be right there with them.

A couple of weeks later, she called on Elsie, whose entire family had been laid off by a neighbouring chain factory. Elsie's husband, Bert, wasn't well, and it seemed only fitting to bring her soup-kitchen stalwart a flask of soup.

Elsie answered the door. She looked distraught. 'The pack of wolves is here, Emma.'

'Pack of wolves?'

'The Public Assistance Committee, PAC. They're going through everything.'

'I brought you some soup. Mutton and vegetable. Can I come in?'

Elsie took the flask and stood back to let her in. 'Thanks, love, but I expect they'll count this as something I could sell, as well.'

Sell? What was going on?

Two men were making notes in a book. 'There's five shillings in the rent jar, and two shillings in the gas jar. Do you have any other savings, Mrs Parsons?'

Before Elsie could reply, she butted in. 'Do you think a family that's been on the dole for the best part of six months has savings? Why do you think I've brought a flask of soup? Try looking in Elsie's larder to see if she can afford food.'

The man looked down his nose at her. 'She has possessions she can sell to raise money for food.' He glanced down at his list. 'A piano, a chair, two saucepans, tablecloths —'

She clenched her fists. 'The piano was her grandmother's, and what will she cook in if you take her saucepans?'

The man smiled a nasty, sneering smile. 'If she has no food, she won't need saucepans to cook it in. Anyway, she has another one, and I don't need to justify my actions to you. I have a job to do. The country can't afford to pay dole to those who have assets.'

'You call a few miserable shillings, some saucepans, tablecloths, and a piano assets? Who the hell in Hawley Heath can afford to buy a tablecloth, never mind a piano? This is ridiculous.'

'I have a job to do, and a piano is not an essential item. Sell it, Mrs Parsons. You'll not get a penny dole until these things are sold. Now, we'll look upstairs, if you don't mind.'

'You'd strip this family of everything they have?'

The man closed his book and headed for the stairs.

She followed him. 'Mr Parsons isn't well. He shouldn't be disturbed.'

The man took no notice but clumped up the bare wooden stairs and opened the door to the cupboard on the landing. 'Blankets, three. Sheets –too worn to be saleable.'

Bert Parsons lay in his bed, visible through the open bedroom door. His pallor showed how ill he was. 'Has the doctor seen him, Elsie?'

'We can't afford no doctor, Emma.'

Bert tried to sit up. 'I don't need a doctor. I'll be right as rain in a day or two.'

'Bert, you need to see one. Send for Doctor Brown, Elsie. I'll see to the bill.'

Elsie's tense mouth relaxed a little. 'God, bless you, Emma. I'll run along now and fetch him if you'll keep an eye on these – gentlemen.'

Doctor Brown was a good man who did what he could for poor

patients, but doctors had to eat as well. It was a pity that wolves were so indiscriminately hungry.

'Who are you? What do you want?' Bert sank back against his pillows.

'Public Assistance.'

'Means test? Is that why you're here?'

'Just doing our job, Mr Parsons.' The two men opened drawers and a small wardrobe and made notes.

Bert coughed into a handkerchief and wiped his mouth. 'You want the shirt off my back? One of my bloody pillows?'

She didn't doubt they'd add them to the list of things to be sold if they felt like it. 'You can't do this. It isn't right. These poor people need money to buy food, not a list of things no one can afford to buy.' Damn it, she'd buy the bloody piano herself if she had to.

'Like I said, miss. Just doing our job.'

She took a deep breath, tried to stay calm, and failed. 'I suppose you'll take the damned guzunder from under the poor man's bed if it hasn't got shit in it.'

She stamped downstairs, tears blurring her vision. It hadn't been Joshua and Son who'd thrown this family out of work, and it wasn't the fault of the chain master who'd been forced to do it. It had been the fault of governments who went to war with no regard for their own people, let alone other country's families, and had instigated a depression that was now affecting everyone. That none of this was her fault didn't stop her feeling she'd failed Bert and Elsie. What good was she as a chain mistress if she was helpless in the face of wolves?

Chapter Fourteen

Hawley Heath, England 1932

Rosie removed a length of iron rod from the heat of her forge and placed it on her anvil to hammer. She felt like hammering it flat, really flat like a spade. The last blow to the shipbuilding industry, and to their hopes of a contract to make anchor cable chain for Hull 534 had landed on Emma's office desk that morning.

I regret to inform you that due to the present economic climate, the building of Hull 534 has been suspended for two years. I shall of course keep your details in the event of construction restarting.

That was the gist of it, and it was yet another blow to the crippled industries of the Midlands and the North of England. The building of the major ocean liner at John Brown and Company's shipyard in Clydebank, in Scotland, would have revitalised these hard-hit areas. Couldn't the government see that investment in projects like this would ease unemployment and take thousands out of poverty?

She dealt another heavy blow. Last autumn's election had given the National Government a landslide victory and Lloyd George was still at the helm, but was he doing anything useful? The iron went back in the forge to reheat. They'd been forced to lay off three workers, and helping Emma choose who, had been the most difficult thing she'd ever had to do. That she'd subjected them to the indignity of having their lives poked and prodded by the Public Assistance carnivores didn't sit well on her conscience.

She let her hammer fall with more than necessary force. All means testing and benefit cuts had done was anger the already struggling unemployed and cause protests across the country – protests that had been met with baton charges by police and the unemployed being criminalised for public-order offences.

It wasn't fair.

The link was the worst she'd ever made. She put it back in the flames and waited for it to glow yellow-red so she could reshape it – Mom had taught her to turn a link when she was six, and how to twist a lay-flat chain when she was ten. Emma had learned the trade the same way: by her mother's side and then in Mrs Kimble's chain workshop. It was a way of life that was disappearing, and hard and long though the hours were, she would be sad to see the trade of hand-made chain disappear and the skills lost forever.

Times changed and Joshua and Son was having to change with them or go under. She glanced across at Jack and a brief smile formed. He'd begun making spades, forks, hoes, trowels, and shovels when Charlie suggested the allotments. Now, Jack had moved into forging chisels, pliers, pincers, hammer heads – anything useful he could think of that could be made from iron. Emma had produced a catalogue with drawings and photographs, and they'd saved one worker's job by appointing him as a sales representative to hawk samples of their wares around the Black Country and beyond.

He'd come back with orders, which the men were now fulfilling, and Emma had placed an order for wooden handles for those tools that would need them. Joshua and Son were struggling, but they were hanging on, if by a thread – a bank loan, with interest rates as they were, was out of the question.

And then there was Emma and Charlie. The man was mad about Emma, but the silly girl couldn't see a good thing when it was right in front of her. What was wrong with her? She yanked the iron from the hearth and put it on her bickon. Taking a deep, calming breath, she turned the link.

Had she put Emma off marriage by warning her so often against men who'd take advantage of her wealth, not that most of her wealth was disposable, tied up as it was in Marion's will and workers' homes and livelihoods? It was more than likely, but Charlie was a hard worker who was an asset to the family, not a scrounger. More than that, he was a genuinely nice person. Oh hell, couldn't she get anything right where the Joshuas were concerned? She'd have to have a talk with her eldest daughter.

The fact remained – fewer women were marrying, or they were marrying much later, and divorce, though still stigmatised, had risen alarmingly. The blame was laid at the feet of feminists, flappers, and the loose morals of the time, but was it that women were escaping abusive marriages? If they were, they had a tough time proving a case against their husbands, even having to prove they were of sound mind, and an even tougher time getting any sort of financial settlement after divorce. There was still much inequality between the sexes. Even Emma, had she wanted a loan for the factory, would have had to find a man to co-sign the agreement.

Emma was a strong, independent woman of means, so perhaps she shouldn't interfere in her love life, or lack of it. Emma knew her own mind and would ask her opinion and advice if she wanted it.

Her final length of chain completed for her order, she made her hearth safe and headed home. Jack would work on to finish an urgent contract, and Emma would come when she was ready.

It was a cold, bright afternoon, and as she passed the end of Willis Street two men with clipboards caught her attention. They were waving their arms at some of the older back-to-back terraced houses. Curious, she slowed her pace.

The man in the bowler hat tapped a pencil on his clipboard. 'These eight aren't fit for human habitation. In fact, this whole terrace needs to come down.'

His colleague nodded and made a note. 'Added to the cottages and chain workshops in Forge Lane, Beggars Lane, and Anvil Road that makes seventy-four slums that can be cleared, so far. This entire area is ripe for redevelopment.'

Most of the houses in question didn't belong to Emma, but "this entire area", delineated by a vague and expansive wave of the man's arm, took in some of Willis Street, which had perfectly good houses.

She approached the men. 'Did I hear you correctly? You're planning on knocking down half of Hawley Heath?' It might not prove to be an exaggeration.

'We're surveying housing stock for the council, madam. The Housing Act of 1930 requires the council to demolish slums and build new houses. These back-to-backs have had their day, and some of the old cottages in Forge Lane have half-collapsed already because of mining subsidence.'

She'd only just escaped with her life before one had collapsed when she was a child. She knew how poor some of the old cottages were – some of them needed demolishing but rebuilding half of Hawley Heath was more than Joshua and Son could ever have afforded. Matthew had re-homed the families from the cinder yard into the terraces he'd had built in Willis Street. 'And where will the families live when you knock down their homes?'

'Not my problem, madam. Eventually, there'll be flats built.'

'Not your problem? Some of these houses belong to my

daughter!'

'She'll get compensation, Mrs Joshua.'

'Mrs Taylor. Rosie Taylor. My daughter is Emma Taylor. She owns Joshua and Son and all this part of town.'

'Like I say, she'll get compensation.'

She doubted that would be the full cost of replacing the homes lost or the rents they produced when tenants could afford to pay. 'How long will it take to build new houses? Years, I dare say. What provision will be made for the families made homeless?'

'You'll have to ask the council, madam. I really couldn't say. Look on the bright side – it's an investment in the future, better homes for workers, and jobs for builders in the area. It's a government initiative to help boost the economy. As I understand it, families will be re-homed according to need.'

The bright side. The houses in question all had outside toilets, many sharing one two-hole toilet and a water pump between several houses, but they were still people's homes: places they'd been born, raised their families, loved, worked, and died. She knew the names of all the families that lived in these streets, and they could be re-homed anywhere. The government was ripping out the heart of Hawley Heath and tearing apart a close-knit community.

Not for the first time in her life, she realised that change was coming unasked, and nothing would be quite the same again.

***

Frankfurt, Germany 1932

Hanne pushed Asher in his pushchair. At eleven months old, he was a big boy and growing fast. He could crawl, sit up, and was standing, if wobbly, if she held his hands. To her delight, his first

139

word was Mutter.

Today, she was taking him to see Uncle Saul in his shop. Her uncle had promised to give Asher a gold Star of David on a chain to commemorate his first birthday, and he was making the pendant himself. It would be something Asher could wear with pride when he was old enough not to lose it.

Uncle Saul was washing his shop window when she arrived. There was a tell-tale of yellow paint on the pavement. She pretended she hadn't noticed.

'Come in, Hanne. I've almost finished the star. Come and see how it's progressing.'

On the workbench lay a partly constructed star and beside it a chain made of fine links, each painstakingly made by hand. Uncle Saul was a fine craftsman. 'It's going to be beautiful.'

She touched the one around her neck that her uncle had made for her on her own first birthday. 'He'll treasure it the way I treasure mine.'

Uncle Saul smiled broadly. 'They will be a link to your pasts when we old ones are no longer here and a reminder of the strength of our faith.'

'Don't talk like that, Uncle. I can't bear to think of a world without you.'

'Yet it must be, child. All this?' He looked around his shop with obvious pride. 'This will be Asher's one day. I hope to train him as a jeweller with your permission.'

'I would be honoured.'

Her uncle smiled. 'Then I shall begin as soon as he can hold a file in those chubby little hands. It's never too soon to begin a craft.'

'Did you hear that, Asher? You're a very lucky boy.'

Uncle Saul's face was sombre. 'I hope so, but I fear there may be difficult times ahead.'

'The yellow paint?'

'Ah, you saw it. Yes. People are jealous of what we have. I understand when so many are suffering, but they can't eat gold or silver, and it is our livelihood in better times.'

'There will be better times, Uncle.'

He huffed a laugh. 'I'm sure there will, child. With six million souls out of work, surely things can't get much worse for Germany. Perhaps Paul von Hindenburg will be a better president. With Brüning resigning, or dismissed, and Franz von Papen forming a new government, I hoped things might improve. The Reichstag was so fragmented, and he faced so much opposition, I suppose it was no surprise he had Hindenburg dissolve the Reichstag.'

Her mind went back to the yellow paint. 'Mutter says Hitler has obtained German citizenship.'

'So he could stand for Reichspräsident in the presidential election. Thankfully, Hindenburg won by a narrow majority. And this year, you will be old enough to vote in the federal election. Use your vote wisely, Hanne.'

'You don't think I should vote for the Nazi Party?'

'You must vote as your conscience dictates for the good of Germany. I don't believe Hitler has the good of Jews foremost in his mind. He blames us for Germany's social and economic problems, and he has promised to put those right. People say he is a man of peace, but I don't believe it. I think he has the Rhineland in his sights. And you heard the Schutzstaffel and the

141

Sturmabteilung have had their token bans overturned? I see men in forbidden uniforms strutting the streets.'

'I expect they are getting ready to protect the Nazi election events and meetings from communist interference.'

'Or disrupt the Communist Party campaign meetings.'

'Maybe. Mutter and I heard Hitler speak last year. He promised to oust the French soldiers and stop paying reparations. Those would be popular moves as would getting back the Ruhr.'

'They would. Perhaps, if we can reclaim our industrial heartland, there will be more money and more jobs, and people won't take out their frustrations on my window.'

Asher began to grizzle, and a grizzle turned to a wail that could wake the dead. 'I'll take him home and feed him, Uncle. I look forward to seeing the star finished.

'Take care, Hanne.'

There had been something in her uncle's tone that made her look both ways before she exited the shop onto the street. Someone had re-daubed yellow words on the cleaned shop window.

Juden raus!

Out with the Jews. She sighed. Sticks and stones…

***

Hanne gasped as she read the newspaper report. She reread it to be sure she had it right.

ALTONA BLOODY SUNDAY

Armed Communists (KDP) attack the National Socialist German Workers' Party (Nazis) at Altona in Prussia. Eighteen dead.

With the election taking place today, feelings would be high. No wonder Hitler wanted his storm troopers at the ready.

'You coming, Hanne?'

'Just getting Asher in his pushchair, Mutter.' She strapped the boy in and gave him the homemade toy dog with long floppy ears that Emma had sent him for an early birthday present. It was his favourite toy.

The streets were busy with people heading for the polling station. She wouldn't vote for the KDP, and neither would she vote for the Nazis. She'd cast her vote for the Social Democrats, which was the only party likely to stand between the far-left and the far-right and might offer some stability.

As they approached the polling station, it was obvious some kind of scuffle was taking place. SS and SA uniforms were forming a line preventing Communist voters from entering the hall, while KDP members targeted pro-Nazi voters. What had happened to democracy?

While the crowd of brawlers grew larger, she and Mutter slipped into the hall to cast their votes.

She marked her ballot paper and slipped it into the ballot box; she'd done what she could. She bowed her head in prayer. 'Some rely upon chariots and some upon horses, but we rely upon and invoke the Name of the Lord our God.' She clenched her fists before continuing her prayer. 'Please, Lord, let the Social Democrats win enough of the vote to keep these extremists at bay.'

Chapter Fifteen

Hawley Heath, England 1932

Emma walked beside her mother towards the factory, wondering how long Hawley Heath would remain the town she loved, and for all its smoke-blackened streets, blast furnaces, rolling mills, and pitheads, she did love it. It was a community that wrapped around her, people she'd grown up with, worked with, laughed and cried with, and the thought of it being destroyed, and the inhabitants scattered to the four winds, was unbearable. If what Mom had heard was correct, families would be evicted and their homes knocked down.

First mass unemployment, poverty, and the indignity of means testing, and now this.

Mom broke the silence. 'Was that a letter from Hanne I saw you with earlier?'

'Yes.'

'Is she well? The baby?'

'Asher's one now, and he loves the toy dog I made him. She and Berek are well, but she writes less happily about Germany.'

Mom broke her stride. 'Trouble?'

'I'm not sure. They've just held elections, and the extremist factions have got a big share of the vote. Hanne says the Nazi Party now has two hundred and thirty seats in the Reichstag, which is a majority of about a hundred over the Social Democrats, but not enough to form a government. The Communist Party gained seats as well. She said there were violent clashes between

144

the Nazi and the Communist paramilitary, and the president is governing by emergency decree under Article 48, whatever that is.'

'So, the country is still split? That's better than the Nazis being in power.'

'That's much what Hanne says. She and her family don't trust Hitler and his storm troopers. There have been anti-Jewish slogans and broken windows in Jewish shops, and the storm troopers are responsible for some of them.'

'I was afraid of this, though why when Jews fought for their country like any other patriotic German. If the Nazis form a coalition government, let's hope the Social Democrats can keep Hitler in check. One thing is for certain, the Nazis won't join with the Communists!'

'Hanne's mother says she can't see any of the other parties supporting the Nazis. They're popular with the people, because of the promises they've made, but not with the rest of the elected members of the Reichstag.'

'If they can't work together, and a minority government is in office, they'll agree on nothing, and it won't be long before they call another election.'

'And what if Hitler gets enough votes?'

'Then I fear Hanne and her family will be in for an unpleasant time.'

'Do you think they're in danger?'

'Not danger, I wouldn't think, so much as more restricted in what they can do, where they can go, and where they can live. That's what's happened in the past. They may not have the freedoms they enjoy now if Hitler uses them as a scapegoat for the country's ills.'

'At least they'll have homes. Mom, what's going to happen to people like Bert and Elsie if their house is demolished?'

'I don't know, Emma. Sometimes, there are battles you can't win, and to be honest, those old cottages need money spending on them we just don't have. The other houses you own are all in pretty good order, so a lot of our tenants are safe.'

'Since most of them can't afford to pay rent, they're safe only because we won't evict them. How long can we continue like this, Mom?'

Mom smiled reassuringly. 'Things will pick up, Emma. It won't be this tough forever, and who knows, the compensation you get might just save the factory.'

'I hope you're right, Mom, really, I do.'

***

'Have you seen this, Mom?' Emma pushed the newspaper towards her mother.

Communists provoke running battles with police. Tensions high.

The National Unemployed Workers' Movement, backed by the Communist Party of Great Britain, is behind violence that erupted in Birmingham yesterday.

'It was on the radio news. There were running battles between protesters and police, and some injuries. And not only in Birmingham.'

Tensions were indeed high. The hated Means Test had united the unemployed and forced them into action.

'Some of the women are collecting signatures for a petition

against the Means Test. I've signed already.' She rubbed her aching forehead, ignoring a knock at the office door.

'You all right, Emma?'

'Elsie. How's Bert?'

Elsie smiled, unaware she was about to be made homeless by the council. When they got notice to quit was soon enough for them to worry about it. 'He's much better, thanks to you, Emma.'

'I wish I could do more, Elsie.'

Elsie cast a sideways glance at Mom. 'You're just like your mom, Emma, always trying to fix the world. Can't be done, love, can it, Rosie? But we survive, nonetheless.'

Mom nodded in agreement. 'You're right, of course. What can we do for you, Elsie?'

'This.'

She took the letter Elsie proffered. 'Ah, you've had your eviction notice.'

'You knew about this?'

'I knew the council was planning to clear slums – it's because of the Housing Act. There's nothing we can do to stop it, but I hoped it wouldn't be so soon. I'm so sorry, Elsie. What are you going to do?'

'My sister will put me and Bert up in her spare room, now young Donny is married and away. We survived the war, we'll survive this, and anyway, an indoor bathroom in our new house will be better come winter than a guzunder, fetching water from the pump, damp, and rats in the pantry and outside privy.'

She envied Elsie's pragmatism. 'Have all Forge Lane residents had eviction notices?'

147

'I think so. Some are planning to fight it, and some reckon they might be able to squat in some semi-derelict houses in Cradley Heath if they're still standing by then – the houses, that is. They can't knock the whole area down at once, surely? Maurice and Evelyn Butterworth reckon they'll have to be dragged out screaming before they'll let them touch a brick or stone of their house. There's others of a like mind.'

'It's going to be a hard fight, and I don't think they'll win.'

'No, neither do I, but this is something we might win.' Elsie pushed a list of names across the desk. 'I wondered if you'd sign my petition.'

'Is this the one about means testing?'

'Yes. What they're doing ain't right, Emma. They've made us sell all but the bloody coats off our backs. A sing-song around that old piano was what kept our spirits up. It ain't right.'

'Of course, I'll sign.' They wouldn't check all the names and discover she'd signed twice. She wrote her name clearly and signed with an angry flourish. She passed the petition to Mom.

'Thank you, both. We're taking it to Ramsay MacDonald. We're hoping for a million signatures countrywide, and we're going to march on London like we did in 1929 and deliver the petition to parliament. Will you be coming with us, Emma? I don't expect you to come, Rosie, not after what happened to you last time.'

She was grateful Mom hadn't argued the point. 'I shall if I can, Elsie, but there's a lot going on here at the moment and people who might need help to be re-homed. I can't be in two places at the same time.'

'You're a good girl, Emma. I know you'll do what's best.'

She smiled, got up from her chair, and gave Elsie a hug. 'Sometimes, it's a job to know what the best is. Thank you for being so understanding.'

'No good blarting over a tipped-up po, as my mom would have said.'

She laughed, but her eyes filled with tears. She would miss people like Elsie if they were re-homed away from Hawley Heath. They were the backbone of the community and everything she loved about the place.

***

Rosie was doing her best to support Emma in her decisions. Compulsory purchase orders had been served, eviction notices issued, and the Joshua and Son empire was shrinking street by street. Emma was using some of the cash paid for the old houses to pay a month's rent up front on new residences for those of the Joshua workforce, past and present, who didn't have relatives to lodge with. Her problem was the lack of available, unoccupied housing that would escape the slum clearance and the fact that many of the slum houses to be cleared were shared by two or more families. Time was running out to find alternative accommodation.

'If the worst comes to the worst, Emma, we can use one or two of the rooms we keep for the sick at Heath Hall, and we could ask if we could house families temporarily in the church rooms.'

'What about the Sisters of Mercy?'

'No harm in asking, though they may only take the sick.'

Emma's eyes shone with tears. 'I feel so helpless, Mom.'

'You're doing more than most employers would, love. You can't magic houses out of thin air. Perhaps some of our Willis Street tenants have a spare room they would let to keep people in the area.'

'That would mean splitting families. You can't expect eight or ten people to share one small room.'

'Some already do, Emma, and it would be better than living on the streets.' An icy shiver ran down her spine. Willis had threatened to throw her entire family out on the streets in winter if she refused to go under the bridge with him. Emma was nothing like her father in spirit.

'We'll ask. Rent for a month for one room will cost us less than a house, and a small regular rent would be a little extra income for those tenants willing to share their homes.' She didn't mention the fact that most of the tenants already owed them rent and really should give it straight back to them. Had the government any idea of the hardship they were causing?

'And have the Public Assistance Committee dock their dole because of their generosity?'

'We'll keep it a secret arrangement then.' Emma's brow creased. 'I'm not giving good money to this damned government with their means testing.'

'Does that mean you're going on this hunger march? I hear the Glasgow contingent has already left for London.'

'They have. No, I feel I'm needed here, but quite a lot of the able-bodied men from here are marching. They'll be back in time to fight these evictions. Did you know, countrywide, they've reached their million-signature target? Not even Ramsay MacDonald can ignore that.'

'I hope you're right.' She didn't share Emma's optimism. Successive governments had ignored the plea for votes for women for around sixty years. Equality of the sexes was an ongoing battle she suspected would rage long after she was dead. Why would they take notice of a petition? But Emma was right about staying; local concerns needed their attention more. There were families who'd vowed to stay in their homes, no matter what, and she didn't want to see anyone injured if council bailiffs forcibly evicted them.

The day of the departure of the hunger marchers dawned bright and clear. It would be warm walking even though it was mid-October. People lined the streets shouting encouragement and waving their menfolk and a few women goodbye. The Hawley Heath brass band struck up a tune, and heads held high, the protesters carried their part of the petition along the High Street and marched out of the town towards Birmingham.

She wished she could march with them, but her last experience, being crushed and trampled, had made her think better of the idea. Her bones weren't as strong as they used to be, and disabled, she was no use to anyone.

The next day's newspaper had an article about the march, but it wasn't front-page news.

Great National Hunger March gets underway. Contingents from England, Scotland, and Wales to converge on London.

There was a brief description of the protesters' demands, but three thousand unemployed out of three million made little impression on the press. During the next two weeks, there was virtually no coverage of the march at all. There seemed little hope it would impress the government, either.

On October 27th, the day the marchers were due to reach London, she turned on the radio to see if there was any news.

'A hundred thousand people gathered in Hyde Park this morning to greet the marchers, who have come from all over

151

Britain to protest at means testing. There has been widespread condemnation of the march on the grounds of public order, especially in the Conservative press. Mounted police are being used to disperse demonstrators as I speak, and I understand violent clashes are taking place across central London. There are serious casualties.'

Voices rose and drowned the reporter's words.

He shouted above them. *'Protesters claim the police are being used to stop the petition from reaching parliament. Wait! The police have arrested a man – he's in handcuffs – and they have the petition. The police have confiscated the petition, and the crowd is furious. Hey, watch out! Ouch...'*

There were sounds of a scuffle, the jeering and chanting of the crowd, the jangle of horse harness and the clop of hooves. The men of Hawley Heath were in the middle of that somewhere.

'This is John Price in Hyde Park handing you back to the studio.'

She switched off the radio, remembering too well the scenes in Birmingham at the last hunger march and being carried off on a stretcher. Thank goodness she and Emma hadn't gone on this one.

Eviction day loomed closer, and she turned her attention back to the housing crisis. The few men who'd remained had emptied the houses of furniture and built barricades across the streets. Some families had already packed and left. Some, like the Butterworths, had stored provisions and had locked and bolted their doors.

The morning of the evictions, she was up at four o'clock, and she drove Emma down to the entrance to Forge Lane. She parked a hundred yards away, anticipating trouble. The hunger marchers were due back today, coming by train paid for by the NUWM and were due in at six in the morning. She wanted to be there to greet them and to lend her support at nine o'clock when the council workers were due to begin work.

A distant clatter of diesel engines made her pause. Early morning delivery lorries? The clatter drew closer along with the rumble of tyres and dimmed lights. Four tractors trundled out of the darkness their large dozer-blades raised. As they reached the barricade, the blades lowered, and they swept away the piles of furniture like so many matchsticks. By the time the men of Hawley Heath arrived, it would be far too late to stop the destruction.

'The bastards.' Emma dashed in front of the first bulldozer. 'Stop. Stop. There are people in some of those houses.'

'Get out of my way, woman.' The driver waved at her to move as he drew closer, but Emma stood her ground.

'Emma!' She charged after her daughter and grabbed her coat, dragging her aside. She raised a clenched fist at the driver. 'Stop, damn you. Stop!' The bulldozer trundled on, followed by a truck full of workers.

As if to demonstrate how unstoppable they were, the blade of the first bulldozer crashed through the garden wall of Bert and Elie's small cottage and came to rest with its blade embedded in the cottage wall. There was a crash and a puther of dust as the front of the house collapsed inwards.

Chapter Sixteen

Frankfurt, Germany November 1932

Hanne put Asher down to sleep and crept from the nursery. With luck, he would sleep for an hour and give her time to read Emma's latest letter and catch up on some chores.

Dear Hanne,

I'm sorry not to have written for a while, but life has been quite hectic. Where to begin? At the beginning, I suppose. First, our government cut the cost of paying the unemployed by introducing means testing. This meant men went into homes and assessed possessions and savings to see what could be sold before people were paid, or they assessed them for a lower payment because, say, a woman was taking in washing and being paid a few pence. As if life isn't hard enough for these people.

A quiet whimper from the nursery made her pause, but Asher went quiet again.

Of course, this caused protests, and a hunger march was organised to take a petition to London. It turned into a fairly bloody affair, much as the last hunger strike did.

England's politics seemed as violent and bloody as Germany's. Tensions were high since Chancellor von Papen had asked Reichspräsident Hindenburg to dissolve parliament to pre-empt a vote of no confidence by the Communist Party – a vote the Nazis would have supported to get another election – at least, that's what the newspapers hinted. Hitler's success in the last election had obviously boosted his confidence. Hindenburg had been governing by emergency decree, but a coalition or one party with a big enough majority could put an end to that.

Secondly, the town council, following a government instruction, have begun clearing the slums to build new homes. While that sounds like a good thing, it had the result of making people homeless. Some of these houses belonged to me, and they bought them under a compulsory purchase order, which means I had no choice but was given compensation, some of which I've used to help families find accommodation.

She loved Emma. She had such a good heart. Her and Mutter's apartment stood on ground cleared when the Judengasse was demolished, long before she was born. Things changed constantly as she was becoming all too aware.

Trouble arose when some residents refused to move out, and the council moved in with bulldozers while the men of Hawley Heath were away on the hunger march. They broke through the barricades and all but flattened a cottage.

Worse, Mom ran into the building to rescue Bert and Elsie, and a section of ceiling fell on her, injuring her shoulder and hip on her left side. She spent a night in hospital, but thankfully no major damage. She's stiff and sore, and I'm helping run around after her, but she isn't a good patient. In fact, she's an impatient patient!

Mom was very shaken up, we all were, but fortunately, Bert and Elsie weren't in the cottage. They'd packed up and moved to Elsie's sister's the day before the bulldozers were due, which the council knew very well. Unfortunately, Mom and I didn't know that, or we could have avoided the accident.

Thank goodness no one was badly hurt.

I stood in Anvil Lane this morning, or what's left of it. I felt as

155

if my world had crumbled around me. It's a wasteland of rubble scattered with discarded possessions thrown out when the people were evicted. All those memories from my childhood wiped out in a matter of days. Life used to seem so safe and unchanging, and now – Oh, I suppose I shall become accustomed to the new homes and probably new faces, and not seeing the friends and acquaintances I would chat to every day, but it feels strange and unsettling.

Anyway, enough of me. How are you and Berek, and Mutter and little Asher? I'm so pleased Asher loves his toy dog. How are things in Germany? I worry about you, Hanne.

Dear Emma, such a disturbing time for her, and yet she still had the heart to think about her cousin in Germany.

She would write back, but first she had to go with Mutter to vote, yet again.

As before, the streets were busy with men and women going to vote, but now, instead of sporting shorts and sleeveless shirts and blouses in sweltering heat, they huddled in long coats with collars turned up against a bitter November wind on an overcast day. Strutting among the residents of the area, as if they already owned the city, were uniformed SA and SS, accosting people to ask how they would vote and turning away those who would vote against them.

If folk answered that they were voting Nazi, she couldn't blame them. To say Communist would probably have earned them a beating.

'Sieg Heil. Heil Hitler!' The loud salutes to their party leader would infuriate the Communist KDP paramilitary.

She turned away from them and pushed Asher's pushchair faster.

'Wait for me, Hanne. My legs can't keep up with yours.'

'Sorry, Mutter.' She slowed her pace. 'Is your back paining you?'

'It's this cold weather. The pain seems to get worse every winter.'

'Oh, Lord, here comes the Communist paramilitary. Quick, this way.' She steered the pushchair into an alley and pulled Mutter after her. 'We'll wait until they've gone. There's bound to be trouble.'

The sound of running feet came closer, and there were sounds of a scuffle. Men shouted in guttural tones, and a shot rang out.

'God of Abraham, Isaac, and Israel protect us.'

'Shush, Mutter.'

More running feet, more shouting, another shot. She gripped the handle of the pushchair to stop her hands shaking. Mutter put an arm around her, and she found her an anxious smile. If the paramilitary found them, and dragged them out into the street, there would be no protection from the violence.

A small whine grew to a wail. She grabbed Asher from his pushchair and buried his face in her coat to quieten him. 'Hush, Asher. Hush, sweetheart.'

They backed deeper into the alley. Mutter tapped her arm. 'There's a way out at the end of the alley. We can go the long way round to the polling station. Take Asher. I'll bring the pushchair.'

'You don't think it would be safer to go home?'

'And not practise our democratic right to vote for someone other than these Communist and Nazi thugs?'

'I was thinking of Asher.'

'So am I, Hanne. Believe, me, if we don't stand up to these people, they will trample us underfoot. Stalin may have condemned anti-Semitism in Russia, but the Communists would do away with democracy, and the Nazis hate Jews. Where then are Asher's freedoms?'

She turned and ran down the alley, followed by the slower feet of her mother. She would cast her vote, and no one was going to stop her.

***

Hawley Heath, England 1932

Rosie sat with her feet up, impatient at having to rest – the pain in her hip and shoulder was much less, but she was having to pace herself and rest frequently. The doctor assured her she would heal, but six weeks of not "overdoing things" stretched like eternity. She picked up the letter from Hanne that Emma had left for her to read while she went to make her a cup of tea. It would occupy a few minutes.

My dearest Emma,

Thank you for your letter. You sound as if you are having a difficult time, and I hope your mother is feeling better. Between politics and the depression, no one is having it easy, it seems.

We have had yet another election. Mutter and I voted, but the streets were terrifying with SS and storm troopers fighting with the KDP paramilitary and intimidating voters. There were even gunshots. How can such an election be free and fair? Mutter and I hid in an alley and managed to get to the polling station without being molested, but it was frightening, especially as I had Asher with me.

Oh, for a stable government. I have had enough of all the

158

parties disagreeing and tearing the country apart!

They announced the results on the radio this morning. The Nazis have one hundred and ninety-six seats now, so they've lost thirty-four. Unfortunately, the Social Democrats also lost seats, twelve, and now have one hundred and twenty-one seats, if I remember the figure correctly, and the Communists, the KDP, have gained seats and now have a hundred.

The major parties are even more equal now than before, and the country is split, so I have little hope of any agreement in the Reichstag. Mutter says two hundred and ninety-three seats are needed for a majority, so the only coalition that would have enough seats would be the Nazis and Social Democrats since the Nazis would never work with the Communists. I'm not sure which is worse, the KDP or the Nazis.

As before, we can only hope that the Social Democrats will keep the Nazis and Communists in order. If there is no coalition, Mutter says she sees Chancellor von Papen asking Reichspräsident Hindenburg to continue to govern by emergency decree.

Men! They are such children. I'm sure we women would do a better job, given the chance.

She smiled. She had to agree. Women would be so much more reasonable – they'd sort it out over a cup of tea and a biscuit.

The letter re-folded, she accepted the cup of tea Emma offered. 'You know, Emma, England isn't so different from Germany. According to a newspaper article I read last week, the police tried to incite violence among peaceful hunger marchers by disguising agent provocateurs as workers and planting them in Trafalgar Square. The police caused some of the injuries and deliberately tried to disrupt peaceful protest. It's an attack on our liberty and freedoms. We can't let our voices be silenced when we see injustice being done by the rich and powerful to the poor and disinherited.'

'You'd make a wonderful politician, Mom. You'd be incorruptible.'

Mom laughed. 'Your father would have a fit. He suffered enough when Mary Macarthur had me bringing the women out on strike against Matthew, and then Marion whisked me off to London, and they threw me into gaol for breaking the War Office windows.'

'You did what?'

'We were protesting about women not getting the vote. I broke a window and spent a fortnight in Holloway gaol. Your dad was furious. No, I'm too old to go gallivanting, and anyway, we have enough problems here to deal with.'

Emma picked up the letter from Hanne and replaced it in its envelope. 'I thought I might visit Hanne and Berek. I haven't met little Asher yet, and I can afford it since I've had compensation money for the houses in Forge Lane.'

'I don't think now is a good time, Emma. Let the dust settle first. I feel very uneasy about the state of things in Germany. Hanne hiding in an alley? Doesn't that tell you something about the tensions there? Meeting Asher can wait, surely.'

'It isn't just Asher I want to see. I need to go, Mom. Charlie loves me, and I can't move on until I know – until I know how I feel about – about the person I met in Frankfurt. I know there was a spark between us, but how can I be sure it's still there unless I find out?'

'And what do you intend to do if it is, Emma?'

'Nothing, Mom.'

'So why go?'

'You don't understand…'

Mom sighed her frustration. 'So, tell me.'

'I can't explain it. It's about me, not them. I fell in love with the wrong person, that's all.'

'You can't help who you fall in love with, sweetheart.'

'No, but – '

'And if the spark has gone out?'

'Then I'll come home with an easier mind and get on with my life. As you said, Mom, there are problems enough here without complicating life further.'

Chapter Seventeen

Frankfurt, Germany 1933

Hanne shivered. It was below freezing and was almost dark, the ice crystals on the pavement sparkling in the light from the streetlamps. She hurried as fast as the slippery surface would allow; Mutter needed the painkillers she'd bought from the pharmacy, but that wasn't the only reason she wanted to be home before dark.

She didn't feel safe.

In December, Chancellor von Papen had been replaced by the defence minister, Kurt von Schleicher, who'd held talks with the left wing of the Nazi Party, led by Gregor Strasser, in the hope of finding centre ground, but Hitler had disempowered Strasser, and now approached the chancellor for coalition talks.

A Nazi coalition, with a man with the persuasive and passionate tongue Hitler had, didn't bode well for the Jews of Germany. A new year didn't fill her with great hope for improvements.

She reached the door to the apartments and relaxed tense shoulders. Home safe. 'Mutter, I have the tablets.'

'Shush.'

She put the tablets on the table and perched on the arm of Mutter's chair to listen to the radio.

'Reichspräsident Hindenburg has appointed Adolph Hitler as chancellor of the German Reich. Franz von Papen will be vice-chancellor of what Hitler is calling the "Reich Cabinet of

National Salvation", which is a coalition of the Nazi Party and the German National People's Party and includes the heads of ten Reich ministries. It is expected that the cabinet will rule through presidential decrees, as before, written by the cabinet and signed by Hindenburg'

She gripped Mutter's hand, fear coursing through her. 'Hitler–'.

'Shush.'

'Hitler said today that he looked forward to bringing Germany out of its present depression and building a powerful nation for the German people with a robust military presence to defend its borders. He further promises to end reparation payments and reclaim the county's industrial heartland.

'Torch-lit parades have been held in Berlin by the SA and the SS to celebrate Hitler's appointment.'

Her heart was racing. 'Mutter, I thought Schleicher was chancellor.'

'He's resigned because of ill-health.'

The voice went on to other news, and she tipped two pills from the bottle and handed them to Mutter. 'I'll fetch you water to swallow them.'

'Thank you, Hanne. Hitler promises much. We shall see if he can deliver on his promises.'

'The news didn't mention Jews?'

'No, not a word.'

'That's a good sign, surely? Did they say there had been attacks om Jewish property, like before?'

'No. I hope that bodes well, Hanne.' Mutter paused. 'You know why the brownshirts were banned last year?'

163

'I remember there was an emergency decree, something about the preservation of state authority.'

'Quite. Prussian police uncovered evidence that the SA was ready to take power by force after an election of Hitler.'

'So why was the ban lifted?'

'Saul says it was part of the deal before Hitler would support a new cabinet in the July election.'

Neither voiced their private fear that Hitler wouldn't stop at chancellor now he had a working coalition. She'd heard the passion and determination in Hitler's voice when he spoke; the man had a vision for Germany that was based on his own lust for power, not the good of the people, but surely, people wouldn't stand for the kind of repression the old man she'd met on the tram had feared.

The next day's report in the *Jüdische Rundschau* affirmed her feelings.

As a matter of course, the Jewish community faces the new government with the largest mistrust, but we are convinced that nobody would dare to touch our constitutional rights.

If the Central Association of German Citizens of the Jewish Faith was convinced, she would stop worrying.

The following week, the new cabinet issued the Decree for the Protection of the German People. While that sounded like a good thing, it placed constraints on the newspapers and allowed the police to ban political meetings and marches.

She took her worry to Mutter. 'How can political parties campaign if they're not allowed to meet?'

'It's a temporary ban after the clashes between the Communists and the Nazis. Things will go back to normal once passions calm down.'

She hoped Mutter was right, but she had a nagging feeling that this was the thin end of what might be a very thick wedge.

***

Hawley Heath, England February 1933

Emma tuned into the new Empire Service broadcast on the radio's shortwave.

'*News from our correspondent in Berlin. An arson attack has badly damaged the German government's Reichstag building in Berlin. The fire is thought to have started around nine o'clock last night, when passers-by heard breaking glass and raised the alarm. Soon after, flames erupted from the building. Fire engines attended the fire all night, but the debating chamber and the cupola have been destroyed.*

'*An unemployed Dutch construction worker has been arrested. Chancellor Hitler was overheard to say "This is a God-given signal. If this fire, as I believe, is the work of Communists, then we must crush out this murderous pest with an iron fist".*'

Hitler was taking advantage of the disaster to further his own agenda. There was a pause and the sound of shuffling paper.

'*News just in reports that Germany's President Hindenburg has invoked Article 48. The cabinet has drawn up the Decree of the Reich President for the Protection of the People and State. This act abolishes freedom of speech, assembly, privacy, and the German press. It also legalises phone tapping and interception of correspondence, and suspends the autonomy of federated states, like Bavaria.*'

Her letters to Hanne were no longer private? Her heart thudded. Hitler was doing more than taking advantage; he was shutting

165

down freedom! She must be careful what she wrote, and Hanne must be careful too; their letters were often very political.

'It is understood that some four thousand people have been arrested and imprisoned. Many of the Communists elected by the German people are among them.'

He'd arrested elected representatives? How on earth could he get away with that? It was unthinkable. The radio crackled and hissed, and she adjusted the tuning knob frantic to hear what else Hitler was proposing.

'The decree also places restraints on police investigations and permits the arrest and incarceration of political opponents without a specific charge being brought. It also permits the dissolving of political parties and gives central government the authority to overrule state and local laws and overthrow state and local governments. With their main opposition in prison, and the future of opposition parties uncertain, Hitler's Nazi Party looks to have free rein in the Reichstag.'

Hitler hadn't waited many hours to use his iron fist; had the Communists really been to blame or had Hitler used the fire as an excuse to crush all opposition? The voice on the radio drew her back.

'Sir Horace Rumbold, British Ambassador in Berlin, was quoted last month as having written "Hitler may be no statesman, but he is an uncommonly clever and audacious demagogue and fully alive to every popular instinct". It is understood he had informed the foreign office that if Hitler eventually gained the upper hand, another European war was within measurable distance.'

War? Dad had gone to war, but many of his friends hadn't come home. She could still feel his arms around her after she'd

166

run along the station platform to welcome him home, and he'd hugged her as if his life depended upon it. She'd been twelve, and he'd been away for what had seemed like most of her life.

Grandma Joshua had given her life to the war as well. There couldn't be another one; there just couldn't. It was madness.

***

Frankfurt, Germany February 1933

Hanne read the Nazi paper, *Der Stürmer* with growing concern, not only because it was virtually the only newspaper still in circulation, but because its motto was "*The Jews are our misfortune.*" Did people really believe that when so many Jews were doctors, musicians, writers, and lawyers? There had been riots across the country, a Communist had died, and hundreds of people had been injured.

The SA had been enrolled as auxiliary police and the Brownshirts were allowed to shoot to kill to quell communist demonstrations. But it wasn't just the Communist Party, trade unionists, the Social Democrat Party, and the Centre Party who'd been targeted by the storm troopers. The entire country had been terrorised by them, and passions were running high; violence, repression, and propaganda had people strung taut like a bow.

Hitler's decisive action saves nation from Bolshevism.

Reichstag fire signal for planned Communist uprising.

Mutter shook her head. 'Sadly, people will believe what they're told, Hanne, but this fire decree smacks of a planned campaign to put the Nazis firmly in control.'

'You were right not to trust Hitler. Civil liberties mean nothing to him, and if he can strip ordinary Germans of their rights, what hope is there for us?'

167

Hitler was Catholic, and an Austrian bishop had already told Catholics to adopt a moral form of anti-Semitism. What was moral about discriminating against faith? Another article caught her eye.

Lebensraum!

The government's foreign policy upholds the plan for expansion to give the German people more living space and to increase the country's food and industrial production. Territories to the east are included in this plan.

'What do they mean by east, Mutter? Poland, Austria, Czechoslovakia, Hungary? Hitler thinks he can annex these countries without a fight?'

'Hitler believes he can do whatever he pleases, Hanne. I fear he may be right.'

She folded the newspaper sickened by what she'd read. Would the German people stand by and let Hitler do this? The federal election, the third in nine months, due to be held next week, would give the people the opportunity to voice their opposition, despite the Reichstag Fire Decree.

On March 5th, she and Mutter once again set out to vote. She shivered, and not just from the icy wind; the Nazi press had repeated claims made by a Canadian priest that Shylocks were causing the depression. One man in Berlin, according to a neighbour, had been given fifty lashes for being a Communist and fifty more for being a Jew. She was glad of her warm coat with its fur collar as she pushed Asher along in his pushchair. Everywhere were storm troopers and SS lurking intimidatingly and accosting voters.

Part of her wanted to go home and forget the election, but Mutter was adamant she would cast her vote, and she wouldn't let Mutter go alone.

A storm trooper approached and grabbed her arm before she could avoid him. 'You will vote for the Nazi Party.' It was a statement, not a question. 'It would be well for you to think carefully, Frau.'

She bowed her head. 'I shall think carefully, sir. Now, please let me cast my vote.'

At the polling station, the scene was the same. Uniformed SS and SA stood by the booths watching how people marked their papers. She wouldn't let them intimidate her – she'd vote against the Nazis if it was the last thing she did.

A man wearing the SS insignia towered over her. She swallowed hard and pushed Asher behind her. Taking her pen from her bag, not trusting the Nazis not to alter a pencil vote, she shielded the paper with one hand, made a bold mark, and pushed the unfolded paper into the ballot box before the man could stop her.

He grabbed her arm and sneered into her face. 'Tod allen Juden! This dirty Jew is voting against the salvation of our country. Against our saviour, Hitler. Tod allen Juden.'

She shook loose his grip, and a woman spat at her. Another group of voters moved away, averting their eyes. Only one woman moved to her defence.

Mutter stepped between her and the Nazi. 'We have a right to vote according to our conscience. You have no right to stop us.'

He laughed in Mutter's face. 'I think you'll find it is you who have no rights, Juden.'

If this wasn't a free election, where was democracy? If it was a free election, and Hitler won, it could be Germany's last.

They reached home thankful not to be lashed for being Jews. It

169

was late next day before the result of the election was announced, assuming someone had actually counted the votes.

'Despite Communist attempts to disrupt polling, the NSDAP, Nazi Party, gained ninety-two more seats, giving them two hundred and eighty-eight seats in the Reichstag. The SDP lost one seat and the KPD, Communist Party, lost nineteen seats.'

The voice on the radio sounded triumphant – had the Nazis taken that over as well?

'Hitler is expected to announce a coalition agreement tomorrow.'

They waited anxiously for news. It was a foregone conclusion that the KDP elected members of the Reichstag wouldn't be allowed to take their seats, and within days, all of them had either been arrested or had gone into hiding.

It was two weeks before Hitler dealt his death blow to German democracy. He persuaded the Reichstag members to pass the Enabling Act, disguised as the Law for Removing Distress of People and Reich, which allowed the cabinet, which in effect was him as chancellor, to enact laws without the approval of the divided Reichstag for four years, which would take them to the next election.

To all intents and purposes, the country had become a legal dictatorship. What future now for democracy and the Jews of Germany?

Chapter Eighteen

Frankfurt, Germany Spring 1933

Hanne looked out of her apartment window onto a street of rioters. Not, as she'd expected, riots against the Nazi seizure of control, but Storm Troopers and nationalist Stahlhelm in their WW1 helmets targeting hapless Jews.

An elderly man was knocked to the ground and kicked. A woman running to his aid was dragged screaming down an alleyway. She shrank back from the window. She ached to go out and confront them, but what could she do against a wave of extremist SA?

The sound of shattering glass meant more broken windows in Jewish homes and shops. What had her people done to deserve such hatred?

The noise of pounding feet, raised voices, and breaking glass faded as the Nazi fanatics moved on, chanting their hatred and leaving behind a trail of destruction. The old man was still lying on the ground, and the woman who'd gone to his aid knelt by his side weeping, her clothes ripped.

Checking Asher was asleep, she locked her front door and ran down the stairs and out into the square. Berek had left for work early and wouldn't be home until late as the pharmacy stayed open until ten at night, but Mutter – where was Mutter? She hurried to the woman's side. 'Is he breathing? Are you hurt?'

The woman was too distressed to answer. The man had a livid bruise on his head, but his chest was moving up and down.

Knocked out? As if to answer her question, he moaned.

She took hold of his hand. 'You've hurt your head. The SA troops have gone. You're safe now.'

He opened his eyes and squinted as if in pain or taking a while to focus. 'Ester?' He focussed on the woman and raised his other hand to stroke the woman's cheek. 'Oh, Ester, daughter, what have they done to you?'

He sat up and put his arm around his daughter. They didn't need a doctor, and she had to find Mutter. Torn between leaving Asher alone and finding her mother, she hurried across the square and past the synagogue. She stopped mid-stride. **Dominikanerplatz**? This was Börneplatz! It had a synagogue, and they'd called it after a Dominican Monastery? She ran on towards Uncle Saul's shop; Mutter would probably be there, and Asher was safer left at home.

The sign on Börnestrasse read **Grober Wollgraben**. When had that been changed? It was as if the Nazis were trying to erase their history, their culture – their very existence. She ran on, heedless of distant shouting.

'Mutter!'

'Hanne, thank God. Where's Asher?'

'I left him at home. Are you hurt? Where's Uncle Saul?'

'Just a few bruises. Saul's putting boards over a broken shop window. They damaged his shutters. Those – thugs!'

'Let's get you home, Mutter. Quickly, before Asher wakes and misses us.'

They left her uncle hammering nails into his window frame to secure stout boards and hurried home.

Mutter shook her head. 'I don't know what things are coming to when you can't go out in your own street and be safe. God of Abraham, Isaac, and Israel protect us from this evil.'

***

Hawley Heath, England 1933

Rosie listened to the news on the Empire Service with growing concern. Emma was still talking of going to visit Hanne, and the news from Germany wasn't good. There had been anti-Jewish protests fuelled by Hitler and his paramilitary. Most of the people who stood against the Nazi Party were in prison or silenced by fear.

'*The first meeting of the Nazi-controlled Reichstag has taken place amid concerns from countries around the world about democracy. Special Nazi courts have been set up to deal with political dissidents, and the Jewish War Veterans of America movement has announced that it will boycott German goods and services.*

'*Elite SS guards are establishing a concentration camp outside the town of Dachau, in South Germany, for political opponents of the regime, and the cabinet have passed an Enabling Act which grants Hitler the powers of a dictator for four years.*

'*In New York City, an anti-Nazi rally is being organised for Monday next, and American citizens are threatening to boycott German goods if the Germans carry out their planned permanent boycott of Jewish-owned stores and businesses.*'

She turned the tuning knob past static crackling to the BBC National Programme.

'*The National Joint Council, which comprises representatives from the TUC, Labour Party, and Co-operative Movement, is*

173

proposing to launch an anti-Fascist campaign. A mass meeting is being called for April 12th, to be held in the Royal Albert Hall. There will be a call for a ban on all German goods.'

She switched the radio off and went to find Emma. She found her in the kitchen making a pot of tea. 'Emma, the news from Germany is getting worse. I don't think it's safe for you to travel there.'

Emma poured boiling water into the teapot. 'There are protests about something or other all the time. These anti-Jewish demonstrations are just the new regime celebrating by puffing out their chests and throwing their weight about. Things will settle down.'

'I don't think you believe that for a moment.'

'Mom, unless Hanne tells me not to go, I'm going.'

Her daughter could be so stubborn sometimes. 'Sweetheart, I really don't think it's a good idea. A young woman alone.' She rephrased that. 'A young woman alone who looks like she might be Jewish.'

Emma's brow furrowed, but whatever she'd been about to say remained behind closed lips. She fetched the second-best cups from the cupboard and set them in saucers. 'Mom, I know the risks, but Hanne will meet me at the station, and we can ride a tram right to Börneplatz.'

'Why are you so determined to put yourself in danger?'

Emma handed her a cup of tea, opened her mouth, and closed it again.

'Is it Hanne you're going to see or someone else? Is this why you won't build a relationship with Charlie?'

Emma stared at her own tea as if wishing to see the future in it.

'It's –'

'Complicated? You said that once before about Charlie. Oh, Emma.' She clattered her cup back into its saucer. 'You haven't fallen for Berek?'

Emma didn't reply, and her silence was as good as a confession.

'You silly, silly girl. How can you go to see Hanne while you have feelings for her husband? You must put him out of your mind for good. Hanne and Berek are married. They have a child, for God's sake. What about little Asher? Emma, I forbid you to go.'

Emma dropped her cup on the kitchen floor, shattering it to pieces and spreading brown liquid far and wide; she ran from the room, footsteps pounded up the stairs, and a door slammed shut.

She got a dustpan and a cloth and began picking up pieces of china and cleaning the floor. Upsetting Emma was the last thing she'd wanted to do, but no one should come between a man and wife and their children. Women who did that were trollops, and the weak men who were flattered by their attention and encouraged them were no better.

***

Emma walked past the devastation that was the slum clearance. Men with rolled-up sleeves were still clearing away debris, but others were digging trenches and still more loaded concrete mixers with sand, gravel, and cement. She hoped new houses would soon take the place of the demolished ones and that the former residents could move back to where they belonged. So far, the cycle factory had escaped the bulldozers, but nothing seemed certain anymore.

She shut out the noise of machinery, and builders' raised

voices, only to hear the hammers and steam bellows when she entered the factory. She hurried to the office and back to what was troubling her heart. Much as she hated to admit it, Mom was right. She couldn't put herself between Hanne and Berek or cause either of them any pain. Besides, she risked Hanne's friendship, and that was worth more than pursuing a spurious and ill-fated dream. The only way to distance herself from that dream was to remain in England.

At least, in Hawley Heath, they had food, even if it was in short supply. There was little fuel to run the tractors, and the horses had been requisitioned during the war: producing enough food to feed the population was now down to the strength of a man's arm, and without proper nourishment, that strength was fading. Going to bed hungry had become a reality again. She'd heard things were even worse in Russia – someone had even mentioned cannibalism. How desperate did you have to be to eat another person?

She pushed the thought away and opened Hanne's latest letter.

My darling Emma,

Hanne did love her. She was right to protect that love.

I hope all is well in England and Hawley Heath in particular. We are all well, and Asher is growing fast, but things are moving apace here and not in the right direction.

At the beginning of April, the SA boycotted all Jewish shops and businesses, even doctors and lawyers, and Jewish students were banned from schools and universities. Thankfully, according to the Jüdische Rundschau, the German-Jewish newspaper, this was limited to one day because of international outrage and the general apathy of the German people. It is comforting that non-Jewish Germans didn't follow where Nazi propaganda led and that other countries oppose Hitler. The storm troopers are a law unto themselves. Perhaps Hitler should have better control over them; certainly, they are responsible for trouble we've had recently.

Hanne was in trouble? If this letter had been opened and read, Hanne would be in more than trouble. She'd be classed as a political dissident and thrown into gaol or worse. She must warn her somehow.

However, we are all wearing yellow badges to show pride in our Jewishness. We shall resist Hitler's attempts to dishearten us. That said, our neighbours to the left of us are planning to emigrate to America, and I've heard others saying Germany is no longer a good place to live. But Germany is our home, and we shall fight to remain here as long as we can.

A new decree has been passed banning Jews and other non-Aryans from the Civil Service and from practising law. Apparently, non-Arian is defined as anyone descended from non-Aryan, especially Jewish, parents or grandparents. So, my dearest Emma, you too are non-Aryan. You are fortunate to have been born in England.

She was beginning to realise how lucky. She couldn't imagine England ever being anything but a democracy, even if the government was full of stuffy old men intent on resisting change for the working man and woman and the unemployed.

Hitler couches these repressive laws in terms like the Law for the Restoration of the Professional Civil Service. Jewish government workers have been ordered to retire! I fear for Berek's employment as a pharmacist, as I'm sure the bans won't stop here.

Indeed, another law, the Law for Preventing Overcrowding in German Schools and Schools for Higher Education, is a cover for restricting the enrolment of Jews and preventing their education. If this law remains in force after Hitler's four-year reign, I worry about Asher's future here. This may be the reason that would force us to leave Germany – education is important.

And if Hanne, Mutter, Saul, and Berek were forced to emigrate, where would they go? America like their neighbours? Palestine? Germany was already too far away; America and Palestine were even farther.

I hear Hitler has set up Nazi training camps. Training them to do what, one wonders. Thuggery? The new Gestapo, a secret-police force set up by Göring, is said to be even more brutal than the SA and SS, although I've had nothing to do with them yet. Can you believe they have even changed our street names? Dominikanerplatz? What was wrong with Börneplatz and Börnestrasse?

Would it be the Gestapo who read letters and tapped telephones? A shudder ran down her spine. These were dangerous times. She must be very careful what she wrote back.

The Nazis may be able to ban our ritual and traditional ways of living, but they cannot destroy our faith and our obedience to God. May the God of Abraham, Isaac, and Israel protect us.

'Amen to that, Hanne.' She felt so helpless and ached to go to her cousin's aid, but she would be another worry for Hanne. No, she would remain in England and help in any small way she could; she had a little personal money she could send if Berek lost his job, but what Joshua and Son had must be used for the good of her workers and business.

She picked up the *Manchester Guardian*, to add to the pile on a chair by the door, ready to be turned into firelighter.

She opened it – local news would be less terrifying than

178

foreign.

A telegram from Berlin informs us that by order of the Minister of the Interior, the Manchester Guardian is forbidden in Germany until further notice.

What on earth had the newspaper written to be banned?

The Brown Terror reigning in Germany continues to be inflicted on Jews, Communists, Trades Unionists, and other workers. The efforts made by the dictatorship to keep the people silent were shown by a case in a Berlin court, yesterday. A Jewish street-vendor was sentenced to a year's imprisonment because he was overheard saying Jews were being maltreated. Future cases of the sort are to be treated with great severity.

People couldn't even state a truth or an opinion anymore?

In Frankfurt, a man and his two sons were arrested and beaten. One son has minor injuries, but the other was badly injured and may be deaf for life. The father is in a grave condition. One man from Oberhessen is said to have been hung by his feet and beaten. He died of his injuries.

Oh, dear God. Had Hitler unleashed this brown terror on his people? He must know what was happening – he must be allowing it, encouraging it.

Thousands of Jews are eager to leave Germany but satisfying the conditions of entry into another country make emigration difficult. When Germany is levying a huge emigration tax, escape has become impossible for many. All Germany feels like a vast prison.

A meeting has been organised on April 19th at the Manchester Free Trade Hall to protest strongly at the

treatment of Jews in Germany.

She sank onto the pile of newspapers. She hadn't realised things were so bad. Why hadn't Hanne told her? If she went to Germany, she'd be vulnerable as a female Jew – she'd been attacked before – and there was no way Hanne, Asher, Mutter, Saul, and Berek could afford to get out.

She let tears trickle down her cheeks. Would she ever see her beloved again?

Chapter Nineteen

Frankfurt, Germany 1933

Hanne lay in Berek's arms, eyes closed but thinking about Emma; at least, her dear cousin was safe in England. For the first time, she felt trapped and fearful in her own country. Her father had given his life fighting for Germany. Why hadn't they left for England when they could, before the huge emigration tax had dashed so many hopes of escape. As a family, they'd had money, now being whittled away at an alarming rate, and Emma would have given them a home until they found work and a place of their own.

Why, why, why? The words spun around in her head.

The truth was that Mutter's health had been deteriorating for a while now, and she wouldn't have been well enough to travel. Nothing would make her leave her mother and Uncle Saul behind without what little protection she and Berek could provide.

She sighed; anyway, it was too late now. They must endure what Hitler threw at them. What was it the old man on the tram had told her? If they couldn't use trams, they would walk – he was right; if Berek couldn't work as a pharmacist, he would find something else. Nothing would break the spirit and faith of the Jewish people.

She heard little but Nazi propaganda on the radio or in the newspapers, and after Emma warned her that post was being opened, she and Emma were being careful what they wrote. Emma's last carefully worded letter hinted at a worldwide condemnation of Nazi repression of its own people, and Jews in particular. And as Mutter had said, it had happened before and they'd survived.

Berek stirred in his sleep, and she opened her eyes. A flickering yellow light shone through the bedroom window. A distant noise grew in intensity. People were singing, banging on doors, and voices rose in protest, followed by the tinkle of breaking glass.

She eased Berek's arm from her waist and crept to the window. Outside in the street, lit by torches held high, a group of young men, students by the look of them, were throwing something onto a bonfire.

Members of the SA, the brown-shirted storm troopers, and the Schutzstaffel, with their black shirts and SS insignia, were going from house to house, raising the occupants from their beds.

She shook Berek's shoulder. 'Berek, the SA and SS are outside. They've set a fire in the street.'

Berek leapt from the bed naked and rushed to the window. 'Wake your mother and fetch Asher. We must be ready to run and hide.'

'You think they want to hurt us?'

'I don't know.' He pulled on trousers and a shirt. 'What are they burning?'

Something angular sailed through the air, landed in the fire, and was followed by another. 'They're burning books! Why would they do that? The SA are coming here.'

A loud, insistent hammering sounded on the door to the street. Judging by the loud voices and thudding feet on the stairs, someone had let them in.

'Quick, Hanne. Get Asher and your mother and hide.'

'What about you?'

'Go, now!'

She turned and ran. 'God of Abraham...' She plucked Asher from his bed and ran into Mutter's room. 'Mutter, storm troopers are coming up the stairs. We must hide.'

Mutter rubbed her eyes and stared around the bedroom.

'Mutter, quickly. We must hide.'

'Under the bed.'

They crawled under, dragging Asher between them and lay listening to the noises from the next room. It sounded as if the door had been broken down and the room was being torn apart.

'God of Abraham, Isaac, and Israel protect Berek.'

Voices demanded, and she caught odd words. 'Un-German spirit – black-list – Einstein – Freud – Brecht – pacifist – Jewish – Bauhaus – Hemingway – Wells' the list went on, each word punctuated with the bang of a book on the floorboards. She tensed her fingers on Mutter's arm. They were taking all her father's books?

Mutter put a hand on hers. 'They're only books, Hanne. There are other copies. They can't destroy the words.'

Footstep receded downwards, and a door slammed. There was an agonising silence, and then light from the living room flooded the bedroom.

'They've gone. You can come out, now.'

She slid out from under the bed and helped Asher and Mutter out. 'Oh, Berek.' His face dripped blood, and one eye was half-closed. She went into the kitchen and fetched a clean cloth and a bowl of warm water.

She bathed his cuts with a gentle hand while Mutter made a pot of coffee and ladled sugar into cups. They sat in silence with the flickering light from the flames of great literature playing across the curtains, no one wanting to go to bed or look at the empty bookshelves or the ruined door. This desecration had brought home to them the precarious position in which they lived and the fact that there was nothing they could do to protect themselves.

Mutter switched on the radio. Goebbels was speaking to German students in Berlin.

'The era of extreme Jewish intellectualism is now at an end. The breakthrough of the German revolution has again cleared the way on the German path. The future German man will not just be a man of books, but a man of character. It is to this end that we want to educate you. As a young person, to have the courage to face the pitiless glare, to overcome the fear of death, and to regain respect for death - this is the task of this young generation. And thus, you do well in this midnight hour to commit to the flames the evil spirit of the past – the intellectual filth and the Jewish asphalt literati. This is a strong, great, and symbolic deed – a deed which should document the following for the world to know: here the intellectual foundation of the November Republic is sinking to the ground, but from this wreckage the phoenix of a new spirit will triumphantly rise.'

The hated voice fell silent, drowned by the cheers of the crowd.

The Nazis had banned their trade unions, boycotted their businesses, prevented their children from having an education, taken Berek's livelihood, changed their street names, burned their books – they were trying to eradicate their way of life. They were even banning opposing political parties. Where would this horror end? She felt rather than heard Mutter's quiet plea for help. *'God of Abraham, Isaac, and Israel protect us.'*

***

184

Hawley Heath, England June 1933

Emma handed the order for garden tools, dog chains, and chains for securing gates to Dad. 'Nash's have given us a big order. They want them urgently, and I promised to deliver it within the fortnight.'

Her father read down the list. 'Spades, forks, hoes, shears, shovels, gate chains, catches, and hinges... How did you persuade them to order all this?'

She winked. 'I drove over there with samples and used my womanly charms.'

Dad laughed. 'It's a wonder you didn't sell them bicycles as well, then.'

She smiled her triumph. 'Actually, I did. Mr Nash ordered one for his son to grow into. He's putting wooden blocks on the pedals so the boy can reach.'

'Emma, you're a marvel.'

'Also, while I was selling him gate fixings, I thought why not make gates? Farm stock has to be kept in, and wood rots in time. And we could make iron railings – and chain harrows – we could make those as well.'

'Gates and fences are traditionally oak or chestnut, which lasts a long while, and iron rusts.'

'Not if it's galvanised.'

Dad's brow creased. 'We'd need a big dipping tank to galvanise gates.'

'It would be an investment and provide more jobs. The more we diversify, the better chance we have of riding out this recession.'

185

'You've convinced me.'

'I'll get a tank ordered and get in touch with suppliers of zinc and chemicals.'

Dad smiled. 'And I'll get the men started on this order.'

She watched her father stride across the factory floor with a straighter back. Hope for the future was more important than money right now. Things had to pick up soon or bankruptcy would put an end to Joshua and Son the way it had to so many other businesses in the area.

She closed the office door against the crash of hammers on iron, returned to her desk, and pencilled out a gate like the five-bar oak ones they had on the farm, estimating dimensions and total length and width of iron section needed. Iron wouldn't need to be as thick as wood for strength. Would five bars be enough to keep in lambs? Make it six. They wouldn't be cheap to produce. Hand gates could be solid iron, but a gate wide enough to drive a tractor through would need thicker iron for strength and would be very heavy. Tube steel like the bicycles? Maybe making farm gates was something Theo, George, and Charlie could experiment with.

She mopped her forehead with a handkerchief. If it was hot in the office, the men must be sweltering. They'd begun work at six o'clock, while it was cool, but it was now noon. She'd order the wooden handles for the tool order and then tell them to go home before they dropped from exhaustion.

The workers downed tools as one, and only the steam bellows, the quiet lungs of her world, broke the exhausted silence.

'Be back at six in the morning and we'll knock off at noon again.'

'See you tomorrow, Emma.' The chorus of voices warmed her

heart to melting. Somehow, she'd earned their trust and respect the way Mom and Dad had.

'Thank you. All of you. You've done a great job today.'

At home, she switched on the radio to listen to the news while she ate lunch.

'Following the Jehovah's Witnesses' rally on Sunday in Berlin to protest at their treatment by the Nazi government, Jews in London today held a massive anti-Nazi rally.

'Jewish organisations in other countries have also held conferences to discuss the safeguarding of the rights of German Jews. When the entire body of German law is being rewritten to Hitler's specifications, and the law and the police no longer protect Jews, it is feared that soon, all opposition to the Nazi Party will be punishable by law.

'While Va'ad Le'umi, the National Committee of the Jews of Palestine, is determined to assist immigrants from Germany, at the present time, Jews may not leave the country.'

She'd pushed her plate away, her appetite lost. For Hanne and her family, there would be no safe haven.

***

Summer's heavy greenery had turned to the yellows and russets of autumn, and Rosie had taken over the office while Emma spent the day at the cycle factory, ostensibly discussing gates. At least, she hoped it was ostensibly; since Emma had decided travel to Germany was impossible for the foreseeable future, and she wasn't about to argue the point, the hoped-for settling down with Charlie seemed more likely.

While she felt sorry for Hanne and her family, especially now the Nazi Party was Germany's only legal political party, Rosie's concerns were closer to home. She was desperately trying to get to grips with what the Anomalies Act meant for her female workforce if she had to lay any of them off.

A married woman (other than a married woman whose husband is incapacitated from work or is unemployed and not in receipt of benefit) who since marriage has had less than fifteen contributions paid in respect of her, or who, if more than six months have elapsed since her marriage, has had less than eight contributions paid in respect of her during the period of three months preceding the beginning of her benefit quarter, shall be entitled to benefit only if, in addition to satisfying the other requirements of the Acts for the receipt of benefit, she also proves:-

She read that again, twice, and her brain still refused to unravel its meaning. She read on, hoping it would become clearer.

(i)   **that she is normally employed in insurable employment and will normally seek to obtain her livelihood by means of insurable employment, and**
(ii) **that having regard to all the circumstances of her case and particularly to her industrial experience and the industrial circumstances of the district in which she resides either –**
(a)she can reasonably expect to obtain insurable employment; or –

With one in three workers unemployed at the present time, what constituted a reasonable expectation?

(b) her expectation of obtaining insurable employment in her usual occupation is not less than it would otherwise be by reason of the fact that she is married. This Regulation shall not apply to married women who prove that they have been deserted by,

or that they are permanently separated from, their husbands.

She gave up and pushed the notification aside, her head thumping. Who wrote these damn silly rules, and why did life have to be so bloody complicated? She needed some air.

She walked out and along to where Forge Lane had been, the fresh breeze blowing her hair from her face and the Anomalies Act from her mind. The first of the new homes, rising phoenix-like from the demolition rubble, a block of twelve flats three-storeys high, had been completed, and she was looking forward to seeing some of the original inhabitants back where they belonged.

While the rents weren't high, as the council hoped to re-home some of the poorest people, they were still more than many unemployed families could afford. It had always been Joshua and Son's policy not to evict their tenants if they fell on hard times, but she couldn't see the council being so beneficent. Council tenancy conditions were strict and would be enforced.

These homes were no longer the concern of Joshua and Son, and there was little they could do to mitigate hardship – there was only so much money they could spare for charity, and anyway, Black Country people were proud and didn't accept charity easily. They were brought up to work and to work hard, the way she had since she'd left school when she was ten.

Would these flats have the sense of community the old terraces had? They had no yards to hang out washing or walls to chat over, there'd be no gossiping on front doors as people walked by, no streets full of playing children, most of whom would be cousins, second cousins, or third cousins. Hawley Heath was changing, but was it for the better?

Chapter Twenty

Frankfurt, Germany Autumn 1933

Hanne shuddered at the latest news, not that it was news in the proper sense – Hitler had gagged criticism from the press as effectively as he'd gagged his political opponents. Political opposition was punishable by law, and Eastern European Jews and gypsies living in Germany had been stripped of their German citizenship. People who were arrested disappeared without trace, possibly to the new concentration camps.

Even more worrying was the government's – Hitler's – law regarding *lebensunwertes Leben*: life unworthy of life. Did Hitler think he was God to have governance over who was fit to live, and who not, who were defective and useless eaters, as if usefulness to the state was the only permissible reason to live and have children?

If he could order the sterilisation of unfit parents and kill children born with defects... The Law for the Prevention of Offspring with Hereditary Diseases was a cloak beneath which the Nazis could choose who lived and who died. She pushed the next thought away. Not even Hitler was so evil, nor would the world at large allow it – there was international opposition to Germany's new leader – except the wretched pope. Pope Pius XI seemed intent on legitimising Hitler's stance: Catholicism against the Jews, and Germany was largely Catholic.

There had been some relief for a few of her faith. The Zionist Organisation had arranged for several Jews to emigrate to Palestine. She'd argued for trying to leave with them, but Mutter's health meant she hadn't pushed the matter. Would they get another chance? Life was becoming more difficult in so many ways. Jews were now excluded as writers and artists, banned from journalism, music, and theatre, and even banned from farming.

How were they to support themselves? They would soon all be unemployed beggars.

The letterbox rattled, and she jumped as an envelope dropped on the doormat. Emma!

My dearest Hanne,

How are you all? It seems ages since I had a letter from you. I expect Asher has grown a lot. How is Mutter? Is Berek still enjoying his work? I do hope you will all be able to find some way to visit soon for a long holiday. We have plenty of room here, room for Asher and Berek to play football, and Mutter and Uncle Saul would love Hawley Heath.

A long holiday? What did Emma mean, and why had she included Mutter and Uncle Saul in this impossible invitation? She reread Emma's words more carefully. Emma knew her letters might be read – she was offering her whole family safe haven if they could escape.

It's a lovely journey by train to Cologne, Brussels, and Ostend on the Belgian coast, and the ferry across the channel is, shall we say, bracing, so bring warm coats when you come. If you lack the train fare, I had some property compulsorily purchased by the council, so I have a little money I could send should you need it. I can't think of a better way of spending it. I so long to see you all again.

I was reading Pride and Prejudice, recently. Do you know the book? I am burning to send it to you. I think you would enjoy it.

"Burning to send" was an odd way of putting it. Emma knew of the book burnings! She was keeping abreast of the repressions. The book title hadn't been chosen randomly – there was certainly prejudice against the Jews. And looking back, Emma asking if Berek was still enjoying his work suggested she knew, or was worried, that Berek had lost his job due to Nazi laws. How could she tell Emma everything that was happening in Germany without leading the SS to their door if her letter was opened?

She couldn't even telephone her; telephones were tapped, and Jews weren't allowed to use public ones.

Oh, Emma. If only they could get to England and away from these damned Nazis.

'Hanne?'

Her heart pounded. Only Mutter. 'What is it? What's wrong?'

Mutter closed the door behind her, gasping, her hand over her heart. 'The Bernsteins have been evicted.'

The Bernsteins lived in the apartment below them. 'Why?'

'They fell behind with the rent. Abram hasn't been able to work for months. His job was given to an Aryan.'

'Have they somewhere to go?'

'No. At least–'

'They could come here if we squeeze into one room and they have mine and Berek's room.'

'It's too late, Hanne. There's been a new law passed. Homeless people are sent to camps. The SA have taken them away.'

'A camp? Where?'

'I don't know, Hanne. I don't know.' Mutter held her hands over her face. 'What's to become of us, Hanne?'

***

Hawley Heath, England 1934

Christmas had come and gone, and with it, much hope of Emma seeing the original residents re-homed to the new flats, now called Forge House. Most of the flats had gone to families with fewer children who could squeeze into the small space – overcrowding wasn't allowed, second-hand furniture, bedding, and rugs that might house vermin weren't allowed, and who could afford new furniture or one of the proposed semi-detached houses with space for a large family?

The new residents were what Grandma Marion might have called upper working-class, not the poorest, disabled, or unemployed who most needed roofs over their heads. What was to become of them? With the poorhouse now turned into a hospital, it fell upon the ratepayers of Hawley Heath to find them homes. Would the council stand by the dispossessed or leave them to rot in other slum areas isolated from extended family and friends?

While slum clearance sounded good on paper, it was proving a disaster for the families who'd been forced out of their homes.

Pulling her warm hat down around her ears, she hurried towards the factory. She could have driven, the snow wasn't thick, but the walk down the hill always cleared her mind. The view across Hawley Heath to the rolling mills, blast furnaces, and pitheads always grounded her and reminded her of her roots and her duty as a chain mistress to the people who toiled day in and day out to help build Britain's industrial heartland and its ultimate prosperity – when they had jobs at which to toil. She had to believe that things were getting better.

Which was more than they appeared to be in Germany. Her letters to and from Hanne were cryptic, and it was difficult to gauge what was happening there, but Hanne seemed to have understood her offer of a home for all her family, should they be able to leave Germany.

More and more, she relied on the radio's Empire Service to glean information about Hitler and his repressive measures. Somehow, news was getting out of Germany to the rest of the world, and things must be bad if Jewish organisations were trying to get aid to German Jews.

A few months ago, Germany had withdrawn from the League of Nations disarmament talks. The November Reichstag election had won the Nazis over ninety percent of the vote, mainly because voting wasn't secret and no other parties were allowed candidates. Germany and the Nazi Party were now the same thing.

And their solution for homeless people made Hawley Heath's problems pale into insignificance. A new law, the Law Against Habitual and Dangerous Criminals, gave Nazi officials the power to put homeless and unemployed people, along with beggars and alcoholics, in concentration camps. What was right about removing Jews from their jobs and banning them from working, and then imprisoning them because they'd lost their homes?

That Jews were desperate to leave Germany was obvious, but even if they could leave, where would they go? Oswald Mosley had a following among Fascists and had held a rally in Birmingham. There were so many Jews who wanted asylum, and already, Arabs in Palestine were rioting in protest at the number of immigrants.

Tensions were high, and Churchill, on the radio, had made it clear that Hitler was re-arming against the terms of the Treaty of Versailles. Hitler, apparently, had ordered four thousand aircraft to be built. Churchill had made no bones about the fact that Britain would do well to increase spending on armaments to face "peril on

194

every side". Could Britain withstand another war and the recession that would inevitably follow it?

What she needed now was some good news!

Charlie met her at the factory gate.

She sighed. 'What now?'

He smiled. 'I need to hire two men, maybe three. I thought you'd be pleased.'

She relaxed tense shoulders. 'You've got new orders? What for?'

'Gates, hinges, catches, and chains. We've made samples, and I photographed them and sent out catalogues to agricultural merchants all over the country. I think we're on to a winner, Emma.'

'That is good news. Find three men from families who are in most need of work as long as they can do the job. Send me their details for wages, and the invoices for materials. Let me know if there are any supply problems. I know a lot of businesses have been refused credit.'

'Joshua and Son have an excellent reputation, and that's rubbed off on Taylor Brothers. There'll be no supply problems.'

'That's good to know, Charlie. You've worked wonders with George and Theo. I'm very grateful to you – we all are.'

Charlie turned puppy-dog eyes on her. 'You'll come to the picture house with me then?'

She laughed. 'Bearers of glad tidings deserve a night out. I'd be honoured to come with you.'

Charlie kissed her cheek and sauntered away, whistling. She did love him, really she did, if only her heart didn't already belong to another.

***

Rosie switched on her radio and turned the tuning knob, searching for a German station. Sometimes she found Nazi propaganda broadcasts in English.

'Germany and Poland have signed a ten-year non-aggression pact, but Hitler insists that our great nation will not be dissuaded from continuing its rearmament programme. Germany will defend its borders and meet aggression with an iron fist. Germany will reclaim its industrial heartland and expand for the good of the people. Germany will once again be a force to be reckoned with.'

The broadcast reverted to German, and she switched it off.

'Papers, Mrs T.'

Paperboys got younger and younger. 'Thanks, Jimmy.' She resisted ruffling his wiry ginger hair and glanced down the page.

Council for Civil Liberties formed.

A hunger march was planned. She longed to march with them, to uphold the right to protest, to hold the powerful to account and defend the working man against the rise of fascism. She was painfully aware of how easily Hitler had stripped the German people of their rights and freedom, but her marching days were over, her fear of being crushed and trampled too great. Younger legs and stouter hearts would have to do what she couldn't.

She turned a page and ran her eye down the articles. One jumped out at her.

Cunard and White Star in merger talks

Following financial difficulties caused by the recession, the two great shipping companies are negotiating a merger. Both

companies have hulls laid down for enormous liners, White Star's Hull 844 and Cunard's Hull 534, but the building of both ocean liners has been suspended due to lack of funds. It is hoped a merger, a condition of government assistance to the two shipping companies, will allow at least one liner to be built. When completed, it will be the largest ocean liner in the world.

The new company, to be called Cunard White Star, will have twenty-five ships in its fleet.

A new ship would need anchor cable and a myriad of fixtures and fittings, and Joshua and Son were ready and waiting to make it. She bounced open the office door and ran along the factory floor.

'Jack. Look!' She waved the paper and the crash of hammers died to silence as faces, their features lit orange by the forges, turned towards her. 'White Star and Cunard are talking about merging. They're going to build a super liner.'

A cheer went up.

'Have we been invited to tender?'

'Not yet, but I'll be writing to them to remind them we want to. This could be a new start for us as well as them. We have to get the contract for the chain. We have to. Our workers need this.'

'Does Emma know?'

'Not yet. I can't wait to tell her.'

She left the newspaper for Jack to pass around the factory and hurried to find Emma. Building such a large ship would revitalise the industrial heart of the north and the midlands. So many companies would be involved during the years it would take to build it. The rolling mills, pitheads, and blast furnaces that had been virtually silent for years would bring life back to Hawley Heath. The smoke, noise, and smells of industry would be welcomed as a saviour, and the workers would revel in the sweat of their brows and food on their tables.

Chapter Twenty-One

Frankfurt, Germany 1934

Someone had pushed an old copy of *Der Stürmer*, said to be Hitler's favourite periodical, through the letterbox. Hanne picked it up, wrinkling her nose in disgust. An article had been ringed and underlined in heavy pencil.

Ritual Murder of Christian Children

It is often forgotten that during the Middle Ages, Jews were accused of committing ritual murders of Christian children and using their blood for religious purposes. How then can we trust the evil nose and the oily, devil's tail with our children if these inhuman practices are part of their perverted religion?

She threw the paper in the rubbish bin; Mutter didn't need to read that. It was exactly the sort of filthy accusation made against Jews down the generations. That people were willing to believe it and spread it was what scared her most.

With ever-increasing speed, people were turning against them, even former friends. Their freedoms were being removed, and they were being excluded from German life. The latest casualty was taking away Jews' entitlement to health insurance. Were her family so evil that they deserved this treatment? What had little Asher done, what had any of them done, other than being born to Jewish parents?

Berek was listening to the radio. He put a finger to his lips, and she sat beside him on the sofa to listen. It was Hitler's strident, self-righteous, and accusing voice.

'On June 29th, accompanied by the SS, I arrived at Wiesse, where I personally arrested Ernst Röhm, leader of the attempted coup.

'Some two hundred senior officers of the SA were arrested in a purge that will be long remembered as the Night of the Long Knives. Sixty-one traitors have been executed, thirteen were shot resisting arrest, and three committed suicide. Why did I not use the courts to bring about convictions, you might ask? In this hour, I was responsible for the fate of the German people, and thereby, I became the supreme judge of the German people. I gave the order to shoot the ringleaders in this treason.'

The broadcast crackled, popped, and stopped abruptly. She shook her head. 'Hitler has the right to be judge and jury? He has the power to decide who lives and who dies without a trial or any sort of defence?'

Berek's face was grim. 'So it would seem. Either he's paranoid about being knocked off his perch, or someone has filled his ears with conspiracies for their own ends. Either way, he's successfully got rid of anyone who might have challenged him for leadership. He's put himself above the law.'

'Is there no stopping him?'

Berek shook his head. 'International outrage may deter him, but –'

'When thousands attend pro-Nazi rallies in New York and Poland, and American congressmen speak out against Jews?' She huffed her disdain. 'Some chance. Even England is having Fascist rallies.'

Berek's fists clenched. 'Why would anyone support him? I don't understand. You know Hitler and Mussolini have been talking about Germany annexing Austria?'

'He makes no secret of the fact that he's building planes and re-arming. He always promised he'd expand Germany eastwards, but if he breaks the Treaty of Versailles, surely there'll be repercussions.'

'You think anyone wants to stir up another war?'

'You think ignoring what he's doing will prevent one?'

'I don't know, Hanne.'

She dashed away tears with the back of her hand. 'My father died for this country, and this is how Hitler repays his sacrifice. Suppose he forces you to fight and die for him? He has no right. He's nothing but a jumped-up little corporal!'

Berek held her while she cried. Hitler had given himself the right, and there was no one, and nothing short of assassination, that would stop him.

She wished another human being dead? Had Hitler brought her so low?

The radio burst back into life. Hitler spouting more of his fearful, almost hysterical propaganda.

'At the risk of appearing to talk nonsense, I tell you that the National Socialist movement will go on for a thousand years! Don't forget how people laughed at me fifteen years ago when I declared that one day, I would govern Germany. They laugh now, just as foolishly, when I declare that I shall remain in power!'

An icy shiver ran down her spine. If she had a gun or a long knife, she'd kill the man herself.

***

Hawley Heath, England 1934

My dearest Hanne,

There was so much Emma couldn't put in her letter. So much of what she wanted to write about was political. A failed attempt by the Nazis to overthrow the Austrian government had resulted in the Prime Minister being murdered. Paul von Hindenburg, the German president, had died, and Hitler had combined the offices of President and Chancellor and declared himself Führer and commander-in-chief of Germany's armed forces. He was now forcing personal oaths of allegiance to himself as leader. How was all this affecting Hanne and Berek?

I hope you are well. How is Asher coming along with speaking English? It must confuse a child so young to have two languages spoken to him, but they say you learn more easily when you are little. It is a miracle to me that any child masters even their own language, yet they do. It will be wonderful to talk to Asher when I finally meet him. I hope it is not too long before you all come to England for a holiday. You must teach me German, too.

If Hanne didn't know that a hundred Jews had been killed in Algeria, it was best she didn't tell her. It would only worry her, and it wasn't a safe subject to be raised by the nib of a pen. The world seemed in turmoil once again, and she wasn't sure she even felt safe in England after Mosley's Fascist supporters clashed with anti-Fascist protesters in Birmingham. Their Nazi-style anti-Semitism was frightening to one who had Jewish blood in her veins, especially as the members of the Fascist group had police protection during their protest. Birmingham was far too close to home.

Great news on the factory front. Cunard and White Star shipping lines have merged and are building a new ocean liner, the largest of its kind, it's to be called the Queen Mary, and Joshua and Son –

She screwed up the letter and began again. Joshua was a Jewish name, and it was best not to draw attention to it.

– it's to be called the Queen Mary, and the factory has a big order for chain and fittings that will keep us going for quite a while. We've been able to give some of our laid-off workers their jobs back. I hope this is a sign of things to come. There's talk of a sister ship.

She wouldn't mention the government was putting money into expanding the Royal Air Force as part of a new air-defence programme. It was best Hitler knew nothing of that. Was she being paranoid? Somehow, she didn't think so, and neither was Churchill who was pressing for re-armament. Much as the thought of war terrified her, government spending had to help the unemployed find jobs, and Britain had to be ready to meet any threat Hitler made.

If the *Twenty-Five Points of German Religion* was anything to go by, the religious heart of Germany was ranged against Judaism. According to its author, Christ was a Nordic warrior put to death by the Jews, sparing the world from Jewish domination; Hitler was the new messiah sent to Earth to save the world from Jews. The man was a megalomaniac, and a megalomaniac, especially one with a hatred of Jews, was to be feared.

Is Mutter feeling any better? I suppose Berek still hasn't found work. How are you managing for money, Hanne? I can send some if it would help. You will let me know, promise me.

She'd offered before and been turned down, but conditions in Germany were worse now, and if Berek wasn't earning, their savings must be dwindling.

If there is anything I can do to help, you only have to ask. Perhaps there are things you can't get that I could send you?

There was so much more she wanted to say, but she signed her name and sent them all her love, and her heart with it.

***

Rosie bent to her work, the sound of hammers on iron ringing in her ears. They had a deadline to meet, and every able-bodied chainmaker was hard at work. Sweat beaded her brow, and she wiped away a trickle before it went into her eye. Snakes of heavy chain wound across the factory floor as the teams of men forged link after link, moving with a precision born of years. To have all the forges lit again and have the steam hammers thudding out their mechanical rhythm was music to her ears.

Even better news was that Cunard would be building a sister ship to the *Queen Mary*, and they were in an excellent position to be invited to tender for providing chain and fittings for that ship as well.

She shovelled a little breeze onto her hearth and pumped the hand bellows, watching the hearth glow red, orange, and then yellow, selected another length of rod from the stack leaning against the wall, and pushed it into the glowing breeze. Today, she was making gate chains while the men toiled over the heavier cable chain.

Her thoughts went back to that week's major news. An explosion at the Gresford Colliery in Wrexham had killed over two hundred and fifty miners and three of the men sent down to rescue them. She took her supply of coal for granted, but it was dangerous work digging it out of the ground. With more explosions occurring and tunnel collapses, it was doubtful they'd be able to recover the bodies. She couldn't imagine what the mothers, widows, and children were going through.

The team of men to her right let their arms drop to their sides and rested on their hammers. Another completed shackle of chain fell to the floor with a crash and a rattle: fifteen more fathoms done.

Jack mopped his brow and neck with a red handkerchief. 'That's the lot, Rosie. The first part of the order completed on time.'

She removed her rod from the breeze with a sigh of relief and laid it on the side of her hearth. 'You look done in, Jack.'

'Just got to get it down to the Lloyds proofing sheds and pray it passes the strength test.'

'Of course, it will pass. I'll tell Emma you've finished, and she can confirm delivery times with Browns.'

'Can we get it to Clydebank in time? We've run it close.'

She nodded. 'We'll get it there. We're not trusting this order to the railways. Emma's promised we'll deliver it ourselves.'

Jack raised an eyebrow. 'I'll go with the order. I know the Clyde a bit from being up there during the war, and I can help load and unload.'

She smiled. 'You mean you want to skive off and revisit old haunts.'

Jack laughed. 'It would be nice to see the place and the big ships again. I have fond memories of HMS *Valiant* and the fellas I served with. A bit of reminiscing won't go amiss.'

'As long as you come back and don't get seduced by the sea.'

He gave her a hug. 'I'm too old now to join the Navy, so you needn't worry.'

'You used to talk about going back to Scapa Flow.'

'It was a beautiful, lonely place, and now it's a ship's graveyard. No, Scapa's too far north. Seeing the *Queen Mary* and
205

the shipyards will be far enough for me. I like my home comforts too much.'

She poked a finger into his belly. 'I can see that.'

He looked down at the offending bulge. 'Muscle. All pure muscle.'

'Oh, yes?'

He leaned closer. 'I'm not too old to show you my muscles.'

She skipped out of his arms, laughing. 'You can have me if you can catch me.'

The challenge was too much for Jack. He ran after her, jumping over the shackles of chain and catching her by the office wall. Pinning her to the wall, he planted a kiss on her lips. She wound her arms around his neck, and a cheer went up throughout the factory.

Her cheeks were red hot and not just from the heat of the forges. 'I love you, Jack Taylor.'

'I love you too, Rosie.'

A love like hers and Jack's was everything she wished for Emma. She looked up at the window into the office. Emma shook her head in mock disapproval and smiled.

Chapter Twenty-Two

Frankfurt, Germany 1935

Hanne tuned the radio into a foreign service, listening for something in English. Foreign stations were hard to receive, but Berek had done something to the radio to improve reception. With the volume low, and her ear next to the speaker, she hoped to hear news from the outside world without being found out.

Their radio, allowed so they could hear Nazi propaganda, was their last lifeline apart from cautious letters from Emma, and confiscation of it, should someone outside the family discover they listened to English news, would be unbearable.

It buzzed, whined, crackled, and faded in and out.

'Britain, France, and Italy have again declared support for the continued independence of Austria...'

The sound faded to nothing, and she searched for a better signal.

'The Saar region, separated from Germany at the end of the war, has been the subject of a regional referendum. While most political parties in the Saar were in favour of a return to Germany, Communists and Socialists in the Saar are supporting a continuation of the League of Nations administration.

'There have been complaints that the Nazis have engaged in intimidation, kidnappings, and espionage, even tapping phones and intercepting letters. Against this background, it is perhaps surprising that the vote is ninety percent in favour of the Saar being returned to Germany.'

People had the chance to be part of France and preferred Hitler? The long-standing dislike of the French ran deeper than she'd thought. The Jews of the Saar would soon discover what life was like in Nazi Germany. Jewish students were now banned from taking examinations in medicine, dentistry, pharmacy, and law. Jewish men were banned from military service, not that she'd imagine any of them had shed any tears over that.

Shouting outside the window made her switch off the radio and go to investigate. A man was addressing a small crowd and holding up a placard that turned briefly towards her.

Wir lassen uns nicht von Hitler vertreiben.

Juden, bleibt in Deutschland!

Don't let Hitler drive you out? With the emigration tax and other countries refusing to take Jewish immigrants, what chance was there to escape? Few Jews wanted to stay in Germany now, and some had left. How? Had they bribed their way across the border? How much money would it take for her family to pay their way to France and on to England and a better life, the life she wanted for Asher?

'Juden sind hier nicht erwünscht!'

Jews are not wanted here. SS officers strode along the pavement. One grabbed the protester by the arm, dashed his placard to pieces on the ground, and dragged the poor man away. She'd known the man – a Herr Engers: he'd owned a factory that made clothes. Her neighbour had worked for him.

Within a month, meetings to persuade Jews to remain in Germany were declared illegal. It was typical of Hitler's warped mind that his policies were contradictory, so a Jew was damned if he did something and damned if he didn't.

She hadn't seen Herr Engers since his arrest; he seemed to have disappeared. Rumour abounded about concentration camps, and his wife feared he'd been sent to Dachau.

But life went on, however difficult things had become. Germany retook the Saarland, and by mid-March, military conscription had been announced. That it was in breach of the Treaty of Versailles seemed not to bother Hitler one iota. That out of France, Britain, and America, only Britain had challenged it was more worrying.

The only people prepared to confront Hitler seemed to be the Jehovah's witnesses, whose religious organisation was banned because they refused to swear allegiance to the state, and as she'd feared, anti-Jewish legislation was quickly passed in the Saar.

As fresh green leaves broke from tight buds on the trees along the river Maine that ran through Frankfurt, Poland's political parties called for sanctions against Jews, and the Polish Catholic Church joined in the discrimination and violence.

Mixed marriages between Jews and Aryans were banned. That Jews were no longer allowed to fly the German flag, only worried her in that it was one more freedom lost, one further action of exclusion from society, and a shrinking of their civil rights – a feeling that they were being shorn to within a millimetre of their skins and herded into a pen like sheep for slaughter.

She put a hand to her throat in a barely conscious gesture; on every side, the anti-Semitic noose tightened.

***

Hawley Heath, England 1935

Emma lay awake far into the night. She wasn't sure if the recent news was good or bad. The government had announced that it was to triple the size of the Royal Air Force in response to Germany's rearmament, and an agreement had been reached to allow Germany to have a navy, albeit only a third the tonnage of Britain's and with no submarines or aircraft carriers. Was it better to be prepared or worse to risk escalating an already fraught situation? Better to deny Germany a navy or to placate them with a small one?

A country needed ships for trade, and Germany's prosperity depended on trade, but she hadn't forgotten the horrific stories Dad told about fighting in the Battle of Jutland, and she didn't believe the journalists who proclaimed Hitler was a man of peace. Was Britain avoiding another war with Germany or allowing her to gain the upper hand?

More and more, she wavered in her intention not to visit Hanne. She had recurring nightmares about never seeing her and Berek again and never meeting little Asher. Only last week, Hanne had written of a man she knew who'd disappeared. At least, that was what she'd assumed from "*Herr Engers had a disagreement in the street, and no one knows where he has gone. His wife is very worried.*"

Suppose Berek had a disagreement with an SS officer and disappeared. Suppose Hanne did. Hanne had previously mentioned concentration camps for those who defied the Nazis, for anyone who didn't meet their idea of Aryan normality – and who was to say Jews wouldn't come to fall into that category as homosexuals already had? Hitler seemed determined to make all their lives as miserable as he could.

She punched her pillow, turned over in bed, and tried to get comfortable. Mom would try to dissuade her, and deep inside, she knew it was foolhardy at best, but her heart dwelt in Germany, no matter how hard she tried to deny it. The factory had work for the next few months, Charlie was safe hands for the cycle workshop, and Heath Hall, the farm, and the rest home had always run smoothly thanks to the capable men and women who staffed it.

Not for the first time, she wondered if she was really needed. If Ramsay MacDonald could retire as prime minister and let Stanley Baldwin take over, she could take a couple of weeks off work. She needed a holiday; the break would do her good.

She would write and tell Hanne she was coming before Mom made her change her mind. She found Hanne's latest letter to copy her new address on the envelope. She could never remember the new name for Börneplatz.

My dearest Hanne,

How are you all? We are all well, and the factory is doing better at last. Charlie took me to the cinema last week, and they showed a film of the Queen Mary being launched last September. Dad went up to deliver chain to the shipyard, and he said she was going to be a beautiful ship. The hull is complete, but it will take another year or two to finish her. She looks huge.

The good news is they are building a sister ship, and we have the contract to make some of the chain and fittings for her as well. It is such a relief to know our workers' jobs are safe for the next few months, at least.

The cinema also showed a new film of the Royal Air Force's latest plane. It looks magnificent and is so fast.

She'd almost said it was a Hawker Hurricane fighter aircraft flying at Brooklands. Perhaps she shouldn't have mentioned the plane at all. No, Hanne needed to know Britain was preparing for the worst.

We have had another election. We have another National

government, though the Conservative Party has the majority of the votes, if reduced somewhat.

If she was honest, she'd begun looking for signs that the Conservatives would do what Hitler had done. What party wouldn't want to be in power and stay there? If it had happened in Germany, why couldn't it happen in England? How safe was democracy?

Anyway, I wanted to ask if I could come and stay with you for a couple of weeks, hopefully very soon. This autumn has been so wet, with flooding in places, and now it has turned quite cold, so I expect I shall need warm clothes if you are experiencing the same weather.

At least cold and wet wasn't deep snow like they'd suffered in May. No one in Hawley could remember ever having had such a snowstorm.

Let me know as soon as you can, as I'd love to see you all again and meet Asher, or he will be grown up and married before we know it.

She smiled at the thought of being introduced as Auntie Emma. His relationship to her was remote, but she felt very close to the little boy she'd never seen. He was part of Hanne and Berek, so how could she not love him already?

***

Frankfurt, Germany 1935

Hanne held Asher's hand as they crossed Börnestrasse – she refused to call it Grober Wollgraben – towards Uncle Saul's shop. A large sign hung beneath the street sign.

Juden nicht willkommen

She didn't need a sign to tell her she wasn't welcome. A new

212

flag, a black swastika in a white circle on a red background, flew from the corner of a building – another unwelcome change.

Two SS officers strode past the shop. One paused, turned, and strode back. 'This shop belongs to a Jew. Buy from a German-owned shop.'

She frowned. 'But Herr Samuels is a German.'

'Herr Samuels is a Jew. Haven't you heard? Jews are no longer German citizens.'

'What do you mean, not German citizens? We were born here.'

The officer smirked. 'A new law, part of the Nuremberg Laws. And Jews can no longer vote or hold any public office.'

'Well, since we can only vote for Hitler, that won't be a problem, and who wants to work for the Nazis or be German?'

The officer struck her across the face. 'You will learn to hold your tongue, Jüdenhure.'

'Hanne, come inside at once.' Uncle Saul grabbed her coat sleeve and pulled her into his shop as she dragged Asher behind her.

The officer turned his attention to a potential customer, shooing them away from the shop.

Uncle Saul shook his head. 'Hanne, what were you thinking, speaking to the SS like that?'

'I'm sick of being treated like a second-class citizen – except we aren't even that now, apparently.'

'We must bear what we can't change, Hanne.'

'How can you be so calm, Uncle?'

Her uncle smiled ruefully. 'What good will I do if I get my

213

head blown off for a wrong remark? And you have Asher to think of as well as your mother and Berek.'

'I suppose you're right.'

'Little Asher is growing, Hanne.'

'You think so?' She looked down at her son, who was clutching the toy dog Emma had sent him. 'He's almost four, but I still think he's small for his age.'

'And when is he going to have a little brother or sister?'

'How can we bring another child into the world, Uncle? We can barely feed this one.'

'Things are that bad?'

'Berek can't work, you have no customers, and Mutter isn't well. What are we going to do, Uncle? We can't go on like this. I worry about Asher's future.'

'I've been thinking of selling up, Hanne. Fleishman's and Heinberg's have already sold their factories and shops. We can't make a living anymore, what with the recession and all the boycotts and vandalism, not to mention the threats and violence. You were lucky not to get worse than a slapped face. They shot old man Kettner.'

'Kettner, the butcher?'

'Yes.'

'Is he –'

'Not dead, no, but he's in hospital, and who will pay for his care? Not the state, that's for sure.'

'But who would buy a Jewish jewellers' with no customers?'

'We can only sell to Aryans. It was a good business, and

without the boycotts and SS bullies, it will be successful again.'

'And if you can sell, would you leave Germany?'

'If I could sell for enough, we could all leave Germany.' He raised a hand to silence her. 'I wish it was so easy, Hanne. Property prices are at rock bottom, and as usual, the Nazis have us over a barrel. I shall only get perhaps a fifth of what it is worth.'

'But even that might be enough – you have precious metals and gemstones. Emma –'

'You don't understand, Hanne. There may be a thriving barter economy, but who wants jewellery – you can't eat it, and it won't keep you warm in winter. We could hide away some of our smaller, precious items in the hope we can sell them later, but there is a huge emigration tax aimed at preventing us from taking wealth out of Germany. The chances are the tax would take most or even all of our money. No country will accept Jewish refugees who can't support themselves. We are a threat to their jobs and a burden to their society. Even if Emma would give us a temporary home, Britain won't let us in.'

'So, we are stuck here, and the Nazis won't be content until we are all destitute.'

'I fear so, and it's a crime to be a beggar.'

'Emma wrote to me. She wants to visit.'

Uncle Saul shook his head. 'Tell her to stay away for her own safety. For God's sake, don't let her come.'

Her eyes filled with tears. 'I was so looking forward to seeing her, but you're right. I'll tell her not to come.' She sighed and hugged her son. 'You'll have to wait a little longer before you meet your Auntie Emma, Asher. One day, you will. I promise. She will love you so much.'

Uncle Saul put an arm around her shoulder. 'This too shall pass, Hanne.'

She hoped so, but she had a sickening feeling in the pit of her stomach that life would get much worse before they could find a way out of Germany, if escape was even possible.

Chapter Twenty-Three

Frankfurt, Germany 1935

A chill breeze blew from the north, stirring the dead, brown leaves around Hanne's feet. Winter had come with a chill that wasn't only the weather. She walked across Börneplatz towards the park, Asher skipping at her side. There was a small playground with swings, slides, and a roundabout, and Asher loved to play there. The familiar sign that was springing up around the city hung on the fence next to the entrance.

Juden nicht willkommen

She strode past it and through the gate into the park. Asher was a child, and children needed to play in the fresh air. Just because the local kindergarten had refused him didn't mean he couldn't play with other children. A group of youngsters ran across the grass shouting and playing tag, and others pushed one another on swings while mothers chatted on a companionable square of benches.

Asher wriggled his hand out of her grip and ran towards a slide. A fair-haired lad of a similar age dashed towards him.

His mother ran after him and grabbed his sleeve. 'No, don't play with him. He's a Jew. Jews killed Jesus.'

'He's a child, and his name is Asher. He's killed no one.'

The woman waved an angry hand. 'Didn't you read the sign? Jews aren't welcome. In fact, you're forbidden to come in here, bringing your disease.'

'Who says? And what disease?'

The woman backed away from her as if she really believed her contagious. 'The government says. Don't you read the news? And everyone knows Jews carry disease.'

Her mouth fell open. 'That's ridiculous.'

Another woman joined the first. 'This playground is for Aryan children only. You must leave, now.'

She wouldn't subject Asher to this intimidation. She waited for him at the bottom of the slide and took his hand firmly in hers. 'Asher, we have to go.'

He dragged his feet, disappointed at missing his playtime. How could she explain to a child the stupidity of racial and religious intolerance? Weren't they all God's creatures, no matter what they looked like or how they worshipped Him?

Even Protestants and Catholics weren't safe from Nazi repression. Now, the Reich Church with its German Christians, preached its Nazi version of Christianity, and the Old Testament had been excluded as a Jewish document. Some Catholic schools had been closed, and young Christians were being encouraged to leave the church and join Hitler youth groups. Hitler was being deified by people still vulnerable from the depression, who had no grasp of the extent of his subversive ideology.

She stamped her anger onto the pavement.

Der Stürmer, a purveyor of hatred and defamation, had printed an excerpt from Martin Luther's book, *The Jews and Their Lies*. It was burned into her mind almost word for word.

They are nothing but thieves and robbers who daily eat no morsel and wear no thread of clothing which they have not stolen and pilfered from us by means of their accursed usury. Thus, they live from day to day, together with wife and child,

by theft and robbery, as arch thieves and robbers, in the most impenitent security.

Was it any wonder people turned against Jews if this sort of centuries-old propaganda was published? Not all Germans or German priests hated Jews; some had been killed or imprisoned for defying the state, but the churches cared only for their own survival, and they knew who was a Christian, and therefore, by default, who was a Jew.

***

Hawley Heath, England 1936

Rosie put down her cup of breakfast tea and turned the page of the *Manchester Guardian*.

RMS *Queen Mary* sets out on maiden voyage.

Cunard White Star's new luxury ocean liner left Southampton yesterday on its maiden voyage to Cherbourg en route for New York. The hopes and fortunes of British shipbuilding sail with her. A sister ship is under construction and is planned to sail in 1938.

She read the trepidation slipped in between the lines. White Star's Titanic had sunk before the war with a tremendous loss of life. Britain needed a successful ocean liner, and completion of the sister ship, Hull 552, would mean the shipping line had two huge transatlantic ships in service. Months of work for the factory, and many other businesses in the north and midlands, were secured – if the first crossing was successful.

Hope for the future allowed her to view the black drapes still hanging in shop windows with a little more pragmatism. King George V had died in January, and the factory and many shops had been closed as a mark of respect. Throughout Hawley Heath, curtains had stayed drawn and people had walked the streets with sombre faces. A nation mourned.

She'd been a child when Queen Victoria had died, and she still remembered the sense of loss Hawley Heath had felt for a woman they'd never met but who had been a strong and constant symbol of stability during most of their lives. England now had a new king, Edward VIII, and his reign was beginning with much instability.

And war seemed ever closer. A new fighter plane had taken to the skies; the Spitfire would be a formidable weapon should war break out again in Europe.

Two days after the Spitfire first flew, Hitler had occupied the Rhineland, in clear breach of the Treaty of Versailles. So far, Britain and France hadn't responded to this breach other than trying to get a peaceful settlement. The British government had always considered French troops depriving Germany of its industrial heartland unreasonable, given the huge reparations France expected Germany to pay, and for a while, Britain's dislike of France had risen to the top like dirty washing in a hot boiler.

According to the newspapers she'd read, the demilitarised status of the Rhineland was the most important guarantee of peace in Europe, as it stood between Germany and its western neighbours.

Despite her reservations over France occupying the Rhineland, she could only see Germany putting armed forces in there as a hostile act, but Hitler had been unrepentant. '*Neither threats nor warnings will prevent me from going my way. I follow the path assigned to me by Providence with the instinctive sureness of a sleepwalker.*'

It seemed Churchill had been right to press for Britain to rearm, and France had been right to build the Maginot Line, a line of concrete fortifications that ran the length of France's border with Germany. Rearming meant work for hands eager to do it, both in Britain and Germany. The thought of war terrified her – Jack might be too old, but George, Theo, and Charlie would be of an age to be conscripted – but, for the millions of unemployed, food on the table would be more of a relief than the threat of another war was a worry.

She cleared away her breakfast things, and Maisie took them from her to wash up.

Maisie bustled around the kitchen. 'Is there anything else you want, Rosie?'

'No, thank you, Maisie. I'd better get off to the factory. Jack and Emma have been gone ages.'

'You work too hard, Rosie. Always have.'

'And you don't?'

Maisie smiled. 'When I'm too old and tired to look after you, you'll be the first to know.'

She laughed. 'I don't doubt it, Maisie.'

She walked down the hill in the early summer sunshine and along Willis Street to the factory. There was a sign pinned to the factory door. She peered closer at the scrawled writing.

JEWS GO HOME

She blinked and looked again, but the message read the same. She ripped the notice from the door and tore it into shreds. Where, exactly, was home for the Jews? The infection of anti-Semitism was spreading beyond Germany, Poland, and Palestine, and there was no telling where it would end.

'*Shylocks*?' Emma tore up the latest anonymous letter and screwed it into a ball, her knuckles white. 'After everything we've done for Hawley Heath, and they dare to call us Shylocks? Why?'

Mom shook her head. 'No one around here would think that, Emma. It has to be someone from away. Someone who's seen the name Joshua and Son and taken offence.'

'You're probably right, but suppose we lose orders because of our name.'

'You think we should change it? Emma, we've built a reputation for quality and getting orders out on time. Joshua and Son is a respected name where it counts.'

'And if these Fascists stir up more hatred of Jews, what then? Will our name work for us or against us? This is too close to home, Mom.'

'So, what do you propose?'

'I don't know. What would you do?'

Mom straightened. 'Stand up for what I believe in, of course. Justice for the under-dog. I wouldn't let myself be pushed about by – bloody Fascists.'

'So you won't object if I go to London.'

'London? What for?'

'I saw a poster on the wall of the post office the other day. I wasn't intending to go, but now...'

'What poster?'

'There's an anti-Fascist rally in London on October the fourth to stand against Oswald Mosley and his British Union of Fascists, who are planning to march through the East End of London.'

'There's a large Jewish population in the East End.'

'Precisely. Residents have petitioned the Home Secretary to ban the march.'

'There'll be trouble if they march, Emma. You know how violent these rallies can get once passions are roused.'

'I'm half Jewish, Mom. Look what Hanne is suffering in Germany – she's too afraid for my safety to let me visit her – and look at the trouble Fascists are stirring in Spain. We can't let that happen here. One Hitler in the world is one too many.'

'At your age, I would have gone, Emma. Nothing would have stopped me, so I can't say you shouldn't go, but for pity's sake, be careful.'

'I will, Mom.'

According to an alteration plastered across the poster, she had to be at Aldgate at two o'clock in the afternoon on the fourth. The early train from New Street plus a journey on the underground, deposited her at Aldgate station in the East End of London like an autumn leaf blown in on a gust of wind – one of a roiling mass of autumn leaves whipped up by a wind of dissension.

She followed the crowd along Whitechapel High Street and along Christian Street where men and women were bringing furniture, crates, and anything else they could lay their hands on to build barricades.

'What can I do to help?'

A woman looked up and wiped her sleeve across her nose. 'Tek this and shove it in a gap somewhere, lovey. We'll keep Mosley's blasted Blackshirts out.'

She picked up the small table and carried it across the road. A man took it from her and threw it up on top of the pile of assorted furniture and shop fittings, presumably borrowed from local shops.

All along the road, on both sides of the barricades, people brandished sticks, chair legs, and bricks, and waved bottles. There were thousands, tens of thousands of people waiting for the Blackshirts to arrive. People were going to get hurt, but Mosley's parody of Hitler's Brownshirts wouldn't march through the East End unchallenged.

Men in uniforms appeared in the crowd, pushing through towards the barricades; not Blackshirts, but police, some mounted on horses, come to clear the road for the Fascist marchers. Protesters fell back before the horses' hooves, and she had a flash of memory of being three-years-old and getting scarily close to the hooves of a huge cart horse when the women chainmakers were picketing the factory.

Men rushed the police, who beat them back with raised batons.

Mom had been trampled...

Shouts, cheers, jeers, and screams – all was confusion. From the windows of houses, rubbish, rotten vegetables, and the contents of chamber pots rained down on the police. She armed herself with a rolling pin someone had dropped on the road and waited, heart thudding.

As police threw down the barricade, angry protesters charged, and a running battle swept her along. She had to keep moving or risk being trampled. Her legs almost buckled beneath her, but she ran on, avoiding the flailing hooves of the horses, ducking police batons, and wielding her weapon against any police officer who tried to arrest her.

Gasping for breath and unable to run farther, she side-stepped into a shop doorway and leaned against the door panting as the tide of anger surged past. A young man with blood pouring from his head slumped at her feet.

She dropped her weapon and knelt beside him. 'You need to get to a hospital. Can you walk?'

He shook his head. 'Best stay here until this calms down, miss. Me head looks worse than it is, I reckon. Me Mam's given me worse with her rolling pin for cheeking her.'

'If you're sure.' She was grateful for not having to brave the current again and sat beside the young man. 'I'm Emma.'

'Nice to meet you, Emma. I'm Ethan.' Ethan mopped at his head with a handkerchief.

'What happened to the Blackshirts?'

Ambulances pulled up by the smashed tumble of furniture that had been the barricade. Men carrying bags tended the worst of the wounded. One came over to them. 'Are you two injured?'

'Ethan has a cut head.'

The man examined it. 'You should get that looked at. Go and sit in the ambulance. I'll be with you when I've checked the people over there.'

'Where are Mosley and his Blackshirts?'

'The police sent them to Hyde Park.' The man hurried away, and Ethan went over to the ambulance.

He left her standing amid a scene of destruction and huddles of injured men, women, and children, police among them, and what had they achieved? Communists, Jews, trade unionists, and dockers had been arrested, and some looked badly injured, but they'd shown the spirit of democracy: they'd come together to fight fascism in England.

Chapter Twenty-Four

Hawley Heath, England 1936

Emma had come home from London more determined than ever to fight fascism and everything it stood for – that the government had allowed Mosley to march in an area so likely to cause violent disagreements was irresponsible, to say the least, and inflammatory. It didn't send a message of hope to the Jewish community.

Letters from Hanne had become more and more cryptic, and more and more worrying. She now understood phrases like '*I didn't take Asher to the park today*' as another restriction placed against Jews.

Between her work at the factory and her responsibilities to the farm, the rest home, and the cycle workshop, she read every newspaper she could lay her hands on and listened to every news broadcast on the radio.

She needed to know what was going on in the world, especially as it impinged on Hanne and Berek, and little Asher. Germany's attempt at pretending everything was normal by hosting the Olympic Games and including Jews in their team hadn't lessened her fear for her cousin. Hanne had sent a new photograph of Asher. He looked like Willis had at the same age: so like she had. He could be her child – no one would suspect otherwise if they didn't know.

She switched from the Empire Service to the British news. '*It is with great sorrow that I broadcast the news that King Edward*

VIII has announced his abdication from the throne of England. It his intention to marry the American divorcee, Wallis Simpson. Prince Albert, Duke of York, will be crowned as King George VI. His daughter, Princess Elizabeth, will be heir presumptive.'

Imaginary hedgehog spines bristled. Presumptive as in if there wasn't a male born to be heir? Women still had much to prove if they were to achieve equality.

Frankfurt and her beloved's face, so beautiful, so alive, with dark eyes and smiling lips, danced between her and the affairs of Hawley Heath. How could she concentrate on the mundanity of work when those she loved were sinking ever deeper into danger?

Poland followed Germany's lead in singling out Jews in every walk of life. Businesses now had to display the owner's name as recorded on their birth certificates, so customers knew if they were dealing with Jews.

Shylocks. Mom hadn't told her about the anti-Semitic sign on the door but piecing together the torn shreds in the wastepaper bin in the office had revealed it. Emma Taylor was as English a name as you could get if Britain insisted on such measures. Surely, it couldn't happen here.

At least, there was one glimmer of hope. Something had come of what was being dubbed *The Battle of Cable Street*. The Public Order Act had banned the wearing of political uniforms in any public place or public meeting, so the Blackshirts could no longer parade their fascist ideology behind quasi-Nazi symbolism. She hoped the copycat Silvershirts of the USA would get the same treatment.

The newsreader hailed the act as a decisive blow against the rise of fascism in Britain and then announced Britain and France's non-intervention appeasement agreement regarding the Spanish

Civil War. It seemed fascism could be tackled or ignored at will. Perhaps the British government hadn't the stomach to stand up for democracy.

***

Frankfurt, Germany 1937

Jews and gypsies had lost their right to vote. Hanne now lived in the country of her birth with no rights and no citizenship. She grew increasingly depressed as more and more hatred was broadcast and more and more restrictions were placed upon her – she could no longer visit a restaurant, swimming pool, or park. Jewish children were banned from German schools and universities.

Couldn't people see it was Nazi anti-Semitism and propaganda? Austria, Poland, Romania: they'd all turned against the Jews amid Christian indifference to their plight. *"The Jews murdered Jesus and deserved God's punishment. Jews are morally harmful."* This was Christian America's verdict with no trial or jury.

Those that could leave were leaving, but it was now more difficult than ever. Not only were countries closing their doors after the initial spate of refugees from Germany, but the Nazi government had increased the tax on all Jewish assets, claiming usury and white slave labour as justification. If a Jew wished to leave Germany now, he would have to leave almost all his wealth behind to fund Hitler's egotistical warmongering. Uncle Saul's suggestion of hiding small valuable items seemed like a good one – should they ever have the chance to escape – but for Mutter's health, they'd have risked it by now, if only for Asher's sake.

She reached Uncle Saul's shop and found him in a state of agitation. 'Uncle, what is it? What's happened?'

He shook his head. 'I have to sell the shop, Hanne. After all these years building it up and I am forced to sell it to an Aryan.'

'They can't force you, Uncle.'

He waved a letter under her nose. 'This came just now. It may not be legal, but it's clear I have no choice. Storm troopers will vandalise and loot the shop, and the government will confiscate any insurance money. I can't afford to keep repairing it and replacing stock when I have no customers.'

She read the letter. Refusal to sell would almost certainly result in the shop being destroyed and would probably see Uncle Saul arrested and imprisoned. 'Those small valuables you mentioned. I think it's time we hid them.'

'I've already put some in the safe and hidden the key.'

'Uncle, they could force you to open the safe. It would be better to hide what we can and leave the safe unlocked. Leave some gems and jewellery on display and blame looting if anyone asks. God knows they've stolen enough from us.'

He nodded and fetched some small velvet bags. 'Take the most expensive jewellery in that cabinet out of their boxes. I'll burn the boxes, so there's no trace. Start with the largest diamonds, and hurry.'

The urgency in his voice made her fingers fumble as she removed beautiful rings set with pearls, diamonds, rubies, sapphires, and emeralds. Uncle Saul had given her a diamond and sapphire ring when she and Berek had married. She took it from the finger where Berek had put it and placed it in the velvet bag with the other rings. It would be safer there – she would be safer with it there.

Brooches followed rings, necklaces followed brooches, and

watches followed necklaces as bag after bag was filled with the most precious and expensive items. Uncle Saul rearranged the display, putting the larger price tags on some of the least expensive items. He smiled. 'No one but an experienced jeweller will know the difference, and it might prevent the SS or the SA looking further into the business.' He smacked his forehead with the palm of his hand. 'Invoices. I must destroy the invoices. There must be no trace.'

He hurried away to add the invoices to the fire. The shop bell jangled, and she swept the jewellery bags off the counter and into the rubbish bin.

A tall, thin man looked her up and down and wrinkled his nose. 'I wish to speak to Herr Samuels.'

'I'll fetch him for you.' She locked the cabinet they'd been working in with an ostentatious turn of a key and put the key in her pocket. 'I won't be a moment.'

'Uncle, there's a man in the shop asking to see you.'

'An Aryan?'

She nodded. 'And not a customer, I'll bet.'

'And the precious items?'

'I threw them in the rubbish bin.' She held out a ringless finger. 'This too.'

He squeezed her hand. 'Good girl. Now, let's see what this Aryan wants.'

She followed her uncle into the shop.

A storm trooper now accompanied the man, who introduced himself. 'My name is Litzmann. I wish to buy your shop.' Herr Litzmann put what looked like a legal document on the table.

'This is the price I shall pay to include all stock, fixtures, and fittings.' He stabbed a finger at a figure she couldn't read upside-down.

Uncle Saul turned the paper to face him. 'But that doesn't cover the cost of the items on display, never mind the building and shop fittings. My business is worth five times that.'

'You will sign here and, given the nature of the goods, you will vacate the property immediately. We wouldn't want expensive jewellery to go missing, would we?'

'And if I refuse?'

The storm trooper fingered a pistol in a holster on his belt.

Herr Litzmann glanced at her. 'You wouldn't want harm to come to this pretty little thing, would you, Herr Samuels? I strongly urge you to sign.'

'Uncle –'

'It's all right, Hanne. I've been thinking of retiring.' Uncle Saul signed the document with a flourish, took the door keys from a chain on his belt and placed them on the glass-topped counter. 'Get your coat, Hanne. We're leaving.'

She scowled at Herr Litzmann and picked up the rubbish bin. 'We have standards, Herr Litzmann. We wouldn't want to leave you our rubbish.'

Herr Litzmann raised a staying hand. 'What have you in there?'

She wrinkled her nose and held out the bin at arms-length, heart thumping. 'Look if you like. A child was sick all over the floor and his mother wiped it up with a napkin she had in her bag. It stinks, so I'd hold your nose and keep your mouth shut.' With luck, he'd suffocate while he did it.

Uncle Saul took a step towards her. 'I should put it on the fire, Hanne. The child could be ill, so who knows what disease the napkin might be carrying.'

Herr Litzmann waved her away. 'Empty the bin and wash it.'

She walked slowly, holding out the bin, her head spinning, and her legs weak. Once outside, she transferred the velvet bags to her own shopping bag and emptied the rest of the contents onto the fire. She returned the washed bin to the shop and took a last look around the place that had supported the family for so long. It was only a building, only things. Things could be replaced.

Except it was more than that. It was years of hard work, a way of life, hopes for the future. To see Herr Litzmann handling the gems in the cabinets with greedy fingers made her want to vomit.

Uncle Saul's eyes glistened with tears. He'd bought this shop with his late wife. It was his home as well as his business, and it held memories more precious than the gems they'd saved from this Nazi thug.

'Come, Uncle.'

Uncle Saul roused. 'I have personal possessions, upstairs.'

Herr Litzmann barely looked up from a showy diamond and sapphire brooch. 'Collect what you need and be quick about it.'

'I'll wait for you outside, Uncle.' She closed the shop door behind them and pointed to her shopping bag. 'They're safe.'

He nodded. 'It's just a few photos and things. I won't be a moment.'

She pulled up her collar against the chilly morning before opening the door to the street. 'Mutter will make us a nice cup of coffee. We'll make room for you in the apartment. This too shall pass, remember, Uncle.'

He put his hands on her cheeks and kissed her forehead. 'I thank God for my family every day, Hanne.' He smiled. 'God is good.'

Chapter Twenty-Five

Hawley Heath, England 1937

Bunting and Union flags hung from lampposts along Willis Street and the High Street. Signs bearing the name King Edward VIII had been painted over, and King George VI had been stencilled over the top. The factory was closed, the workers given the day off, and hastily produced commemorative mugs and plates adorned shop windows. Today was the coronation of King George VI and Queen Elizabeth, and a celebration like this hadn't been seen since the end of the war. There was an air of expectancy blowing through Hawley Heath.

Rosie was hoping for good weather for the garden party arranged in the grounds of Heath Hall, but the sky was overcast and threatening rain. It was a good job they'd hired a marquee. She'd splashed out tuppence on a copy of the Radio Times as the BBC was covering the coronation. The front cover was in colour and showed a drawing of the view from a window as ranks of guards on horses rode past.

Spots of rain splashed into a puddle. The wind was from the west and the sky looked lighter there. Hopefully, it would be fine in London later. She carried her bags of shopping up the hill to Heath Hall; the butcher had delivered cold meats and pork pies for a buffet, the baker had donated loaves by the dozen, and the milkman had delivered gallons of milk for tea, but the grocer's van had broken down, so she'd collected the cheese rounds herself, and damned heavy they were. Glasshouses would provide salad courtesy of the gardeners and local allotments.

Emma was helping lay a long trestle table, while Jack and Charlie carried in chairs borrowed from houses in the town. They'd all been up since dawn preparing a grand affair to which everyone was welcome.

'I've brought the cheese, Emma,'

'Thanks, Mom. Can you put it on the side table by the cold meat?'

She looked around. 'What are we doing about tea?'

'Theo's fetching the big urn from the kitchen, and George is setting up a paraffin stove borrowed from the church room. You could put out the milk jugs on that table over there if you like.'

She unpacked milk jugs from a box, glad Emma had thought to ask people to bring their own plates, cups, saucers, and cutlery. She had a small stock of paper plates and cups for those who forgot.

As people filled the marquee, music filled the air from loudspeakers, bringing the radio broadcast of the procession and service into the marquee. Outside, children played games and ran races organised by some of the fathers. Today, they forgot the problems of unemployment, poverty, and the threat of war; they were making memories that wouldn't soon be forgotten.

The coronation service went on in the background for what seemed like hours: some listened, some chatted, and some had only come for the food. She smiled, grateful that they had food to offer. There were unfamiliar faces among the visitors, and some old faces were missing; the new houses hadn't done what they were intended to do, and a new class of resident had moved in who hadn't known the hardship of working for Matthew Joshua at the turn of the century. The community she'd grown up with had changed, and with it, the loyalty she'd built over the years.

***

Frankfurt, Germany 1937

Hanne sat with her family listening to the radio, which was turned very low. Since Jews had been banned from having electrical or optical equipment, and even records, bicycles, and typewriters, she'd lived in fear of the radio being discovered and confiscated – it spent much of its time hidden under the bed behind a pile of blankets. She'd tuned it to Britain's Empire Service, her only link with the sanity of the outside world. The coronation had been the chief topic all day, and they'd listened to much of it, but this evening, Britain's new king was to address the nation live on radio.

Emma would be listening to the speech, and that made her feel close to her cousin, closer to England.

The king spoke slowly. *'It is with a very full heart that I speak to you tonight. Never before has a newly crowned King been able to talk to all his people in their own homes on the day of his coronation. Never has the ceremony itself had so wide a significance. For the dominions are now free and equal partners with this ancient kingdom.'*

Free and equal was something she would never be while she lived in Germany. Her world had shrunk to little more than her apartment and the closest shops that sold food. She longed for England and the haven Emma offered.

The king's speech was different to the speeches Goebbel's Ministry of Enlightenment and Propaganda spouted daily. If Hitler had been God, he wouldn't have been worshipped more. The government had taken over art, literature, theatre, film, and music, and allowed nothing that didn't further Nazi ideals. Germans were being brain-washed in every sector of their lives.

The broadcast ended, and she tuned back to the Reich Broadcasting Corporation's programme; it was as well to keep abreast of developments.

Goebbel's hated voice invaded the room, and she turned the volume knob anti-clockwise to quieten his strident tones. *'Without fear, we may point to the Jew as the motivator, the originator, and the beneficiary of this horrible catastrophe. Behold the enemy of the world, the annihilator of cultures, the parasite among nations, the son of chaos, the incarnation of evil, the ferment of decay, the formative demon of mankind's downfall.'*

'What catastrophe? The catastrophe is Hitler!' Tears stung her eyes. 'Why does he hate us so much?'

Mutter dry-washed her hands. 'Hanne, you and Berek should take Asher and leave.'

'Mutter, I can't leave you and Uncle Saul, and anyway, where would we go? Who will take us in?'

'The Cohens are going to Palestine – someone, they won't say who, but I believe he is English, is getting them visas and false papers and will hide them until he can get them out. Frau Cohen said she would put us in touch with him.'

'But, Mutter, it's no safer in Palestine. Last month, Arabs attacked Jewish property and killed twenty-one Jews. If we go, we must go to England because Emma will vouch for us.'

Mutter took her hands in her own. 'Then go to England. Berek, make her see sense.'

Berek shook his head. 'Hanne is right. We're family. Either we all go, or we all stay.'

Uncle Saul ran knobbly fingers across his forehead. 'But think about Asher. He's even forbidden to go to school. What future has the boy here? Take some of the gems and gold we rescued and see if you can use them to bribe border guards. You may be able to get to Holland. You'd be safe there.'

'But who do we know in Holland who'll give us a home? Asher needs his family, and those gems were meant to look after all of us. Mutter, Uncle Saul, please – I can't leave you even if I could get out.' She'd almost said *could get to safety*. They might be in dire circumstances, but so far, they weren't in imminent danger. 'And anyway, you said it yourself, no one can eat jewellery. We need cash. Perhaps we could send some jewellery to Emma, and she could send us reichsmarks. She may be able to get them from a bank in England.'

Uncle Saul threw up his hands. 'And if our parcel is searched? Or Emma's letter is opened and the money discovered? There are spies everywhere looking for signs that people are trying to get out, because the Nazis know they must have money they can confiscate. It wouldn't work, Hanne.'

'Isn't it worth taking the risk? What's the worst that can happen?'

Her uncle shook his head. 'I promised your father I'd look after you and your mother if the worst happened. You're not my responsibility now you're married, Hanne, but I'll see your mother is safe if you choose to leave. We'll be all right. Take Asher and go.'

She bit her fingernail. Any choice she made would be wrong for someone, and she'd never forgive herself if anything happened to Asher, Berek, Mutter, or Uncle Saul.

***

Hawley Heath, England 1937

238

The newspaper carried a report of the marriage of the Duke of Windsor to Wallis Simpson. Emma folded it neatly and turned to Maisie, who'd bustled in and looked as if she was eager to bustle out again.

'Post boy brought these, Emma. They look foreign.'

'Thanks, Maisie. I expect they're from my cousin, Hanne, in Germany.' There was a small packet and a letter. She opened the letter eagerly, smelling the familiar lavender scent.

My darling Emma,

I hope you like the little gift I am sending to you as promised. Uncle Saul has been forced to retire and has sold his shop. Although he didn't get as much for it as it is worth, he let me choose some trinkets for myself, Mutter, Berek, and Asher, and this one is for you to value, as I know you will, as we may not be able to visit as planned. Uncle Saul will find retirement hard, and I hope you will send some note of worth to console him in his need.

Emma read the letter twice more. What an odd message. Hanne hadn't promised a gift, and why would Berek and Asher want trinkets. Some note of worth? What was she supposed to write to console a man she barely knew? She opened the small packet that had accompanied the letter. Inside some cotton wool lay a ring. It looked like a diamond and several emeralds, but they couldn't be real. A genuine diamond that size would be worth a lot of money.

She placed it on her ring finger, imagining it as a token of love from her heart's desire. Of course, she would value it. Forcing herself to drag her eyes from the ring, she tried to read between the lines of the letter. There was no visit planned, and why say the present was promised? *This one is for you to value* was an odd way of putting it when Hanne's English was excellent. What was she trying to tell her? More to the point, what was she trying to ask her?

She was asking for help?

Some note of worth. Bank notes? Hanne needed money, but daren't say so? She'd refused offers of help in the past, so why now? The newspapers had written about Jews not being able to make a living and a huge emigration tax being levied, making it impossible for many to leave Germany. *Forced to retire* and *not be able to visit.* And he'd sold the shop for less than it was worth. Her eyes were drawn back to the ring – a trinket for her to value. Value… It was a real diamond? Real emeralds?

Hanne needed her to sell the ring and send her the money, and she had more trinkets she needed selling. Given the possible opening of packets and letters, it was a miracle the ring had arrived. Hanne had taken an enormous risk, and that itself should have told her this wasn't a simple gift.

She would have the ring valued and sell it for Hanne and her family, but how could she be sure bank notes would arrive safely? Hide them in something, a book, maybe? Even a book might be searched. Hanne couldn't give her clear instructions by letter or telephone. Phones were tapped in Germany.

There was only one option: Hanne needed cash, and she would have to take it in person and smuggle out more jewellery, if necessary. Her heart thudded. It could prove dangerous, but she was clear in her determination: Hanne needed her, and she would go.

Chapter Twenty-Six

Hawley Heath, England 1937

Emma stepped off the train at New Street, Birmingham. She'd reasoned that the best place to get a good valuation and price for Hanne's ring was from someone sympathetic to German Jews, and who better than a Jewish jeweller? The place to ask would be a synagogue, and she'd passed one at Singers Hill, close to the station, last time she was in Birmingham.

She patted her pocket for the tenth time to ensure the precious ring was still there in its envelope. At least, she hoped it was precious and she'd read Hanne's request correctly.

The door to the synagogue stood open. Should she cover her head or remove her shoes? She kicked off her shoes, pushed them to the side of the entrance, and walked bare-headed into the shadows.

A bearded figure turned to greet her. 'Shalom. Rabbi Abraham Cohen at your service. How may I help you?'

'Shalom, rabbi. I'm Emma Taylor. My grandfather was Matthew Joshua of Hawley Heath.'

'Joshua...' The rabbi stroked his beard. 'Matthew Joshua, the chain master?'

'Yes. I have a favour to ask. I have a cousin in Frankfurt, Hanne Bergman. She and her family want to leave Germany and come to England.'

He nodded. 'Terrible times for German Jews, for Jews everywhere. I'm not sure how I can help – the British government is wary of taking in refugees, and German Jews have passport restrictions, I believe. The Birmingham United Jewish Benevolent Board may know how it could be done. I can give you an address.'

'Thank you, that would be helpful. I wanted to sell this for Hanne.' She brought the packet from her pocket and unwrapped the jewel.

Rabbi Cohen scribbled an address on a piece of paper and handed it to her. His eyes opened wider when he saw the ring. 'That looks valuable. It has sentimental value, too?'

'Hanne's uncle is a jeweller. He had to sell his shop for much less than it was worth but has saved some jewellery. At least, I think that's what her letter means. She daren't write openly as letters are being intercepted, but the Nazi government has brought in huge taxes on Jewish wealth, and Hanne's family has little or no money. I hoped you might know of a jeweller who would give me a fair price.'

'There's one in Hurst Street. The owner is one of my flock, a Mr Friedman. He's a good man and fair. You can trust him.' He frowned. 'I have heard of these taxes. Hitler is forcing Jews to sell their businesses at, maybe, a fifth of their value, and then stings them with a tax of twenty-five percent of the true value. Many are left destitute, even owing the government money. The German authorities mustn't get to know about these jewels. If letters are being intercepted, how will you get the money to your cousin?'

'I plan to take it myself.'

He raised bushy eyebrows. 'A Jewess walking into the furnace of the devil?'

'My surname is Taylor, and I have a British passport. Why would they think I was Jewish?'

The rabbi smiled. 'Why would they think you were not?'

Did she look so Jewish? She'd never thought about her looks, but she took after her father. 'I think the British ambassador would have something to say if a British citizen was robbed of her money by a German while in Germany. I shall not be dissuaded.'

He bowed his head. 'May it be Your will, God of our God, God of our fathers, that You should lead this child in peace, and direct her steps in peace, and guide her in peace, and support her in peace, and cause her to reach her destination in life, joy, and peace, and return her in peace. Blessed are You, God, who hearkens to prayer.'

'Amen.' She smiled apologetically, unsure of the correct response.

'Go in peace, child.'

She left him praying for the Jews of Europe and Palestine. She hoped God was listening.

The jewellers' in Hurst Street had a glittering window display, and the prices had to be seen to be believed. Could Hanne's ring be worth so much?

'Mr Friedman?'

'I am he.'

She placed the ring on the shop counter. 'Rabbi Cohen said you would give me a fair price for this.'

The jeweller put a loupe to his eye and held the ring close, examining it minutely. 'It's an excellent piece. It's yours to sell, miss?' He removed the loupe from his eye and put the ring down. 'I'm an honest trader. I don't deal in stolen goods.'

'It belongs to my cousin in Germany. She has more that she

wishes to sell to raise money for her family to emigrate. I only ask for a fair price and that perhaps you will buy more if I can bring them to England.'

Mr Friedman waved a hand at the window. 'Those are retail prices. I have to make a profit – I have costs, rent, rates, wages…'

'I understand that. I'm a chain mistress. I know about running a business.'

'A chain mistress? I only know of one such. Joshua and Son. You're Matthew and Marion's granddaughter?'

'I am, sir. Emma Taylor. Willis Joshua was my father.'

'Sad affair, young Willis drowning. Very sad affair. Matthew and Marion were devastated.'

'You knew my father?'

'I did. I valued Matthew and Marion as customers and friends. They all came to synagogue when they were in Birmingham. A lovely family.'

That wasn't how Mom would have described them, but this man had seen another side of the Joshuas. 'What was he like? My father, that is.'

'An impetuous young man. Very charming and good looking. I expect he swept your mother off her feet – all the ladies loved him. You never knew him, then?'

'He died before I was born. Mom married Jack, and he brought me up as his own. Matthew died when I was very little, but I knew Grandma Marion. She was very good to me, and I inherited Heath Hall and the factory when she died.'

'She was a kind woman.' Mr Friedman's eyes went back to the ring. 'I will give you its trade value, plus a little extra for your cousin. Any relation of Matthew's is a friend of mine.' He pursed his lips. 'And if you bring me more, the deal is the same. This is between us, yes?'

He held out his hand, and she shook it. 'A deal between us. Thank you.'

He opened a safe behind the counter and handed her a bundle of notes and a receipt, which she pushed into her handbag, fastening the catch securely. When she left the shop, the jeweller was putting the ring in the window. Out of interest, she waited for him to add the price ticket. It was only five shillings more than he'd given her. So much for his profit.

Mr Friedman winked, and she smiled in gratitude.

***

The ferry docked at the port of Ostend, on the Belgian coast, and Emma picked up her luggage, ready to disembark. She'd hidden the precious reichsmarks in various places. Some in a book, some in a box of sandwiches, and some sewn into her clothing. She hoped they wouldn't find all of them if a German border guard or some other official searched her.

She'd walked into the bank a fortnight earlier with the equivalent of six-months' wages for the average chainmaker and had asked for it to be converted into German reichsmarks. According to the exchange rate, a hundred reichsmarks was worth about eight pounds, and eight pounds was around three-weeks' wages for the average working man. With this in mind, but with an eye to weight, she'd ordered ten and twenty reichsmark notes and some five reichsmark silver coins.

She'd collected them on her way to the station, which was only a couple of hours after she'd informed Mom what she was planning. Mom's words still rang in her ears. *"Emma, for God's sake, what are you thinking? You've read the news and heard the radio speeches. You know how dangerous this is for a Jew.*"

She wasn't a Jew, or at least, she was only half-Jewish and not a practising one. The rabbi had thought she was…

Mom had made her promise to telephone home as soon as she arrived in Germany. She'd conveniently forgotten that Jews weren't allowed to use public telephones in Germany, and she might meet with opposition if she attempted to use one. Did Hanne have a telephone? If not, someone would allow her to use theirs, surely – it would be worth a reichsmark to put Mom's mind at rest.

'Paspoort, juffrouw.'

She handed over her document to be stamped. As before, the border guard looked her up and down. Had she changed so much from her passport photograph in nine years? Would Hanne and Berek have changed so much that she wouldn't recognise them? The face of her beloved that she'd held so close to her heart all these years had faded. Would the spark she'd felt still be there, and if it was, what would she do about it?

The border guard thrust the passport into her hand. 'Volgende.' He waved her on with an impatient hand. 'Vlug, vlug.'

She boarded the Ostend to Vienna Orient Express, claimed a compartment and bunk, and stowed her luggage before making her way to the dining car. She was starving, not having eaten the sandwiches that hid some reichsmarks, and wanted to be sure of a table. Her luggage would be safe, wouldn't it? She'd locked it, tested the catch, and had the key in her pocket. Her heart thumped, and she half-turned back. Should she stay with her luggage or risk eating? She had to eat; it was too long a journey to go without food. She hurried on along the corridor.

The dining car filled quickly, and she was joined by an elderly man who complained about the weather, the food, and the cramped state of his compartment. She gobbled her meal, made her excuses, and ran back to her compartment to watch over her luggage and attempt to sleep. Not easy, as she discovered the grumbling man was in the next compartment and was now sharing his woes loudly with his companion.

Pulling her blanket over her ears, she let the rhythmic motion of the train lull her to sleep. A change in motion, and the sound of rattling chain and shouting, woke her.

She heard the familiar word "*paspoorten*" so they must be at the German border. Her heart thumped. There would be German border guards.

Doors banged along the corridor and boots thudded barely heard over the thumping of her heart. What had possessed her to travel to Germany?

'Reisepass.'

Taking a deep breath, she handed over her passport. She could do this.

'Wohin gehst du?' He frowned. 'Jüdisch?'

She knew what that word meant, at least, and last time she'd travelled, the guard had wanted to know where she was going. Edith had been a tremendous help, but this time, she had her compartment to herself. 'I'm English. I'm going to Frankfurt.'

He gripped her precious passport. 'Was hast du in Frankfurt vor?'

'I don't understand. I'm English.'

He repeated the question more loudly.

'It's no good you shouting at me. I don't speak German.'

He shrugged, gave her back her passport, and moved on to the next compartment.

Sleep evaded her; Aachen, Cologne, and Wiesbaden came and went through the long night with stops, and shunting, shouting, and whistles.

'Frankfurt Sud. Frankfurt Sud.'

She must have slept, after all. It was four-thirty in the morning, and the station lights shone through the window blind. She gathered her luggage and stepped down from the train.

Several soldiers in smart uniforms and shiny boots marched along the platform, pistols in holsters. They didn't wear brown shirts, so they weren't storm troopers. They weren't black, so not French, like the soldier who'd attacked her before. Were these the SS Hanne had spoken of?

She followed the other passengers, keeping close to them, out onto the street. She didn't know if trams ran so early, but she knew the way to Börneplatz, or Dominikanerplatz as it was now. Shop windows bore signs that read **Juden Verboten**, and there were posters like she'd seen before, depicting large ugly Jews trampling on people.

She raised her head and walked on, unashamed of being half-Jewish. She rested on a bench under some trees. Hanne wouldn't be up for hours.

A man pointed to a sign above the bench. **Keine Juden Erlaubt**. 'Drecksjude.' He spat at her and waved his arm at the sign. 'Juden verboten. Kannst du nicht lesen?'

She knew what Juden verboten meant. She wiped spittle from her face with the back of her hand and got to her feet. It was no use denying her Jewish heritage; it was written all over her face. And anyway, why should she? She walked on, her luggage getting heavier and heavier. Everywhere, strode armed men in uniforms, and every building bore signs saying Jews were forbidden.

Somehow, she had to help get Hanne and her family out of Germany.

Chapter Twenty-Seven

Frankfurt, Germany 1937

Hanne opened the door to a knock, unsure who it could be so early. 'Emma? What are you doing here?' She grabbed her cousin's arm and pulled her inside the house, luggage and all. 'Why didn't you tell me you were coming?'

Emma put down her bags. 'I knew you'd tell me not to come, and I didn't trust German post with bank notes.'

'You sold the ring?'

Emma nodded. 'Was that what you wanted me to do? I got a good price for it, I think, and the jeweller is prepared to buy more from me.'

'I knew you'd understand. Uncle Saul said it was too risky, but you did it.' She threw her arms around Emma and hugged her. 'You are wonderful.'

Emma blushed bright scarlet.

'Now, I've embarrassed you.' She kissed Emma on the cheek. 'I'm so pleased to see you. I love you so much, Emma.'

Emma's eyes shone with unshed tears. 'I love you, too, Hanne. It's so good to see you again. Are you all well? Tell me what is happening here – trying to judge from your letters is hard.'

'All in good time, cousin. First, we shall have breakfast, and you shall meet Asher.' She picked up one of Emma's bags and took her by the hand. 'Mutter, Berek, Uncle Saul, look who's here. Emma has sold the ring.'

'Emma, child.' Uncle Saul kissed Emma on both cheeks. 'Thank you, but you shouldn't have risked yourself for us.'

'I didn't meet with any trouble, apart from a man who objected to me sitting on a bench.' Emma frowned. 'There are an awful lot of posters and signs forbidding Jews. Is it like this everywhere in Frankfurt?'

'Everywhere in Germany, Emma.' Berek's face showed his concern. 'Emma, the man objected, because you look like his idea of a Jewish woman. We know the places to avoid, but people are being arrested all the while for doing nothing wrong. It was very risky for you to travel alone.' He smiled. 'But very brave.'

Emma blushed even more scarlet.

'Come, Emma. You must want to freshen up after your journey. You know where the bathroom is. I'll make breakfast. Berek, take her bags to our room. She and I can share a bed. You won't mind sleeping on the sofa, will you, Berek?'

'And where will Uncle Saul sleep?'

'Oh, well, you'll have to sleep on the floor, then, Berek.'

Emma looked mortified. 'I'm putting everyone about. I'm so sorry, I didn't realise Uncle Saul was staying with you – I don't mind sleeping on the floor, or I can stay in a hotel.'

Berek picked up Emma's luggage. 'I can't let a guest sleep on the floor, Emma. And you won't find a hotel that will take a Jew.'

Emma clutched her handbag tighter. 'I have a British passport.'

'They won't risk it, Emma. Jews are forbidden from all kinds of things, and anyway, most hotels are in Aryan hands, now. You wouldn't be welcome.' Berek's voice was bitter. 'We're not welcome anywhere. We can't work, we've lost our businesses, and what we had left they've taken in taxes. What are we

251

supposed to do?'

Berek and Emma disappeared into the bedroom, still talking, and she set the kettle to boil. The apartment had become crowded, but they'd manage. Emma had brought with her a possible lifeline, and maybe even a way of future escape for them all. A little inconvenience was a small price to pay for freedom.

Over breakfast, talk turned to the state of Germany. Emma wanted to know all the details.

Emma took a sip of coffee. 'I heard Germany has sided with Italy in the war in Spain.'

Mutter's cup paused before it reached her lips. 'They bombed Guernica. We heard reports of it on the radio. And they seem determined to destroy Madrid.' Mutter put down her cup. 'You mustn't mention we have a radio, Emma.'

'I won't. Hitler really has geared up for war?'

'So, it would seem, Emma. Hitler and Mussolini signed a treaty. They call it the Berlin-Rome axis. They're supporting Franco's Fascists. And Hitler has also signed a treaty with Japan to fight Soviet communism. He's gathering allies.'

Emma shook her head. 'And all Britain can do is agree with France on a non-intervention policy.' She smiled briefly. 'We have a radio, too. We hear news of Germany on the Empire Service.'

Uncle Saul changed the subject abruptly. 'You didn't have trouble selling the ring Hanne sent?'

'A local rabbi recommended a jeweller, a Mr Friedman.'

'And you say he'll take more jewellery. You trust him?'

Emma nodded. 'He's Jewish and wanted to help. I saw the

price he put on the ring in his window. He'll make hardly anything for his trouble.' Emma fetched her bag and placed a bundle of notes and some coins on the table. 'I hid some in a book, and some I sewed into my clothing. I shall need a needle and thread to make repairs.' She held up a few rather damp looking notes. 'And I had to wash these in the kitchen sink. I hid them in my sandwiches. 'If you trust me to do it, I can smuggle out more jewels the same way.'

'Of course, we trust you.'

There were murmurs of assent. She would trust Emma with her life, with all their lives. It was the Nazis, who followed Hitler like a flock of mindless sheep, she didn't trust.

***

Emma had fallen in love with Asher at first sight. Was that her penance in life, her atonement to quell the Joshua curse, to fall in love with people she couldn't have? She'd never have a child of her own, not now. At thirty, she felt she was too old to raise a child even if she did find a man she wanted to father it. Charlie would have made a great father, but she'd never managed to persuade herself it was right to have sex with a man just to become pregnant. Love had to feature in the equation, and she didn't love Charlie in that way.

She'd promised to send Asher something for his sixth birthday later that summer. It had been a spontaneous promise before she'd thought of the likely possibility of parcels being opened. Would border or postal officers search a child's toy? Might it be a way of secretly getting money to Hanne?

She undressed and shrugged into her nightdress, feeling oddly embarrassed in front of Hanne, who had no such qualms. Hanne was beautiful with evenly tanned, flawless skin, and childbearing hadn't spoiled her figure.

'Asher is a lovely child, Hanne. Didn't you want more children – I'm sorry, that's a personal question.'

Hanne slipped into her own nightdress. 'I'd have loved more children, Emma, but Berek and I discussed it and decided we shouldn't. With Germany as it is at the moment, I regret having Asher. No, that's not true. I could never regret Asher, but I fear for him.'

'I can see why. Germany has changed since I was last here. It must be frightening to live this way, never knowing what discrimination you'll face next.'

'Christians think Hitler is God's punishment on the Jews, and we deserve it. Even the pope hasn't denounced Hitler, in fact, he says we killed God, because Catholics believe Jesus was the son of God and therefore God.' Hanne brushed a stray strand of dark hair from her face. 'It isn't our belief, and anyway, why should we be punished for our forebears' crimes? Catholics have killed enough people who didn't share their beliefs. No religion or people are entirely innocent.'

She glanced at the bed, waiting for Hanne to invite her. To lie where Berek laid seemed too much of a liberty. She looked away. 'People are always searching for someone to blame for their own inadequacies and insecurities. I've heard some of Hitler's speeches on the radio. The weaker his argument, the greater his rhetoric, and the louder he shouts.

'But people listen, and anti-Semitism has spread to Austria, Poland, Romania, America... Where are we supposed to live, Emma, if not in Germany?'

'England, Hanne. You should all come to England.'

254

'I wish we could, but Britain doesn't want us either.

'But if you have money and can prove you can pay your way.'

Hanne shrugged. 'Maybe, but anyway, Mutter isn't well enough to travel so far. They accept some children, on a temporary basis, because they're not a threat to jobs, but children need to be sponsored, and some are sent on to America.'

'I would sponsor Asher, you know that, but you wouldn't send him to England alone?'

'No, of course not. Not unless things get much worse. He's too young to be away from us.'

How much worse did they did need to get? Could she be parted from her child if she had one? No, Hanne was right; it would be a last resort.

Hanne climbed into bed and patted the sheet beside her. Last time she'd stayed, Hanne had given up her single bed and slept on the floor. Now it was poor Berek.

'Honestly, Hanne. I don't mind sleeping on the floor. I feel awful turning Berek out of his bed.'

Hanne laughed. 'He wouldn't hear of it, Emma. He would do anything for you. We all would.'

She gave in gracefully and slipped beneath the covers. 'Then maybe you'll use some of the money I brought to buy a camp bed. If I'm coming again with more cash, we shall need one. In fact, if Uncle Saul is staying permanently, buy two camp beds.'

'We'll see to it first thing in the morning.' Hanne's eyes filled with tears. 'I wish you didn't have to risk yourself so much, Emma. You look too Jewish to escape notice.'

'Oh, Hanne.' She put her arms around her cousin and let her

nestle her head on her shoulder. 'It'll be all right. We'll find a way to get you to England.' Mutter looked so frail compared to nine years ago; could the woman endure such a journey?

Hanne looked up at her as she reached out to switch off the bedside light. 'I'm glad you're here, Emma. But whatever you do, don't lose your British passport.'

She held Hanne in her arms listening to her quiet breathing as the house slept. This was the challenge she'd been given, and she would rise to it. She would get Hanne and her family to safety if it killed her.

Next morning, Uncle Saul laid out a selection of jewellery on the table. 'I'm concerned about giving you too much to take at a time, Emma. If you are caught with it, they'll know you are trying to get Jewish wealth out of the country, and that's forbidden. One or two items, three maybe, you could say are personal jewellery. In fact, wearing them openly might be the best deception.'

Mutter dry-washed her hands. 'Saul, isn't that risking her being robbed? If she was fair-haired, Aryan-looking, I wouldn't worry, but she isn't. Suppose the SS attack first and ask to see her passport later? It's too risky.'

Uncle Saul raised a questioning brow. 'Emma?'

Berek raised a hand to stop her answering. 'It isn't fair to ask her, Saul.'

'Emma's safety comes first.'

She smiled at Hanne's concern, but she needed to help. 'I don't mind wearing them if that's what you think is best, but I managed to get coins and bank notes here undetected. I can get gems out the same way. We can sew them into my clothing and hide them in bread rolls.'

Hanne wasn't deterred. 'But too many at once risks you carrying a lot of money next time you come.'

Berek ran a hand across his brow, his eyes full of worry. 'And too few means the risk of extra journeys when the situation is getting worse all the while.'

'Berek, what if I sent instalments hidden in toys for Asher? Would they search a child's toy coming into the country?'

'I don't know. I suppose they're more likely to search items leaving the country. It's taking money out they're trying to stop. They want to confiscate everything we have in order to fund rearmament. They must have stolen millions already.'

Uncle Saul chose six rings with the largest diamonds and pushed them towards her. 'These are small enough to be sewn into the hem of your dress or coat.' He pushed a brooch after them. 'This doesn't look as if it's worth much, so you would be safe to wear it. An honest jeweller will give you its true value. And this–' He stood with a beautiful sapphire necklace laced between his fingers, brushed her hair aside, and fastened the necklace around her neck. '–must not be sold. It's yours to keep come what may.'

She fingered the sapphires her vision blurring. 'I shall treasure it always. Thank you.'

Once the jewels were safely hidden, she announced her intention to return to England. 'The train leaves just after two o'clock in the morning from the main station.'

Hanne frowned. 'Must you leave so soon?'

She'd have loved to have stayed longer, but she was in the way, and Berek needed his wife back. 'I want to get the money to you as soon as possible. Look out for a small parcel for Asher, let me know as soon as you get it, and I'll send another.'

Berek nodded. 'Someone must go with you to the station.'

'I'll go.' Hanne was quick to volunteer. 'We can get the night tram, and I'll come back the same way. At that time in the morning, I'll be quite safe.'

'I should go with Emma, Hanne. If something should happen to her –'

'You're needed here, Berek, to look after Mutter, Uncle Saul, and Asher. Suppose we get another gang of hoodlums trying to break in? Two men in the apartment stand more chance of stopping them than one. Think of Asher, please. Emma and I will be fine on the tram.'

Berek didn't look happy. 'I'll walk you both to the tram, at least, and meet you off it when you come back, Hanne.'

None of them went to bed that night. Just after midnight, she said her tearful goodbyes to Mutter and Uncle Saul, and then to Berek. She and Hanne boarded the tram and rode in silence to the station. The train was standing at the platform. They had a matter of minutes before she left, maybe forever.

Hanne broke the tense silence. 'Emma, about Asher. You offered to sponsor him. Can you find out how I could get him to England? If things here should get worse, I could send you a message.' Hanne swallowed tears. 'If things get worse, will you take my son to England?'

She hugged her cousin her cheeks wet with Hanne's tears. 'Of course, I will, Hanne.'

'People have been arrested for no reason and sent to camps. If something should happen to me and Berek, you'll look after him as your own?'

'Hanne, please, don't say that. I couldn't bear to lose you.'

Hanne's eyes sparkled with tears and echoed the love she felt in her own heart. 'I love you so much, Hanne.'

'I love you too, Emma. I've loved you since the first moment I saw you.'

Their lips met, tentative at first, and then with a passion she'd never known before. They drew apart as the train whistle sounded and carriage doors began to slam.

She gathered her luggage and ran, leaving her heart with the woman she loved.

Chapter Twenty-Eight

Frankfurt, Germany 1937

The train rumbled through the night, accompanied by snoring from the overweight woman on the bottom bunk, who'd been fast asleep when Emma boarded the train.

She couldn't sleep. Her lips still felt the pressure of Hanne's upon them, and the thrill in the pit of her stomach reminded her of the first real sexual stirrings she'd felt. She hadn't meant for that kiss to happen; she'd determined to leave her cousin in blissful ignorance of her true feelings, but she hadn't reckoned on Hanne feeling the same way about her. What did this mean for Berek and Asher? What can of worms had her moment of weakness opened?

'Oh, Hanne. Shall I ever see you again?' She let her tears fall. Mom had been right to berate her for tearing Hanne's family apart. How would her mother feel if she knew it was Hanne, not Berek, who was the love of her life?

She'd long accepted that she was a lesbian and doomed to a single and lonely life, but society swept the subject of female sexual perversions under the carpet in England; it wasn't fashionably or excitingly outrageous as Oscar Wilde had made being a homosexual male even if sodomy was a criminal act. Lesbianism wasn't illegal, but it was still judged scandalous behaviour that would reflect poorly on her family.

Germany seemed more liberated, unless you were a Jew, of course.

'Weisbaden. Weisbaden.' The voice grew louder along the

corridor and faded as the guard hurried past.

The train stopped, and she peered at her watch in the light of the carriage lamp. Two-forty-five. Doors slammed, feet thudded past her window, and the train juddered into life again.

She drifted to sleep; Hanne was in her arms, her skin smooth, her lips sweet.

'Nächster Halt Köln.'

Cologne. Five-thirty. She punched her feather pillow and yawned. It was light outside. Her companion snored on.

An hour later, they reached Aachen. Next would be the German border with Belgium. Once over the border, she'd feel safe. She pushed aside the blind and peeped through the window. Judging by the sun, they'd turned south-west towards Herbesthal in Belgium.

She threw on her clothes. Not long now.

Strident German tones echoed along the corridor, and their compartment door flew open. 'Zehn Minuten bis zur belgischen Grenze. Halten sie ihre Pässe zur Kontrolle bereit.'

The door slammed shut, and another door crashed open along the carriage. If the whole train wasn't awake by now, it would be a wonder.

The woman on the other bunk stirred and opened her eyes. 'Where are we?'

'Belgian border.' Never had her heart thundered so loudly, not even when Hanne had kissed her, or had she kissed Hanne? She took her passport from her bag and took a deep, calming breath.

The train rattled to a stop, and she raised the blind to see barriers, wire, and a guard tower. They would change engines, for from here, they'd be pulled by a Belgian engine. Belgian border guards, the dreaded Nazi SS among them, flung open carriage doors and stormed along corridors.

'Paspoort, mevrouw.'

Her travelling companion handed over her passport and the border guard examined and stamped it, but the blond SS officer pushed the guard aside.

She cringed as the man's blue eyes fixed on hers. 'Jüdin, das ist dein Gepäck?' The man pointed to her luggage with his pistol. 'Diese?'

She nodded, and he pulled the bag down and opened it, spreading her belongings across the carriage and examining each one. He opened the tin that held her bread rolls and lifted one to his lips. She stopped breathing; if he took a bite… He wrinkled his nose in disgust and dropped the roll back in the tin, snapping shut the lid.

'Aufstehen!' He made a sign with his pistol for her to stand, so she got to her feet. Holding the pistol to her throat, he ran one hand across her body, lingering on her breasts before caressing her hips and stomach. She shuddered but remained still, trying to focus on the finger on the trigger and stop shaking. Sweat trickled between her breasts. He licked his lips and raised the hem of her dress to put his fingers between her legs.

Her instinct was to clamp her legs together, but she had to distract the man from the hem of her dress. She shifted her weight and slightly parted her legs. He smiled and probed deeper. Satisfied she wasn't hiding anything of value in her underwear, his eyes focussed on the necklace Uncle Saul had given her. She took a deep breath and her chest heaved. He lifted the necklace from where it lay between her breasts and then yanked it off, breaking the fine gold chain.

'That's mine. Give it back.'

'Was musstest du dafür tun, Jüdenhure?'

He thought she was a whore? 'It was a gift. Give it back.' She thrust her passport in his face. 'English, nicht Jüdisch. Give me back my necklace.'

Whatever you do, don't lose your British passport. Without it, she was lost, and she'd just denied her Jewish heritage; Grandma Joshua would turn in her grave.

He snatched the passport and handed it to the border guard without looking away from her. The guard stamped it. 'Ze is Engelse, officier.'

'Englisch?' He looked at the passport and handed it back to her.

'And my necklace? Do you steal from British citizens?' She pointed to the woman. 'I have a witness. I shall report you to the British Embassy.'

He threw it at her feet and stamped out of the compartment and into the next. Sinking to the floor, her courage spent, she dissolved in a flood of tears.

'There, there, dear.' The woman passed her a clean handkerchief. 'You did well. Those SS officers are a law unto themselves. He'd have shot you just as easily as return your necklace if you hadn't been British.'

She swallowed bile and picked up the broken necklace. 'I should never have worn it, but if it had been found in my luggage, he might have thought I was smuggling it out.'

'And you're not?' The woman smiled. 'I know my jewellery, and that's a very expensive piece to wear on a train journey.'

'Is it?' Sapphires glittered in her hand. 'It was a gift from a friend.'

'He must be a very good friend, dear.'

She smiled, remembering Uncle Saul's kind face. 'Yes, he is a very good friend.'

The sudden movement of the train brought her back to the present. The guard post drifted behind them in a pall of smoke and steam. She was over the border and into Belgium. She was safe.

***

Hanne listened to the secret radio in her bedroom to distract her from her inner turmoil. Emma had turned her fragile world upside-down and waiting to hear that she'd arrived home in England safely was tearing her apart. Guilt tore her apart even more effectively. Not because of her faith: while it expressly forbade male homosexuality, it didn't forbid intimate relations between women. Many Jewish lesbians lived as such openly in Frankfurt, but that wasn't the point; she should never have kissed Emma when she loved Berek.

She couldn't be a lesbian when she enjoyed sex with her husband, yet if she'd allowed herself to admit her feelings for Emma when they first met, if she'd known Emma had felt the same about her, would she have married Berek? Probably not, and she'd have missed loving a wonderful man, and she wouldn't have had Asher.

She couldn't regret her life's path despite her present pain. She must push Emma to a corner of her heart, knowing her future lay with Berek and it could be years before it was safe for her and Emma to meet again, but it was hard, so hard.

Was this why Emma had never married and why she hadn't

come to her and Berek's wedding? Oh, poor Emma, to have loved her for so long without hope of a relationship. Did she hope for one now? If so, Emma would be heartbroken, because she couldn't hurt Berek. She loved both Berek and Emma, and she must take her and Emma's secret love to her grave.

'*Neville Chamberlain, Britain's new prime minister, is proposing to partition Palestine. Arab and Jewish states, separated by a mandated area incorporating Jerusalem and Nazareth. Arabs are demanding a single state with minority rights for Jews.*'

The mention of Palestine had interrupted her thoughts. Could Arabs and Jews live peaceably side by side?

'*Japan has launched an attack on China. Earlier this year Germany signed a pact with Japan to fight Soviet communism. Communism is finding a foothold in China, and Hitler's Germany will not tolerate Bolsheviks or Jews.*'

It seemed no one was going to live in peace. Not for the first time since Emma left, she'd wished they'd agreed a code to alert Emma she was sending Asher to safety. That kiss had driven all thoughts of danger from her mind.

A knock on the door had her taut as a bowstring. Heart in mouth, she opened it a crack.

'Parcel for Master A Bergman.'

Only the postman. She opened the door wider and recognised Emma's handwriting. 'Thank you.'

He looked at the stamp. 'It's from England.'

Emma had got home safely. Her heart thudded, and she held out her hand to take it; it didn't look as if it had been opened, and it could be full of banknotes. 'Yes, it's probably a present for my son from my cousin.'

The postman didn't hand it over but moved forward to step inside the hallway.

Her hands trembled. 'He'll be six. My son will be six. It will be a toy.'

'Yes, a toy. I wondered if I might have the stamps. I collect stamps.'

'Yes, of course.' This was a complication she didn't need. The postman would notice parcels from England. How could she explain the next one and the next? If he grew suspicious, he'd report it, and she'd have German intelligence breaking down her door. 'I'll fetch scissors to cut them off.'

He placed the package on the table, and she cut open the wrapping. The parcel inside was wrapped in pretty paper with a label addressed to Asher. Thank goodness Emma had thought to do that.

She cut off the paper with the stamps on and handed it to the postman. 'Emma sends Asher small gifts from time to time. She's very generous. If you're not on duty, I'll keep the stamps for you, if you like.'

'Thank you, Frau Bergman.' He smiled, something she'd become unaccustomed to, and left whistling.

She checked through the window that he'd left the building before opening the parcel. Inside was a toy lorry. Asher would love it, but where were the notes? There was a letter.

My darling Hanne,

I hope you are well and Asher likes his present. I had an eventful journey home, but arrived safely with luggage intact. I met our mutual friend, Mr Friedman in Birmingham the week before last. He sends lots of love to you. His love is worth having in small doses, but he can be a bit overwhelming in large doses! Anyway, I shall feel warm inside to think of Asher playing with his new lorry and carrying his precious items around in it.

I miss you, Hanne. I hope what I said at our last meeting hasn't caused you sleepless nights. I would hate to think I'd upset you. You and Berek and Asher are very special to me. I am wearing the lovely necklace Uncle Saul gave me. Mom is quite envious.

I hope we shall meet again, but it may not be for a while, I fear. Hold me in your heart as I hold you in mine. Stay safe, Hanne.

All my love

Emma.

She ran her fingers across the words imagining Emma writing them, feeling the connection. Emma was being cryptic about their love and the cash, as she must.

Emma had got home with the jewels, that was fairly clear. Mr Friedman was the name of the jeweller she sold the gems to, so his love must be money. *Small doses* was their agreement not to send all the notes in one consignment but there was no indication that the money would be delayed, so what had happened to it?

Asher didn't have precious items to put in the lorry. Bank notes? She picked up the lorry. It had back doors that opened, and inside was a package decorated to look like a stack of boxes; inside that was a bundle of notes.

'Oh, bless you, Emma.' She brushed away tears. 'May the God of Abraham, Isaac, and Israel protect you, my love.'

Chapter Twenty-Nine

Hawley Heath, England 1938

My darling Emma,

Emma smiled and held the notepaper to her lips to taste and breathe in the smell of lavender, the scent that reminded her of Hanne. It was six months since her return from Frankfurt, six long months away from the woman she loved, laced with loneliness, happiness, fear, and pain.

It was fear that killed her smile. The noose around the necks of Jews in Europe was tightening, and it wasn't just Jews who were suffering.

Another concentration camp had opened, this one at Buchenwald near Weimar, and those who spoke out against Nazi rule found themselves arrested and interned.

Then, Jews in Czechoslovakia were accused of sacrilege in the town of Hummené, and there'd been vicious assaults on Jews in Poland.

A radio report in September had chilled her to the bone. Six hundred thousand troops paraded at Nuremberg in front of Hitler, the number terrifying and mind-numbing. Hitler had declared an end to the Treaty of Versailles, and the rally at Nuremberg was a very public renunciation of the military restrictions placed on Germany at the end of the war.

Roosevelt, the American president, had tried to warn the world of Hitler's evil intent, but his words fell on deaf ears. The British policy of appeasement avoided facing the threat Hitler posed head on. If she, a young chain mistress from the Black Country, could see it, why couldn't the government? Maybe it was because they hadn't fallen in love with a Jew.

Maybe they hadn't heard speeches by people like Goebbels. *"The Jew is the plastic demon of decomposition. Where he finds filth and decay, he surfaces and begins his butcher's work among the nations. He hides behind a mask and presents himself as a friend to his victims, and before they know it, he has broken their neck."* According to Goebbels, Jews were responsible for all the ills in the world.

More disturbing was an article in a Nazi newspaper Hanne had cut out and sent to her.

The Eradication of the Less Valuable from Society seemed to be an ongoing argument centred around the cost of keeping mentally ill patients in hospitals. It followed on from a Nazi Marital Health Law, which forbade people with hereditary diseases from marrying 'genetically fit' partners, and the Law for the Prevention of Genetically Diseased Offspring, a desire for *"racial hygiene"*, which allowed the legal sterilisation of people with genetic diseases.

While she could see the logic on a purely practical or economical level against preventing the births of children with debilitating genetic problems, on an emotional and humanitarian level, there was much more to consider. With Hitler in charge, the whole subject of the less valuable in society took on a more sinister aspect. What gave Hitler the moral right to judge whose life was worthless? Did he think he was God?

That he'd do it legally, by passing an abominable act, was not in doubt. What did the future hold then for the sick, the physically or mentally handicapped, or for Jews?

She put the article down, wiped her hands on her dress as if her fingers were tainted, and turned back to Hanne's letter.

Your last gift arrived safely. Asher so loves opening your little presents. I hope the recipe book I sent was of use to you. Mutter's bratwurst is the best I've tasted.

The book had had gemstones hidden in its spine, although she'd had to tear it apart to find them. She had yet to take them to Birmingham to sell. She blessed the day she'd met Mr Friedman; he'd mended the chain on her sapphire necklace and refused to let her pay for the repair.

Asher keeps asking when he can see his Auntie Emma. Perhaps he could come to stay with you when he's a little older. It would be an experience for him, but I'm not sure if you can prepare for such a visit or what the journey would be like. I've never travelled across Europe as you have. Perhaps, we could arrange for you to meet him partway? I would come with him if Mutter didn't need me here. I so long to see you again.

Hanne seemed to be preparing to send Asher to England, but when? If only they'd discussed this in more detail instead of blowing caution to the winds with that kiss. She read the letter again. Hanne was asking her to discover how it might be done and to put things in place should it be necessary. There were organisations in England that might know. He'd need papers and a safe route if things got desperate enough for Hanne to send him. She wished Hanne would come as well, but if her mother needed her, she would stay behind.

Storm clouds are gathering. I fear we may have thunder.

Was that a comment on the weather or a warning? Japan and China were at war. Germany had signed a pact with Italy and Japan, and before Christmas, Japan had captured Nanking and massacred tens, if not hundreds, of thousands of Chinese. With the Treaty of Versailles in tatters, were Hitler and his allies preparing for war?

***

Rosie pushed the order book aside with satisfaction. Business had picked up over the last twelve months with several large orders for cable chain. Swan Hunter and Cammell Laird in the north of England, and in Scotland, Fairfield's at Govan, Yarrow's at Scotstoun, Denny's at Dumbarton, not to mention Brown's at Clydebank were all building ships again.

The crash of iron on iron and the soft whoosh of the steam bellows had once again become the heartbeat of her life. Every forge was lit, every man and woman employed, and the smell of breeze, iron, and sweat filled the hot air with comforting familiarity. Once again, men held their heads high, families had food on their tables, and with the mines, rolling mills, and blast furnaces working to capacity, the town prospered.

Satisfaction came at a price: America, Japan, and Germany were also building ships. Joshua and Son would not be tendering for Japanese or German ships, that was for sure. If it came to another war, she didn't want the company stamp on enemy anchor cable.

The thought of war terrified her, but it was fairly obvious that Hitler was planning for it, and Britain was preparing for it as a precaution. At least, she hoped it was only a precaution. Jack had been lucky to come home uninjured, although he'd suffered nightmares for months and still did occasionally.

She fingered the strap of one of the cases that had arrived that morning, one for every man, woman, and child in the family, praying they'd never have to use them. Gas masks – she'd heard men tell of the friends who'd died of gassing in France and knew men who still suffered from the effects. George was twenty-eight and Theo twenty-five, and if they were conscripted, they'd have to fight. So many young men's lives had been wasted during the war, and the dread of losing her sons kept her awake at night.

Britain had begun operating a naval base in Singapore in response to the terrible massacre of Chinese citizens by Japan, and Nazi Germany's Wehrmacht had crossed the border into Austria. She'd seen a news bulletin about Austrians gathered in Heldenplatz in Vienna to hear Hitler's declaration of Austria's annexation. He spoke of Anschluss – a united Austria and Germany. Hitler had taken Austria peacefully, but with a large show of force.

And force to prevent it was something Britain and the rest of Europe were reluctant to use. She took a gas mask from its case and put it on, adjusting the strap to fit. It would be horrible to wear, like being shut in a coffin with no air. She ripped the hateful thing off. War must be a threat if the government thought these were necessary.

At least Emma seemed happier since she'd been to visit Hanne. She spent little time in the factory nowadays, and more and more time with the Jewish community in Birmingham. Selling Hanne's uncle's secret jewels and getting money to her beleaguered cousin in Frankfurt had given her a mission in life. If it kept her happy and in England, it was all to the good.

She picked up the leaflet that had come with the gas mask. Advice on its fitting and use, what to do in the event of an air raid, and a plea to turn over any spare land to growing food. Air raids? Gas? Rationing? War had come calling. She fingered the gas mask again. There had even been talk of evacuating women and children from danger areas. Was anywhere truly safe?

Jack poked his head around the door. 'Is Emma about?'

'She's gone to Birmingham.'

'Oh. There's a man here says he's taking the railings.'

'What railings?'

'Any iron gates and railings that aren't keeping in livestock.'

'What for?'

'They're to be melted down for munitions.'

Her heart thumped. This was happening, and no amount of denying the fact would change a thing. Britain needed to be ready to stand against Hitler. 'Tell him to take them. We can bring any outside iron stock inside. I take it he isn't requisitioning our iron rod?' She wished she hadn't used the word requisition – it would remind Jack of the loss of his beloved horses to the last war.

She'd talk to Emma when she got home about turning over the rest of the lawn to cultivation and extending the allotments. And she'd see about forming a Hawley Heath branch of the new Women's Voluntary Service set up to help the Air Raid Precautions organisation. If war with all its associated dangers and hardships was coming to Hawley Heath, they had to make sure Hawley Heath was ready.

***

Frankfurt, Germany 1938

The radio, turned low, played English band music while Hanne stuffed two diamond necklaces with matching bracelets into a cloth bag, tied the neck with ribbon, and pushed the bundle inside a small mantel clock. The clock would never run again, Uncle Saul had removed part of the movement to make room for jewellery, but it looked the part and wasn't expensive enough for

273

anyone to take notice of. It was just a cheap clock without a winding key.

Mutter had taken to her bed. The Jewish doctor had called and declared her heart was failing; the stress and fear of being a Jew in Nazi Germany had taken its toll on her frail body. And now, Hitler had declared himself supreme commander of the Wehrmacht, which meant the armed forces were directly under his command. He had made himself unchallengeable. What hope remained for peace?

The funds hidden in the apartment were growing, but did they have enough to get the entire family out of the country? Emma's letter suggested border guards had searched her on her way home, so what were the chances of them getting their carefully garnered money out with them? And that supposed Mutter was fit to travel, and they could find a country that would take them.

Sweden had tightened its immigration control, Romanian Jews had had their citizenship revoked, and in Austria, now annexed to Germany, Jews had had their businesses taken over by Nazis. Poland, too, was threatening to revoke the citizenship of Polish Jews in Germany. The whole of Eastern Europe was closed to them, and Austrian Jews were being forced to emigrate, but to where? Those who wanted to leave were competing for increasingly fewer places.

She packed the clock in a cardboard box and chewed the end of her pen.

My darling Emma,

How I miss you. I hope this little clock will remind you of me and the time we spent together. It doesn't keep good time, I think it needs something adjusting inside, but it's a pretty piece. Maybe you will make it work better.

She leaned closer to the radio to catch the news.

'Anti-Jewish riots are continuing in Poland. Many Jews have been killed or injured.'

Sweat beaded on her brow, and the back of her neck felt sticky. Anti-Semitism was like a disease, spreading from person to person, and country to country, with no conscious thought of the victims. Jews across Europe lived in constant fear. How long before violence erupted again in Germany, in Frankfurt, on Dominikanerplatz?

As if to answer her question, shouting erupted down on the Platz, and she crossed to the window. SS officers were beating a man around the head and threatening to make him scrub the street like Jews had to do in Austria.

The man was kneeling in fear and picking gravel from the ground. Powerless to help, she drew the curtain, but she couldn't block out the image, the shouting, or the fear.

'Asher?' Her son was beneath the table, holding a kitchen knife in his hand. He had seen so much hatred and violence. 'It's all right, Asher. No one will hurt you.'

She was no longer sure that was true. Without a pre-arranged a code for Asher's escape from danger, she must write something that Emma would understand.

Asher is becoming more impatient. He so wants to see his auntie again.

The radio announcer made her pen pause midway to the paper. *'In Germany, Jews are now excluded from the economy. They must register assets of over five thousand reichsmarks, and Jewish assets are being seized. In Austria, it is reported that Jews in Vienna are being made to eat grass.'*

Grass? That couldn't be true. 'Oh, God, protect us from these Nazis.' Their hiding places must be fool proof. If they didn't declare their hoarded money, and it was discovered, the repercussions didn't bear thinking about. Men had been sent to Dachau or Sachsenhausen for less.

'The Jewish community in Britain has asked the government to intercede on behalf of the Jews of Europe.'

Help couldn't come too soon. Her family were playing a dangerous game.

Chapter Thirty

Hawley Heath, England 1938

Emma stood with her hands on her hips. 'But there must be something we can do.'

The rabbi opened his hands palm upwards in a gesture of futility. 'The influx of Austrian Jews has put an immense strain on the government. They examine every visa, looking for a reason to refuse entry.'

'But the Jewish community must be able to put their case. My cousin and her family are in danger in Germany.'

'And so are many others. Emma, my child, what will happen if too many Jews are allowed into England? We are universally feared and hated. Hitler has made sure of that. People will turn against us. You think we do nothing, say nothing, but Jews have no voice.'

'Is that true, or are you just concerned for your own businesses? Is it that you don't want your peaceful lives here upsetting by immigrants? We were all immigrants once.'

The rabbi bowed his head. 'There is something in what you say. Established communities don't welcome strangers easily. We become inward looking, withdrawn, and defensive. I suppose it's a natural phenomenon in a minority group.'

'Hanne's family has money. They could support themselves until they find work.'

The rabbi raised an eyebrow. 'They are fortunate from what I have heard about others. That would help their application, but there you have it – until they find work – adults are a threat to jobs despite unemployment having decreased. The fear of the recession still hangs over us.' He sighed, making her feel even more helpless. 'Children are easier to get into England if we can prove they won't be a burden on the country.'

'I will sponsor Asher. Hanne knows that. Her last letter sounded as if she might send him. I know she doesn't want to, but she daren't write openly of her plans.' She clenched and unclenched her fists. 'How it's to be done, I don't know. Hanne suggested I meet him partway, but unless I know the route he will take and the time…'

'God will find a way, Emma. I will pray for them.'

She bit back a retort about her lack of trust in God. 'Thank you, Rabbi.'

'You could contact the Jewish Refugees Committee in London and the Children's Inter-Aid Committee. I know they have brought in a few children. Contact Mrs Skelton and Mrs Bendit. They may be able to help you. The Central British Fund and the Save the Children Fund support the children's committee, I believe.'

'Thank you, Rabbi.'

'And if all else fails, Rabbi Solomon Schonfeld is the Chief Rabbi's son-in-law. He has strong views on bringing in refugee children. He has been to Austria to that end with some success.'

'He sounds like a man to approach. Thank you again, Rabbi.'

'May the god of Abraham, Isaac, and Israel go with you and keep you all safe.'

'And you, Rabbi.' She drove back to Hawley Heath, wondering

if the entire world had its head buried in the sand, hoping the problem of re-homing Jewish refugees would go away if they ignored it.

***

A warm, dry spring had been followed by June gales that had seen bedsheets flapping on lines and a wet July where washing had dripped from rails over baths, ranges, and fires.

Emma looked out across the new areas put down to food production, and the men digging an air-raid shelter at the bottom of the hill, to dark blankets of smoke and threatening rain, wondering if even the weather had turned against them. The beans were producing basketfuls of long, green pods, now that the wind had stopped battering them to the ground, but slugs were playing havoc with the potatoes and salad crops, and Cabbage White butterfly caterpillars had enjoyed more of the greens than the family had. Who'd be a gardener?

She would. Tending a patch of ground, under the guidance of anyone who knew more about the subject than she did, was a source of calming comfort and a haven of quiet from the incessant noise of the chain factory. Hoping the rain would keep off a little longer, she hoed weeds between alternating rows of carrots and onions with a methodical motion. Knowing the food produced at Heath Hall could once again mean the difference between the town eating and starving, should there be war, made it all the more worthwhile. The soup kitchens of the depression that she'd hoped were a thing of the past might yet need bringing back into being.

War, with Hanne stuck in enemy territory, didn't bear thinking about, but it was feeling inevitable. After the German invasion of Czechoslovakia, Britain had given a guarantee that if Poland was attacked, she would come to their aid.

Spurred on by this worry, she'd written to the various organisations Rabbi Cohen had suggested. All had said much the same thing. Visas to get into England were difficult to come by, and people wanting to emigrate from Europe needed to go to the British Embassy of their country. Children were easier to bring into Britain, but only if they would not be a burden on the country, and charitable funds to support them were limited.

Sponsoring Asher wasn't a problem, but Hanne and her family obtaining visas could be difficult.

The hoeing finished, she went back into the house. She would have to write more openly than she liked if Hanne was to understand the situation.

My darling Hanne,

I hope you are keeping up your spirits. We are very busy preparing for the future and have turned over more land to growing food. I wish you could see the results of all our hard work and taste the fresh vegetables. I wish I could send you some to try.

Concerning the large package you are thinking of sending. If I were dispatching a parcel of this nature abroad, I would seek the advice of a representative of the destination country to be sure it was acceptable. You may need import documentation.

The British Embassy was in Berlin. Could Hanne and her family travel so far? There was a British Consulate General office in Düsseldorf, which was closer to Frankfurt and towards the Belgian border. They had the money for train fare. How could she tell Hanne that many women had come to England under the auspices of being domestic servants? Cash had got through hidden in packages, so why not a letter? She had to risk it.

She screwed up the letter and began another telling Hanne what she knew about immigration and that they must apply in person to either the British Embassy in Berlin or the British Consulate in Düsseldorf and try to get a visa for herself and Mutter as domestic servants. Asher should be granted one, as Hanne's child, but could Berek and Uncle Saul use the same ruse? If they needed jobs in England in order to get a visa, she was in an ideal position to provide them. Farmhands, gardeners, servants, chainmakers, welders. Hanne needed to know she would guarantee them work to help their visa applications.

Feeling more hopeful, she walked down to the town to post her parcel, a knitted jumper for Asher with the letter sewn inside it. Asher was small for his age, but he would grow into it.

The postmistress smiled apologetically. 'Papers were late, this morning, Miss Taylor. Young Danny had gone to school before they arrived. My Bert's out delivering some now.'

'Do you want me to take our copy with me, Mrs Darby?'

'That would save him some steps, dear. Thank you.' Mrs Darby folded a copy and handed it to her. 'I see Roosevelt is doing something about those poor Jews across the channel. Mr Matthew Joshua would turn in his grave if he knew their plight, may he rest in peace.'

'It's about time someone helped.' She handed over her parcel to be weighed.

Mrs Darby looked up the postage rate for Germany in her booklet. 'Another present for your young cousin? You spoil that child.'

She smiled. 'He's a sweet boy.'

Mrs Darby stuck on the postage and cancelled them with a metal stamp. 'You must worry about them.'

'All the while. I'm hoping to sponsor them to come to England.

Things are awful for them out there.'

'They'll be very welcome, I'm sure.'

'I hope so.' She handed over some coins. She'd done what she could until she heard from Hanne again.

Outside, she opened the newspaper, eager to see what solution was being offered.

Roosevelt Meets with Europe's Heads of State at Evian-les-Bains to discuss Jews.

President Roosevelt has met with heads of countries across Europe to discuss the problem of re-homing Jews presently being harassed by the Nazis.

Where are these Jews to go? Anti-Semitism is as entrenched in America as it is in many European and Middle Eastern countries, and Switzerland and Italy have already refused to take Jewish immigrants.

The American spokesman, Myron C. Taylor, was cautious about promises of aid, only assuring the committee that America's 30,000 immigration quota could include Jewish refugees.

Britain has agreed to accept a few thousand German Jews, and Australia has promised to take 15,000 over a three-year period.

The Australian representative, T.W. White, remarked that as they had no real racial problem, they were not desirous of importing one. This appeared to be the opinion of many delegates.

Only the Dominican Republic agreed to accept 100,000 refugees.

Her heart fell. She didn't even know where the Dominican Republic was. How many was a few thousand? Two, three, ten? It was a drop in the ocean. It appeared most of the world was shutting their doors to Jews, not opening them.

***

Frankfurt, Germany 1938

Hanne helped her mother down from the train in Düsseldorf while holding on to Asher's hand. Berek and Uncle Saul carried the bags they'd brought with them in the event of having to stay overnight, although no hotel was likely to allow them in. The British Consulate wasn't far from the station, and they'd waited for Mutter's health to improve before travelling, but she still couldn't walk far without getting breathless.

There was a queue outside the door. They took their place and shuffled forward slowly in tense silence. What was taking so long?

At last, they were inside and were directed to a room. A stiff-backed, grey-haired man in a dark suit looked over his spectacles at them. 'Passports.'

Berek laid their passports out on the desk. 'We wish to go to England. We have relatives there.'

'You wish to visit or to stay in England?'

'To stay, of course.'

The man sniffed and perused the first passport. 'Hanne Bergman. Which is she?'

Did she look so like Mutter in her photograph? 'I am. This is my mother, Frau Samuels, my husband, Berek Bergman, our son, Asher, and this my Uncle Saul. We wish to travel together. My mother and I are to be domestic servants.'

'You realise that the number of visas issued is very limited for immigration into Britain?'

'Yes, but my cousin Emma will vouch for us.'

'We'll get to that in a moment. First, you will need to enter all the relevant information on these application forms.' He passed a form to each of them. 'Name, age, address, past and present employment, health, etcetera.'

Mutter glanced at her. Mutter's health could prevent her from being accepted? If so, they were wasting their time here. None of them would leave Mutter behind. She tightened her grip on Asher's hand; she'd harboured hopes that they could all travel together. Would she have to send him to England alone, after all?

'I shall need your fingerprints and various documents as listed on the form. I need proof of sufficient funds to support yourself and your family – a bank statement or bankbook, proof of residence in Germany – a rental agreement or proof of home ownership will suffice. Do you have a letter of invitation from this cousin? Sponsorship for the child?'

'Emma –'

He cut her off as if he didn't want to give her a chance to put their case. 'Do you have proof of an offer of employment in England, and if so, of what kind? Not all trades are wanted. I shall need all this information if I am to consider your applications, and I should warn you that you may not be accepted. I have to satisfy my government you won't be a burden on the state and that you will assimilate into our society in a way that is an asset to us, not a liability or a threat to British labour, however deserving a case you may be.'

'Emma has already agreed to offer us employment.' She handed him the letter Emma had sewn into Asher's jumper.

He read it and tapped it with the back of his hand. 'This doesn't give details of what role each of you will have. I need to know the full name of the employer, the name of any company involved, the wages to be paid, and an address where you'll be living.'

'But she guarantees us employment and will sponsor Asher. We can prove we have funds.'

'Then come back when you have all the necessary documentation. Take the forms with you. I don't have the final say – your applications have to be approved by the Home Office. It will take several weeks. As you can imagine, we have thousands of applicants.'

The interview was at an end, and the man hadn't sounded apologetic: he'd sounded relieved to have someone else decide their fate. They trailed out, heavy with disappointment. It was obvious by the man's attitude that the British government would put every obstacle in their way.

'At least we weren't turned down out of hand.' Mutter always looked on the bright side.

Uncle Saul's brow furrowed. 'If they need proof of funds, we shall have to pay some of our hidden money into the bank, which will mean it will have to be declared. We could lose it all before we have a chance to escape.'

She'd been thinking the same thing. 'We don't have a choice, Uncle Saul.'

Berek nodded. 'We have to abide by the rules, so there's nothing more we can do today. We may as well get the next train home. Hanne, you must write to Emma and ask for this letter of invitation and a detailed promise of employment for each of us and an address for where we'll be living.'

'As soon as we get home.' Emma would send the information they needed by return of post, but "several weeks" sounded ominous. This building, this little piece of Britain, had felt like a safe haven, but her hope of speedy rescue had evaporated like rain on a hot day, and now they had to go back outside and face whatever Hitler threw at them next. The wait for Emma's letter, so they could complete their applications, would be hell, and the next few weeks after that would be agonisingly slow.

They walked past a news stand. A Nazi newspaper had a headline in huge letters.

JEWS FOR SALE AT A BARGAIN PRICE – WHO WANTS THEM? NO ONE

.

Chapter Thirty-One

Hawley Heath, England September 1938

Emma paced the office floor. There'd been no good news from Hanne, and every indication she'd picked up from the radio and newspapers suggested the British government was dragging its heels and tying up the immigration process in needless bureaucracy. Didn't the smug, self-obsessed pigs realise people's lives were in danger? But for the money she'd been able to smuggle Hanne, she and her family would starve. There must be people who were destitute and homeless – and if she was truthful, they needed rescuing more urgently than Hanne did.

She paced across the office, stared out across the factory to the sound of a country preparing for war, turned, and paced back again. The government was more concerned with placating Hitler and allowing him to terrorise the Jews than condemning his insanity. There'd even been an article in The Times calling on Czechoslovakia to cede him the Sudetenland. How was that concession going to halt his avowed expansionism?

Stopping in front of her desk, she reread Neville Chamberlain's latest efforts.

Prime Minister in talks with German Chancellor.

The Prime Minister, Neville Chamberlain, is meeting German Chancellor, Adolph Hitler, in Berchtesgaden today to negotiate an end to German expansionism in Europe. This follows Hitler's proposal to partition Czechoslovakia and annex the Sudetenland. The refugee crisis will worsen should

Czechoslovakian Jews join the hundreds of thousands of Jews from Austria and Germany now seeking a home outside of Greater Germany.

The chances of Hanne, Berek, Mutter, Saul, and little Asher being among the few thousand to be let into England became remoter by the day. Could she have said more in her letter to persuade immigration of their plight and their value to the Hawley Heath community? She could have written a separate letter to warn Uncle Saul not to put jeweller or shopkeeper as his past employment: Britain had enough shopkeepers. And she should have told Hanne not to say Mutter had a bad heart: Britain didn't need invalids.

She clenched and unclenched her hands and tried to relax tense shoulders. She'd guaranteed employment in domestic service and in horticulture, which she'd heard were the most likely jobs to be accepted, those least likely to compete with and threaten existing jobs.

Her shoulders tensed again of their own volition. It was the waiting that was killing her, and if she felt stressed, how the hell must Hanne be feeling? She wanted to drag them all here by force, shout at the border guards, and harangue Neville bloody Chamberlain, but she was helpless in the face of snail-pace bureaucracy, and – she grabbed the newspaper and tore it in half and half again– it was driving her insane.

She buried herself in work, pushing Charlie to greater efforts to diversify as iron tubing became scarcer because of the government requisitioning iron stocks to make guns, tanks, and armaments. She worked evenings in the allotments, all day in the chain factory, and spent half the night writing letters to anyone who might help get German Jews into England.

And life went on regardless of her worrying.

The British government informed the Czechoslovakian president they wouldn't fight Hitler to protect the Sudetenland, and Winston Churchill warned of the grave consequences to European security if Germany partitioned Czechoslovakia.

They were on a knife edge, and the blade was razor sharp. She'd become addicted to the radio news.

'*The government has announced today that it has ordered the Royal Navy to sea.*'

War took a step closer, and the country held its breath.

Two days later, came better news. RMS *Queen Elizabeth* had been launched at Clydebank. Joshua and Son had supplied chains for what was the largest ship in the world, and she felt justly proud. The *Queen Mary* and *Queen Elizabeth* had saved Joshua and Son from bankruptcy, and she was thrilled the ship had finally been launched. Whether it would be the luxury liner they had intended it to be was up to Hitler.

Neville Chamberlain was in Munich attempting to defuse tensions, and she waited restlessly for news. The outcome could affect the difficult decision she'd been agonising over. Should she do as Mom had during the last war and turn part of their operation, possibly the cycle workshop, to a munitions factory? Should she risk her workers? It was dangerous work, as she knew. Mom had never forgiven herself for Grandma Joshua's death.

The next evening, the family gathered around the radio to hear a news bulletin about Neville Chamberlain waving a piece of paper outside number ten Downing Street.

The announcer relayed Chamberlain's words. '*We regard the agreement signed last night, and the Anglo-German Naval Agreement, as symbolic of the desire of our two peoples never to go to war with one another again.*

'My good friends, for the second time in our history, a British Prime Minister has returned from Germany bringing peace with honour. I believe it is peace for our time. We thank you from the bottom of our hearts. Go home and get a nice quiet sleep.'

'Peace.' Dad breathed his relief. 'George and Theo won't have to fight.'

Mom squeezed Dad's hand. 'Thank the Lord. Oh, thank God.'

She massaged knots from her neck and shoulders, and tension drained out of her. Peace must help Hanne and her family. She went to bed that night and slept soundly for the first time in months.

***

Frankfurt, Germany October 1938

Hanne sat with Mutter, Berek, and Uncle Saul huddled around the radio. Tuned to the British Empire station, they'd listened intently to Chamberlain's speech.

'Peace?' Berek's low tone showed his effort to stay calm for Asher's sake.

Uncle Saul shook his head. 'They've turned their backs on us. Britain, Italy, France – they don't give a damn about Czechoslovakia and the Jews of Europe. Anything to keep the peace.'

She had to agree. 'If Chamberlain trusts Hitler to abide by his promises, he's over-estimated the man's morality. I don't trust Hitler one inch. His poison still spreads across the world.'

'Now we must all have identity cards and Jewish names.' Mutter dry-washed her hands in a too-familiar gesture. 'Men must add Israel to their names and women must add Sarah. I must now be known as Julia *Sarah* Samuels.'

The walls of the apartment closed in on her, and she moved across to the window to stare out across Börneplatz – *Dominikanerplatz* – at the few hunched figures of her neighbours trying to scratch a bare living or bartering goods for food. Nothing in her world was right anymore. Berek, Mutter, and Saul were sick with worry. Asher, picking up on their anxiety, was wetting the bed.

A synagogue in Nuremberg had been demolished on the spurious grounds that it was ugly. A Jesuit publication, controlled by the Vatican, had called Jews sinister and accused them of trying to control the world. Would they have voiced that opinion but for Hitler's insidious propaganda? Who were they to talk with their history of intimidation, inquisition, and torture? The devil is the Jew's master? They are a standing menace to the world? Look closer to home, Pope Pius XII!

The radio announcer drew her back. '*The German Wehrmacht has occupied the Czech Sudetenland under the terms of the Munich Agreement.*'

Berek reached out a hand to her to sit by him. 'God help the Jews of Sudetenland.'

The newscaster paused before the next news article.

'*Following a request by Heinrich Rothmund, head of the Swiss federal police, all passports of German Jews are to be recalled. They will be marked with a J for Jew. This is to prevent German Jews from passing as Christians and smuggling themselves into Switzerland.*

'*Poland has revoked the passports of all Jews who have lived outside of Poland for over five years, rendering them stateless.*'

Uncle Saul switched off the radio, and silence settled over the room. Mutter twisted a piece of her skirt into a knot, Uncle Saul stared at the backs of his hands as if the future could be told there, and Berek ran his fingers through his hair. They had no words left to describe their feelings of helplessness.

Without passports what hope of escape remained? She checked the doormat for mail for the third time in as many hours, awaiting a reply to their applications for visas.

There was nothing from the British Consulate. No news was good news, she kept telling herself, but in her heart, she knew the British Home Office would find any excuse to prevent them from reaching England and safety. Emma had done her best for them, but would it be enough?

***

Hanne had all but given up hope of obtaining visas. There had been an anxious wait until their invalid passports were returned to them – each one now stamped with the proscribed large red 'J'.

The only replies from the British Consulate had been requests for more documentation and answers to obscure questions, like if they were selected for a temporary visa and transmigration, which country would they like to go to from England? They wanted to stay in England where they had offers of a home and jobs – what was it the British Consulate didn't understand about that? Perhaps, they should have lied to gain entry into England?

Had their applications got lost among the thousands of expelled Polish Jews now trying to get into Britain? Seventeen thousand had been stranded, homeless and stateless, at the border town of Zbaszyn when Poland had refused them entry. It was the sort of Nazi ploy she'd come to expect. First, remove their Polish citizenship because they lived in Germany and then expel them from Germany. Doing it in winter was a typical sadistic twist. How she hated Hitler and everything he stood for.

Fog obscured the streets, and with the damp November murk had come a bone-chilling cold. Surely, the final decision on whether they could travel to England would come soon.

She hardly dared turn on the radio, but she had to know what was happening in the world, and especially England and Germany. The Munich Agreement had promised peace, but she didn't trust Hitler one bit.

'*In defiance of the Munich Agreement, our glorious leader today ceded large parts of Czechoslovakia to Hungary and Italy. The Transcarpathian Ukraine is to be annexed by Hungary.*'

Mutter spat her disgust. 'And Britain and France trusted Hitler's word? He's torn up the agreement and trampled on it.'

'I'll try the Empire Service.' She twiddled the tuning knob. What had Britain to say to this?

Clipped tones delivered Britain's verdict. '*Deported by Nazi Germany, the Jews of Poland have been denied entry into their own country after being deprived of Polish nationality. They are surviving in bitter winter weather with little help, food, or shelter. The United States of America have responded to the humanitarian crisis by sending aid to the Polish refugees at Zbaszyn.*'

Mutter clenched her hands together, her knuckles standing out white against red washday hands. 'At last, someone has done something.'

The radio crackled and whined. She adjusted the tuning knob. '*Neville Chamberlain was not available for comment after Germany's breaking of the Munich Agreement contrary to Hitler's September promise.*'

'Mutter, the British and French governments won't sit back and let this happen.'

Mutter huffed disagreement. 'Hitler thinks he's invincible. If no country risks any action to show him otherwise, what's to stop him doing whatever he pleases?'

What value was peace if it meant tyranny and brutal dictatorship? She'd rather have war.

The Jewish community across Europe held its breath, but war didn't come.

The following week's news brought her out in a cold sweat.

'A young Jew, Herschel Grynszpaan, whose family was deported from Germany and stranded in the Polish border town of Zbaszyn, has entered the German Embassy in Paris and shot Third Secretary of Legation, Ernst vom Rath. It is feared his injuries are life threatening.'

Part of her wanted to cheer; a Jew had dared to fight back, but at what cost? Whether or not Ernst vom Rath died, Nazi retribution against the Jews of Germany would be swift, far reaching, and brutal.

'May the God of Abraham, Isaac, and Israel protect us.' She crossed to the door of the apartment and locked and bolted it.

Chapter Thirty-Two

Frankfurt, Germany 1938

November 9th was a day Hanne would never forget. There had been an air of tension in the Platz all day. News had trickled in regarding the barring of Jewish children from schools, the banning of all remaining Jewish newspapers, and the forbidding of any Jew to possess any kind of weapon, on pain of twenty years in a concentration camp.

The air grew thick with fear as they waited for the next move against them. Goebbels' rancid voice, once gentle and friendly, screamed abuse from the radio. '*Jews should feel the anger of the people.*'

Ernst vom Rath was dead, and Goebbels had just given the German people permission to vent their hatred. She shuddered; Nazi Germany was set on revenge.

As daylight faded, the sound of distant voices rose. An orange glow lit the dusk sky. Somewhere across the city, something was burning. The voices were coming closer. Another orange glow was spreading across the skyline, and smoke rose into the night; she could almost smell it. It reminded her of the day soldiers had forced their way into the apartment and burned her father's books.

The voices were shouting. She could make out words now. '*Juden raus.*' Where was Berek? 'Mutter, lock the door.'

'But Saul and Berek are still out, Hanne.'

As if she didn't know. She couldn't take her eyes from the window. 'I'll watch for them. Lock the door and take Asher into the bedroom.'

The key turned in the lock. She kissed Asher. 'Go with Oma, Asher, and you must stay very quiet if you hear shouting. Promise?' Her son's eyes were wide with fear, but he nodded. 'It will be all right, Asher. Just hide and stay quiet with Oma. I'll be with you once Papa and Uncle Saul are home.'

Mutter lifted a sharp knife from the kitchen table and went into the bedroom with Asher.

She opened a drawer and armed herself with a rolling pin. 'Where are you, Berek?'

The tramp of heavy boots thudded across the Platz. Not men in uniforms, but a mob of angry Germans wielding weapons. Loud voices followed the familiar tinkle of breaking glass. '*Juden raus! Juden raus*!'

Shops and houses across the Platz were under attack from men with sledgehammers, sticks, and axes. The sound of running feet came closer; two men were approaching the apartment.

Berek and Uncle Saul!

She crossed to the door and unlocked it as the feet thundered up the stairs. Berek pushed Uncle Saul into the room and slammed the door behind him. She turned the key and threw herself into Berek's arms.

He kissed her. 'Where's Asher?'

'In the bedroom with Mutter. I told them to hide and stay quiet if they heard shouting.'

'You should go with them. They're breaking into Jewish shops and houses. They're burning the synagogues.'

'God of Abraham...' As she watched, men were breaking down

the doors of the Börneplatz synagogue. Flames licking the night sky told of other houses of God burning.

Across the Platz, the house belonging to Kettner, the butcher, was also in flames. Uncle Saul unlocked the door.

She put her hand against the door to stop him. 'What are you doing?'

Uncle Saul pushed her aside. 'Kettner and his family may be inside. We have to get them out.'

Berek re-buttoned his coat and elbowed past her. 'I'm coming with you, Saul.'

'Berek, no—'

'Lock the door, Hanne.' The door slammed in her face and footsteps thundered down the stairs. She turned the key and watched Berek and Uncle Saul dash across the Platz and into the oncoming storm.

Flames leapt from downstairs windows; the Kettners could be upstairs. Berek and Uncle Saul disappeared into the burning house as a hoard of angry men surged forward. One old man was being dragged along by his beard.

There was a crash of sledgehammer on wood, and heavy boots thudded up the stairs. She dragged the kitchen table across the room to bar the door and shrank back against the wall. Something flew through the window and shards of glass cascaded across the room. The doorknob turned, and a second's silence was followed by the splinter of wood as an axe head broke through the panelled door.

She hammered on the bedroom door. 'Mutter, let me in.'

A hand came through the front door, feeling for the key. She dashed back, brought down the rolling pin on the man's wrist, and was rewarded by a yelp of pain and a curse.

'Hanne, quickly!'

She ran and slammed the bedroom door behind her. 'Help me push the bed across the door.'

Together they heaved the heavy oak bed across the room, jammed it against the door, and then crawled beneath it. She clutched her rolling pin, Mutter clutched her knife, and both of them clutched Asher, who began to cry.

'Shush, Asher. Quiet, remember.'

Thumping, banging, shouting. Table legs screeched on floorboards, and the front door crashed open. Heavy footsteps crossed the kitchen and the living room. It sounded as if cutlery drawers were being emptied, crockery smashed, and furniture upended and broken.

She gripped her rolling pin tighter and Asher tighter still. 'Keep behind me, sweetheart. Whatever happens, stay here, and don't come out. Unless you smell smoke. If you smell smoke, you run outside. Do you understand, Asher?'

He didn't answer, he just clutched the toy dog Emma had sent him when he was little, but he had to understand. He had to. Mutter's lips moved, praying to a God who seemed to have deserted them. Were the Nazi's right when they said the Jews were cursed because they killed Jesus? Was this divine retribution?

'God of Abraham, Isaac, and Israel, keep Berek and Uncle Saul safe and protect us from this madness.'

The bedroom doorknob rattled, something heavy thudded against it, but the bed didn't move. The familiar sound of splintered wood suggested it wouldn't be long before the Nazi thugs destroyed the entire door. She was shaking so much she could barely hold on to the rolling pin.

Mutter changed the grip on her knife and wriggled forward. She grabbed her mother's jumper and whispered through clenched teeth. 'No, Mutter, please. Stay here.'

The bed springs bounced above their heads and Mutter shrank back, too late for her surprise attack. All they could see from the light of the streetlamps and burning buildings were jackboots: Nazi jackboots.

She held her breath and put one hand over Asher's mouth. The wardrobe door banged open, and the man threw clothes onto the bedroom floor. The sound of a zip was followed by the acrid smell of urine.

A boot kicked a bed leg. 'I know you're under there. If you want to live, come out. All of you. Now!'

She pushed Asher behind her and exchanged a glance with Mutter; if the man looked under the bed, he would see Asher. Mutter nodded and began crawling forward. If she tried to use her knife, the man would kill her. She motioned to Asher to stay still and quiet and followed Mutter out from beneath the bed, still clutching her rolling pin.

'What have we here? Two dirty Jews. One each, Gustav.'

She knew this man. He was no civilian as his clothing suggested. He was a Brownshirt. This was no spontaneous riot; it was an orchestrated military attack. She raised her rolling pin. 'Leave my mother alone, you Nazi pig.'

The man's fist connected with her cheek, and something cracked as her head snapped to the side. 'That's for trying to break my wrist.'

He hit her again. 'You can have her after me, Gustav.'

'And you can have the old one after me, Hans.'

'I'm not into old flesh, Gustav. She's all yours.'

Hans threw her backwards onto the bed and grabbed at her clothing, ripping her dress. She kicked out and flailed her arms, trying to hit him, but he grabbed her wrists, knelt over her, forcing her legs apart with his knees, and held her down. Mutter lunged forward, knife raised, but Gustav grabbed her knife hand, beat her about the head, and forced her to the floor.

Please God, Asher stayed silent. She bit back a scream, her arms getting weaker and weaker as she struggled. These men were too strong; fighting would only get them hurt worse. She turned her head aside as he yanked off her knickers and thrust inside her. Mutter was crying. She couldn't see her, but she knew from Gustav's grunting what was happening.

God of Abraham, Isaac, and Israel protect my son.

***

The men had gone. They'd taken their pleasure with their conquests, but Gustav had been gentler with her than Hans; she'd accepted her fate and put herself in God's hands. Red and orange light flickered through the ruined bedroom door and onto the walls. Börneplatz was burning. Hanne clutched her clothing around her and rolled off the bed onto the floor. There was nowhere she didn't hurt. 'Ash –' Her jaw didn't work properly. Mutter lay where Gustav had left her, her eyes staring. 'Mutter?'

Asher lay curled into a ball in the far corner. She crawled under the bed. 'Asher. It's all right.' She winced at the pain in her jaw and face and stomach. 'It's safe to come out now.'

Had he heard her? 'Mutter...' Her mother moaned quietly.

'Mutter.'

'Hanne?'

'They've gone, Mutter. Can you move?'

'Oh, Hanne, my darling Hanne, what have they done to you?'

'I'm all right.'

'Asher?'

'He's still under the bed.'

'Asher, the men have gone. You can come out.'

Asher uncurled and wriggled out from under the bed. He clung to her, his eyes bright with tears. 'That bad man hurt Oma. I want Papa. Where's Papa?'

He'd seen her mother being raped? 'I don't know, sweetheart. I can't hear anyone in the house.'

Mutter rolled onto her hands and knees and pulled herself to her feet, using the bed for support. 'We must move the bed so we can get out. We have to find Berek and Saul.'

Moving the bed was beyond them, and Asher screamed when they tried. They climbed over it and out through the ruined bedroom door. Furniture lay smashed and overturned, paintings and curtains slashed, and not a piece of crockery was unbroken. She sank to the floor and stared at the photograph of her and Berek on their wedding day, the silver frame bent and smashed, the image torn.

The chill night air blew billowing smoke through the broken window, while flames danced across the Platz. The Kettner's house was a smouldering ruin, and the synagogue was burning.

Dark shapes lay on the ground. A man ran among them, not to help the injured but to steal what little they had left. She had to find Berek.

'Mutter, stay here with Asher.' Holding her stomach, she crept down the stairs and out onto the Platz. She wove her way between bodies – people she'd known all her life. Good people.

'Berek! Uncle Saul!' She'd last seen them going into the Kettner's house. Please, God, they'd got out alive.

'Hanne?'

She turned, heart in mouth. 'Herr Kettner, thank God you're safe. Where are Berek and Uncle Saul?'

He shook his head. 'I don't know. They rescued me and Greta, but I haven't seen them since.'

'But they got out?'

'Yes.' He looked at her more closely. 'Child, what's happened to you?'

She shook her head.

'Oh, my poor child. And Julia?'

'Mutter is alive. They –' She couldn't say the words.

'Nazischweine. And the boy?'

'They didn't find him. I left Mutter trying to comfort him.'

'I'll help you look for your husband and uncle.'

Together they searched the Platz. Shards of broken glass lay everywhere; there wasn't a Jewish home or business that hadn't either been broken into or set alight. Only Aryan houses and shops had escaped. No fire engines tried to put out the flames. No police or ambulances had answered any summons for help. It was as if they were under orders to let the fires burn and the people die.

She knelt by a body lying in a pool of blood, and Herr Kettner turned it over. Not Berek or Saul. They moved on. A group of men sat huddled against a wall, many with bloodied hands and faces. 'Have you seen Berek Bergman or Saul Samuels?'

'The SS arrested a lot of the younger men and marched them away.'

'Berek has been arrested?'

'I don't know if he was among them.'

One man raised a limp arm and pointed. She followed the direction of his finger to an alley. Please God, they'd hidden.

Herr Kettner held her back. 'I'll look. Stay here.'

She held her breath, waiting for Herr Kettner to emerge from the shadows and muttering the all too familiar and ever more desperate prayer. 'God of Abraham…'

Herr Kettner's bowed head and slumped figure answered her question. 'Oh, dear God, no.'

He walked slowly towards her and raised his head. 'I'm so sorry, Hanne.'

She didn't want to believe what he was saying. 'Not Berek? No.'

'Both of them, Hanne.'

She pushed past him, and he grabbed her arm and gripped it tight. 'No, Hanne. You don't want to see. There's nothing you can do to help them, now.'

She couldn't say the ritual words, but Herr Kettner spoke them for her. 'Blessed are You, Lord, our God, King of the Universe, the Judge of Truth.'

He held her as her fragile world fell apart and she wept.

Chapter Thirty-Three

Frankfurt, Germany 1938

Hanne and Mutter stood in the centre of Börneplatz. Hanne refused to think of it as Dominikanerplatz. One wall of the synagogue still stood, and smoke rose from the smouldering ruins of Jewish shops and houses, while Aryan properties were untouched. Unburned fragments showed sacred scrolls and prayer books had been thrown out into the Platz and set alight. Glass crunched underfoot and sparkled in the morning sun like a myriad of tiny diamonds, and women swept the pavements with brooms.

With the banning of Jewish newspapers, the community was isolated, not knowing if this was a local riot or something that had taken place all across Germany. If it was widespread, the government had to be behind it. News was by word of mouth and not reliable.

She felt numb, her mind unable to process what had happened and unable to answer Asher's questions. Herr Kettner had taken charge, insisting he would wash the bodies of Berek and Uncle Saul according to their custom and dress them in simple shrouds. He also insisted he would stay with the bodies and recite the psalms until their burial. He said it was his way of repaying his debt to them, but she knew he wished to prevent her from seeing the mutilated bodies of those she'd loved. She was grateful for that mercy.

Graves were being dug, and the burials would take place in the Jewish cemetery that afternoon. With the rabbi among the injured, Jewish custom would be observed as best they could, and she would lay to rest the only man she'd ever love.

Asher stood between her and Mutter, bravely trying to be the head of the family in his father's place. Tears welled in her eyes; she loved him so much, and she knew in her heart what she had to do.

The decision she'd been putting off had been made for her. If she or Mutter were denied entry to England, she would have to get Asher to Emma on his own. She couldn't leave her mother.

'Hanne?' A neighbour, not a Jew, approached her. 'I am so sorry. I am ashamed that my countrymen have done this to you.' She looked up at the broken windows and the lone candle guttering in the breeze. 'You and Asher and Julia must come and stay with us. Please say you will. You can't live there in this cold with no windows.'

They'd spent the night huddled in one bed in the back bedroom, which had escaped with an unbroken window, with a heap of broken furniture wedged against the door. 'We have nothing left, Mia. They destroyed everything. They even spoiled our food.'

'You've not eaten? I'll prepare something for you. Come when you are ready.'

She wiped away tears at such kindness. 'Thank you, Mia. We bury Berek and Saul this afternoon.'

'Then you must have something warm inside you to sustain you. Gunter and I will come to pay our respects if we may?'

'You will be very welcome, Mia.'

The woman nodded with an expression of relief and squeezed her hand. 'When you are ready, then.'

'Thank you.'

Mia hurried away to cook, and she turned her attention back to the Platz. There were no young men, in fact, no men except the elderly, like Herr Kettner. How many had been arrested? Rumour abounded. The men had been sent to a camp – Lodz or Dachau. No one knew for sure. How were they to survive without their menfolk?

She didn't ask what was in the food Mia provided. They had to eat, although pain in her jaw and cheek made chewing difficult: life came before faith. The stew warmed her as she stood at the graveside with her mother and her son.

There were no caskets, too many had died to make enough coffins in time, but Herr Kettner had draped a tattered prayer shawl over the bodies of Berek and Saul who were to lie together. He had cut a tassel from the corner of the shawl; every minor detail of custom he could perform had been carried out with respect.

Graves had been dug alongside one another, a too-long row of death, and the close-knit community had come together to mourn their dead as one. Mothers, fathers, sons, daughters, uncles, cousins… Although dug in haste, every care had been taken to honour the dead.

An elder of the synagogue led the psalms and prayers, and she bowed her head, letting the calming words flow over her and into her. Beside her, Mutter made a tear in her dress above her heart. She followed suit; for Asher's sake, she had to be strong.

Eulogies were spoken, old men spoke with frail voices, shoulders hunched. Women held their children and wept. The bodies were lowered into the ground while quiet voices sang a dirge and each of the mourners stepped forward in turn to take a shovel and put earth over the shrouds.

'God, full of mercy, who dwells in the heights, provide a sure rest upon the Divine Presence's wings for Berek Bergman, son of Solomon, and Saul Samuels, son of Jacob.'

The elder went along the row reciting the names of the dead for each family who mourned.

'Therefore, the Master of Mercy will protect them forever, from behind the hiding of his wings, and will tie their souls with the rope of life. The Everlasting is their heritage, and they shall rest peacefully upon their lying place, and let us say: Amen.'

'Amen.'

It was done. Now she had to observe the ritual of mourning – she wouldn't bathe for a week, she wouldn't wear leather shoes, and if she'd had mirrors unbroken, they would have had to be covered. Living with Mia, she couldn't respect all the rituals, but she would adhere to those she could, help Asher learn the Torah to honour his father, and face the rest of her life without the man she loved.

***

Candles burned in windows around the Platz. Mia had made them welcome, and somehow, life went on. The Nazis had done their worst, so maybe now they'd leave them alone.

Der Stürmer, the Nazi newspaper, brought news of the widespread disaster to befall the Jews of Germany. The Rothschild Museum of Judaica had been vandalised, the precious collection destroyed. Every city had been attacked, hundreds of Jews were dead, over twenty thousand imprisoned, and hundreds of homes and synagogues had been burned to the ground. Tens of thousands were homeless, and the rush for visas to leave Germany had intensified to more than a thousand a day.

Herman Göring criticised the material destruction and pointed out that German insurance companies would bear the cost of repairs unless there was government intervention.

The next day's copy bore a stark headline she should have expected, yet it shocked her to the core.

Jews to Blame for Anti-Semitic Riots across Germany.

A fine of one billion reichsmarks has been levied on the Jewish community in Germany. Insurance pay-outs for loss or damage to Jewish property during the recent riots will be confiscated by the government, and Jews will bear full responsibility for the cost of all repairs to homes, businesses, and possessions.

She stared at it in disbelief. How were Jews to blame? And when they'd had almost everything taken from them, how were they supposed to pay for repairs to their property, let alone pay a huge fine? This had Hitler's twisted mind written all over it.

She and Mutter still had money. The rioters had been too intent on rape to search the bedroom more thoroughly, and they hadn't found their secret hoard so painstakingly collected – and thankfully, neither had they found Asher.

They wouldn't have money if they spent it replacing all the damaged items and repairing doors and windows. How then could they afford train and ferry fare to get to England? Without money, what might she be forced to do to bribe a guard to let her, Mutter, and Asher across the German border?

They needed those visas from England, and they needed them now.

***

Hawley Heath, England 1938

Cold sweat trickled down Emma's back when she read the morning headlines.

Jewish Homes Fired, Men Killed, Women Beaten.

She read on, heart thumping, head swimming.

Berlin, Thursday – After what is being called Kristallnacht, the Night of Broken Glass, Jews are cowering in terror. Throughout Germany, mobs of Nazis rampaged through the cities, breaking windows, looting, and burning Jewish businesses and homes. Hundreds of synagogues have been destroyed in the wave of violence, and it's thought almost a hundred people have been killed with many more imprisoned or injured and women raped.

Not even Dr Goebbels could stop it after his acid attack on the Jews incited the violence following the death of Ernst vom Roth. In Berlin, the entire police force was called out.

The Nazi government has already laid the blame for the riots at the feet of the Jews. With this as an excuse, they are likely to order foreign Jews to leave Germany and inflict even more penalties on the remaining Jewish population.

Foreign embassies have been besieged by desperate Jews seeking permits to enter Britain, her Dominions, or the USA. They crowded the corridors, waiting for their turn, only to be asked "How much capital have you?" Most have nothing.

Even those with money were turned away on other grounds. Very few were successful in their pleas.

There have also been reports of suicides. Some 30,000 Jewish men are reported to have been arrested and transported to camps at Dachau, Buchenwald, Sachsenhausen, and Lodz. The pogrom has evoked worldwide condemnation.

Men killed and women beaten and raped. What of Hanne and her family? There was no way to find out other than to write and pray for an answer. She could hardly hold her pen for shaking.

My Darling Hanne,

The newspapers are full of the terror inflicted on German Jews by Nazi mobs. I am so worried about you all. Please let me know you are safe and well. Have your British visas arrived yet? Do you need more money sending? I can get some to you by return of post.

I am praying for you,

Your loving Emma.

It was a brief letter and to the point. She stuffed it into an envelope and drove to the post office to catch the morning post. Then she drew some cash from the bank and took it home to hide in a present for Asher, along with another letter should the first fail to arrive. She would send money whether or not Hanne needed it.

That evening, the radio news described the destruction. It was far worse than anything she could have imagined. Dear God, how could anyone do this to innocent people?

Hanne and her family were in the midst of a violent pogrom.

She waited, tossing and turning through several nights, but no letter came from Frankfurt. She tried to think of reasons. Her letter might not have arrived if services had been disrupted, or Hanne might not be able to get to a post office to post a letter, or she might be injured and in hospital – or dead.

She couldn't concentrate on work, and nothing Mom or Dad said to comfort her made a scrap of difference. She wouldn't rest until she heard from Hanne. 'Please, be safe, Hanne.'

She listened to the Empire Service on the radio constantly, hoping to hear news of Frankfurt.

'Emma!' Mom ran into the room waving a newspaper. 'The British government is waiving visa requirements for unaccompanied Jewish children from Germany.'

She snatched the newspaper from Mom's hands and spread it on the table. 'We could get Asher to safety? Aid agencies are working to bring children out. I need a phone number, an address. I can't find an address –'

'Calm down, Emma. Deep breaths.' Mom put her arm around her. 'Sit down and read the article properly.'

It had taken a disaster to spur the government into action, but it seemed as if they would now accept children for eventual resettlement in other countries, probably Palestine. Surely, anywhere was better than Germany, and once Asher was here, maybe she could keep him.

There was mention of the Movement for the Care of Children from Germany, set up by Norman Bentwich and his wife, Mami. There was no address or telephone number, but he was connected to London County Council, and they would surely have contact information.

Two hours later, she was speaking to Mr Bentwich and had given him Asher's name and address in Frankfurt. He assured her he would add Asher's details to his list and consider his case according to the criteria if his parents were willing to let Asher travel to England unaccompanied.

She put down the telephone receiver, wiped away tears of relief, and grabbed a pen and notepaper. She had to let Hanne know what could be put in place for Asher, even if she couldn't help the rest of the family, and she'd write the letter twice and put

311

the copy in with another present for Asher in the hope one of them would arrive. Please, God, help would come, and that it wouldn't come too late.

Chapter Thirty-Four

Hawley Heath, England 1938

Within days, there were newspaper and radio appeals for people in Britain to foster German Jewish refugee children, and representatives from the Movement for the Care of Children from Germany had travelled to Germany and Austria to organise the transport of those children chosen to travel. The movement assured potential foster parents that the children's stay would be temporary, and they would provide fifty pounds for each child to assist their onward emigration.

America's proposal to admit twenty thousand children had come to nothing. Apparently, they believed that *"allowing children without parents goes against the laws of God"*.

Further details emerged that doused Emma's hope for Asher. Although monetary aid was promised by the Jewish Refugee Committee and other community efforts, and the Central British Fund for German Jewry was funding the rescue operation, precedence was being given to those in greatest need – orphans, those with a parent in a concentration camp or with parents too poor to keep them, and teenagers in concentration camps.

Asher didn't fall into any of those categories – unless Berek had been one of the men arrested.

Again, she was awaiting news from Hanne. The letter arrived the next morning, and the shaky writing on the envelope didn't bode well for her news.

My darling Emma,

Thank you for your letters and the gift for Asher. I have terrible news to impart. You will have read of the events of what the radio is calling Kristallnacht. They came during the night and burned Jewish houses and businesses and the synagogue on Börneplatz. The mobs destroyed everything we had. Berek and Uncle Saul rescued the Kettners from their burning house, but rioters killed them.

Killed the Kettners?

Berek and Uncle Saul are dead, Emma. Our home is uninhabitable, and we have been taken in by a kind Aryan neighbour. I am distraught, and Mutter has taken to her bed again. I have to get Asher out somehow; the poor child is terrified we shall be killed too. I'm praying Herr Bentwich's organisation can help me. Please press Asher's cause with him as best you can.

You can write to me care of Frau Mia Lautner at 23 Dominikanerplatz, Frankfurt am Main.

Your loving cousin,

Hanne

She let her hands fall into her lap and stared out of the window. Poor, poor Hanne. She took a long, shuddering breath and let it out again. For Hanne to lose the man she loved, the father of her child, was too cruel. Poor Mutter, and poor little Asher. No child should see such awful events. Would this change Asher's case with the aid movement?

She telephoned the exchange and asked to be connected to the movement's number.

'Hello. The Movement for the Care of Children from Germany. How may I help?'

'Can I speak to Mr Bentwich, please?'

314

'I'm sorry, Mr Bentwich is in Amsterdam. Can I help?'

'I don't know. My name is Emma T… Emma Joshua. I gave the details of my cousin's son, Asher Bergman, to Mr Bentwich. The boy is in Frankfurt. His father and uncle have just been killed during the Kristallnacht riots. His mother is desperate to get him to England.'

'As are hundreds of other mothers, Mrs Joshua.'

'Miss Joshua.'

'Miss Joshua. I'm sorry, but orphans take priority over those with a parent.'

'But she's destitute. They destroyed everything she had, and Asher is traumatised. He's terrified they'll be murdered.' Destitute might be a white lie, but it was one criterion that prioritised children, and she didn't know if the Nazis had stolen Hanne's secret store of gems and money. What she'd sent hidden in the toy for Asher wouldn't last long.

'Destitution would push his name further up the list. How old is he?'

'Six. No, he'll be seven now, but he's small. Is there a representative of your movement in Frankfurt?'

'The chosen children from south-west and southern Germany will be assembled in Frankfurt for the journey to England. I can pass Asher's details to the central office dealing with those areas.'

There had to be something more she could do. 'Tell them that if they make sure Asher is on the first transport from Frankfurt, I'll give a home to him and four more boys at my own expense. I have a large house, a thriving business, a farm, and sufficient funds. I can offer employment and apprenticeships as well to older boys. Asher's mother, Frau Hanne Bergman, can be contacted care of

315

Frau Mia Lautner at 23 Dominikanerplatz, Frankfurt am Main.'

'That's a very generous offer, Miss Joshua. I shall certainly pass that on. We are desperate for foster parents and children's homes to take these poor mites.'

'Will it help get Asher to England?'

'It very well might. Try not to worry, Miss Joshua. I'll do everything I can to get Asher and the other four boys to England and into your care.' There was a rustle of papers. 'I don't seem to have your details.'

Oh hell. Had she used Taylor as her name when she'd spoken to Mr Bentwich? 'I may be in your files as Emma Taylor. My father was a Joshua, but my adoptive father's name is Taylor. It's a long story.'

There was a further rustle of paper. 'Yes, I have your details here. Heath Hall, Hawley Heath. Is that correct?'

'Yes.'

The woman confirmed Hanne's name and address. 'Someone will be in touch with you soon, and if Asher is chosen, Frau Bergman will be notified of the travel arrangements.' The woman hesitated. 'Mr Bentwich is talking to Dutch authorities in the hope of setting up an escape route through Holland to avoid trying to get the children out through German ports. As soon as that's in place, we'll begin bringing out German children. Good luck, Miss Joshua.'

'Thank you.'

The conversation at an end, she put down the receiver and massaged her tense neck. Now, all she could do was wait – yet again.

The news was full of the plight of German Jewish children with

316

appeals for homes going out daily. Even newspapers held heart-breaking pleas in the form of small advertisements

Will someone give a home to two children? A girl age four and a boy age seven from a respectable Jewish home.

Home needed for well-behaved boy aged fourteen. Willing to work. Speaks a little English.

It made her realise how desperate Hanne must feel and how bewildering it would be for those children, alone in a strange country, many with no English at all. Thank goodness Hanne had been teaching Asher the language. He would be an enormous help in translating for the other boys until she could teach them. If they couldn't understand English, they couldn't go to school.

The enormity of the task before her hit her like a brick through a window. Her impetuous offer in order to save Asher was going to cause difficulties she couldn't possibly foresee except she'd thought to ask for boys. They could share a room and not take up two of the bedrooms that might be needed in the home for sick women, not that the home was so desperately busy now that women had better working conditions and general health.

Boys would need beds. Even the largest room wouldn't have room for five. Bunk beds. She needed a carpenter, mattresses, bedding. And they wouldn't be able to bring many clothes or shoes. The task grew and swallowed her.

She took a deep breath. It could be weeks before they arrived. She'd put out an appeal for outgrown clothes and shoes, pester her brothers for clothes they didn't wear much, and buy whatever else was needed when the boys arrived.

And in the meantime, perhaps she could persuade other members of the community to open their homes to the refugees.

It was December 2nd when the first Kindertransport, or children's transport, docked in Harwich, bringing two hundred children from a Jewish orphanage in Berlin. She listened intently to the news report.

'The children, some only toddlers, stand on the dock looking bewildered, all with tags around their necks, some clutching a small suitcase, and some with nothing.'

Her heart went out to them. Whatever difficulties lay ahead, she was doing the right thing.

***

Frankfurt, Germany 1938

Hanne opened a bulky envelope with trembling fingers. It wasn't Emma's handwriting on the envelope, and only one other person knew her new address.

She unfolded the letter and several things dropped to the floor.

Dear Frau Bergman,

We are pleased to say your son, Asher Bergman, has been given a place on a Kindertransport to England, London, Liverpool Street station, via Holland, on December 15th. I enclose his numbered identity tag and a visa exemption certificate.

Children to leave on this transport will be taken to Frankfurt Hauptbahnhof station for 6am on December 15th. Parents may not accompany their children to the station, so a group of children will be collected at 5.30am from outside the Römer, the Town Hall. Please make sure your child is there on time.

Your child is allowed one small, locked suitcase. No valuables are permitted and only ten reichsmarks. Please mark the suitcase with the child's name and number and hang the enclosed labels around your child's neck.

She stooped to pick up the dropped items. A manilla label with a number, and the other held his name, sex, date of birth, and her name and address and stated:

This document of identity is issued with the approval of His Majesty's Government in the United Kingdom to young persons to be admitted to the United Kingdom for educational purposes under the care of the Inter-Aid Committee for Children.

This document requires no visa.

Both had lengths of twine attached. Asher would look like a parcel. Tears streamed down her face. How could she send him away? He was so little, still her baby.

She straightened, swallowing her grief. She had to be strong. This was a holiday – a visit to Auntie Emma – and she and his grandmother would follow him very soon. That's what she'd told Asher, and he needed to believe that.

And he also needed a suitcase, small because he would have to carry it – and a change of clothes, a spare pair of shoes, soap, flannel, toothpaste, toothbrush, and a comb. And something to put a drink in and a tin for sandwiches. And the photograph of her and Berek and Mutter when he was five. He needed something to remember her by, because she was all too well aware that once on that train, she might never see him again.

Mia found her a small leather case, and she packed his favourite clothes. Was the case too heavy? She took out a thick jumper and replaced it with a thinner one. England was cold in winter. She removed the thin one and put back the thick one. Maybe he didn't need spare shoes, but what if he got his feet wet? She wouldn't be there to tell him to change them.

She sat on the bed and buried her head in her hands.

319

A gentle hand touched her shoulder. 'It's hard, Hanne, but you're doing the right thing.'

She looked up into Mutter's kind face. 'It doesn't feel like it.'

'I'd have sent you, had the circumstance been the same.'

'What if I never see him again, Mutter?'

'You will, Hanne. Emma will look after him like her own until we get there. Have faith.'

Mutter looked so frail. Would she make the journey to England? She had to believe it.

She was up at four o'clock on the morning of the fifteenth, having tossed and turned all night. There was breakfast to have, sandwiches to make, and last-minute items to pack. It had snowed in the night, and the streetlights reflected off the white blanket. It would be cold.

She couldn't eat.

At a quarter to five, they bade Mutter a tearful goodbye and began their trudge through the snow to the Römer. A small group of children and parents had already gathered, huddled together for mutual comfort, all attempting to be cheerful in the cold pre-dawn wind. Asher held his favourite toy in one hand – the dog Emma had sent him as a baby.

A woman approached with a paper in her hand. 'Asher Bergman?'

'Yes.'

The woman ticked off a name on her list. 'Good. We're waiting for one more, Frau Bergman, and then you must say your goodbyes. Ah, this must be them.' She hurried away to greet the late-comers.

She took a deep breath; she had to do this. 'You have to go with these children and this lady, Asher. You're going to have an exciting journey on a train and then on a big boat. This lady will look after you, and when you get to England, Auntie Emma will be there to meet you. Oma and I will join you very soon. We have things to do here before we can come.'

He gripped his toy dog tighter. 'Promise you'll come, Mama.'

She swallowed. 'I promise. I love you, Asher. I'm going to miss you so much. Be a good boy for Auntie Emma.'

He clung to her, and she hugged him tight and kissed him, his cheeks wet with her tears.

'We must go now.' The woman smiled. 'Don't worry. We shall look after them. Come along, now, children. We're off on a grand adventure.'

She gave him a last hug and handed him the suitcase. 'Don't lose this, and don't take off your labels. There's food and drink in the suitcase, and the key is in your pocket, remember. I'll see you very soon.'

'Asher, come along now.'

He trotted after the woman with his suitcase in one hand and the toy dog, ears trailing to the ground, in the other.

'I love you, sweetheart.'

He turned. 'I love you, too, Mama.' The night swallowed him, and he was gone.

Chapter Thirty-Five

Hawley Heath, England 1938

Emma and Charlie boarded the train for Liverpool Street Station. Emma's heart was in her mouth. Her charges were due to arrive that afternoon, and Asher and the other boys would have been travelling for about thirty-six hours: train from Frankfurt to the Hook of Holland, ferry to Harwich, and then another train to London. They'd be exhausted.

She took the list of names from her handbag, having tried to remember them all but failing. She had their numbers as back up if she needed to identify them quickly.

Elijah Hirsch, Wilhelm Herzfeld, Levi Wolff, and Joseph Berkowitz They were aged between four and fifteen, Joseph being the oldest and Elijah the youngest. While she hoped the older boys would help look after the younger ones, if they couldn't speak English, she'd be relying on Asher, who'd be as exhausted and traumatised as they were. With this in mind, she'd asked Charlie to go with her. Not that he spoke German, but a friendly male face might reassure them.

They disembarked onto the platform at Liverpool Street and joined a group of adults, all of whom seemed to be waiting for the coming train from Harwich. Several men with cameras stood nearby. Newspaper reporters or television crews? She wished they could get a television signal in Birmingham.

The newspapers were doing their best to highlight the plight of the Jews in Europe, especially Jewish children. One headline had warned that the Nazis would wipe out Jews across Europe unless democracies evacuated them.

She ran through the things she'd put in place for the boys, hoping she hadn't forgotten anything important. Hanne would be anxiously waiting to know if Asher had arrived. So would the other parents. The first thing the boys must do was write a letter home, if they had anyone to write to. If they hadn't, they could write and thank Mr Bentwich.

Charlie put an arm around her. 'It'll be all right, Emma.'

She flashed him a brief smile. It was all she could do to stop herself pacing up and down, and she hadn't realised she'd been shifting her weight from foot to foot like a captive wild animal.

A distant rumble heralded a train. She gripped Charlie's hand, and he squeezed hers back.

Children of all ages stepped down from carriages and looked around them, lost, tired, and bewildered. She stood on tiptoes, looking for Asher while Charlie held up cards with the boys' names on them.

A tall boy pushed towards them. He was holding a small boy by the hand. He pointed to himself and then to the small boy. 'Ich bin Joseph. Das ist Elijah.'

She smiled and pointed to herself. 'Ich bin Emma Taylor.' Then she pointed at Charlie. 'Das ist Charlie.' She put her hand at what she thought was Asher's height. 'Asher. Have you seen Asher Bergman?'

The boy shook his head and shrugged. He hadn't understood her. And where were Levi and Wilhelm? Charlie shouldered through the crowd his cards held high. He returned with two boys in tow. 'Wilhelm and–' He looked at the child's label. 'Levi. This

323

little one is Levi.'

'Have you seen Asher? Small, dark hair...' It could describe many of the children. 'I'll recognise him if I see him. Can you look after the boys while I find him?'

The platform was emptying, the engine puthering steam in readiness to leave. Where was he? She stared along the platform and then turned back to see a small boy standing alone and abandoned like an item of lost luggage, dwarfed by the suitcase in his hand and holding a toy dog by one leg. 'Asher!' She ran along the platform and gathered him into her arms. 'Asher, are you all right? Do you remember me?'

'You're my Auntie Emma.' His lower lip wobbled.

She smiled through tears of relief. 'Come along, Asher. Let's get you all something to eat and drink, and then we'll go home with your new brothers. Come and meet Charlie. You'll like Charlie.' She was jabbering. The poor boy looked bewildered, so she gave him a brief hug. 'It will be all right, Asher. You're safe now, and your mother and grandmother will come and join us soon.'

He managed a smile, and together they walked along the platform to begin a new life. *He's safe, Hanne. Asher's safe.* Could Hanne pick up on her thoughts? *I'll guard him with my life, my beloved.*

***

Frankfurt, Germany 1938

Hanne sank into the chair in Mia's living room. 'He's safe, Mutter. Asher's safe. He's in England with Emma and four more boys she rescued.'

'God of Abraham be praised.' Mutter hugged her. 'Thank

324

goodness for good news at last.'

She opened the other package the postman had dropped through Mia's door. The typewritten address was her old one.

'It's from the British Consulate about our visas.' She read on. Berek Bergman. She swallowed; Berek wouldn't need his visa now, but she'd been accepted. 'I have a visa. I can be with Asher.'

Mutter sat up straighter. 'What about me?'

'Oh no.' Her dream shattered. 'Yours and Uncle Saul's applications were turned down.' She dropped the useless visa in her lap.

'You must go, Hanne. You promised Asher.'

'I can't leave you, Mutter. How can I leave you here alone?'

'I have Mia and her family.'

'Mutter, nowhere in this accursed country is safe for a Jew. Mia can't protect you.'

'And you can?'

There was no answer to that.

'Hanne, I'm your mother, and I'm asking you, telling you to go to Asher. He needs his mother.'

'And I don't need mine?'

'Look at me, Hanne. My life is worth nothing unless I know you are safe in England. Please, leave me and go.'

'Oh, Mutter. I can't. I just can't. How could I forgive myself if anything happened to you?' She gulped back tears. 'Asher has Emma and a new family.'

'Emma is not his mother. It's your job to do the right thing by him, just as it's my job to do right by you.'

She pushed the visa back in its envelope, torn between her son and her mother. 'You can't make me go.'

'No, I can't.' Mutter sank back into her chair with a sigh of defeat. 'Go and make a cup of coffee, Hanne, and think about your responsibilities.'

'Perhaps I can appeal the decision.'

'And that will only delay your departure. You said it yourself, Hanne. Nowhere in Germany is safe for a Jew.'

Mia was busying herself in the kitchen. She filled the kettle and put it on the hob to boil. 'I overheard what your mother said. She can stay here for as long as she wants, but maybe the consulate would listen to an appeal. It's worth trying, surely?'

Mia didn't live in constant terror. 'It could take months. Is there any way we could get her over the border and into Holland?'

'Only if you were to leave the train near the Dutch border and cross on foot at night away from a border post. Even then, there'd be patrols. The Nazis are terrified of anything of value being smuggled out of the country. You might be young enough to do it, but she isn't fit to travel other than by train and boat. And you'd still have to cross the channel and have her allowed into England.'

'At least Holland is sympathetic to Jews.'

'That's true. What are you going to do, Hanne?'

There was a thump from the living room. Had Mutter fallen? She hurried through the doorway. Mutter was lying on the floor clutching her chest.

'Mutter, what happened?'

Her mother moaned. 'Hanne?'

'I'm here. Are you hurt? Is it you heart?' Blood seeped between

Mutter's fingers. She was clutching something. 'Mutter?'

Mia gasped. 'I'll fetch the doctor.'

'He won't treat a Jewish patient, and they arrested the Jewish doctor on Kristallnacht.'

She moved Mutter's hand to reveal a small fruit knife, the silver handle of which was protruding from between her mother's ribs just above her heart. 'Oh, Mutter, no. No…'

'Promise me you'll go now, Hanne. I can die knowing you'll be safe.'

'You can't die. I won't let you.'

Her mother coughed. Blood oozed from the corner of her mouth. 'I'm doing the right thing, Hanne.' She coughed again. 'Now you do right by Asher.'

She cradled her mother in her arms, careless of the blood that wet her dress. Mutter's eyelids fluttered and her body went limp.

'I promise, Mutter.' She held her mother close; Mutter had made the ultimate sacrifice for the daughter she loved.

***

Frankfurt, Germany 1938

Jewish law decreed Hanne must mourn her mother for a year. She stood at the graveside alone and watched the candles she'd placed on the graves of her mother, uncle, and husband gutter in the breeze. It was so cold. Her bag was packed, and what wealth she had left, she'd hidden in her clothing. She would mourn those she'd lost for the rest of her life. Berek, Mutter, and Uncle Saul would live in her heart forever.

Mia stood by the cemetery gate, waiting for her. 'I shall tend their graves for you, Hanne. They will be honoured.'

327

She hugged Mia. 'I can't ask that of you. It might not be safe to be seen being sympathetic to Jews, even dead ones, but thank you for being a good friend.'

'Don't blame yourself, Hanne. Your mother knew she hadn't long to live. This way, her suffering was cut short, and she died happy in the knowledge that she'd done this thing so you might live. You would do the same for your child.'

'I hope I would have her courage, but I feel anger towards her.'

'For leaving you?'

'I suppose so. I don't know.'

'That will pass. When you see Asher again, you will see the value of her sacrifice.'

She smiled bleakly. 'Part of me wants to flee, and part of me wants to stay.'

'They're dead, Hanne. You can't do anything for them now. Go, and make your mother's sacrifice worthwhile.' Mia took her hand in her own. 'And be happy, child. Be happy with Emma.'

She frowned when Mia winked. 'You know?'

'I could see it in her eyes and in yours. Don't think you are betraying Berek. He would want you to be happy. He loved you and you loved him, but that part of your life is over. Make a new one in England. You will write to me when you get there?'

'Of course, I will. Thank you again, for everything.'

Mia wiped a tear from her cheek. 'Go now. You'll miss your train.'

She kissed Mia's wet cheek and turned and walked away. There was nothing here for her now.

She walked to the station, following in Asher's footsteps. The

328

route would be the same, via Cologne and Dusseldorf to the Dutch border, and then across the Netherlands to the Hook of Holland, and then a ferry to Harwich. She'd written to Emma to say she was on her way and when to expect her in London.

Her spirits lifted. She would see Asher again and Emma. This was a new start, and she wouldn't let Mutter's sacrifice go to waste.

Although she was early for the train, the carriages were busy. She found a seat, stowed her luggage, and let the monotonous sound of wheels on track lull her to sleep.

The train jolting to a halt shook her awake. The light was failing towards dusk. 'Where are we?'

The elderly Jew next to her looked up from his book. 'We're nearing Bonn. A few hours yet to the border.'

'Are you heading for England?'

'No. I have relatives in Arnhem. I'm to stay with them for a while. The sooner I'm over the border, the happier I shall be.'

She echoed his sentiment.

'Do you have gloves?'

She looked at her hands. 'Why?'

'I would cover that ring before you get to the border. The SS officers will search the baggage and remove anything of value.'

She covered her wedding ring with the fingers of her other hand. There was nowhere safe to hide it if they were going to search the baggage. She took it off and turned away from the man to raise the hem of her dress and push the ring inside her knickers. Would it even be safe there?

Her heart thudded at the possibility of another rape. 'Thank you for the warning.' She had money and odds and ends of jewellery carefully hidden in her luggage and in her clothing. She needed it for the ferry and the train to London. What would she do if they found it?

The lights came on in the train, and the windows reflected faces tense with worry. Cologne and Dusseldorf fled behind her as the train sped north to the border. It was two o'clock in the morning when the train shuddered to a halt.

The man beside her shielded the carriage light from his eyes and peered into the darkness. 'SS officers everywhere. We must be at Emmerich. We're almost at the border.'

The train jolted forward and then slowed and stopped again. Another hundred yards, and she'd be in Holland. Doors slammed open, and the all too familiar sound of jackboots thudded along the corridor.

The door opened and an SS officer strode in. 'Border inspection. Passports, please.'

He inspected several passports and returned them to their owners. She handed him hers. Stamped with a red J, there was no way she could deny being Jewish,

He returned it to her, and she put it back in her handbag with her precious visa, a picture of Mutter, and the torn wedding photograph of her and Berek. 'Give me that.'

'It only has my passport and visa and a few reichsmarks.'

He emptied it out, took the money, and pushed the rest towards her. 'Get down your luggage and turn out your pockets. If you have items of value, declare them now. You are not permitted to take valuable items out of the country by order of the Führer.'

She took a deep, shuddering breath and swallowed her fear.

Sitting with her suitcase on her lap, she waited to be searched. *God of Abraham, Isaac, and Israel...*

Chapter Thirty-Six

Emmerich, German/Dutch border 1938

While the SS officer emptied Hanne's case, and went through everything with a fine-tooth comb, another officer guarded the compartment door with a rifle. She'd emptied her pockets. A handkerchief, a small tin of boiled sweets donated by Mia for the journey, and a comb.

'What's this?'

The SS officer held up a warm cardigan.

'Isn't it obvious?'

The officer struck her across the face. 'I mean this.' He held the garment up and turned it inside out to show a diamond brooch pinned to the inside.

'It was my mother's.'

He examined every item of clothing, feeling hems and collars and pulling out her store of valuables. 'You Jews think you are so clever at hiding jewellery.' He picked up a book she'd packed, and she held her breath. He opened it and shook it, and banknotes fluttered to the floor.

'Hans, take her outside and shoot her.'

The officer with the rifle gestured her to leave the compartment. The rifle didn't give her a choice. Her knees felt weak; this was where she died.

She grabbed her handbag – she wasn't going anywhere without

her passport and visa – even dead, she would have an identity. He pushed her off the train and towards a clump of trees. Even in the dark, she could see the land was flat and featureless but for clumps and rows of trees, and the moon glinting off water. The smell of smoke and steam mingled with the sweet smell of earth and the bitter stench of lost freedom.

She turned to face him, and he pushed the barrel of the rifle beneath her chin. If she was to die, she would die bravely like Berek and Uncle Saul – and Mutter. 'Does your mother love you, Hans? Would she want you to kill an innocent woman? I've done you no harm.'

Hans lowered the rifle barrel and then raised it again. 'Orders are orders, Fraulein.'

'Frau Hanne Bergman, widow of Berek, mother of Asher. At least know who it is you are murdering in cold blood. My mother died, so I might live. I sent my little boy to England so he might live, and I promised him I'd join him. Would you waste a mother's sacrifice? Destroy a mother's promise? What kind of man are you?'

He motioned her into the bushes. 'Go, and make sure you're not caught anywhere near here. You're dead as far as he knows. Go!'

She fled into the undergrowth and didn't stop running until she was out of sight of the railway. A distant rifle shot – she smiled despite her predicament. Hans had given himself time to have raped her before he killed her. His fellow officer wouldn't suspect he'd let her go.

She retrieved her wedding ring and put it back on her finger. 'Thank you, Lord, for giving Hans a heart.'

She had no idea where she was or which direction she'd run.

From maps she'd seen, the Hook of Holland was to the northwest. It was a clear night and the Pole Star shone brightly. She'd been walking back into Nazi Germany! Changing direction, and stumbling over undergrowth, she headed towards what she hoped was the Dutch border. The road she reached ran straight as an arrow and led in the right direction, but there would be no cover from Nazi patrols.

She would stick to it while it was still dark and hope to cross the border during the night, or the following night, leaving the road if she came across a border post. People did manage to cross into Holland, so it must be possible. A signpost at a junction read Arnhem, and Arnhem was in the Netherlands.

Emma would be waiting for her at Liverpool Street Station at noon, and she'd be frantic when she didn't turn up. She'd send her a telegram from Arnhem. She rubbed her head tiredly; telegrams cost money she didn't have.

Just before dawn, she left the road and took to the fields, negotiating drainage ditches and rough ploughed land. She had to rest. And she didn't know if she was in Germany or Holland. She headed towards a stand of trees and pushed her way into the shadows. She'd be safe there until dusk.

Something jumped out at her, and everything went black.

***

Hawley Heath, England 1938

Today, Emma would see her beloved Hanne again. She smiled as she peeped in on the boys in their bedroom. They'd taken a while to settle, there'd been tears, anger, withdrawal, and wet beds, but love, kindness, and giving them small tasks to make them feel valued had resulted in some kind of workable relationship. After yesterday's digging over part of the garden so the frost could break down the soil, they'd slept like logs. She'd let them sleep on a little longer.

Charlie had moved in temporarily to help with the refugees and had spent his nights on the sofa. He was up and dressed when she came down the stairs. 'Emma, I'm worried about the boys.'

'They seem to be settling. Asher is an enormous help with translating.'

'It's not that. They have temporary visas. They'll be expected to emigrate to, I don't know, Palestine or America if their parents don't turn up to collect them, and the more I read of the news, the more convinced I am that won't happen.'

'That's a pessimistic view, Charlie.'

'Even if it is, I hate the thought of them being uprooted and having to start again with strangers in a strange land. This has been hard enough for them.'

'So, what do you suggest?'

'Adoption if their parents don't claim them.'

A family of her own? 'Would they let a single woman adopt four refugees?'

'Maybe not, but you don't have to be single. You know how I feel about you, and these boys feel like my own children, now.'

She had to tell him the truth. 'Charlie, if there was a man I would marry, it would be you, and not just for the boy's sake. I can't marry any man. I love –' Her tongue stuck to dry lips. 'I love Hanne.'

'But Hanne's your cousin and she's...' His voice trailed into silence.

'She's a distant cousin and yes, she's a woman. I'm a lesbian,

Charlie. That's why I can't marry you.'

'But –' It wasn't often Charlie was speechless.

She took her opportunity to avoid discussing her sexuality, a subject no one but Hanne knew about. 'I have to meet Hanne in London at noon, and I don't want to be late. We'll discuss this later, Charlie.'

She hurried away before he gathered his wits.

***

Dutch/German border 1938

Hanne woke with a thumping headache to see a pair of dark brown eyes in a pinched face framed by black curly hair.

She sat up and wished she hadn't. 'What happened? Who are you?'

The small girl cocked her head to one side like an inquisitive sparrow. 'I'm Ingrid, and I'm nearly three. Who are you?'

'I'm Hanne. What on earth are you doing out here by yourself?'

'Ursula hit you on the head.'

'Whose Ursula?'

The girl pointed. Two more girls, one about nine or ten and one younger, were peering into her handbag.

'Here, that's mine, you thieving scoundrels.'

'We were looking for food.'

She brought the tin of sweets from her pocket. 'Haven't you eaten? Where are your parents?'

'They're dead. We're trying to get over the border like the others.'

'Others?' There were more?

The girl pointed. 'There are loads of children hidden in the wood waiting to cross tonight.'

'Alone? Some must have parents with them.'

'Their parents brought them almost to the border and left them.'

Parents were that desperate? 'Have any of you any food?'

'We ate it yesterday.'

'I'm hungry.' Ingrid rubbed her stomach to emphasise the point. 'I'm cold.'

'We're all hungry and cold, Ingrid. Which of you do I have to thank for the bump on my head?'

Ursula, the eldest, bit a grubby fingernail. 'I thought you were a Nazi. This is Monika.'

The younger child smiled a gappy smile. 'We want to go to England. Are you going to England?'

'Yes, but I have a visa. Do you have papers to say you can go to England?'

Ursula shook her head.

Oh, hell. She couldn't just leave them here. 'We'll cross the border together and see if we can get to England. I have a cousin there. She may be able to help.' Emma would have realised she wasn't coming by now.

She must somehow get a message to England; Emma would do all she could to help these poor children. She might be able to persuade Mr Bentwich to get them visas like Asher had, and in the meantime, Holland was supposed to be sympathetic.

Just before dusk, she woke Ursula. 'It's time we thought about moving, and we'll be warmer once we're walking.'

As the light faded, shadows emerged from the trees. There must be fifty children. Some carried small cases, some had nothing, all looked tired, cold, and hungry. The first pale stars twinkled. She led the way back to the road and began walking towards Arnhem, Ursula carrying Ingrid at her side.

She took the little girl from Ursula's arms, balanced her on one hip, and glanced behind her to see the ghostlike figures of children following her. The low moon sparkled the frost on the road. It would be a bitterly cold night. Silhouetted against the moon were soldiers. There was a barricade across the road. They were at the border.

She bent down to whisper to Ursula. 'Run back, quiet as you can, and tell everyone to keep low, stay quiet, and take to the field on our right – and mind the ditch.'

Ursula turned and ran to spread the message, and carrying Ingrid, she led Monika off the road. Children scattered into the ditch behind her and melted into the field. She felt like the Pied Piper of Hamelin in a bad dream that had just turned into a nightmare.

***

Hawley Heath, England 1938

Emma paced the living room. Hanne hadn't arrived at Liverpool Street Station, and she had no way of finding out what had happened to her or where she was. She wouldn't sleep, so there was little point in her going to bed except to escape Charlie.

Charlie wasn't to be escaped so easily. 'About Hanne.'

She turned to face him. 'You've thought of a way to find her?'

'No. I'm sorry. Look, I realise you love her, and you're worried about her, but until we hear from her, there's nothing we can do.' He raked his fingers through his hair. 'I've been thinking. I meant what I said about adopting the boys and getting married.' He raised a hand to stop her objection. 'Let me have my say, Emma.'

She sat on the sofa beside him. 'Go on then.'

'I've accepted you love Hanne, and you'll never love me that way, but I live alone, I've no family, and I'll never marry or have children of my own. Your family and these boys are all I have. All the family I'll ever have. I'm not asking for a relationship, just to belong somewhere and look after these kids. If a marriage of convenience, so we could adopt them, guarantees them a home while they need one, I'm prepared to do that. Are you?'

'That's an enormous commitment, Charlie.'

'Not for me. For me, it would be a privilege. And if you wanted to keep yours and Hanne's relationship private, marriage would be a fine disguise.'

'You're a good man, Charlie.' He really did love the boys, and it was obvious they loved him. 'If that's what it takes to keep them here and Hanne agrees – I've already broken the sexual chains by loving a woman. A marriage in name only? What's one more chain of convention to break? Maybe I'll have to alter the factory name to Joshua and Sons.'

He smiled. 'Together we could found an empire.'

She wagged a cautionary finger at him. 'Only if it's necessary. You'll always be a part of the family, Charlie, married or not.'

He kissed her on the cheek and went off whistling. She got up, Charlie forgotten, and began pacing the room again. 'Where are you, Hanne? Where on earth are you?'

339

Chapter Thirty-Seven

Dutch/German border 1938

Hanne crouched in the field and tried to make out how many soldiers there were and where they were patrolling. A searchlight swept across the road and swung its beam over the field on the other side of the road.

She glanced behind her and gestured the children into the ditch, sure there were more furtive figures than she'd started out with. She crawled into the ditch and bit back a curse as icy water lapped at her knees. Ingrid squealed, the dirty water up to her middle, and she held her breath, praying the noise would be mistaken for a night bird or a wild animal.

'Shush, Ingrid. We mustn't make a sound.' With three children in tow, she'd had a small chance of getting across the border, but with what looked more like a hundred and three, and Ingrid, what were the chances?

The beam of light swung over them and she ducked. Her only hope was that if any Nazi saw a hundred small heads bobbing above the ditch in the dark, they'd assume they were hallucinating or had drunk too much Schnapps.

If Asher had been among these children, she'd have wanted whoever had their safety at heart to do their utmost. She crawled forward, keeping a firm grip on her bag that held her precious visa, and checking behind to make sure the children were following. To their credit, the moans and gasps of disgust at the icy, filthy water were quiet as mice squeaks.

Keeping moving would keep them warm, but her hands had already lost all feeling. She crawled on. German voices grew louder. The smell of cigarette smoke wafted towards her and a tall, dark shape loomed over her. She froze and felt Monika stop behind her.

The sound of a zip, a grunt, splashing water, and the stench of urine. The soldier went back to his post, and she breathed out again. A large car loomed out of the night, catching the soldiers in its headlights. Only two of them, and they were busy with the occupants of the car. There seemed to be an argument.

She motioned Monika past her. 'Keep going until I catch up with you.' Monika crawled past, followed by Ingrid, and she waited while small bodies crawled by on their hands and knees.

She wanted to know they hadn't left anyone behind, and she needed to do a head count. It seemed ninety-one children had joined her and the three girls, making ninety-four. Where had they all come from? More to the point, how was she going to feed them and keep them safe?

When she was sure there were no strays, she scrambled after them. The light from the border crossing swept the road and fields behind them. She climbed out of the ditch and ran, crouching, along the field edge. A stand of trees bordering the far end would give some cover despite the bare branches. She stooped to pull a child from the ditch. He was shivering with cold. 'Hide among the trees and wait for me.' He nodded, teeth chattering, and ran for cover.

Beside her, a tall youth helped younger children out, pointing them towards the trees. She tried to keep a tally. 'I think, we're two short.' She stared down the length of the ditch, trying to spot movement.

The youth squinted. 'I'll go back and check. I'll meet you in the wood.'

'Thank you.'

The youth disappeared. She should have asked his name. Suppose he didn't make it back, and she didn't know whom to inform? Suppose she'd miscounted and sent him back on a wild goose chase?

She ran to the wood, lined up the children in rows of ten and recounted. Three were missing. Two and the boy who'd gone to find them. She went to the edge of the wood and stared out, hoping to see the missing children. An arc of light swept across the road and fields. Was that them caught on the very edge of the beam? The light fled past them and arced back again. She must have been mistaken.

'Got them.'

The voice behind her made her jump. 'We dodged the light and came round the far side. There are German guards all along this stretch of road.'

'Thank goodness you're safe. I'm Hanne, by the way, from Frankfurt. I'm heading for the Hook of Holland. I intend, somehow, to get these children there.'

'I'm David. I'm from Nuremberg, and I'm here with my sister.'

'David, I have to keep these children moving, or they'll freeze to death. I can't do it by myself. Will you be our rear-guard and make sure no one gets left behind?'

'Of course.' He was shivering, too. 'We'll have to keep off the road.'

She'd been hoping travelling would be easier once past the guard post. She addressed the cold. wet, tired, and muddy bunch before her. 'David says there are German guards on the road. It must be right on the border, so we'll keep to the fields. Once it's safe, we'll head back to the road, and when we get there, we run. If I hoot like an owl, lie flat on the ground or take to the ditch.'

Did they know what an owl sounded like? Some of them would, and when they dropped to the ground, the others would copy.

Leaving the safety of the wood behind, she swung Ingrid onto her hip and set off across the fields. The searchlight was behind them – to the east, judging by the Pole Star that shone in a gap in the clouds. They seemed to have been walking for miles. Surely, they were across the border now.

'Ursula, creep onto the road and tell me if you see soldiers.'

The girl clambered gamely across the muddy ditch and up onto the road, standing for a moment, her dark figure visible in the pale moonlight. 'No Germans, Hanne.'

She beckoned the children closest to her. 'Up onto the road.' She led the way, confident that David would see they left no one behind, and started off in a slow jog. The sound of small feet pattering behind her kept her running. The road was straight and flat, and there would be no hiding while they were on it.

Despite her fear, she slowed to catch her breath and look behind her. The straggle of children, some running, some walking, some carrying other smaller children, trailed back along the road. They were flagging, and she had to keep them moving.

Ursula stopped beside her. 'Are we in Holland, yet?'

'I don't know. We must keep going.'

She marched on, feeling more than ever like the Pied Piper. They'd turned slightly north, which had to be away from the border. They must be in Holland by now. She had to keep their spirits up. She began singing, and after a moment Ursula joined in, her high voice carrying in the night air. Others joined in, and soon there was a chorus of voices.

'Alle meine entchen, schwimmen auf dem See...'

Her ducklings swam behind her. There were lights ahead and her voice fell silent. She slowed her pace. Should she approach and hope for help or avoid human contact? It was getting light, and the children couldn't go any farther, desperate as they were for rest, food, and water. She couldn't go farther, either.

She put Ingrid down on the ground and straightened her sore back. A man walked towards her. He stopped in front of her, and she tensed.

'Wie ben jij? Wie zijn al deze kinderen?'

Her tired brain made no sense of the words.

'Je ziet er uitgeput uit. Waar ga je naar toe?'

'You're Dutch?'

'Nederlands.'

She tried English. 'These children are German Jews seeking refuge in the Netherlands. We've been walking all night. Can you help us.?'

'Help, yes. How many?'

'Ninety-four. We need water, food, warmth, somewhere to sleep.'

'Come.'

He led the way into a small village and knocked on several doors. 'Deze kinderen hebben voedsel, water, en een slaapplek nodig.'

The villagers opened their doors and three or four at a time, they were taken into people's homes.

The kind Dutchman beckoned to her. 'Come. My wife will find you clean clothes, food, a bath, and a bed. The children will be cared for.'

'I can't thank you enough. Their parents can't thank you enough.' She hesitated. 'The border guards took everything I had. I can't pay you.'

He brushed aside her gratitude, along with her concern. 'I have children. You have done a great thing bringing them out of Germany.'

She raised a weary smile. 'I was bringing myself out. They just tagged along.'

He laughed. 'Then they tagged along with the right person.'

'Can I ask one more favour?'

'Ask.'

'I need to get a telegram to England. These children need British visas.'

'And you have no money. After you bathe, you will write me the message. I shall cycle to Arnhem to the telegraph office.'

She wiped away a stray tear. 'Thank you. Thank you so much.'

The thought of a warm bath and a bed was bliss. Tonight, she would sleep in safety for the first time in a long while.

***

Hawley Heath, England 1938

Emma answered a knock on the door. 'It's all right. Asher. No one's going to hurt you.' A door slamming in the wind had sent the child hiding under the kitchen table with a knife in his hand. It had taken her five minutes to persuade him out.

She opened the door to the post boy. 'Telegram, miss.'

'Thank you.' She hurried into the living room to open it.

94 CHILDREN NEED BRITISH VISAS STOP CONTACT BENTWICH STOP HOOK OF HOLLAND IN ABOUT 2 WEEKS STOP NO MONEY STOP HANNE

Hanne was alive! The telegram had been sent from Arnhem, so she was safely over the border and into Holland. She let out a held breath and read the telegram again. Ninety-four children? Where on earth had Hanne found ninety-four children, and why had she left the train? And what was she supposed to do with them all – turn the church rooms into a dormitory? If Hanne was bringing children, it was because they'd needed bringing.

And they needed British visas. She read the telegram over the phone to the helpful woman at the Movement for the Care of German Children.

'Ninety-four children. And where are they now?'

'The telegram was sent from Arnhem this morning.'

'And they're with this Hanne? Who is Hanne?'

'Hanne Bergman. She's a distant cousin. You helped get a visa for her son, Asher.'

'Ah, yes, I remember. Asher's father was killed and his mother was destitute. Does Mrs Bergman have a visa?'

'Yes. She was on her way to England but didn't arrive. Somehow, she's got caught up with these children.'

'And they're making for the Hook of Holland.'

'Yes. On foot, by the sound of it. How far is it from Arnhem to the port?'

The woman was silent for a moment. 'Looking at the map on the office wall, I'd say just short of a hundred and fifty miles.'

'Good God. They can't do that in winter. They'll die.'

'They'll have to go via Rotterdam. It should be possible to work out a rough route and find them. That large a group won't pass unnoticed.'

'But they have no money, and probably no food.'

'Leave it to us, Miss Joshua. Rescuing children like these is what we were set up for. We'll find them.'

'What will happen to them?'

'We'll launch an immediate appeal for British homes and this is just the story to capture the public imagination. Please don't worry. Dutch people have shown themselves to be very supportive of Jewish children travelling through their country. I'm sure they won't lack help until we find them.'

'And the visas?'

'I'll get on to the Home Office immediately. I know the best person to speak to and what pressure to apply. In an emergency like this, he won't drag his heels. I'll telephone you back when I have news.'

'Thank you.'

'You're very welcome. It's what we do.'

The phone went dead. All she could do now was wait – yet again. At least this time, she didn't feel alone. The movement and the Dutch people would help get Hanne and the children across Holland to England.

Chapter Thirty-Eight

Holland 1938

Hanne and the children spent the day and the night with the villagers. The next day, they assembled in the street. The children were clean, their clothes had been washed and dried, and they looked rested and eager for the journey ahead.

She clutched her bag; her visa and passport had been covered in mud, and Bram's wife, Lotte, had helped her clean and dry them. She hoped they were legible enough to pass as official documents.

Bram, the gentle Dutchman who'd welcomed her into his home, stood beside her. 'Arnhem is not far – a day's walk. I shall walk with you, Hanne. I have a cousin there who may take you farther. You must go due west from Arnhem.'

'That's kind of you, Bram.'

'I will harness my pony to the trap. It can carry the food people have given you for the journey, and the little ones can ride, yes?'

Was there no end to this man's kindness? 'Thank you for everything, Bram. Please thank everyone for their care.'

The smallest children loaded onto the trap, they took their leave of the villagers, waving their gratitude.

'Veilige reis.' It was a cry from many lips.

She raised a questioning eyebrow.

'They are wishing you a safe journey. Come, we will make better time with the little ones riding.'

The closer they got to Arnhem, the more built up the surroundings became. They'd left behind the patchwork of flat fields and the stands of trees. The early winter dusk was falling when they crossed the river into the city.

People stopped and stared at the odd procession trudging along the city street. Some pushed sweets into the children's hands, others gave out drinks in paper cups.

'My cousin is expecting you. I telephoned him while you slept.' He'd stopped the pony and trap in front of a large building.

'Where are we?'

'This is a meeting hall. You can stay the night here. People have donated blankets.'

Bran's cousin stood in the doorway. 'Welcome. You must all be cold and tired. We have bread and hot soup for the children. Come in. Come in.'

Inside was brightly lit and welcoming. A stove in the centre of the room radiated comfort. The smell of hot soup was enticing and piles of blankets lay on a table. It was all she could do not to burst into tears.

Bran approached with his cousin. 'This is Sem. He wishes to speak about tomorrow.'

She sipped her soup and cupped her hands around the warm mug, hoping Sem's English was as good as Bran's.

Sem smiled. 'I have a truck. I can't take everyone, but I could take some children on to Rotterdam.'

'That's kind of you, Sem, but who would look after them?' She'd formed a bond with these children she couldn't just break. They called her Tante Hanne, and she'd promised to get them to England. She could ask if they wanted to go with Sem, but she

349

was the adult here, and they were her responsibility. 'Thank you, but no. My cousin is arranging visas for them to go to England, and they stand a better chance of getting them if we all stay together.'

***

Hawley Heath, England 1938

Ninety-Four Jewish Children in Epic March Across Holland in Freezing Weather.

Reports are coming in about a group of Jewish children who escaped from Nazi Germany a few days ago. The children, all unaccompanied by their parents, seem to be with Mrs Hanne Bergman, a German Jew whose husband was killed in the anti-Semitic riots on Kristallnacht.

Mrs Bergman's seven-year-old son is already safe in England, but it is known that desperate parents unable to leave Germany take their children to the German border and abandon them in the hope they can make it into Holland alone. Mrs Bergman was due to have entered Britain to join her son two days ago, but she failed to arrive.

A telegram received from Mrs Bergman from Arnhem suggests she is bringing these children on foot one hundred and fifty miles across Holland in freezing conditions and hopes to reach the Hook of Holland in about two weeks. It isn't known exactly where the children and Mrs Bergman are at present, but it is known that she has no money to feed them or herself, and the Movement for the Care of German Children is mounting a rescue operation to find them and bring them to England.

Pressure is being put on the British government to issue special visas to allow them into the country, and a plea is being

broadcast on the radio and television for British foster parents to take these brave children into their homes.

Emma put the paper down. A hundred and fifty miles in December. If this was what the woman at the movement meant by putting pressure on the Home Office and launching an appeal for homes, she hadn't been joking. If this story didn't capture the public imagination, nothing would. And she could finally tell Asher his mother was out of Germany and on her way to him.

Eager for more news, she'd driven down to the newsagent. She couldn't miss the message on the board outside.

Heroine Widow Brings 94 Jewish Children out of Germany. Homes needed URGENTLY

A newspaper had similar headlines. Everywhere she looked, Hanne was heralded as a heroine, and the newspapers loved her. The Home Office surely couldn't refuse them a home in Britain now.

***

Holland 1938

Hanne changed Ingrid to her other hip and put one foot in front of the other with dogged determination. If she was tired, the children were exhausted, and she'd wondered if she'd been wrong not to let some of them go on alone, but word of their journey had gone ahead of her, and the generosity of the Dutch people gave all their legs the will to keep moving.

All along their route, people came out of their houses to offer food or drink. Men and women joined them to carry the smaller children on their shoulders for a mile or two before handing over their burdens to others. Farmers brought carts and tractors, and the exhausted gratefully accepted a ride to the next farm or town.

Hay barns and town halls were turned over to them to sleep, and soup kitchens appeared as if by magic. Someone was anticipating their route and organising aid.

In Nieuwegein, a banner fluttered in the breeze, and a crowd of people waited to greet them. A camera flashed.

WELKOM TANTE HANNE EN DE VIERENNEGENTIG KINDEREN

She recognised the words Tante Hanne, but the rest meant nothing. She smiled tiredly at the well-wishers.

Rotterdam was still two or three days away, and it would be the same again to reach the Hook of Holland. Uncertainty plagued her. Would they make the rest of the journey, would Emma have managed to get permits for the children, would her own visa even be legible? The thought of them all stranded on the Dutch coast haunted her.

A man approached her and kept pace with her. 'Hanne Bergman?'

She nodded.

'I'm James Abrams. I'm a representative of the Movement for the Care of German Children.'

She stopped in her tracks. 'Emma sent you? You have visas for the children?'

'We've been following your progress in the Dutch newspapers along with the whole of Holland. You're quite the celebrity.'

Children clustered around her like chicks around a mother hen. 'But do the children have visas?'

'We're hopeful.'

'Hopeful?'

'Very hopeful.'

'We haven't walked all this way for you to be hopeful or even very hopeful. These children are homeless and stateless. They need visas.'

'It's all in hand. The movement is working hard on your behalf.'

She walked on and the children followed. They wouldn't reach the coast by talking.

The man caught up with her. 'I brought a bus. There's room for all of you if we squeeze up a bit. You don't have to walk any farther. The publicity has done its job.'

'Publicity?'

'Your story has melted hearts. We've had hundreds of offers of homes. You can stop walking.'

She strode on angrily. 'You mean you've known about us and have let these children walk in this weather for a publicity stunt? They have blisters, chilblains, cold sores, coughs, grazed knees…'

'It wasn't just a publicity stunt. We organised food and shelter. We've found foster homes and there will be visas. Wasn't the walk worth that? Isn't that what you're trying to achieve?'

She stopped, and a child bumped into her: Ursula, never far from her side. She put her arm around the girl. 'You mentioned a bus?'

'It's around the corner.'

The bus was old, but it was a welcome relief to tired legs and sore feet. She counted the children onto the bus, David bringing up the rear. 'They're all here, David. You've done a great job.'

He smiled and climbed onto the bus. There were children

sitting on children, squashed in five to a seat. She squeezed in beside Ursula and Monika and put Ingrid on her lap. James climbed into the driver's seat.

'When will we reach England, James?'

'Tomorrow. We've arranged beds for the night and the special permits are due to arrive in the morning. We'll catch the morning ferry and be in London by noon.'

'Which station?'

'We'll dock at Harwich and take a train to Liverpool Street Station. You'll get a hero's welcome, Mrs Bergman.'

She leaned forward, holding out her visa. 'This got wet. Do you think it'll be accepted?'

He took it from her, looked it over, and handed it back. 'If the Home Office doesn't let you in, there'll be a public outcry. It'll be fine, I'm sure.'

'One more thing before we leave.'

He turned in his seat. 'What?'

'Can you stop at the next telegraph office and send a telegram to my cousin? She'll meet me at the station.'

He smiled. 'Of course.' The engine burst into life and the bus bounced onto the road.

She sank back into her seat, tears brimming. Once in London, she'd be saying goodbye to these children forever. Ingrid, Ursula, and Monika, in particular, had burned a hole deep into her heart. She'd carried Ingrid for more miles than she dared to contemplate, feeling the warmth of her body against her own, her little arms around her neck, and her soft breath on her cheek.

Tante Hanne? She felt more like her mother.

354

***

Morning dawned sunny, and Hanne was up early. Breakfast was like a banquet, the children hungry, rested, and happy.

James slid onto a bench beside her. 'The special visas have arrived. We have to fill in the names of the children on these labels, so we know who is who and no one gets lost. Also, we'll be able to tell their parents they're safe and give them an address to write to once the children are settled in their foster homes. I'll set up tables over there to process the children if you can help organise them into families. The ferry leaves in two hours, and the sooner we do this, the sooner we can get them on it.'

She cleared her plate and began ushering the children into rows, brothers and sisters together. She didn't know the names of many of them, and most of those she did she got wrong. It didn't matter. They were here safe and excited that they were going to England.

'Tante Hanne?'

'Ursula?'

'Where will go when we're in England?'

'I don't know, Ursula.'

'Will Ingrid and Monika come as well?'

She blinked back tears. She couldn't bear the thought of them being separated, but she couldn't lie to the child. 'I hope so.'

Ursula's face betrayed her anxiety.

A tall figure pushed towards her. 'David.' She hugged him. 'I shall miss you. Look, I'll write the address of my cousin on a piece of paper. If you or your sister need anything, please contact me there.'

355

He hugged her back. 'Thank you for bringing us to safety.'

'I couldn't have done it without you, David.' She wrote Emma's address and handed it to him. 'Take care. And remember, anything you need.'

He nodded wordlessly and joined his sister in the queue of refugees.

The children labelled like luggage, they led them towards the dock. The ferry was already there, smoke puthering from its funnels, the sun gleaming off its sides, a picture of hope.

She took a deep breath, picked up Ingrid, and led the children up the gang plank and onto the deck. Children spilled around her, running to the sides of the ship to look into the water.

She stopped dead, and Ursula and Monika stopped with her. 'Emma?'

'I couldn't wait to see you, Hanne. I had to come.'

Ingrid put her arms around her neck, and Ursula and Monika clung around her waist. Tears ran down her cheeks. 'It's so good to see you, Emma. How's Asher?'

'He's well. He wanted to come with me, but I daren't risk him not being allowed back into England. Where's your mother?'

She hadn't been able to write the words to tell Emma of Mutter's sacrifice. She shook her head, unable to stop the tears. 'She's dead, Emma.'

'Oh, Hanne. I'm so sorry.' Emma wiped away her own tears. 'What will happen to these children?'

'All ninety-four have foster homes to go to. You did a great job, Emma.'

Ingrid began to cry. Monika clung tighter. Ursula looked up

with soulful eyes. The children didn't understand English, but Ursula voiced their fear. 'We want to stay with you, Tante Hanne.'

And she desperately wanted to stay with them. She put a protective arm around Monika. She didn't need to translate Ursula's words. 'Tante Emma?'

Emma smiled and took Ingrid from her tired arms, kissing the little girl on the cheek. 'What's three more children? We can squeeze them into Heath Hall, somehow.' Emma reached out a hand towards hers. 'Let's go home, Hanne.'

The End

Fact from Fiction

While Emma and Hanne's families and businesses are entirely fictional, the broad events portrayed in this novel are based in fact. The worldwide recession following the end of World War One and the Wall Street crash threw whole families out of work, and soup kitchens were a reality that saved people from starvation. It was so bad in Russia that there were reports of cannibalism.

That women were allowed to vote in the 1929 election was a major breakthrough that took some sixty years of campaigning by women to achieve. The determination and resilience of ordinary people never fails to amaze me.

The rise of Hitler was something I never understood until I began researching this story, and the comparative ease with which he took power and planted hatred into the minds of people is terrifying. There are parallels in the world today that should not be ignored.

The flight of refugees from Germany is also paralleled by flights from war zones in several countries at the time of writing. War goes on even during 'world peace'. That parents were desperate enough to leave their children at the German border in the run up to World War Two, and tell them to walk into Holland, is a measure of the terror under which Jews lived in Nazi Germany.

That the rich countries of the world were reluctant to give homes to refugees is also mirrored today: truly, 'when you are accustomed to privilege, equality feels like oppression'. (Franklin Leonard)

The persecution of Jews leading up to and including Kristallnacht on November 9th/10th 1938 is well documented and factual.

The Movement for the Care of Children in Germany was a real movement, and Mr Bentwich was a real person. With funding from the Central British Fund for German Jewry, he and the movement, along with others such as the Quakers, were instrumental in rescuing thousands of Jewish children from Nazi-occupied Europe. Ten thousand children were brought by the Kindertransports from Germany, Austria, Poland, and Czechoslovakia to safety in England.

Hanne's journey is fictional and the movement's publicity stunt a figment of my imagination – no criticism of the Movement for the Care of Children in Germany is implied or intended – but the courage and dedication shown by Hanne reflects the courage and dedication shown by members of the charitable groups who went into Nazi Europe to bring Jewish children out.

Not all the children brought into Britain found homes as secure or loving as the one Emma, Charlie, and Hanne provided. Some found temporary respite in England and were sent on to America or Palestine. Some were used as cheap labour, some spent their childhoods in children's homes, and some were doubtless abused by their foster parents, but many were adopted by loving families.

In any event, the courageous choice parents made to send their children alone to England turned out to be the right choice. It is a sad truth that few of the rescued children saw their parents again. Of the Jewish children and adults still in Nazi-occupied Europe at the outbreak of war in 1939, most were sent to concentration camps where some six million Jewish men, women, and children were murdered.

Dominikanerplatz was destroyed by Allied bombing in World

War II. The Museum Judengasse and the memorial on Neuer Börneplatz now commemorate the Jews of Frankfurt lost in the Holocaust.

***

Other titles

Fantasy

http://mybook.to/ChildofProphecy

Mystery

http://mybook.to/SilenceoftheStones

Historical Fiction

http://mybook.to/TouchingtheWire

http://mybook.to/DandelionClock

http://mybook.to/KindredandAffinity

http://mybook.to/Revenge1705

The Chainmakers series

http://mybook.to/ChainmakersDaughter

http://mybook.to/ChainmakersWife

http://mybook.to/Chainmistress

http://mybook.to/ChainmakersTrilogy

http://Chainmakersboxset

For Their Country's Good Series

http://mybook.to/OnDifferentShores

http://mybook.to/BeneathStrangeStars

http://mybook.to/OnCommonGround

http://mybook.to/FTCGtrilogy

http://mybook.to/FTCGboxset

Non-Fiction by my alter-ego, Ruth Coulson

http://mybook.to/WatercolourSeascapes – a step-by-step guide to painting seas in watercolour.

http://mybook.to/AnimalPortraits - a step-by-step guide to painting animals in watercolour and ink, and pastel.

Thank you for reading. If you've enjoyed The Chainmakers' series, please leave me a review at one of the Chainmaker links above.

Printed in Great Britain
by Amazon

29455695R00201